Saintly
Murders

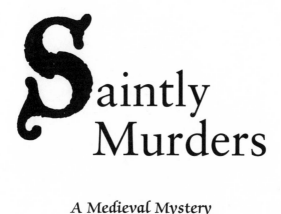

Saintly Murders

A Medieval Mystery
Featuring
Kathryn Swinbrooke

C. L. Grace

St. Martin's Minotaur
New York

www.minotaurbooks.com

Library of Congress Cataloging-in-Publication Data

Grace, C. L.
    Saintly murders : a medieval mystery featuring Kathryn
  Swinbrooke / C. L. Grace—1st ed.
       p. cm.
    ISBN 0-312-26993-5
    1. Swinbrooke, Kathryn (Fictitious character)—Fiction.
  2. Great Britain—History—Lancaster and York, 1399–1485—Fiction.
  3. Canterbury (England)—Fiction. 4. Women physicians—Fiction.
  I. Title.

PR6054.O37 S25 2001
823'.914—dc21

                            2001019578

First Edition: August 2001

10 9 8 7 6 5 4 3 2 1

To a marvelous and brave young lady,
Lisa Monaghan
of Kesh, County Fermanagh, Northern Ireland,
a brilliant student who died 23 December 2000;
in loving memory

'My theme is alwey oon, and evere was—
Radix malorum est Cupiditas.'
—Chaucer, 'Prologue to The Pardoner's Tale,'
The Canterbury Tales

In the Middle Ages women doctors continued to practise
in the midst of wars and epidemics as they always had, for
the simple reason that they were needed.
—Kate Campbellton Hurd-Mead,
A History of Women in Medicine

Historical Note

By May 1471, the bloody civil war between the Houses of York and Lancaster had ended with Edward of York's victory at Tewkesbury. The Lancastrian King, Henry VI, was later murdered in the Tower by Yorkist henchmen; and Edward of York, rejoicing in the regal title of Edward IV, assumed full power. Edward was supported by his beautiful wife, Elizabeth Woodville, and his two powerful brothers, George of Clarence and Richard of Gloucester, together with their gangs of henchmen. The Yorkist faction settled down to enjoy the fruits of peace, even though old grievances and hatreds still simmered and often surfaced.

In France, the sly, shrewd Louis XI, 'the Spider King,' watched with trepidation the growing strength of his country's old enemy. Louis was ever ready to interfere and check England's ascendancy, whatever the cost. . . .

List of Historical Characters

Henry VI: Henry of Lancaster, son of the great Henry V, regarded by some as a fool, by others as a saint, by a few as both. His weak, ineffectual rule led to vicious civil war between the Houses of York and Lancaster.

Margaret of Anjou: French Queen of Henry VI and the real power behind the throne; her hopes of victory were finally quashed by two outstanding victories by the Yorkist forces at Barnet and Tewkesbury in the early months of 1471.

Beaufort of Somerset: Leading Lancastrian general and politician; reputed lover of Margaret of Anjou, killed at Tewkesbury.

Henry Tudor: Last remaining Lancastrian claimant. By 1473, in exile at the Courts of France and Brittany.

Nicholas Faunte: Lancastrian Mayor of Canterbury; later captured and executed in his own city.

THE HOUSE OF YORK

Richard of York: Father of Edward IV. Richard's overbounding ambition to become king led to the outbreak of hostilities between York and Lancaster. He was trapped and killed at the Battle of Wakefield in 1461.

Cecily of York (nee Neville): 'The Rose of Raby'; widow of Richard of York; mother of Edward, Richard, and George of Clarence.

Edward IV: Successful Yorkist general and later King.

Edmund of Rutland: Edward's brother, killed with the Duke of York at Wakefield.

George of Clarence: The beautiful but treacherous brother of Edward IV; a prince who changed sides during the Civil War.

Richard of Gloucester: Youngest brother of Edward IV; he played a leading part in the Yorkist victory of 1471.

FRANCE

Louis XI 'The Spider King': Responsible for the strengthening and centralisation of the French monarchy in the last quarter of the fifteenth century.

Jeanne d'Arc 'La Pucelle': The visionary leader of the French resistance to England till the English captured and burnt her at Rouen in 1431.

ENGLISH POLITICIANS

Thomas Bourchier: Aged Archbishop of Canterbury.

William Hastings: Henchman to Edward IV.

Francis Lovell: Henchman to Richard of Gloucester.

Saintly
Murders

The Prologues

'O cursed synne of alle cursedness!
O traytours homycide! O wikkedness!'
—Chaucer, 'The Pardoner's Tale,'
The Canterbury Tales

Death had come for Roger Atworth, the former soldier now a member of the Friars of the Order of the Sack in Canterbury.

'Oh, Jesus miserere!' the old man murmured.

He stared across at the light streaming under the narrow door. Death had slipped in like an assassin, scuttling padded feet down a gallery, striking quickly from the shadows of an alleyway. Death had sprung his trap. Atworth knew a great deal about suffering: the pains running across his chest and down the left side of his body were like a tocsin warning that he had only a short while to live. Atworth tried to move, but his legs, hands, and arms felt as if they were encased in lead. His mind wandered. What day of the week was it? He had lost all sense of time. He recalled the good brothers preparing to celebrate the Feast of the Annunciation, which came nine months before Christmas. Atworth coughed deep in his throat and licked the phlegm forming on the corner of his mouth. He wouldn't see another Yuletide. He wouldn't kneel in adoration before the crib, help decorate it with holly and ivy, and wonder, once again, if the bright red berries truly symbolised the blood of Christ. Atworth tried to concentrate. He knew enough about physic to recognise the symptoms of delirium tremens. Isn't that how Brother Simon the infirmarian described it? His whole body was wracked with pain. His throat was dry. Atworth hadn't even been able to eat the meagre scraps the mysterious cowled figure had brought him.

'Who was it?' Atworth murmured into the darkness. Yet what did it matter? He was going to die, and like a good soldier, he was prepared for that. He tried to recall the words of the death psalm, the 'De Profundis.' What was it now, Psalm 130?

> ' "Out of the depths have I cried unto you, O Lord!
> Lord, hear my voice! Let your ears be attentive to the
>   voice of my supplications.
> If thou, Lord, shouldst mark iniquities . . ." '

Atworth coughed. He tried to raise his head, but the effort was too much. He stared up into the gathering gloom. Guilt! Oh, Atworth felt guilty! He couldn't stop the nightmares from pouring back, like black, fetid waters, souring his soul. They were nightmares of the days of his youth, of fighting in the Free Companies under a gold-and-red banner in northern France. It was a time of great plunder and rapine, whole villages put to the torch! Men, women, and children were cut down like lilies in the field.

Roger Atworth shook his head. He recalled a young woman he had taken. Where was it now? Just north of the village of Agincourt, where King Henry had won his great victory. She had been fleeing, with a fardel or bundle over her shoulder, and stumbled into the clearing where Atworth and his men were resting. He had raped her, and so had his men before they let her go, a miserable, bleeding bundle of flesh scarred in mind, body, and soul.

'Oh, Jesus miserere!' Atworth pleaded for the mercy he so desperately needed and yet didn't deserve. He and his men had been cursed for that. An old crone living in the forest had heard the girl's screams and come hurrying to find out. The woman had stood on the edge of the clearing, her grey hair streaming down her shoulders, her old face vivid with disgust and fury. Even then Atworth had admired her courage. She had walked forward like some prophet of old, bony finger jabbing the air. At first she talked in a patois they didn't understand, but then, surprisingly enough, she'd lapsed into English.

'Cursed ye be,' she'd shrieked, 'in your eating and your drinking! Cursed be ye in your sleeping and waking! Cursed be ye in riding and walking! Cursed be ye in your lying down and getting up! Cursed be ye at the dawn and at the depth of night! Cursed be ye by my death!'

Atworth closed his eyes. He recalled the incident as if it had happened only an hour ago. He had drawn his sword and driven it straight through the old woman's belly, spiking her like he would a rabbit or a pig. Afterwards they'd hung her upside down from one of the outstretched branches of an elm tree. They'd all stood round and laughed at her vein-streaked, scrawny body dangling from the tree like an animal's cadaver on a butcher's stall. They had gathered their boots, saddled their horses, and left that blood-soaked corpse without a second glance. How had one of his men described Atworth? 'A fiend who fears neither God nor man.' Well, the old woman had been right. From that day on nothing had ever gone right. Two days later they had been ambushed by a group of German mercenaries, Lorrainers who had killed six of Atworth's men and captured most of their plunder.

Atworth opened his eyes; the pain had subsided. Perhaps someone would come to help. He strained, listening for a sound; the light coming under the door was now fading. No one would come! Atworth returned to his reverie. Every member of his troop had died a violent death, killed amongst the hedgerows and ditches of northern France. They had been taken up in the great disaster that had engulfed the English forces as the armies of France, led by that eerie Maid of Orleans, 'La Pucelle,' Jeanne d'Arc, had driven the Goddamns out of France. Atworth had been in the market place at Rouen when they'd burnt the maid. He had watched her thin, emaciated body bubble in the heat, yet her voice remained strong, praying aloud even as her waiflike face was hidden by the sheet of flame. And afterwards? Those sombre days in the castle at Rouen, bodyguard to Duchess Cecily of York, a bond had been forged there which lasted even now. Nothing had changed it, not even when Atworth was captured by the ruthless Vicomte de Sanglier, a young, Godless man. In de Sanglier Atworth had seen his own soul, and again, a bond had been formed, a chain forged and linked; it stretched across the years, and Sanglier still had his hand on it.

After his escape from France, Atworth had returned home to his small village outside Canterbury. He became a man haunted

3

by his demons. Atworth had brought great plunder, set himself up as a prosperous tenant farmer, and become betrothed to a manor lord's daughter; but it had all turned sour. The girl had died in one of the sudden fevers which swept the shire. Atworth's businesses never prospered. More importantly, everywhere Atworth went he would glimpse those ghosts: that old crone staring at him from across a tavern room. Or, in the dark watches of the night, he would glance through his casement window and see the harridan's face, framed by her iron-grey hair, glaring up at him with soul-less eyes and red-rimmed mouth. She was a frightening apparition on the moon-dappled lawn before his timber-and-plaster house. Atworth had known no peace.

'I became like a bottle in the smoke,' he murmured.

He had hastened into Canterbury to seek consolation. He had prayed and fasted. One of these brothers had heard his confession. The monk had wept at Atworth's litany of sins: murder, rape, robbery, and arson. He had refused to give absolution until Atworth had completed a pilgrimage. Atworth travelled to Outremer, experienced the searing heat of Palestine, and returned by way of Rome to seek absolution from one of the Pope's own confessors; the priest had enjoined upon him a life of strict observance.

Atworth had returned to Canterbury. He had joined the Friars of the Sack and committed himself to a life of prayer, fasting, and penance. Even here his past would not let him out of its iron grasp. He had been ordained a priest and won a name for holiness and for being a shrewd confessor.

Dame Cecily of York, the King's own good mother, had recalled their earlier bond and hastened to place her soul in his care. Atworth's jaw tightened. She had good cause to come and seek his absolution. He murmured a prayer. He was being too hard! Now he was a prisoner, taken secretly and questioned about the past! The letters in his wallet had disappeared, yet he had not betrayed his Duchess; she did not deserve that. Atworth wondered what would happen now. He paused in his reflections and shuddered as a fresh spasm of pain coursed through his chest. He couldn't breathe. He heard a sound and glanced round, breathing in and flinching at the fetid smell of this place. His eye caught a shadow. Was someone standing before the door?

'Who is it?' he croaked.

Perhaps it was Jonquil come searching for him. The figure came forward. Atworth tried to scream but found he couldn't. Was it a phantasm? He closed his eyes, yet even in his pain-filled mind, Atworth recognised those pus-covered rags, the wooden sabots, that harridan's face, the steel-grey hair, and those black, soul-less eyes.

'Ah, Jesus!'

Atworth's head went back, and the death rattle sounded strong in his throat. He fought for breath, but he'd lost his last battle. Father Roger Atworth of the Friars of the Sack shuddered and died.

' "From sudden death.
Lord, deliver us.
From famine.
Lord, deliver us.
From pestilence.
Lord, deliver us.
From the evil which stalks at mid-day.
Lord, deliver us.
From fire and sword.
Lord, deliver us.
From the scourge of the Evil One.
Lord, deliver us." '

On the eve of Sts. Perpetua and Felicity, a solemn procession of friars from the Order of the Sack left their house and processed dolefully through the main gate out into the streets of Canterbury. The friars walked in solemn file, preceded by a cross-bearer and two thurifers swinging censers from which poured grey, perfumed clouds of incense.

They walked down the centre of the street making their Procession of Rogation, pleading with God to intervene in the great scourge which now afflicted the city. At first their prayer in the busy thronged streets and alleyways of Canterbury went unheard. However, the rise and fall of their chanting, like the solemn beat of a drum, soon made itself felt: it reminded the good burgesses how this truly was a time of evil. The shopkeepers, the pedlars, the hucksters, as well as the pilgrims on their way to Becket's glorious shrine paused in their business and drew aside. Some knelt

5

on the muddy, cobbled ground and crossed themselves. They eagerly watched one friar who, with a stoup of holy water and an asperges rod, was busy sprinkling either side, as if this would save them from the scourge which had so suddenly appeared in their fair city.

Even as one thread-maker knelt, he gazed across the street and glimpsed the small, black, furry body dart out from a needle-thin alleyway and race to hide itself in a small gap beneath the timbered pillar of a house. The thread-maker clutched the wooden handle of the dagger pushed into his belt. If it wasn't for the good brothers, he would have pursued it! Rats, black and slimy, spike furred with twitching snouts and pattering feet, seemed to infest the city. What was it now? Almost the end of March. Soon it would be April. The air would be spring fresh. The trackways and roads would harden, and the pilgrims would come pouring like a river into the city. They all wished to kneel before Becket's jewel-encrusted shrine, press their hot faces up against it, and make their petitions to Canterbury's great saint. But what would happen now? Over the last three weeks, the city appeared to be infested by a plague of rats causing chaos and confusion.

The line of Friars of the Sack passed, and the thread-maker got to his feet. He walked on into the small ale-house which stood on the corner of Black Griffin Alley. Somewhere behind him he heard a child shriek, 'Rat! Rat!'

The thread-maker just shook his head. He stared round the dingy tap-room, a ramshackle place with dirt-stained table and unclean stools. The ale-wife, standing behind the cask, beckoned him forward, creasing her greasy face into a smile, wiping her hands on a dirty apron. The thread-maker would have declined, but he was thirsty. He sat on a stool, and the ale-wife brought across a black jack, white and frothing at the top. The thread-maker was about to snatch it out of her hand, but she stood back.

'Pay first, drink second!'

The thread-maker fished into his wallet and took out a coin.

'I'll take two,' he offered.

The ale-wife's smile returned, and the black jack was placed on the table beside him. The ale-wife went to the door and stared down the street as if trying to catch sight of the procession.

'Much good that will do.'

The thread-maker whirled round at the voice from a shadow-filled corner. The man sitting there got to his feet and came forward, quiet as a ghost, and, without invitation, sat on a stool on the other side of the thread-maker's table. In fact he did look like a ghost, with his pallid face, greying hair, deep-set blue eyes, furrowed cheeks, thin nose, and bloodless lips. The man was dressed in a none-too-clean shirt under a moleskin jacket tied with a cord, his breeches were worsted, pushed into mud-stained leather boots, yet his fingers and face were clean. The thread-maker, who prided himself on his sharp eyesight, noticed that the war-belt slung over the stranger's shoulder was of fine leather with close purple stitching; the sword and dagger in their sheaths seemed to be of shiny, grey steel.

'Don't you believe in prayer, Brother?' the thread-maker asked.

The uninvited guest grinned: His teeth were fine, sharp and even. He stretched out a hand. 'My name is Monksbane.'

The thread-maker clasped the hand.

'You are a scholar?'

Monksbane's smile widened. 'I like that,' he murmured. 'I used to be at the Inns of Court in London until I became a rat-catcher.'

The thread-maker toasted him genially with his black jack of ale.

'So you know all about this pestilence?'

'There are two types of rats'—Monksbane cradled his own drink, a faraway look in his eyes—'black and brown. Neither has a right to be in the kingdom. Oh no.' He didn't pause at the thread-maker's questioning look but tapped the side of his nose. 'People are so clever. Do you know that there weren't even rabbits here until the Conqueror came? And the same is true of rats! Brought by ship they are. The brown is all right but the black—' He pulled a face. 'Some people claim they bring pestilence whilst they breed worse than flies. In one year two rats can produce many litters.'

The thread-maker sipped at his ale. He now considered himself fortunate to have stepped into this ale-house and met such an interesting teller of tales. Was the man true or a counterfeit? A cunning man? Despite his drab apparel, his war-belt, sword, and dagger looked of fine quality, and when he moved, the thread-maker heard the clink of coins.

'You really are a rat-catcher?'

'Was,' Monksbane replied.

'Is that your real name?'

The smile disappeared.

'Are you here to catch our rats?'

The smile returned.

'Nowadays I hunt different quarry.'

'But you were saying about the rats?' The thread-maker didn't want to upset his mysterious guest.

'Ah, yes. I was chief rat-catcher in Farringdon Ward in London a number of years ago.' He stretched out a hand and pointed to the scars on the back of his wrist. 'Rat bites,' he declared proudly. 'Oh, ale-wife, bring two more fresh stoups! I'll be paying!'

'Can I have my coin back?' the thread-maker shouted.

The ale-wife turned in the doorway, came back, and threw the coin into the thread-maker's outstretched hand. She smiled flirtatiously at Monksbane and waddled back to the great cask standing against the far wall.

'Rats,' Monksbane continued, 'breed like flies, especially the black ones. They swarm all over the place.' He lowered his voice and leaned across the table. 'Do you know I have heard stories how, at sea, they have eaten away the planks of ships and made them sink?'

'And what can they do here?' the thread-maker asked.

'Worse than the plague of locusts in Egypt,' Monksbane declared. 'They'll get into the cellars. They'll eat everything! The more they eat, the more powerful they become, and they breed even more.'

'What about poison?' the thread-maker asked.

Monksbane spread his hands. 'God knows why, but they become used to it.'

'And cats?'

Monksbane sipped from the fresh tankard the ale-wife had placed in front of him.

'You might not believe it, but I have seen three rats attack a cat. Dogs are good, a rat-catching pack, but'—he sighed—'there's a short supply of them in Canterbury.'

'Is it a plague?' the thread-maker asked.

'No, it's an infestation. A mysterious one as well. You see'—

Monksbane leaned across the table, his voice low—'I've been in Canterbury since the Feast of the Purification,' he tapped the side of his nose, 'on the business of the Archbishop, though I've always got an eye out for rats. I can smell them, no matter how rank the odour is in a place like this! You see that table over there?' He pointed across the room. The thread-maker followed his gaze. 'The ale-wife doesn't know it, but there are two under there.'

'You said it was mysterious?'

'That's what I'm saying.' Monksbane preened himself. 'At the end of February . . .' He pulled a face and shook his head. 'Nothing. Oh, the usual ones. Now, down the Mercery, in the market place, even in the Cathedral close, rats swarm as if they had popped out of the earth!'

'So the good brothers are right to pray?'

'Yes,' Monksbane answered, 'though prayer won't get rid of them. Something else has to be done. Certainly if the brothers pray hard and long enough; then God, in his goodness, might reveal the source of this "devilish infestation," as I call it.' Monksbane drained his tankard and got to his feet; he undid the buckle and strapped the war-belt round his waist. 'The Devil's children: From Satan they come; to Satan they can return! But how, when?' He patted the thread-maker on the shoulder. 'Only the good Lord knows.'

Going back to pick up his cloak, Monksbane left the frightened thread-maker staring at the two dark shapes lurking beneath the table beyond.

In the Falstaff Inn, just outside the west gate of Canterbury, the royal spy Robin Goodfellow eased himself up on his bed and rubbed his face. He heard a rap on the door and recognised it as the sound which had roused him from sleep. He slipped his hand beneath the bolster, took out his Italian stiletto, and holding this behind his back, walked across and pulled back the bolts.

'Who is it?' he called.

'Master Goodfellow, your supper.'

The spy turned the key in the lock. He pulled the door open a crack and stared at the young slattern. She was comely enough, with long, blonde hair almost hiding her dirt-stained face. Her drab gown was open at the neck, and its ragged hem hung just above her bare feet. The tray she carried bore a goblet, a large jug of wine, and a wooden bowl of steaming pottage steeped in herbs with a small, white manchet loaf placed on the top. Robin Goodfellow studied the girl closely. She smiled again.

'Your supper, sir.'

Goodfellow pulled the door open and waved the girl in. The slattern placed the tray on the table, picked up the jug, and filled the goblet. She turned, hands provocatively on her hips, and tapped her foot on the floor.

'Is there anything else sir requires?'

'There's nothing else sir requires.' Goodfellow gestured to the open door. 'But if there is, you'll be the first to know. Tell Master Taverner it was good of him not to forget me.'

The girl flounced out. Goodfellow locked and barred the door behind her and stood for a while listening to her receding footsteps. He walked to the window shutters, lifted the bar, opened them, and stared out. It must be about six o'clock, he thought; darkness was already falling. He had taken a chamber overlooking the yard behind the tavern. He closed his eyes and relished the smell of the spring, the sweet fragrance of the herb gardens, the perfume of the early flowers. He stared to his left and then to his right. The shutters of the chambers on either side were closed, as were the shutters of the chambers above. He looked up. The spy noticed how the walls of the tavern, an ancient place, were slightly crooked. He would have preferred glass-filled windows.

Goodfellow grinned; he was becoming soft! This was not some sumptuous manor here in Kent or a château along the Loire Valley. The shutters were sturdy enough; the bar would keep it locked. Goodfellow closed them and peered through the crack: it was narrow enough. The leather hinges were thick, strong, and secure, whilst the wooden bar felt as hard as iron. The spy felt his stomach rumble with hunger and walked back to the table. He sat on the stool, took his horn spoon from his pouch, and began to eat the pottage. He smacked his lips. The meat was fresh but highly spiced; the thick gravy had been enriched with herbs and diced vegetables. He heard a sound in the far corner of the room; he picked up a boot and threw it in the direction of the sound: a squeak and a scampering of feet were the only responses. The spy returned to his meal. The rats didn't bother him. He had eaten and slept in worse places. He put down the horn spoon and picked up the goblet of wine, sniffed at it carefully, and sipped.

'Robin Goodfellow!' he murmured and laughed to himself.

That was no more his name than it was the rat's which had disturbed him. He went back to his meal. He had been born Padraig Mafiach at Clontarf, near Dublin. He had entered the service of the Duke of York as an archer and soon found he had a gift for both languages and disguise. Now he worked for England, bearing important messages for the House of Secrets in London. However, the King was on pilgrimage to Canterbury, staying at his palace in Islip just outside the city. Padraig was to meet the King's Master of Horse, Colum Murtagh, the following morning and then be taken out to meet the King and deliver his message.

Mafiach heard a sound in the passageway outside. He put down the spoon and picked up the stiletto, but the sound receded. The spy continued with his meal. He felt tired and battered, his nerves fretting and on edge. Surely he was safe? Very few people knew of his arrival, and he had been careful to keep himself safe. Again he heard a sound, this time outside. Padraig put down the horn spoon, opened his wallet, unrolled the greasy scrap of parchment, and studied what he had written. A quotation from the prophet Zephaniah (1:16):

The day of the Lord,
The Kings of Kings most righteous, is at hand:
A day of wrath and vengeance, of darkness and cloud:
A day of wondrous, mighty thunderings:
A day of trouble also, of grief and sadness:
In which shall cease the love and desire of women:
And the strife of men and the lust of this world.

Mafiach studied this carefully and the Latin version underneath.

Regis regum rectissimi prope est dies domini
dies irae et vindictae tenebrarum et nebulae
diesque mirabilium tonitruorum fortium
dies quoque angustiae meroris ac tristitiae
in quo cessabit mulierum amor ac desiderium
hominumque contentio mundi huius et cupide.

11

No one but him would understand this cipher or the code scrawled below: 'Recto et Verso,' front and back, or "Veritas continet Veritatem, The truth contains the truth."

Padraig smiled to himself. His eye caught the phrase 'A day of wrath and vengeance'; although he did not know it, for Robin Goodfellow, baptised Padraig Mafiach, that day was very close.

Chapter 1

'Allas,' quod she, 'on thee, Fortune, I playne,
That unwar, wrapped hast me in thy cheyne.'
—Chaucer, 'The Franklin's Tale,'
The Canterbury Tales

The Great Hall of the Archbishop of Canterbury's palace was a sombre building with its deep-vaulted, groined roof and soaring walls. Even the cloths of Montpellier scarlet hanging against the walls did little to dispel the gloom. The windows were mere holes. On that April evening, the Feast of St. Isidore, all the candles, oil lamps, and chafing-dishes had been lit to fend off the icy gloom. The far part of the floor, near the great double doors, was covered in green rushes perfumed by fresh lilies and spring roses, mint and lavender. Further up, near the great mantelled hearth which thrust into the room, Saracen carpets were strewn to fend off the cold seeping through the flagstones. The place was the despair of the Archbishop's chamberlain, who had ordered a great fire of pine logs to be lit. This provided light and heat and sent the shadows dancing. Even the goshawks, perched like sentinels on their wooden stands, heads covered in little leather hoods emblazoned with the Archbishop's escutcheon, felt the cold and moved restlessly to the jingle of jesse bells. The great mastiff, stretched out in front of the fire, red tongue lolling between white teeth, moved occasionally to catch the heat, yet he was as quiet as the three people who sat before the fire.

In the centre, on a chair of state, his slippered feet resting on a footstool of red satin, sat the aged Bourchier, Archbishop of Canterbury, prelate and politician. He was a priest who had quietly confided to his own confessor that, now past his eightieth year, he constantly prepared for death. Bourchier's face showed his age, with its dark, liverish blotches; spotted, sallow, sunken cheeks; and slack mouth with abscesses on the gums. His hair was gone apart from a few wisps, though his eyes were bright and sharp as any young man's. 'He was a true falcon,' as one critic commented. Bourchier's mind was as agile, his wits as nimble as those of any young serjeant-at-law at the Inns of Court. Now he sat, eyes watering, staring into the fire, ears pricked for that dreadful sound he and his two companions were waiting for. One vein-streaked hand was raised; the beautiful episcopal ring, once worn by Thomas à Becket, shimmered in the light. Bourchier stretched his other hand out to the fire. He wore a hair shirt against his skin; that was penance enough! The cold he couldn't stand, and he was dressed in two thick, woollen houpelandes and, over these, a cotehardie with a round neck edged with fur. Around his bony shoulders hung an ermine-trimmed military cloak.

On Bourchier's left, Luberon, clerk to the City Council, perched on the edge of a seat like a little pigeon, eyes bright in his red, cheery face, prim lips pursed. Dressed in a long, grey robe with a white pelisse, Luberon didn't feel the cold and quietly prayed that this meeting would not be too long as the heat from the fire was intense.

On a high-backed chair to the Archbishop's right, Kathryn Swinbrooke silently shared Luberon's discomfort. At first the fire had been welcoming enough, but she wore a thick, woollen dress of dark murrey. She had already loosened the top button and discarded her cloak, which lay across her lap. She pulled her feet, shod in thick buskins, under the chair and tried to relax. Kathryn Swinbrooke, apothecary and physician to the City Council, decided to distract herself by watching Luberon. The little man always amused her: kind-hearted and generous, Luberon was also proud as a peacock and constantly tried to hide the fact that his eyesight was beginning to fail. Only when Kathryn pressed him would Luberon agree to wear the spectacles she had specially bought for him in London.

For the umpteenth time since she had arrived an hour previously and been left to kick her heels in an antechamber, Kathryn wondered why both the council and the Archbishop required her presence. She had a litany of tasks waiting for her at her house and shop in Ottemelle Lane, whilst Thomasina—not to mention Alice and Wulf—would be worried about where she was and what had happened. She leaned back and winked at Luberon. The city clerk blushed and glanced away.

You are beautiful, he reflected. The physician was dressed so elegantly: the white, high-collared pelisse blending subtly with her olive-skinned face. The cowl-like wimple round Kathryn's head discreetly hid her raven-black hair though revealing the slight grey above the temples—*a product,* the clerk reflected, *of those violent days with her husband.* Luberon felt his face flush with embarrassment. Alexander Wyville, Kathryn Swinbrooke's first husband, was one of the reasons for this meeting. Bourchier, once he had made his point, would come to that soon enough. And how would Kathryn take it? Luberon glanced at his friend: Her young-looking face was serene, her large, dark eyes calm, her generous mouth slightly smiling at Bourchier's dramatic manner. Luberon knew Kathryn. Despite the pert nose and smiling lips she could, when provoked, be hot-tempered and very passionate and give free rein to her tongue. Kathryn moved her hands, peeled off her pearl-studded samite gloves, and wiped at the bead of sweat coursing down her forehead. She started as Bourchier abruptly exclaimed, 'There! There! Do you hear it now, Kathryn, Simon?' He glanced at Luberon.

They had both heard and nodded.

'Rats!' Bourchier exclaimed. 'Rats all over Canterbury and all over my palace!'

He turned, glaring down the hall as if, by look alone, he could excommunicate and drive off this sudden plague on both his city and church.

'Halegrins!' the Archbishop declared.

'What are those, Your Eminence?' Kathryn asked.

'An old word'—Bourchier sat back in his chair—'for the violators of tombs and the devourers of human flesh!'

Kathryn thought he was being dramatic but held her peace. The Archbishop gestured at Luberon. 'Come on, Simon. Give me your report.'

'We are now at the beginning of April.' The clerk steepled his fingers. 'By the end of this month, Your Eminence, Canterbury will be full of pilgrims. His Grace the King is already at Islip.'

'Yes, yes, I know about that.' Bourchier gestured at Luberon to continue. 'This plague? This plague?'

'Canterbury has always had rats,' Luberon declared sonorously.

'I know that!' Bourchier snapped. 'Some of them have two legs!'

Luberon glowered at the Archbishop; Kathryn bit her lower lip.

'Come to the point, Simon!'

Luberon winced at the pain in his stomach and wondered again if the meat he had eaten at that city tavern had been rancid. He quietly promised himself to have a word with Kathryn. Perhaps she could help? Or had the meat been tainted by these rats?

'Simon?' the Archbishop purred.

'The rats appeared,' Luberon continued, 'at the beginning of March, around the Feast of St. David of Wales. We first had reports of an infestation beyond the city walls near the river Stour, followed by similar reports of infestations in Westgate and Northgate Wards.' He shrugged. 'By then it was too late. They are seen everywhere. As you know, Your Eminence, ancient sewers and tunnels run beneath the city. The rats use these. Once they surface on the streets'—he held out his hands—'they have food enough, mounds of refuse, the offal in the Shambles, the poulterers, the refuse which litters every alleyway. They are doing great damage to food stocks, particularly grain—indeed, anything stored in the cellars of houses. If hungry, they will attack what's available. Vintners and taverners are complaining how the rats will gnaw at wood: casks, tuns, and vats are ruined.'

'Is that possible?' Bourchier turned to Kathryn.

'Your Eminence, I am a physician, not a rat-catcher.'

'I know, I know, but . . .'

'Rats will eat anything,' Kathryn hurriedly continued. 'Normally they will not gnaw at wood or baskets; but if that wood has been drenched in food or drink, like a wine vat, yes, they would. They are great devourers. They live to eat and procreate . . .'

'Like many sons of Adam,' Bourchier interrupted drily.

'Each pair can breed at least four litters a year,' Kathryn declared. 'This is an infestation the city has never witnessed before.

16

Rats can live anywhere, move anywhere. They can swim; they will eat anything. Some physicians claim they are the carriers of malignant diseases.'

'Why?' Bourchier asked.

Kathryn forgot about the excessive warmth. She leaned forward, emphasizing the points on her finger.

'First, where there is dirt and refuse, disease and rats always flourish. We do not know what is the cause and what is the effect. Secondly, their urine and faeces must be tainted.'

Luberon swallowed hard, hand to his lips. He did feel a little queasy.

'And?' Bourchier demanded.

'My father—God rest him, Your Eminence—loved to talk to Italian visitors, particularly physicians. He met some who claimed how the very breath of a rat is fetid and polluted.'

'So what is our danger?' Bourchier wanted to know.

'As summer comes, the incidence of disease will increase; it always does in hot weather. The rats will make it worse. Secondly, they may have an effect on foods, though last year's harvest was good and plentiful. . . .'

'And?'

Kathryn gestured at Luberon to explain.

'Canterbury, Your Eminence, is the pilgrimage centre of the kingdom. If this news is bruited abroad, the number of pilgrims may well fall; and the effect on trade,' Luberon added, 'would be disastrous.'

Bourchier leaned back in his chair and stared at a gargoyle carved in the centre of the mantelpiece, a monkey's face shrouded in a cowl. *The sculptor,* Bourchier reflected, *must have had little love for monks or priests,* a sentiment Bourchier himself often shared.

'So what do you recommend?'

Luberon stared at the floor. Kathryn played with her pair of gloves. The rats concerned her. Only this week she had dealt with three children who had been bitten; even her house and shop, swept and cleaned, had been visited by what Thomasina called 'those damnable slinkers of the night.' Kathryn had discussed the problem with the Master of the King's Horse, Colum Murtagh, who lodged with her. Murtagh, who had served in the Royal

Wars, knew a great deal about rats and had expressed his surprise at how intense this infestation had become.

'What,' he'd asked, 'has brought so many rats to Canterbury in so short a time?'

Thomasina had replied that it was a judgement of God. Kathryn couldn't decide, but the topic was on everyone's lips, particularly amongst other members of the Apothecaries' Guild who had precious stocks to guard.

'We have rat-catchers.' Luberon broke the silence. 'And the City Council has been approached by one Malachi Smallbones.'

'Who?' Bourchier demanded.

'Principal rat-catcher from the city of Oxford,' Luberon explained. 'He claimed a similar infestation occurred there last year: Both Town and Gown hired his services. Apparently he was very successful.'

'You have proof of this?'

'Your Eminence, he brought letters of recommendation.'

'And what does he advise?'

'That the council,' Luberon glanced sly-eyed at the Archbishop, 'with the help of the Cathedral, allocate monies to hire a veritable army of rat-catchers under Malachi's command; that he be allowed to buy potions and powders, not to mention small hunting dogs; that he be given a commission to enter all dwellings and go where he wishes to wipe out these vermin from hell.'

'It will be very costly,' Bourchier growled.

'Malachi well deserves his reward,' Luberon answered.

'Kathryn, do you agree with this?' Bourchier extended his fingers.

'If this Malachi is as organised and skilled as he claims to be,' Kathryn shrugged, 'I would accept. Canterbury is divided into wards. Every citizen should be alerted, a small reward placed for every'—she raised her hand—'two-dozen rats brought in. Allow Malachi and his confederates to go through the streets and kill where they wish. But these potions?' She glanced across at Luberon.

'Poison, henbane, belladonna, foxglove.'

'He will have to be careful,' Kathryn replied. 'Domestic animals, not to mention children, must not pick up such bait. He should also be prudent.'

'How's that?' Luberon snapped.

'Poisoned baits can be eaten by humans,' Kathryn declared. 'But I have some knowledge of rats: If they eat certain poisons, eventually they become impervious to them.'

'Impossible!' Luberon jibed.

'No, no. I have seen men and women with a similar condition. Powders and potions which work on others seem to have little effect upon them.'

The Archbishop still looked askance.

'Your Eminence, I only report what I know. It is important,' Kathryn warmed to her topic, 'that Malachi be given every help. It's not enough that rats are killed.' She smiled. 'You know what I am going to say, Simon? More city scavengers must also be hired, rubbish cleared from the streets, sewers cleaned. The Butchers' and the Poulterers' Guilds must co-operate: offal should be collected, taken outside the city gates, and burnt, and heavy fines imposed on those who dump refuse or fail to clean latrines and cesspits.'

'You are enjoying this, aren't you?' Luberon glared across at Kathryn.

'You know why, Simon. If the council spent more money on clearing refuse and keeping the water supply sweet . . .'

'This will cost so much,' Luberon declared mournfully. 'Perhaps Your Eminence will approach the King and ask for a respite on taxes and levies? Perhaps the King, in his infinite compassion, will make a grant to his city of Canterbury . . . ?' Luberon faltered.

Infinite compassion! Kathryn thought. Edward IV and his two brothers, George of Clarence and Richard of Gloucester, were men of war. 'Wolfish men' was how Colum described them, with more sins on their souls than hairs on a woman's head. Kathryn had met them all: Edward, standing over six foot, beautiful face, blue eyes, his blond hair like a golden aureole round his well-shaped head. George of Clarence was just as handsome, except for that smirk on his lips which betrayed a venomous, even murderous nature. Finally, Richard of Gloucester, dwarfed by his brothers, with his russet hair and white, pinched face, was a man who could never stay still. Richard was the King's right-hand man, and if Colum was to be believed, a ferocious warrior who'd played a great part in his brother's late victory at Tewkesbury in the West Country.

'Infinite compassion.' Bourchier smiled at Kathryn as if he could read her mind. 'I will see what I can do. The King's mother, the Duchess Cecily, has a soft spot for this city. Yet it seems,' he sighed, 'that only gold will cure this pestilence; so gold must be spent, eh, Kathryn?'

'Your Eminence, it's either that or fire.'

'What!'

'Fire.' Kathryn pushed her chair further from the hearth. 'A fire would burn out the nests and the hunting runs of these rats.'

'We can't burn the city!' Luberon screeched.

'I am not saying that. Yet Malachi must not only kill rats, he must search out their nests. . . .'

'It's so strange,' Bourchier mused. 'Do you know, Kathryn, the rats were first seen in the Cathedral grounds?'

'Some people see it as a visitation from God,' Luberon interjected, 'the scourge of His anger.'

'Why is that?' Bourchier glared at Luberon.

'I speak discreetly, Your Eminence. I trust you and Mistress Swinbrooke.'

'Spit it out, man!' Bourchier growled.

'The King'—Luberon looked around as if he was frightened lest the walls had ears or the King's eavesdroppers lurked behind the arras—'the King is coming to Canterbury,' Luberon chose his words carefully, 'to give thanks for his great victory, that God has given him the crown and confirmed his rule.' Luberon paused.

Bourchier began playing with the episcopal ring. He glanced quickly at Kathryn and stared at the fire. 'I think you've said enough,' Bourchier whispered.

Kathryn stared across at Luberon and shook her head, a sign that the clerk should say no more. Yet Luberon had simply voiced what other people thought. The House of York had been victorious at Tewkesbury, and a savage blood-letting had occurred. Their great rivals, the war chiefs of Lancaster, had been killed or barbarously executed in market places up and down the kingdom. Even here in Canterbury, Nicholas Faunte, the Mayor, who had thrown his lot in with the Lancastrians, had died a hideous death on the gallows near the market-place cross. More sombre news had arrived from London: how the saintly Lancastrian King,

Henry VI, had been taken prisoner and housed in that dark, narrow place, the Tower. Edward and his brothers had sworn great oaths that not a hair of his head would be hurt; yet shortly after the victorious Yorkist leaders had reached London, Henry had died suddenly and mysteriously. Some people claimed he had taken a fall; others that he had been knifed most cruelly to death by Yorkist henchmen. His body had been moved to Chertsey, and already pilgrims were visiting his tomb, claiming miraculous cures. Bourchier himself had been petitioned that Henry VI had died a martyr's death and should be proclaimed a saint.

'If God wished to punish any house,' Bourchier had replied slowly, 'he has other, more subtle ways than punishing our city of Canterbury. Do you not agree, Kathryn?'

The physician held her peace.

'Whatever.' Bourchier stirred in his chair and extended his hands towards the fire. 'Kathryn, Mistress Swinbrooke'—he smiled—'you will give this Malachi every help and sustenance.'

He paused and stared up at the black wooden crucifix fixed on the wall above the mantel hearth.

'Martyrs and saints,' he murmured. 'Let us now leave the rats to their rat-catcher. Malachi Smallbones has three weeks to prove his boast.' He drummed his fingers on his thigh. 'Do you believe in miracles, Mistress Swinbrooke?'

'God can do what he wishes.'

Bourchier leaned across and squeezed Kathryn's hand. 'You would make a good theologian, Mistress. You know the Friars of the Sack?'

Luberon winked quickly; now he was warning her.

'They had a brother, a member of their order,' Bourchier continued, 'a Roger Atworth, a man well past his seventy-fifth year. A former soldier, he became a merchant; then he gave up all his wealth and entered the friary. Atworth soon won a name for sanctity, austerity, and prayer. People were astonished at the change, particularly those who had known him in France, including Cecily, widow of Richard, Duke of York, and mother of our King.' Bourchier paused.

Kathryn glanced across at a small shelf beneath the crucifix holding a sacred relic. Murtagh had once fought for Richard of

York. The Irishman had often discussed Duchess Cecily, a haughty but very beautiful woman. In her youth she had been known as 'the Rose of Raby.'

'That explains,' Luberon murmured, 'why Duchess Cecily so often visited Canterbury.'

'Atworth became her confessor, even adviser,' Bouchier said.

'Was he a charlatan?' Kathryn asked.

'Oh no! Prior Anselm considered him a very good, holy man, noted for severe discipline against himself but compassion for others. Atworth's life at the friary was austere: He wore a hair shirt, fasted, and prayed. However, Prior Anselm conceded that Atworth was haunted by his past. Hideous deeds were perpetrated in France,' Bourchier murmured. 'Have you ever heard of "the Ecorcheurs," Kathryn?'

'Who hasn't?' she replied. 'Homo lupus homini: Man became wolf to man.'

'I would agree with that.' Bourchier cleared his throat. 'Simon, Kathryn, do you wish some wine?'

Both shook their heads and smiled at each other. Any cup of wine, coupled with the heat from the fire, would have sent them to sleep. Bourchier patted his stomach.

'I would love one, but my physician has told me'—he grinned at Kathryn—'to wait until after vespers. Ah yes, "the Ecorcheurs,'" he continued. 'They were Free Companies who fought under the banners of the great English lords. They won their name because they supposedly flayed Frenchmen alive. No wonder the English were called "Goddamns" or "Devils without tails"! Anyway, Atworth was one of these; but like Saul on the road to Damascus, he saw the error of his ways and came back to God. To cut a long story short, Atworth died on the Feast of the Annunciation.'

'How old was he?' Kathryn demanded.

'Around his seventy-eighth summer, almost as old as me,' Bourchier joked. 'He was found dead in his chamber. The door was locked and bolted from the inside so his manservant, the lay brother Jonquil, called for help. The door was forced. Inside Atworth lay on the bed; apparently he had died in his sleep.'

'Was he in good health?'

'Sickly,' Bourchier replied, 'but of a very robust constitution.'

He bowed his head. Kathryn noticed how the Archbishop had

drawn mother-of-pearl paternoster beads out of his pocket and was gently threading these through his fingers.

'Prior Anselm and Brother Simon the infirmarian were the first to see the corpse. It bore no mark of violence except'—Bourchier scratched his chin—'here.' He tapped his wrists and, leaning down, his ankle, 'The stigmata.'

'What?' Kathryn exclaimed.

'The Five Wounds of Christ,' Bourchier declared. 'Holes, the size of nails, through his wrists and on the instep of each foot just beneath the ankle, and a similar wound to his left side.'

'Impossible!' Kathryn breathed. 'The same marks of the crucifixion? Christ was nailed by his hands and feet to the cross and a spear thrust through his side.'

'Were the wounds bleeding?' Luberon asked.

'No, just filled with blood. Prior Anselm described them as "sacred rubies," the blood frothing round the cut, though it hadn't flowed. There's more. As you know, our Saviour was crowned by the heathens with a coronet of thorns thrust into his scalp. Similar marks were found around Atworth's scalp.'

Kathryn stared in disbelief. She had heard of such miraculous manifestations but never really believed in them.

'Was a physician called?'

'Brother Simon is a skilled physician,' Bourchier retorted. 'I understand your disbelief, Kathryn, but other members of the community were called to act as witnesses. The body was stripped; the stigmata were clear to see.'

'And Brother Simon ascertained the cause of death?'

'Atworth's face was serene, his skin slightly discoloured: Failure of the heart is quite common in a man of his age.'

'And these wounds had never been seen before on Atworth?'

'Never, though he had often complained of pains in his wrists and ankles and similar pains in his left side.'

Kathryn held her peace. She remembered her father's advice: "Never ascribe to God," he'd declared, "what can be the work of man."

'I wish I could have seen that,' Luberon declared.

'Yes, that's a good point.' Kathryn paused. 'Why didn't Prior Anselm broadcast the news through the city?'

'Because he was under strict orders not to.' Bourchier patted the gold pectoral cross against his chest. 'I am the leader of the Church of England. I do not take kindly to every corpse being claimed as the relic of a saint. Prior Anselm did send a message to me; I went to view the corpse myself.'

'You saw this?' Luberon exclaimed.

'With my own eyes. I tell you: marks of thorns on the forehead, the wounds on the wrists and insteps, the jabbing cut just under the rib cage. Atworth's clothes were on the floor: a hair shirt, linen drawers, his brown robe and girdle, and nothing else. I questioned Prior Anselm closely. He claimed Atworth had been ill, kept to his chamber two days before he died, but nothing untoward happened. There was more. When Anselm greeted me at the door, he asked me to comment on whatever I found remarkable in Atworth's chamber. He was careful not to suggest anything.'

'And?'

'I was only in the chamber a few seconds, more concerned with inspecting the cadaver, when I became aware of the strongest perfume. It seemed to pervade the entire chamber. Now, Mistress Swinbrooke, you have been in rooms where people have died. You can almost smell death. Atworth's chamber was different: Its one window still remained shuttered.'

'What was the smell?' Kathryn demanded.

'Like sweet roses and lilies crushed and distilled. I knelt and said a requiem for Atworth. I noticed how his flesh had a slightly cold, waxy feel. Prior Anselm asked me what we should do. I gave orders for Atworth's corpse to be buried immediately. Anselm objected. Duchess Cecily had to pay her respects, so I agreed. A scurrier was sent to Islip. Duchess Cecily, accompanied by her son Clarence and a small group of retainers, slipped into Canterbury. The Duchess, too, was full of wonderment at what she saw. The following morning, the twenty-sixth of March, Atworth was buried beneath the flagstones before the Lady Chapel in the friary church.'

As a physician Kathryn was full of interest in such a remarkable case. She only wished she could have inspected the wonderful phenomenon. In her time she had met men and women who claimed to be saints, even angels, but there had been nothing wrong with them which a good dose of valerian wouldn't cure.

'And this fragrance, you couldn't trace the source?'

'The chamber was simple: wooden floor, stone walls, a broken coffer, a table, a battered chair, nothing more than you could load into a small cart. Atworth died a very poor man. Now, as I have said, the burial took place on the twenty-sixth of March. The friary returned to its normal routine, but Jonquil, the lay brother, was very upset. In the evenings, just before sunset, he went and prayed before Atworth's tomb. On the thirty-first of March, the Feast of St. Ceadda, Jonquil was praying there when he claims to have smelt the same wondrous fragrance I had smelt in Atworth's death chamber. The Lady Chapel glowed in light: He saw a figure, dressed all in white, a cowl pulled over its head. . . .'

'Oh no,' Kathryn interrupted, 'he saw an apparition of Atworth?'

'Jonquil stood petrified. He heard a voice ordering him to tell Father Prior what he had seen. Jonquil obeyed. Terrified, he fled the church. Prior Anselm, Brother Simon, and others hastily returned to the Lady Chapel. They saw nothing, but once again, they smelt that fragrance.'

Kathryn lifted up her hand. 'Of course,' she whispered, 'I've heard of this. My maid and nurse, Thomasina, always brings me the chatter of the city; she talked of wondrous doings at the Friary of the Sack.'

'The news has spread throughout Canterbury. Atworth's tomb has been visited, and miracles have occurred.'

'Miracles?' Kathryn enquired.

'You don't deny God's work?' Bourchier smiled.

'No, I don't, Your Eminence, though I am more concerned with men's credulity. What sort of miracles?'

Bourchier hid his grin behind a hand. 'A young bridegroom worried about his impotence lay over the flagstones.'

'Oh no!'

'Listen!' Bourchier continued. 'He said he had rubbed his genitals against the stone. When he returned home, his potency had returned.'

Luberon sat straight in the chair, a look of disapproval on his face.

'Simon, Simon'—the Archbishop leaned across and tapped him on the wrist—'these things happen. There have been others. A young woman with a skin disease visited the friary. She suffered from scrofula; that disappeared. An old soldier who suffered an ailment of the bowels also claimed to be cured, as did a mother whose infant had been bitten on the wrist by a rat.'

'Any more?' Kathryn asked.

'Why? Do you disbelieve, Kathryn?'

'I don't, Your Eminence. I am just intrigued.'

'The Duchess Cecily?' Luberon chimed in.

'Ah yes, Simon, the Duchess Cecily.' Bourchier peered at the hour candle on its great, black iron stand. 'The flame has almost reached the seventh circle,' he remarked. 'Our visitors will have arrived.'

'What visitors?'

'The Duchess Cecily is very pleased at all these reports. She has sent her henchman, Walter Venables, to meet us here, along with Cardinal Peter Spineri.'

'The White Cardinal!' Kathryn exclaimed. 'The papal legate?'

'The same,' Bourchier confirmed. 'He has travelled up from London to be the King's guest at Islip. Duchess Cecily is demanding that the life, death, and miracles of Atworth be investigated. Cardinal Spineri has promised to place Atworth's case before the Holy Father in Rome for beatification.'

Kathryn's stomach clenched. She half-suspected what was going to happen next.

'You know the process,' Bourchier murmured. 'Spineri will be the Advocatus Angeli, the Advocate of the Angel: his task will be to prove that Atworth is truly a saint and now enjoys the vision of God.' He leaned across and grasped Kathryn's wrist. 'Mistress Swinbrooke, you are an excellent physician, a wise woman, nobody's fool. I have heard of your reputation.'

'Other excellent physicians work in Canterbury.'

'They can be bought,' Bourchier smiled, 'either by being frightened or bribed. Kathryn, I want you to be the Advocatus Diaboli, the Devil's Advocate. It will be your task to prove that Atworth's life, death, and so-called miracles do not warrant beatification and canonisation.'

Kathryn studied the watery, shrewd eyes of this old Archbishop. 'A true fox' was how Colum had described him.

'Surely,' she whispered, 'Canterbury can afford another saint?'

Bourchier's eyes wrinkled in amusement.

As cunning as a serpent, Kathryn reflected. Bourchier would concede to Duchess Cecily's demand and do everything he could do to assist, but that glance told her everything. Bourchier was Archbishop of Canterbury, and his cathedral housed the sacred remains of Thomas à Becket.

'What are you thinking, Kathryn?'

'Why, Your Eminence, I am sure you know. Canterbury can only afford one saint. If the Church of the Friars of the Sack holds the remains of a holy man, pilgrims might become diverted, take their offerings elsewhere.'

Bourchier's eyes widened in mock innocence.

'Oh, Kathryn, how could you?'

'Quite easily, Your Eminence.'

'But will you accept the task?'

'Duchess Cecily is a powerful woman.'

'Aye, Kathryn, but Colum Murtagh also has the King's ear.' Bourchier raised his hand and sketched a blessing towards her. 'I am eighty-two years old, Kathryn.' His voice dropped to a whisper. 'I have seen kings and princes come and go, but the power of the Church remains. I will protect you.'

Not waiting for an answer, Bourchier leaned over the arm of his chair, picked up a small hand-bell from the floor, and rang it vigorously. The door at the far end opened. 'Your Eminence?' a servant called.

Bourchier leaned his head against the back of the chair. 'Have my visitors arrived?'

'Both are waiting in the antechamber.'

'Then let them wait no longer.'

Huffing and puffing, Bourchier eased himself up. Kathryn and Luberon hastened to help; and flanked by both, Bourchier walked down the room across the multi-coloured Saracen carpets, and paused half-way. Servants carrying sconce torches came in, followed by a cross-bearer and a chamberlain. Whilst the servants took up positions on either side of the hall, the chamberlain walked forward.

'Your Eminence, Cardinal Peter Spineri, Bishop of the Church of St. Sebastian in Rome, and Walter Venables, equerry to Her Grace, the Duchess of York.'

'Then let them come forward.' Bourchier's voice was soft but carrying.

The cross-bearer and chamberlain stood aside. Kathryn was immediately taken by how short and plump Spineri was: He had a tonsured head, and his small, round face was as brown as a nut. He had merry eyes, a snub nose, and a generous mouth. She could tell why he was nicknamed 'Cardinal Albus, the White Cardinal.' Spineri was dressed in the pure white robe of a Carmelite, buskins of the same colour on his feet, a silver girdle round his plump waist, and a black cowl thrown back over his shoulders; he rested on an ebony-topped walking-stick. Face wreathed in smiles, he came forward and exchanged the 'osculum pacis,' the kiss of peace, with Bourchier.

Venables was a young, dark-faced man, clean-shaven, his black hair cropped close above his ears. He was dressed in a long gown of blood-red scarlet with full sleeves, the cuffs and collar fringed with fur; on his legs, green hose were pushed into soft, brown leather boots with silver buckles. *A soldier,* Kathryn thought, *but also a man used to the silken subtlety of the court.* He wore a silver chain round his neck; the silver medallion on the end was emblazoned with the Yorkist arms. A thick, broad leather warbelt hung over his shoulders, and he handed this to the chamberlain as he came forward to kneel and kiss Bourchier's ring.

Further introductions were made. Venables and Spineri, born courtiers, each in turn took hold of Kathryn's hand and kissed it lightly. Spineri was effusive, his English tinged with a strong accent and the occasional Italian word. Venables was soft-spoken, watchful, tense as a cat. He seemed more interested in Kathryn than the other two, as if in a hurry to take her measure, discover who she really was. Kathryn coloured with embarrassment at his long, searching look.

'Have we met before, Master Venables?'

The henchman's severe face broke into an affected smile. 'No, Mistress, but I wish we had.'

Further gallantries were halted by Bourchier ordering the servants to place more chairs around the fire. A tray of cups and a dish of comfits were brought in. Kathryn was glad to see a jewel-encrusted goblet. It had been deliberately chilled, and the white

German wine was cool and fragrant. They took their seats, this time further away from the fire, Spineri next to Kathryn, Venables beside Luberon.

'The hour is growing late,' Bourchier began, 'so I will not tarry long. Mistress Swinbrooke has accepted the commission I have given to her.'

'May I say,' Spineri broke in with a smile, 'I have never met such an attractive Advocatus Diaboli.' His voice dropped to a melodramatic whisper. 'I look forward to meeting you in the lists, not sword against sword, but wit against wit, eh, Mistress?'

'How long will this take?' Venables broke in. He seemed to resent Spineri's closeness to Kathryn and the gallantry he showed her.

'How long is a piece of twine?' Spineri asked. 'Mistress Swinbrooke, I will not bore you with Canon Law. However, the Advocatus Diaboli is the initiator. You can demand whatever you want.'

'Are there documents on Atworth?' Kathryn demanded.

'A few, probably held by the friars.'

'And people from his former life?'

'A number of old soldiers in and around Canterbury.'

'I will not visit them,' Kathryn declared. 'They may, if they wish, come to me.'

Venables was watching her intently. Spineri seemed more concerned with drinking his wine. Kathryn had the measure of the plump, merry cardinal. He was a King's man through and through: If Cecily of York wanted her cat canonised, Cardinal Spineri would scarcely object.

'And these miracles? They must be local people?'

Bourchier nodded.

'I wish to examine them carefully.'

'Are you denying the miracles?' Venables asked hotly.

'Sir, I'll deny nothing. I will simply put forward evidence so His Eminence can decide for himself. But above all,' she continued, 'I must question Prior Anselm and others. Finally, Atworth's body must be exhumed.'

Venables smiled across at her, nodding in agreement.

'Is that really necessary?' Spineri protested.

'If the body hasn't decayed, Your Eminence . . . ?'

Spineri pulled a face.

'In the end,' Kathryn concluded, 'the Church needs evidence of sanctity. I believe Brother Atworth's corpse may yield the truth.'

Kathryn sipped from her wine and repressed a shiver. She would keep her own counsel amongst these cunning, secretive men. Yet she had an unknown fear: This matter hid many secrets, and she wondered how powerful Bourchier's protection truly would be.

Chapter 2

'Though ye prolle ay, ye shul it nevere fynde.'
—Chaucer, 'The Canon's Yeoman's Tale,'
The Canterbury Tales

The Conventual Church of the Friars of the Order of the Sack was a place of dappled-white and shifting shadows. Its soaring, vaulted roof caught and echoed all sound; round, squat pillars along the nave guarded gloomy transepts where former members of the order lay buried under carved sarcophagi awaiting the final resurrection. Sculpted statues stared blindly down from niches in the walls. Gargoyled faces grinned maliciously from the tops of pillars. Night had fallen. Most of the candles had been doused. The incense-fragrant air was chilly. A fine mist had seeped under the doorway; its wisps coiled along the nave like thin, meagre ghosts searching for a place to hide. It was a gloomy church with its shadow-filled corners; but the three friars, who knelt in their small pool of light before the Lady Chapel, were oblivious to the shifting shapes and shades around them. They blew on their fingers and rubbed their arms in a futile attempt to keep warm. The only light was the candles lit before the statue of the Black Madonna, an ancient wooden image of the Virgin Mary holding the Divine Child, his arms outstretched to an ignoring world. The friars stared down at the flagstones. The words freshly etched there seemed to leap up: HIC IACET FRATER ROGER ATWORTH OBIT . . ." The inscription ran on: How Brother Roger had lived the life of a holy friar and died in the odour of sanctity in the year of Our Lord 1473.

'If not the odour of sanctity,' the friar in the centre murmured, 'then at least something akin to it.'

'Is it right, what we are doing?' one of his companions asked.

'We have no choice,' their leader replied, his face hidden deep in his cowl. 'We must take the oath, all three of us, to keep all silent. We must revere our great saint.'

He placed the sacred chalice in the centre of the flagstone and laid on top the square white paten. He touched this with his fingers and whispered the sacred words. His companions, in a more faltering manner, followed suit: As they did, they quietly prayed that the Blessed Roger, now surely in a place of light, would understand what they were doing.

The meeting in the Archbishop's palace had finished. Kathryn, Venables, and Spineri had all agreed to meet the following day for the solemn exhumation of Roger Atworth's corpse. Kathryn was intrigued, and her reluctance had now disappeared. She was genuinely curious and kept wondering about the phenomena Bourchier had described.

'I can see,' she declared after Spineri and Venables had withdrawn, 'that our eminent cardinal has already made his mind up.'

'Oh, I am sure he has.' Bourchier sipped at the goblet. 'When Spineri returns to Rome, I am certain he will lead a sumpter pony heavily laden with gifts, both for himself and his friends in the Curia.'

Kathryn stared longingly at the hour candle. It now showed the eighth hour; it really was time she should leave. However, Luberon and Bourchier still remained seated. The little clerk was agitated: He kept shuffling his feet and clearing his throat, his usual habit when nervous.

Kathryn made to rise. 'Your Eminence, the hour is drawing late.'

'I'll see you safely back to Ottemelle Lane,' Bourchier gestured at her to remain seated, 'Kathryn.' He looked down as if fascinated by the collar on the sleeping mastiff.

'Your Eminence, surely we are not here to await your dog?'

Bourchier lifted a hand. 'I stand rebuked. I think it's best, Simon, if . . .'

Luberon coughed. 'Kathryn, you are well?'

'For the love of God, Simon,' she retorted sharply, 'I am *not* well. I have had a busy day, a long line of patients. Now, seated in front of this fire, I feel one side of me is burnt; the other is freezing.'

Bourchier laughed apologetically.

'Oh, come to the point, Simon.'

'You are not married?'

Kathryn threw her head back and laughed. 'Very perceptive, Simon.'

'You live in Ottemelle Lane?'

Kathryn glowered at him.

'You are a reputable physician, well liked by many. His Eminence trusts you, as does the City Council. . . .'

'Enough!' Kathryn interrupted.

Luberon closed his eyes. Kathryn's face had that stubborn, pugnacious look.

'I think I've heard this hymn before,' she declared. 'Kathryn Swinbrooke, member of the Apothecaries' Guild, physician to the City Council, adviser to His Eminence Bourchier Cardinal Archbishop, is living in a house in Ottemelle Lane'—Kathryn's eyes rounded in mock innocence as her voice dropped to a harsh whisper—'and a man lives there, Colum Murtagh, an Irish soldier, Master of the King's Horse, keeper of the royal stables out at Kingsmead. He's not married either. Thomasina also lives with me, and God knows how many times *she* has been married. Agnes, my maid, is not married, and neither is my apprentice, Wulf. We used to call him "Wuf" till he objected. He much prefers Wulf after the saintly Wulfstan, who I believe, Your Eminence, was a bishop of the Church? I am the head of a large household. I do good business as a physician and as an apothecary. However, what I do at night between the sheets'—Kathryn's face flushed with anger—'is my own business! Widow Gumple, with her stupid head-dresses, her fat face, and her malicious tongue, does not concern me!' Again she made to rise.

'Kathryn, Kathryn'—Bourchier leaned across and clasped her hand—'in my eyes you are a daughter.'

'In my eyes, Your Eminence, you are a snooper!'

Bourchier grinned. 'They say you have a rough tongue, Kathryn.'

The physician glanced across at Luberon and felt a pang of regret at her outburst. He sat crumpled on the edge of the chair like a little boy, eyes staring, mouth open.

'I meant no offence, Mistress,' he whispered.

'None taken'—Kathryn forced a smile—'but I wish you'd come to the point. I do my best to heal bodies; I cannot be held responsible for wagging tongues.'

'Do you love Colum Murtagh?' Bourchier's voice was surprisingly harsh.

Kathryn felt her throat go dry. If it had been any other man, she would have stormed out; but Bourchier was a good priest, a shepherd who genuinely cared for his flock and not just its fleece. Luberon refused to meet her gaze.

'Tell me, Kathryn, please.'

'Yes, Your Eminence, I do,' she declared hotly. 'I am not his leman; I am my own woman.'

'Are you handfast, betrothed?'

'I am not, but Colum wishes it was so.'

'And why not?'

'You know why not.' Kathryn sat back in the chair. 'I was married to Alexander Wyville. The story is well known: Two years ago Wyville decided to join the Lancastrian forces; he left Canterbury and never returned.'

'Have you searched for him?'

'Yes, I have. Sometimes I suspect he is dead. Other times I dismiss that as wishful thinking.'

'Do you want him dead?'

'I married him, Your Eminence, because I thought I loved him, because my late father wanted it. Wyville proved to be a ruffian—a man who smiled and pretended to be a saint—but in his cups he was a villain free with his fists. His tongue and heart were soaked in wormwood. He had great dreams of profiting from the war. I was glad to see him go, and God forgive me, I pray he won't come back. Is that sinful?'

'No.' Bourchier shook his head. 'No, it isn't!' He patted her hand. 'But what if, Kathryn, Wyville is dead? According to Canon Law,' the Archbishop continued hurriedly, 'should her husband disappear and no trace is ever found, a woman has to wait ten years before she can remarry. Do you want to wait ten years?'

Kathryn closed her eyes. In her mind's eye she saw Colum: hair black as night, dark-blue eyes crinkling with amusement, laughter lines around his mouth, his strong hands as he tried to mend a bridle or a halter, the smell of leather . . .

'Kathryn?'

She opened her eyes.

'You have done good work for the council and for me,' Bourchier continued. 'Oh, we pay a fee. Now I wish to reward you, not pry or snoop.'

Kathryn's heart beat a little faster.

'Your private life is a matter for confession and the priest who shrives you, but as you know, I have great influence.' Bourchier explained. 'I have already despatched letters to all the priests in the villages and towns the Lancastrian forces passed through on their way to Tewkesbury. I have asked them to make careful search if they know anything about a man called Alexander Wyville.'

'He could have gone under another name!' Kathryn responded. 'He joined Faunte's forces outside Westgate. Even then he was pretending to be what he wasn't.'

'I know.' Bourchier scratched his chin. 'Nicholas Faunte, the late but not lamented Mayor of Canterbury, raised a force for the Lancastrians and led them west. They wanted to be present at the great victory. On their way they also hoped to enrich themselves through pillage and plunder. In an attempt to escape the clutches of the law, many took different names, aliases, including the names of herbs such as Feverfew, Hellebore, Verben. Now we know,' Bourchier paused, 'some of these forces reached Tewkesbury, where King Edward and his brothers inflicted a devastating defeat and the House of Lancaster went into the dark.' He picked up the hand-bell and rang it.

Kathryn heard the door at the far end of the hall open.

'Bring him in!' Bourchier shouted. 'Tell Master Monksbane that I will see him now!'

Kathryn stared at the curious individual who marched up the hall. Bourchier didn't move as the grey-haired man came round and knelt before the chair of state. He kissed Bourchier's ring and took the stool opposite, a wiry, pale-eyed man dressed in a moleskin jacket and leggings, though his boots, wallet, and ornate war-belt looked costly. He was the sort of man Kathryn might glimpse in a crowd yet be unable to describe in great detail: almost faceless, indistinguishable. When he smiled, however, Kathryn felt a warmth; Monksbane was apparently proud of his profession, whatever it was, and was clearly trusted by the Archbishop.

'Mistress Swinbrooke,' Bourchier moved in his chair, 'may I introduce Monksbane. I don't think he was baptised that at the font, but that's what he likes to be called now. A former student at the Inns of Court in Chancery Lane. A man who fell on hard times but picked himself up and rose to be one of the principal rat-catchers of the capital . . .'

'Farringdon Ward precisely, Your Eminence,' Monksbane broke in; his voice was cultured and as calm as any priest's.

'Yes, that's right,' Bourchier agreed. 'Very proud of his old profession is Monksbane.'

'You've come to Canterbury to catch rats?' Kathryn asked.

'No, Kathryn.' Luberon sat more relaxed, although he found it difficult to hide his deep upset at Kathryn's open declaration about Colum Murtagh.

'Yes, Simon?' Kathryn leaned forward.

'He's not here to catch rats.' Luberon smiled.

'Monksbane is *my* man'—Bourchier patted Monksbane as he would his mastiff—'my man in peace and war. He's a bounty-hunter, Kathryn! Tired of killing rats, he came to Canterbury and offered his services to me. You would be surprised how often the Church has to go hunting. Isn't that right, Monksbane?'

'Yes, Your Eminence. We live in a vale of tears.'

Monksbane's voice turned lugubrious. Kathryn found it difficult not to smile.

'Truly the preacher says you cannot serve God and Mammon! Many a priest flees his parish and takes the offertory box and the sacred plate with him.'

'Especially now.' Bourchier sighed. 'During the war many priests left their livings: monks, clerks, and friars. When they flee, they always take the Church's possessions with them.'

'And Monksbane hunts them down?'

'Yes, Kathryn, he's my lurcher. He sniffs them out, grasps them by the nape of the neck, and brings them back.'

36

Kathryn stared at this curious man; she now realised and was grateful for what Bourchier intended.

'And you will hunt down my husband, Alexander Wyville?'

'Yes, Mistress.' He held a gloved hand up. 'And His Eminence will pay me. Believe me.' Monksbane's face grew hard. 'If Alexander Wyville is still alive, I'll bring him back.'

'And if he's fled?'

'Then, Mistress, I'll tell you.'

'And if he's dead?'

'Why, Mistress, I'll show you his grave.'

'How long will it take?' Kathryn asked.

'Not long.' Monksbane grinned. 'But I need to know everything about him.'

Bourchier heaved himself out of his chair, a sign that the meeting was over.

'Kathryn, the hour is late. Monksbane will take you back to your house. The only people who know about him are the four of us and anyone else you may wish to tell.'

Kathryn took her farewell and followed Monksbane out through a postern door. The cloisters outside were cold and dark, lit here and there by a sconce torch or an oil lamp in a niche. Monksbane strapped on his war-belt. Kathryn noticed how silently he walked; with no clink of arms or clatter of boot, she felt as if she were accompanied by a shadow. He led her down stone-vaulted passageways, across a silent garden, and out through a side gate. They paused to put on their cloaks, Monksbane hurrying to help her.

'You are well, Mistress?'

Kathryn shivered and stared up at the clear night sky. 'The Archbishop likes his fire,' she said.

'His blood runs thin.'

'Are you a physician? Do you know physic?' Kathryn teased, now curious about this enigmatic man who would learn so much about her.

Monksbane did not reply but gallantly offered her his arm. Kathryn took it. They walked down the alleyways, high walls on either side, and onto Palace Street: This was deserted, its cobbles still glistening from the rain earlier in the day. The stalls had been put away, shops closed, windows shuttered, but lantern-horns had been slung on hooks outside doors, and candlelight glowed through cracks and crevices. A few dogs roamed. Cats sat like kings on the mounds of refuse piled high, waiting for the scavengers to come. They passed a small stocks standing at the mouth of an alleyway. The drunk, his hands and head tightly fastened under heavy slats of wood, had still not regained consciousness, despite the little boy who stood beneath him, a bowl of water in his hands. Kathryn paused and tried to help.

'He's not usually drunk,' the lad whined. 'But he had too much ale and fell asleep here in the middle of the street.'

Kathryn patted him on the head and gave him a coin.

Monksbane looked intently back the way they'd come then led her on. He paused outside the Glory of the Sun, a large tavern on the corner of Palace Street.

'Master Monksbane, I am tired,' Kathryn declared.

'I need to speak to you,' he explained. 'It's best done here.'

Kathryn shrugged and followed him inside. The flagstoned passageway was clean and smelt sweet. Instead of taking her into the noisy tap-room on their left, Monksbane led her up the wooden staircase, pushed the door open at the top, and ushered her into a small chamber. It was empty except for a table, two stools, and a glowing brazier in the far corner. Tallow candles, thick with fat, stood in steel bowls along the table. Monksbane made Kathryn comfortable, went back downstairs, and returned with two pewter tankards of ale.

'Mistress, I leave Canterbury tomorrow. I will not keep you long. You live with the Irishman, Murtagh? Do you love him?'

Kathryn coloured, but Monksbane's eyes stayed level, his face composed.

'I'm not snooping, Mistress. I just want to know.'

'I love him.'

'If you were free, you'd marry him?'

'If he asked, yes.'

'And what if your husband returns?'

Kathryn sipped from the tankard. She pressed its coldness against her warm cheek.

'The law of the Church is quite clear. Alexander was a malicious man.' She continued in a rush, 'If he knew how happy I was now, he would take great pleasure in spiting me. Like a spoilt child, what he doesn't want, he won't let anyone else have.'

'Was he wicked?'

'No, he was weak. In his cups, yes, he could become wicked.' She tapped the tankard. 'This was the key to his soul; and when turned, all sorts of evil tumbled out.'

'And in bed. Was he lusty?'

Kathryn would have slapped the face of any other man, but Monksbane talked like a physician searching for symptoms.

'No, he was not. He blamed me. He could become very violent.' Kathryn touched her grey hairs. 'A little legacy, a gift from my husband.'

'Was he a merchant?'

'Of sorts. Master Monksbane, you should have been a priest.'

'I nearly was'—the fellow grinned—'but I like a pretty face.'

'Then why not a lawyer?'

His expression didn't change. 'I was married once myself. I can call you Kathryn, can't I? I had a wife and two children.' He blinked, the only sign of any emotion. 'Three beautiful flowers.' He snapped his fingers. 'All gone, Kathryn, like tears in the rain, taken by a fever. They talk about the descent into hell. I went down and came back. I was drunk, I was violent, and when I awoke, I was sickly and very poor. First a scavenger, then a rat-catcher.'

'And now?' Kathryn asked.

'Memories,' he replied. 'We all have to do something, Kathryn, to keep the door locked, barred, and secured.' He drank deeply from the ale. 'So if Alexander Wyville came back, he would spoil everything?'

'Yes.' Kathryn nodded her head vigorously. 'Like a spoilt child in a garden he would uproot and tear down.'

'Wouldn't Murtagh kill him?'

'No, not unless Alexander provoked him; and Wyville would be too cunning for that.'

'Of course,' Monksbane agreed. 'Such men choose their opponents carefully. What did he look like?'

'Of medium height, reddish hair, pale face, and green eyes. Lightly built with a slight paunch. He liked his ale.'

'A church-goer?'

'We are all church-goers.'

Monksbane smiled wolfishly. 'Did he believe, Kathryn?'

'I don't think he did. Deep in his heart Alexander Wyville liked nothing.'

'Yet you married him?'

'We wear masks, Monksbane; you are wearing one now. Sometimes it's difficult to separate the mask from the face. I made a mistake, a terrible mistake, and I paid for it.'

'And if I find him dead?'

'Then God rest him.'

'And if alive?'

'Then God help me!'

'Shall I kill him, Mistress Kathryn?'

Kathryn went cold. Monksbane's face didn't change a whit; his voice was matter-of-fact, as if he were discussing some errand to the market place.

'Why not?' he whispered. 'From what you say, earth doesn't want him, but God does.'

'Are you asking me to pay for my husband's murder?'

'Execution, Kathryn.'

She shook her head. 'No, I'll not have his blood on my hands or his soul on my conscience.'

Monksbane smiled. 'I thought you'd say that, Mistress.'

She caught the shift in his eyes and, leaning over, grasped his wrist. 'Please!' she insisted. 'You must not do it. You must not take the law into your own hands. If Alexander Wyville is alive, then let the law take its course.'

'And what happens if he's an outlaw, Mistress?'

Monksbane released her hand and placed it gently on the table. *'Utlegatum, wolfshead,* beyond the law?'

'What makes you ask that?'

'He's a violent man, Mistress, a drinker.' Monksbane ticked the points off on thin, slender fingers. 'He may have gone into hiding; that is, if he's still alive.'

'What would he be hiding from?'

'He may have killed a man. According to the law, a *wolfshead* guilty of homicide, rape, or robbery can be slain on sight.'

'Not Alexander Wyville,' Kathryn said. 'He must face justice, don't forget!' Kathryn drank from the tankard; the ale was good and strong. 'He may have married again and be hiding from Church law rather than the King's.'

Monksbane pulled a face.

'I want you to swear,' Kathryn persisted, 'on the souls of your dead wife and children that if Alexander Wyville's alive, you will bring him in alive.'

Monksbane pursed his lips. 'I agree. Mistress, you wish another tankard?' He pushed back his stool.

'No, I have drunk and spoken enough.'

'I have one favour to ask you,' he continued. 'You are a physician?'

'Yes, and you should have your own.'

'Quacks and leeches!' he jibed. He pushed back the stool, put one foot up on the table, and tapped his ankle. 'I get cramps here and along the back of my leg; it feels tight.'

Kathryn rose and went round to take a look. Using the edge of the table, Monksbane eased off his boot; the hose beneath was clean. Kathryn felt the toes, foot, and ankle. She could find no swelling, but then when she felt the muscles at the back of the leg, they were tight and taut, like a knot being pulled fast.

'Do you suffer from this often?'

Monksbane lowered his foot and put his boot back on. 'Sometimes, particularly when I sit.'

'Show me how you sit.'

Monksbane did so, but Kathryn realised he was simply acting. She recalled the bounty-hunter sitting in the Archbishop's palace; the right leg had been constantly still, rigid.

'When you drink, the pain goes?'

'Yes.'

'And when you rise?'

'Again, no discomfort.'

Kathryn studied his pale face. His complexion was clean, but she noticed the nervous gestures, the way Monksbane kept rubbing his stomach.

'You are anxious.' She smiled. 'Agitated, yes?'

Monksbane glanced away.

'But you hide it well. After all, you are a hunter of men, and you must wear your mask. Yet I would wager a silver florin that you sleep badly. Do you find the hair at the back of your head tangled when you awake?'

Monksbane grinned in embarrassment. 'I toss and turn.'

'And your stomach is agitated. You will pay for the ale you have just drunk?'

'Mistress, you should tell fortunes.' Monksbane eased on his boots to hide his embarrassment.

'You suffer from cramps and pains elsewhere, yes?'

'I think you know the answer to that.'

'There is nothing wrong with your leg,' Kathryn declared, 'except the way you sit. Your humours are nervous and agitated. Next time you sit in a tavern, particularly when the meeting is unpleasant or danger threatens, reflect on how you sit. You will find you are pushing your foot into the ground, tensing your leg. The sinews tighten; cramps ensue. You should bathe your leg in hot water with soothing herbs. Exercise gently; walk with a stick.'

Monksbane gazed in admiration. 'Which schools did you attend, Mistress?'

Kathryn laughed and drained her tankard. 'I have my licence from the City Council, but my tutor was my father. He suffered the same ailment. It's quite common in men of your condition. Now, Master Monksbane, I have a favour to ask of you. You were a rat-catcher in Farringdon Ward. You've heard of the infestation here in the city? Do you know the cause?'

'It could be due to anything,' Monksbane replied, choosing his words carefully. 'Rats live in nests, colonies. Sometimes they swarm. They can be driven out, as we can be, by persecution, fire, and sword. They swim, clamber on board barges which sail along the river Stour. Or there're the ruins outside Canterbury. God knows why they come, how, or from where. You mentioned fire. That's the best cure: to burn their nests, harry them day and night. One remarkable thing, Mistress. I've been round the city and sat in the taverns and listened to the chatter and gossip. In Farringdon infestations occurred, but not like this. Usually you see one or two at first. People ignore them as nothing serious. "Ah yes," they'll say, "I saw the first on the Feast of St. Matthew the Apostle, and then I left it for a month." However, our Canterbury rats seem to have appeared suddenly, outside Westgate and then to the north of the city.' He spread his hands. 'More than that I cannot say.'

Kathryn was about to pick up her cloak when they heard a scratching at the door; a small, greasy-haired pot-boy came running in. He ignored Kathryn and plucked Monksbane by the sleeve. 'A man downstairs, a man downstairs, wishes to see you! The taverner wouldn't let him come up.'

'For me?'

'No, no.' The boy stuttered. 'For the fish, fish . . .'

'The physician,' Kathryn interjected.

The boy gave her a beaming, gap-toothed smile. 'Yes, the woman, fish . . .'

Kathryn laughed.

Monksbane went downstairs and came hurrying back; the man who followed was cloaked and cowled. When he pulled back the hood, Kathryn started in surprise.

'Why, Master Venables!'

She introduced Monksbane; Venables nodded at him.

'Do you have the gift of sight?' Kathryn smiled. 'How did you know we were here?'

'You followed us, didn't you?' Monksbane accused him. 'I thought that after we left the Archbishop's palace.'

Venables was about to turn away, but Monksbane abruptly drew a dagger; in one swift movement it pricked Venables's chin.

'No!' Kathryn raised her hand as Venables's hand fell to his war-belt.

'I hired this chamber, Master Venables, because I wished to talk to Mistress Kathryn. I don't like being followed. And I don't like being ignored, especially by uninvited guests.'

Venables gently pushed away Monksbane's hand. He stepped back and bowed. 'In which case, sir, you have my apologies. I need to speak to Mistress Swinbrooke on a matter of urgency. True, I did follow you from the palace. I waited outside thinking you were simply supping a tankard; but as time drew on, I became impatient. I would appreciate a word alone with Mistress Swinbrooke.' He smiled at Kathryn. 'It is the King's business.'

'I told His Eminence I would see Mistress Swinbrooke safely home,' Monksbane retorted. 'Do you wish to speak to him, Kathryn?'

Kathryn nodded. Monksbane picked up his cloak. 'In which case I shall wait for you downstairs.'

And taking the pot-boy's hand, Monksbane left the chamber.

Venables sat on the stool on the other side of the table. He took off his cloak and loosened his war-belt, his close-set eyes studying Kathryn. 'You've had a busy day, Mistress.'

'And it gets busier,' she remarked drily. 'Master Venables, what do you want?'

'You are the Advocatus Diaboli in the case of Roger Atworth?'

'I know who I am, Master Venables.'

'Atworth was Duchess Cecily's confessor.'

'I know that, too.'

'He was hale and hearty.' Venables ignored Kathryn's brusqueness. 'Duchess Cecily is deeply affected by Master Atworth's death. He was a member of her husband's household in France, a good soldier, a skilled man-at-arms. On at least two occasions he protected the Duchess from enemies, and believe me, Mistress, she has many. He gave up the pleasures of this world'—Venables's voice was precise, clear, his eyes never leaving Kathryn's—'and became a friar. Duchess Cecily continued their relationship and chose him as her confessor. Now you know, Mistress, how her husband, Richard of York, was barbarously slain at Wakefield some twelve years ago at the beginning of the bloody feud between York and Lancaster. Duchess Cecily was not only York's wife but his closest confidante and counsellor.'

'And Atworth became the keeper of her conscience and the treasure-chest of her secrets?'

'In a word, yes.'

'But Atworth has gone to God. I understand the Duchess's grief so . . .'

'Duchess Cecily does not believe Atworth's death was by natural causes.'

'That could just be a woman's grief, a refusal to accept the inevitable.'

'No, it isn't. You see, the Duchess and Brother Roger often corresponded.'

'I hope the Duchess was prudent in what she wrote?'

'Oh, she was,' Venables confirmed. 'Just letters between two old friends.'

'But Roger Atworth was her confidant? Her letters have been returned?' Kathryn asked.

'No, they have gone missing. Atworth kept them upon his per-

44

son'—Venables tapped his war-belt—'in a large wallet which he wore on the cord of his gown. When Atworth's corpse was discovered, the wallet had gone.'

'And did these letters contain anything delicate?'

Venables pulled a face. 'Mistress, I cannot say; the Duchess will not tell me.'

'But there is more?'

'Yes. Brother Roger Atworth was found dead on the morning of the Annunciation, on the twenty-fifth of March. According to Prior Anselm, he had felt sickly the day before and kept to his chamber. Now Brother Roger had written to the Duchess at the beginning of March, the Feast of St. David of Wales. He promised he would write again later in the month, on the feast day of St. Joseph, the nineteenth of March, and despatch it to her at Islip. No such letter came.'

Kathryn rested her arms on the table and stared down at a wine stain in the shape of a wolf's head.

'But Brother Roger's corpse bore no marks of violence? You've heard the stories?' Kathryn asked. 'Stigmata, a beautiful fragrance? Are you sure the Duchess is not just saying this out of grief? The Friars of the Sack have their own physician, and he discovered nothing untoward.'

Kathryn glanced up and continued. 'That's why Duchess Cecily is so keen on this beatification process. She wants Atworth's corpse exhumed, doesn't she, examined by an independent physician? The King knows of Colum Murtagh, and he also knows me. Dame Cecily would press this matter with her son.'

Venables nodded.

'So, tell me, sir, why should someone want to kill Roger Atworth, an old friar immured behind monastery walls?'

'Atworth led a very interesting life,' Venables replied. 'During his campaigns in France, when the Dauphin's forces, commanded by "La Pucelle," began to re-take Normandy, Atworth was captured by a rather sinister French nobleman, the Vicomte de Sanglier. Sanglier kept Atworth in his dungeons and treated him barbarously. He was tortured in hideous ways, his flesh plucked with irons or kept in freezing water.'

'Why?' Kathryn asked.

'Well, Atworth led one of the Free Companies: The French had issued an edict proclaiming all English soldiers captured under the red-and-gold banners of such companies would face torture and summary execution. For some reason Sanglier kept Atworth alive. After a while he released him and began to treat him as an honourable guest.'

'Why the change?'

'Duchess Cecily never got to know. The story is that Atworth feigned sickness and managed to escape. Duchess Cecily believes his imprisonment began the change in Atworth's life.'

'But when Atworth was captured, he was a soldier, not a friar or confessor to the Queen Mother?'

Venables ran his finger through a pool of spilt ale. 'Mistress Kathryn, have you ever heard of "the Ecouters"?'

'It's French, isn't it?' Kathryn translated. 'To listen?'

Venables smiled. 'Skilled in tongues?'

'No,' Kathryn replied. 'But we do have French exiles in Canterbury; I was a good student with my horn-book.'

' "The Ecouters," ' Venables explained, 'are Louis XI's spies; they are, literally, his listeners. Louis has more spies, "Ecouters," in England than there are rats in Canterbury. And, by strange coincidence, they are controlled by the Vicomte de Sanglier, now a leading member of Louis's council. Three months ago, Duchess Cecily found one of her servants, a groom of the chamber, a Gascon, going through her private documents. I had to question him. He was eventually tried before the Marshal of the King's household, found guilty as a spy, and hanged from the common gallows. He was a redoubtable man, difficult to break; but one thing we did discover: He was searching for correspondence between the Queen Mother and Roger Atworth.'

Through the cracks in the shutter Kathryn could hear noises from the street, almost drowned by the singing and shouting below. Someone must have brought a set of bagpipes, and the wailing, eerie sound carried up from the tap-room, interspersed with raucous bursts of singing.

'Why was he looking for letters?'

'We don't know.'

Kathryn bit her thumbnail.

'And that's all he confessed?'

'Yes. We were puzzled. Why had Sanglier singled out Atworth, his former prisoner? The matter was debated in the King's Council in the Chamber of the Green Cloth at Westminster.'

Kathryn recognised the name of the room. Colum had often reported how King Edward, his brothers, and their henchmen used that chamber for their most secret discussions.

'It's curiously shaped,' Murtagh had claimed. 'Thick walls and a door which can be guarded; that and the Tower, not to mention the House of Secrets in London, are the only places the King really trusts.' He'd laughed. 'If only the walls could talk.'

'And these deliberations?' Kathryn asked.

'Richard of Gloucester,' Venables dropped his voice to a whisper, 'put forward a startling theory that Atworth may have been a cunning man, that his conversion was false.' Venables pulled a face. 'Even if it was genuine, Atworth, according to Gloucester, may have been a French spy.'

'But that's ridiculous,' Kathryn retorted. 'If Atworth had been a spy, there would have been no need to go through the Queen Mother's papers. Atworth would have told the French everything.'

'Duchess Cecily argued the same most passionately. As you know'—Venables lifted his eyebrows—'Richard of Gloucester is not his mother's favourite: She calls him the whelp of her litter. Gloucester would not be moved. He argued that perhaps Atworth had, because of infirmity or some other reason, stopped sending messages to France, hence the spy in the royal household. The House of Secrets, which controls our spies in France, also reported on two matters. First, the French did have a spy very close indeed, at the heart of the English Court and Royal Council. Secondly, there could also be a French spy in the priory of the Friars of the Sack in Canterbury. This spy might either be Atworth himself,' Venables sighed, 'or someone else put in to watch him.'

'A Frenchman in an English priory would stand out like a bruise on a pale face!'

Venables shook his head. 'Apparently Vicomte de Sanglier was more careful and subtle than that. Look, Mistress, we sit only a short walk from the greatest shrine in Christendom. Everybody and anybody comes to Canterbury. French kings and queens, nobles and merchants, they all congregate here. Some are genuine, some are spies laden with gold and silver to turn the minds and hearts of the King's loyal subjects.'

'You are claiming this happened at the Friary of the Sack?'

'Possibly.'

'And this same person subtly murdered our holy Roger?'

'Yes, Mistress.'

'A maze of shadows, eh, Master Venables. So Roger Atworth's death . . . ?'

'It hides more, Mistress Swinbrooke, than any of us think.'

Chapter 3

'For deeth, that taketh of heigh and logh . . .'
—Chaucer, 'The Man of Law's Tale,'
The Canterbury Tales

M istress Swinbrooke, you are much in demand.'

Monksbane stood in the doorway; behind him was Colum, shrouded in a military cloak and cowl. Kathryn gave a cry of pleasure and sprang to her feet, knocking over the stool in her hurry. Colum pulled back the hood. Kathryn could see he had washed and shaved, his black, curly hair damp against his head; his tanned, weather-beaten face was smooth except for a razor cut high on his cheek. So pleased to see him, Kathryn forgot about Venables and Monksbane and clasped Colum's hands, kissing him on each cheek.

'You've been looking for me?'

'I've been looking for you, Kathryn.' Colum's eyes crinkled in amusement. 'We have business,' he whispered.

Kathryn stood back.

'Everything is well at home. Thomasina is baking bread but is quietly cursing. Wulf is busy with mortar and pestle. Agnes is laying out the linen sheets in the airing room. . . .'

'Master Murtagh.' Venables came across, hand extended. 'You remember me? The march to Tewkesbury?'

'Of course.' Murtagh clasped his hand. 'You are well?'

Introductions and pleasantries were exchanged. Colum asked what was happening; Kathryn put her finger to her lips and smiled. 'I'll tell you later.'

'I can see you have no need for an escort.' Monksbane kissed her hand, nodded at Murtagh, and, followed by Venables, left the chamber.

Kathryn picked up her cloak and put it round her shoulders. Colum stood chewing the corner of his lip.

'What's the matter, light of my heart?' Kathryn teased.

'Murder.' Murtagh shook himself free from his reverie. 'I'll explain as we go.'

'I am hungry, and I am tired,' Kathryn moaned. 'My legs feel like lead. I could lie down and sleep on the floor.'

'I wouldn't do that.'

Colum took his own cloak off. He was wearing a leather cotehardie over a white linen shirt, his dark-green, weather-stained hose pushed into riding boots which he always insisted on wearing, despite Kathryn's teasing. He put his cloak on a peg and came across and undid the clasp of Kathryn's.

'I understand from the landlord that Monksbane hired this chamber. We might as well eat and drink, then go about our business.'

He went to the door and shouted down the stairs. The potboy came hurrying up. Colum ordered a beef and vegetable pottage, some baked chicken stuffed with grapes, and a jug of Gascony wine.

'There, Mistress.'

Murtagh made her sit. For a while they chatted about the ordinary events of the day; Colum quietly cursed one of the warhorses out at Kingsmead.

'A lovely animal,' he mused, 'but as hot-tempered as Thomasina. Oh, by the way, she crossed swords with Widow Gumple in the market place. Thomasina's threatening murder or at least to cut the woman's tongue out. . . .'

'And this murder?' Kathryn asked.

Colum held a hand up as the door opened and a slattern brought in a tray with two earthenware bowls and the spiced beef piled high; a linen cloth contained two loaves and a pot of butter. Colum paid and waited until the door was closed behind her.

'They've forgotten the wine.'

Colum left the chamber and came back with a jug and two goblets. He filled the cups, and they blessed themselves. Colum seemed as hungry as Kathryn. For a while they ate in silence. On one occasion Colum got up and opened the door to make sure there was no eavesdropper.

'You keep strange company, Kathryn. Venables is the Queen Mother's henchman, a fighter and a plotter but loyal to the Yorkist cause. What business does he have with you?'

Kathryn put down the horn spoon and told him succinctly about her meeting with Bourchier and Luberon. The more she talked, the more agitated Colum grew.

'By all the saints in Paradise!' he whispered when she had finished. 'Be careful, Kathryn. One day I'll tell you a little more, but the Duchess Cecily is a very dangerous woman: proud and beautiful with a vindictive streak. She adores her eldest son, Edward, and does not brook opposition. Her husband, Richard, God rest him, was of similar ilk.'

'Were you at Wakefield when he was killed?' Kathryn asked.

'No, I was with the reinforcements. We didn't march fast enough; the lanes and trackways were clogged with snow. Richard of York ignored all advice and went out to meet the Lancastrians. His army was butchered; his boy Rutland was caught in the Wakefield market place and stabbed to death. The Duke insisted, like some paladin of old, in fighting to the finish with his back to a tree. The Lancastrians killed him. They chopped off his and Rutland's head, decorated them with paper crowns, and slung them over Micklegate Bar at York. When Duchess Cecily heard this, she proclaimed Edward his father's heir to both the duchy and the English Crown. She never forgot Wakefield: God help any man who fought for Lancaster at that battle falling into her hands.'

'But that does not affect the present situation?'

'Yes and no,' Colum replied. 'Since her husband's death, Cecily's bitterness has grown. If she thinks, for a minute, that you are going to blacken the Blessed Atworth's memory ... yet,' he sighed, 'the hunt's begun, and there is nothing we can do. Just be careful, particularly if you meet the Duchess.'

He wanted to question her further, but Kathryn leaned across and pressed a finger against his lips.

'Much more important is Monksbane,' she declared; and as she described Bourchier's offer of help, Colum's face broke into a smile.

'At last,' he whispered. 'Do you think this time, Kathryn . . . ?'

'From the little I have learnt about Monksbane, Colum, yes I do: Alexander Wyville, alive or dead, will be found!'

'And, God forgive me, Kathryn; but if he is dead, would you, could you marry me?'

He stretched out his hand, but Kathryn withdrew hers coquettishly.

'No, I could not,' she murmured. 'No, I *should* not!'

The smile faded from Colum's face.

'But I shall and I will,' she teased him.

If she hadn't moved quickly enough, Colum would have lurched across the table and seized her. As it was, jugs and platters went flying, bouncing on the wooden floor, provoking faint shouts of protest from below. Colum went to the door, opened it, and bawled that all was well and he would pay for any breakages. He slammed it shut and pulled across the bolt. He went across and knelt before Kathryn. He grasped both her hands, squeezing gently, eyes searching.

'You are sure, Kathryn?'

'Well, of course I am.' She fluttered her eyelids. 'I love you, Colum Murtagh. I think I always have, and I know I always shall.'

He pulled her gently down to kneel on the floor beside him. 'I haven't a ring,' he confessed soberly. 'Not yet.'

'And, Master Murtagh, I am not a free woman, not yet.'

He let go of her hands and clasped her face, kissing her hungrily on the mouth, cheeks, and eyes. Pulling her close, he kissed her again, dislodging her wimple. Kathryn broke free and tapped his face playfully.

'Oh, sir, how dare you!' She kissed him back just as hungrily. 'I would wager a shilling to a shilling,' Kathryn whispered, 'that we have now roused the interest of some of the customers. I've been here over an hour,' she grinned, 'and entertained three men!'

Kathryn got to her feet, smoothing down the creases in her dress and re-arranging her wimple. Colum wanted her to share a loving cup, but she shook her head.

'We'll talk later,' she murmured. 'Colum, this business of yours; we'll talk as we go.'

*　*　*

A short while later, cloaked and cowled, they left the tavern, the pot-boy's cries of pleasure at Colum's generosity ringing in their ears. The streets and alleyways were now deserted except for the occasional wandering dog and the furtive slithering of rats across mounds of refuse. Colum grasped Kathryn's hand.

'They are becoming bolder by the day, even out at Kingsmead. They'll wreak terrible havoc amongst our supplies of horse-feed.'

'What's the cure?' Kathryn asked, stepping gingerly over a puddle.

'Fire, Kathryn,' Colum answered. 'Tomorrow, God willing, I am going to search their nests out and burn whatever I find. Now'—Colum paused and stared up at the spire of St. Swithin's Church, a long, black finger against the starlit sky—'you've heard me talk of Padraig Mafiach?'

'Yes, a countryman of yours.'

Colum stared down the alleyway to ensure no one was following.

'A merry man, Padraig. He could play the lute and dance as nimbly as a squirrel on a branch. A good swordsman, an excellent spy.'

Satisfied that they weren't being followed, Colum grasped Kathryn's hand, and they moved on. They avoided the main thoroughfares and used the lanes leading down to Westgate.

'A born mimic, Padraig; he had a gift for tongues. When the House of York had to flee abroad, Padraig became skilled in German, French, Italian, and Flemish. God have mercy on him, but he could change his appearance like any actor in a masque.'

Colum paused, but the shadow which lurched out of an alleyway was only a drunken beggar, bleary-eyed, hands out begging for alms. Colum threw a coin, and they walked on.

'Padraig was sent on an embassy to Paris. He changed his name to Robin Goodfellow. He acted the part of an English traitor'— he laughed abruptly—'or rather an Irishman who wished to betray English interests. At first the French were suspicious, but Padraig could persuade a bird out of its nest. The Frenchman, the Vicomte de Sanglier, took him into his household.'

'Why?' Kathryn asked. 'Why all this?'

'Well, it links in with what you've told me about Venables. Our noble king, God bless his golden locks, truly believes a spy, high in the English Court, is giving information, not about trade or the movement of ships, but about what the King and his Council deliberate in secret—in particular, Edward's desire to get his hands on the remaining Lancastrians who have fled abroad. This information is allowing King Louis to interfere in whatever he wishes. Louis holds his hands up, cries he is innocent, that Edward our King is his noble cousin whom he loves dearly, that he would never dream of harbouring English traitors, and so on and so on.

'Padraig's task was to find out who the traitor was. He may have been successful. He passed a verbal message to one of our merchants in Paris that the information was too dangerous to write or send by any other way until his return. One night, two weeks ago, Padraig kissed Sanglier's household good-bye and slipped out of Paris. The Vicomte pursued him. They tried to block the roads to Calais, but Padraig went by secret routes and reached safety. A few days ago he sailed for Dover. Now Padraig is a cunning man. He would go backwards and forwards like a fox evading his pursuers. Of course, a message arrived at Islip that he had landed. I was supposed to meet him tomorrow and escort him safely to the King. Yesterday evening Padraig lodged at the Falstaff under the name of Robin Goodfellow. He kept to himself and had a meal in his room. He paid well and remained quiet. The taverner, Clitheroe, stabled Padraig's horse and looked after his harness, but late this afternoon he became suspicious; he'd had neither sight nor sound of this mysterious guest. He and his servants went through the usual routine, knocking on the door, going out to the courtyard; but the window shutters were closed. Eventually the taverner became suspicious, and the door was broken down. Padraig lay in an empty room, cloaked and booted, with a terrible wound to his head from which both blood and brains oozed out.'

'Have you been there?' Kathryn asked.

'Very quickly. I ordered the door to be re-hung and locked. I placed my own seal on it; then I came looking for you.'

'How did the taverner know how to tell you?'

'I had told him two days ago that a man, Padraig Mafiach, would be arriving, and when he did, to contact me and only me. God knows for what reason, Padraig chose to use his alias, Goodfellow. The taverner is sharp-witted. Concerned about a murder in his hostelry, he recalled the victim's Irish accent. He became suspicious and sent for me.'

'Is the taverner innocent?'

'Old Clitheroe?' Colum withdrew Kathryn's hand, put an arm round her shoulders, and pulled her close. 'I'd trust Clitheroe with my life. He knows me well from the business I do at his tavern. I often meet the King's scurriers there.'

'Will you be blamed?'

Colum shook his head. 'No. Padraig made one mistake: He used his alias and paid for it with his life.'

'So the murderer must be someone on the King's Council?'

'Yes,' Colum agreed. 'That's the hymn going to be sung, but there again,' he added crossly, 'we are not sure. Did a member of the Council unwittingly let slip some information, or was the Vicomte de Sanglier more astute or cunning than we thought? He could have sent agents in hot pursuit or even had someone waiting for poor Padraig in Dover. From what I can gather, Padraig sought security with a group of pilgrims coming to Canterbury. He left them at Westgate, made the short journey to the Falstaff Inn, and kept to himself. He should have been safe.'

They turned the corner into Pound Lane, a wide thoroughfare where braziers glowed half-way down the street and cresset torches lashed to poles showed the approach to Westgate, a sharp contrast to the silent streets they had passed through. Merchants, packmen, and traders gathered there, seeking permission to leave, even at that late hour, so they could lodge either in the fields or in barns outside the city. Colum showed his pass, and the city watch let them through a postern gate. They walked up St. Dunstan's Street to the welcoming warmth and light of the Falstaff, a spacious building with a red-tiled roof, its black-timbered and white-plastered front lit up by torches. They went through the main entrance. The tap-room had by now emptied. Clitheroe, the taverner, with his slatterns and pot-boys, was busy cleaning up the mess. He greeted Colum and shook Kathryn's hand. 'We've met before, Mistress Swinbrooke.' He pointed to a healed scar on his wrist. 'Last May Day I was a bit stupid with a fleshing knife. But come, I'll be glad to have this business over.'

He wiped podgy hands on his blood-stained apron and led them up the side stairs. He took out a bunch of keys and unlocked a door in the centre of the gallery. Kathryn stood on the threshold as the taverner went in; boards creaked as he lit the candles.

'Strange, isn't it?' Kathryn whispered. 'Such places not only experience death but hold its smell.'

Colum grasped Kathryn by the wrist and led her in. The candles and oil lamps had been lit. They found themselves in a comfortable chamber with a small, four-poster bed, coloured cloths on the walls, and a painting of the Virgin and Child; woollen rugs covered some of the shiny black floorboards. It contained a table, chair, stool, and a lavarium with a jug and bowl, and a peg for napkins. Nevertheless, the homely atmosphere was shattered by the corpse, hidden under a sheet, sprawling on the floor. One lifeless hand hung exposed; a pool of blood had seeped out and dried. Kathryn's stomach churned at the squeak and scurry of rats in the far corner. She composed herself by looking round the room. She noticed how the sword and dagger, probably the dead man's, lay neatly near the bed.

'He'd drawn these?' she asked.

'I put them there,' the taverner replied. 'He had definitely drawn them to defend himself, yet no one heard a sound: not the slap of feet or clash of steel.'

'You are sure?' Kathryn insisted.

The taverner shrugged, picked up the sword and dagger, and clashed them together. The sound echoed like a bell through the chamber.

'It would carry through the room,' Clitheroe explained, 'and down the stairs. We've had sword-fights, Mistress. I have a sharp ear for them.'

He placed the weapons carefully on the bed. Kathryn stared up at the timbered ceiling, its white plaster interspersed by black, heavy beams. She noticed a hook with a lantern swinging on it.

'Was that lit?'

'No, it wasn't.'

'And the candles?' Kathryn asked. She noticed how the candelabra were full of new tallow wicks.

'Oh, they'd burnt low. I've replaced them.'

Kathryn tapped the floorboards with her foot.

'There are no secret entrances?'

'Mistress'—the taverner's sweaty face broke into a smile—'I

have been in the Falstaff since the day I was born. My father owned it and his father before him. I know its every nook and cranny. There's a secret entrance into the tap-room below that was used by smugglers in the old times to bring in the odd barrel of Gascony.'

Kathryn paused as Colum found a foot-rest, brought it across, knelt by the corpse, and crossed himself, mouthing a prayer in Gaelic under his breath.

' "Failte romhat, a Rina naingeal." '

'What's that?' Kathryn asked.

'A prayer my mother taught me.'

Kathryn turned away and walked carefully around. She stopped at the window. This was not some luxurious room in a palace—the window was a plastered square with a wooden timber frame, sealed by loose-fitting shutters, which allowed in a draught of cold air. The bar was fixed to the shutter on the right. She lifted this up—it was rather stiff—pulled it back, and opened both shutters. The night air gushed in, bringing with it the farmyard smell from the stables below. Kathryn peered down and saw a cobbled yard lit by a pool of light from a lantern slung on a beam. She could make out a water conduit to the entrance of the stables. Some-where a groom was singing a love song.

' "My lord, I wish I were,
In the house of my own true love!" '

Kathryn recognised the sweet sentiment and smiled to herself. 'Amen,' she murmured. –

She looked at the wooden windowsill, which showed no sign of scuffing. At her request the taverner brought across one of the oil lamps. Kathryn carefully studied both the inside and outside of the shutter. The wood had been strengthened and protected by black paint; a number of pilgrim badges depicting the Falstaff had been nailed to it.

'Has this wood been freshly treated?' Kathryn asked.

'Oh yes,' the taverner replied, 'once the Feast of the Purification has come and gone and the worst of winter is over.'

Kathryn felt the wood. She could not see, or detect, any mark. She closed the shutters and pulled the bar down.

'And this is how it was when you entered the room?'

'Mistress, I'd take an oath: The shutters were closed and barred.'

Kathryn walked across and examined the door. Of heavy oak, the outside was reinforced with iron studs; the inside was equally strong-looking. It hung on three thick leather hinges. Kathryn could see where it had recently been repaired. The door also had bolts and clasps on top and bottom; its lock was old-fashioned but sturdy enough.

'And this?' she asked.

'I know my own tavern.' Clitheroe scratched his balding head. 'Mistress, that door was locked and bolted, the key was turned, the bolts pulled across. This is a busy place, and we do good trade, especially now spring is here. Maids, scullions, slatterns, and pot-boys go up and down. Next door is a family, and on the other side were three merchants from Hainault who got themselves befuddled and had to be helped up. Oh yes, Mistress, I know a drunk when I see one. They were all drunk.'

'And the room above?'

'A married couple on pilgrimage to Canterbury; they were returning to London. Homely enough: He was old, rather sour-looking; she was much younger, prettier.'

Behind her Colum was still murmuring a prayer. Kathryn stood back. 'Tell me precisely what happened?'

'The gentleman arrived; he paid for a chamber. He also lodged his horse and harness in the stables. I asked him if he wished to eat at the common board. He replied, "No." His food was to be brought direct from the kitchens by one of the slatterns. He said he was expecting someone, but that's all he'd say. Dark-faced, secretive, very soft voice, as if trying to hide his accent. He was sober and respectable. Mistress, as I have said, we are a busy place. He went to his chamber, and that's the last I saw of him. The room was well prepared, the water-jug full, clean sheets. A slattern apparently brought up some food and drink.'

'Where's that now?' Kathryn asked.

'I took it down. He ate and supped well and used the jakes pot, which I've also emptied.' He waved his hand. 'Anyway, the day wore on; it wasn't until after noon that I became suspicious. We left it for a while, and then the usual routine began: tapping on the door, going out to the yard and looking up at the window. I remembered Master Murtagh's request and became suspicious. So I and a few of the stable lads forced the door.'

'Tell me precisely what you saw.'

'I told them to stay outside and came in. The candles had burnt out. The poor fellow lay on the floor in a pool of his own blood. You can see the wound yourself: sword and dagger not far from his body.'

'Had he been asleep?'

'No, the bed hadn't been turned over.'

'And his possessions?'

The taverner pointed to a far corner; Kathryn could make out saddle-bags.

'I haven't touched them; I don't want to be accused.'

Kathryn stared across at the small black crucifix fixed against the wall.

'Colum, have you finished?'

The Irishman got to his feet.

'How could it happen?' Kathryn asked.

'Padraig was a good fighter, nimble as a dancer, often had to be,' Colum replied.

'A man who would defend his life?'

'A man who would fight to the death,' he answered.

Kathryn walked across the room; she took the foot-rest and used that to pull back the sheet. The face beneath made her heart skip a beat. In many ways Padraig looked like Colum, although the swollen face was now a ghastly hue, the half-closed eyes lifeless, and the black, curly hair matted with blood from the hideous wound on the right side of his head. Kathryn peered at this closely, touching it with her fingers.

'The side of the head has been crushed,' she observed. She wiped her fingers on the sheet. 'Blood and brains have seeped out.'

Kathryn found it hard to distinguish the full area of the wound. She could feel fissures and cracks in the skull.

'A club,' she declared. 'A mace or a Morning Star.'

She opened the man's mouth and sniffed but could detect nothing untoward except the acrid taste of wine and the man's last meal. The white teeth were unstained; the tongue was whitish but not swollen or bitten. She then felt the rest of the corpse: stomach, chest, and legs. Helped by Colum, she turned the body over but could detect no other wounds or marks. Assisted by the taverner, they lifted the corpse onto the sheet. Colum, murmuring a prayer, obeyed Kathryn's instructions and began to strip the corpse, revealing a muscular, white-skinned torso. Kathryn could make out healed scars but no other wound. The stomach was slightly distended, bloated; the limbs were stiffening and heavy; the flesh was a clammy cold.

'Rigor mortis has set in,' she remarked.

Kathryn noticed how the shirt beneath the leather jerkin had been buttoned wrongly and the hose points tied clumsily. She pointed that out to Colum.

'Perhaps he was tired?' Colum said sadly.

Kathryn got to her feet, went across the room, and washed her hands with water from the jug. The taverner asked if they wanted any further help. Kathryn shook her head, so he left, closing the door behind him.

Kathryn sat down on the stool. Colum brought a chair across and sat opposite. Kathryn, lips tightly compressed, shook her head. 'Here we have a fighting man,' she began. 'Padraig Mafiach, a spy, a soldier, a man born and trained to be wary as any fox on the hill. He arrived at the Falstaff and immured himself in this chamber. He is cunning and aggressive. The door is locked and bolted; the window is shuttered.' She glanced across; through a narrow chink in the centre of the shutters, she could see the darkness beyond. 'A man who would sell his life dearly, yes? No one came into this chamber except a slattern bearing his food. He must have been convinced about her; otherwise he wouldn't have let her in. Let's pause there. Colum, who's responsible for the food?'

'Why, the taverner is. He prides himself on his culinary skills. He's one of the best cooks in Canterbury. He is helped by maids and pot-boys but . . .'

'Bring him back up!' Kathryn ordered.

Colum left. A few seconds later he returned with an exasperated-looking taverner.

'Yes, Mistress?'

'Did you cook the dead man's supper?'

'I must have done!' he exclaimed. 'I am the only cook here, helped now and again by my wife and others.'

'And what did he eat?'

'A meat pottage, some bread, some wine.'

'Did he order it?'

'He must have done; otherwise it wouldn't have been brought up.' The taverner paused. 'Yes, yes, he did. He said that he'd have an evening meal in his chamber. He said he'd tell me when.'

'And who brought it up?'

'Why, one of the maids.'

'Can you find her?'

'Mistress, I can try, but my servants come up and down those stairs like a bucket at a busy well. It must have been . . .' He continued, 'One thing is certain, on that evening'—the taverner gestured at the corpse—'he never left his chamber. I know that.'

'How?'

'Oh, we have pot-boys at the foot of the stairs. No one goes up except slatterns, maids, and paying customers. We have had the occasional whore come looking for custom, not to mention the local footpads hoping for an unlocked chamber. I tell you this, Mistress, the only people who went up those stairs last night were guests, maids, and pot-boys carrying trays and other necessities.' He pulled a face. 'I hire many a casual labourer.'

Kathryn, satisfied, told him to go. She waited until the door was closed. Colum went across and turned the key in the lock.

'I am satisfied with that.' She sighed. 'Mafiach would be careful what he ate or drank?'

'Oh, yes.'

Kathryn beat her head against the palm of her hand. 'Colum, that taverner will lose his temper. I have one more favour. Go down and ask him what was left on the tray. I want to make sure of that.'

Colum, quietly protesting, left the chamber. She heard him call for the taverner and go downstairs. Kathryn gazed across at the waxen-faced corpse; going across, she pulled back the sheets which covered the dead man's face.

'I wonder if he sees us now?' Colum mused, coming back into the chamber and locking the door behind him.

'Who?' Kathryn glanced up.

'Why, Padraig. In my country they say the ghost of a murdered man lingers for days beside his corpse.'

'Then this is one occasion,' Kathryn declared crossly, going back to the stool, 'I wish a ghost could speak. Well?'

Colum grinned, took off his war-belt, threw it on the bed, and sat opposite.

'I don't think we should ask the taverner any more questions; he is rather busy and getting angry. He declared how, when they broke through the door this morning, the meat and bread had all been eaten and the wine cup was empty; but he reckoned Padraig must have had one, perhaps two goblets. A lot of wine still remained in the jug. The taverner sniffed at the goblet, said there was nothing untoward. When he took it down to the scullery, he and the servants finished off what was left of the wine with no ill effects. In fact, they said it tasted very pleasant. Why, what are you thinking, Kathryn, that Padraig was poisoned before he was murdered? I tell you this,' he added. 'If Padraig ate and drank something and the poison made itself felt, no matter how malignant, he would have unlocked that door and cried for help.'

Kathryn rubbed her face.

'I am tired,' she declared, 'but this intrigues me. We have a fighting man in this chamber. The door was definitely locked and barred. No one could come through there. There are no secret entrances or passageways: Even if there were, Padraig would meet his assailant and fight for his life. The only other means of entering this chamber is the window, but that's shuttered with the bar brought down. Colum'—she grinned—'lie down on the bed. No, I am not going to visit you. Pretend to be Padraig.'

Colum shrugged and went and lay on the bed. Kathryn waited for a while.

'Light of my life,' Colum teased, 'are you going to let me sleep here all night?'

Kathryn eased off her own soft brown leather boots and tiptoed across the chamber. Even as she did so, the floorboards creaked. She grasped the bar across the shutters and pulled it up. Not being properly oiled, it creaked slightly. Kathryn opened the shutters, flinching at the cold night breeze; she then tip-toed across to the bed. Colum lay, eyes closed. Suddenly he opened them and lunged for her, but Kathryn was too quick and stepped back.

'I heard your every movement.' Colum sat on the edge of the

bed. 'You took your boots off and crept across to the window. I heard the bar go up, the shutters open, and you tip-toe back.'

'Padraig may have been in a deep sleep?'

Colum laughed abruptly. 'Padraig was like a cat. He could relax, but he'd slept in too many dangerous beds not to keep an ear or eye open on what might spring out of the darkness.'

Kathryn went across and pulled on her boots. Colum brought across Padraig's sword and dagger. Kathryn examined these carefully. The handles were of coiled wire beneath a leather sheath. The blades of both weapons were sharp and shiny.

'Go outside, Colum.'

He obeyed. Kathryn closed the door behind him. She lifted the weapons, clashing sword and dagger together.

'As loud and clear as a mortuary bell,' Colum declared, coming back into the chamber. He took both weapons from Kathryn's hand and, stooping, kissed her. He held the tip of the sword in mock threat against her throat. 'I could have my evil way with you, Mistress.'

'And tomorrow,' she replied, 'I would serve you food you'd never forget, Irishman!'

Colum remembered where he was, glanced at the corpse, and crossed himself quickly.

'I am sorry, I forgot. I do see the problem, Kathryn. Padraig apparently knew the killer was in the chamber. He had his boots on and drew his sword and dagger, yet no one heard a sound. There must have been blows, parries, lunges. Now Padraig lies with his brains dashed out, and we have no knowledge of who his assailant was, how he got in, or how he got out.' Colum glanced towards the window. 'There is one possibility. What if, Kathryn, Padraig was sitting on the bed or at that table? He hears a scrabbling sound at the shutter. He draws sword and dagger, goes across, lifts the bar, and opens them. His killer is outside. Either he has climbed the wall using a rope ladder or something else.'

Kathryn walked across to the shutters.

'What are you saying, Colum? That Padraig said, "Oh, do come in." '

'No.' The Irishman went across, opened the shutters, and pulled them back. 'Padraig sticks his head out; his assailant is on a rope beside the window. He hits him with a club. Padraig staggers back. The assailant follows him in.'

Kathryn closed the shutters and leaned against them.

'A possible solution,' she mused. 'But, Colum, think! If you were Padraig, this scrabbling at the shutters. What would you do? Would you open them? I mean, at the dead of night? How do you know your assailant, hanging onto some rope or ladder, doesn't have a club or a crossbow-bolt?'

'Very good, my little soldier!' Colum conceded.

'And would Padraig, even if he opened the shutters, stick his head out? I mean, how often in a chamber on the second gallery do you hear someone knocking at your shutters? Why should Padraig even open them? What if his assailant had missed? Why should his assailant be so gracious as to use a simple club when a crossbow-bolt would be more deadly? If Padraig was as cunning a man as you say, he'd let the mysterious rapper continue his noise, take his sword and dagger, race downstairs, and go out into the yard whilst, at the same time, rousing the rest of the tavern.'

Colum glowered at her. 'It was just a theory.'

'I know. I know.'

Kathryn stared down at the corpse.

'One thing I do suspect is that the assailant entered this chamber without Padraig's knowledge.'

'He may have been already hiding here?'

'We still haven't resolved the problem of Padraig resisting, shouting for help. And, as regards both your theories, Colum, how did the assailant leave so quickly and quietly, locking everything behind him?'

They paused at a knock at the door; the taverner came in.

'I have asked amongst the maids. They are not too sure. Some who worked that night are not here, the rest have vague memories of food being sent up.' He raised his eyebrows. 'Any more than that I cannot say.'

'Tell me,' Kathryn said, 'was there anything disturbed? Stool or chair overthrown?'

The taverner shook his head.

'Mistress, if I wasn't a God-fearing man, I'd say a demon came through stone, plaster, and wood; surprised that poor man; and clubbed him to death. Nothing was disturbed. No sound was heard. Well, apart from the usual ones, doors closing, but certainly no alarm was raised, no clash of steel, no cries or shouts.'

The taverner left. Kathryn went across to the saddle-bags. She placed them on the bed and emptied their contents.

'He was carrying a message, Colum?'

'Probably.'

The possessions were paltry: a small purse full of coins that bore witness to the taverner's honesty, a change of clothing, a small dagger, a crucifix of hollowed metal, warrants and licences showing Mafiach had come through Dover, a belt and a set of ave beads. Kathryn searched for any hidden pouch or lining but could find nothing. Colum had picked up the rosary.

'Nothing much,' he murmured, 'for a life of fighting and struggle, not to mention loyalty to the House of York.'

'Did he have wealth?' Kathryn asked.

'The King had granted him a small house and garden in London,' Colum absent-mindedly replied. 'Padraig would have money with the goldsmiths, perhaps here or at York.' He glanced sadly at Kathryn. 'A wandering minstrel boy, our Padraig. He once said he wanted to meet a good woman and settle down. He had dreams of returning to the Blessed Isle.'

Colum stared down at the ave beads and began to search under the bolsters on the bed.

'What's the matter?'

'A psalter,' Colum snapped. 'Padraig once met a beautiful woman. He described her: hair of fire and eyes as green as the sea. He pressed his suit upon her. She claimed to have dedicated her life to God. She gave him these ave beads. They are made out of coral, but she also gave him a psalter. Kathryn, Padraig would no more give up that book than he would have life itself. It was *his* psalter: It contained some psalms and prayers in Gaelic. Come on!' he urged.

Kathryn joined him in the hunt—pulling back bed sheets, lifting the mattress, searching beneath the table, Colum swearing quietly under his breath.

'If he carried a message'—Colum paused—'Padraig would have copied it into that psalter, and the assassin took it. But Padraig was a knowing man: He had seen the days, as we say in Ireland.'

He went back to the bed and picked up the brass crucifix.

'What?' Kathryn demanded.

'Padraig always made a copy: That was the way of the man.'

Colum examined the crucifix carefully. Both the stem and the crossbar were made of hollowed bronze. Colum exclaimed as he prised the top off and shook loose the thin, white scroll from the stem.

'His ghost is still here,' he whispered.

Colum added something in Gaelic, making a gesture with his hands as if Padraig were standing beside him.

'Kathryn, we can do no more. I'll send a messenger to Cuthbert at the Old Priests' Hospital. He'll attend to the corpse and see to Padraig's burial.' He held up the scroll. 'Padraig's death was not totally in vain.'

Chapter 4

'Wel bet is roten appul out of hoord
Than that it rotie al the remanaunt.'
—Chaucer, 'The Cook's Tale,'
The Canterbury Tales

The Council Chamber in the royal palace at Islip, despite the
late hour, was a blaze of light and vivid colours: Hundreds of
beeswax candles in their black, iron stands had been lit. A fire
burned in the great hooded hearth. Braziers had been wheeled in;
herbs sprinkled on the top evoked the fresh smell of summer. Yet
this was no festive occasion. The shutters had been drawn against
the mullioned glass windows; knight bannerets wearing the livery
of the Royal Household thronged the corridors and galleries leading to the chamber. Inside, Edward of England, seated at the top
of a long, polished, oval table, had even dispensed with clerks.
Only 'Friends of His Chamber,' as he called them, had been per-
mitted to attend this Council meeting. On his left sat Bourchier,
eyes half-closed; Edward thought the old Archbishop was asleep,
though he knew better. Bourchier was a wily old spider. He would
keep his own counsel and weave his webs. On Edward's right sat
his widowed, still beautiful mother, "the Rose of Raby," Cecily of
York, Mother of the King. He idly wondered what mood his tempestuous mother had assumed. She gave nothing away. She wore
a dark-crimson velvet dress trimmed with white fur, its bodice and
sleeves tight and clinging; Cecily had loosened the brocaded strap
beneath the high waist-line and dispensed with the short train at
the back. On her hands gleamed beautiful sapphire rings; round
her throat a jewelled necklace, containing the same stones, shim-

mered brightly. Edward had always thought his mother a most beautiful woman, and age had not withered her. She had the same porcelain, delicate face, that mouth which could display a variety of moods, and above all, those dark-blue eyes which could be full of laughter or glare in hateful menace.

Edward sighed and stared down at the pieces of parchment on the table before him. Mother still clung to a pattern: her shaved eyebrows, the light, white paste on her face, and the soft red blush high in her cheeks. Many claimed Edward of England had been pursuing his mother all his life. More than one courtier had whispered on the likeness between Cecily of York and Edward's own wife, the striking beauty Elizabeth Woodville. Edward closed his eyes. He wished he was in his bedchamber with Elizabeth, arms round her cool, alabaster body, his face nuzzling between her breasts.

'Your Grace, we are waiting!'

'Sweet brother.'

Edward raised his head and smiled at George, Duke of Clarence, his handsome, treacherous brother: gold hair falling down to the nape of his neck, that beautiful oval face marred by the rather heavy chin, the cynical blue eyes, and that pouting lower lip.

'Have you been drinking, brother?' Edward asked sweetly.

'Deep and full of the waters of life, Your Grace.'

The man beside Clarence laughed abruptly. Unlike his brothers, he was not dressed in the blue, red, and gold of the Royal Household. Richard of Gloucester had been hunting in the forest around Canterbury. He still wore a green, weather-stained jerkin over a white linen shirt. A delicate, narrow-faced man, Richard could be charming when he wished and implacable to those he opposed. Now he sat twisting a feathered cap in his hands or glancing at the ring displaying his emblem, the Boar Rampant.

'You are amused, brother?'

Edward just wished he hadn't drunk so much himself; his belly felt tight, swollen. He loosened the brocaded jacket as he gazed round at the rest, men who had fought shoulder to shoulder with him at the bloody battles of Towton, Mortimer's Cross, Barnet, and Tewkesbury; dark-brown Hastings, with whom he'd shared many a mistress, his companion in lechery; Francis Lovell, seated across from Richard of Gloucester, eyes watching the King's brother like a greyhound would his master. *Shifting alliances,* the King thought; he groaned quietly to himself. He had fought valiantly for the Crown. Now he had to struggle against the jealousies of his own victorious war party as it fragmented into factions, lost in court intrigue, each choosing their own master.

Edward beat a tattoo on the table. His mother watched and tried to control both her rage and fear. *You are getting fat, Edward,* she thought, noticing how his rings were tight, lost in dimpling folds. Edward the Beautiful, over six foot two in his stockinged feet, once called 'the Royal Leopard,' 'the Golden Lion,' 'York's Sweet White Rose,' had feasted and drunk a little too deeply. All the fault of his wife, that jumped-up Woodville who preened and prinked as if she were the Queen of Sheba! And she, Cecily, the widow of the great hero of York, had to play second fiddle, but not now! She had roused her son, demanded this council, and glaring across at the smiling faces of her other sons, Cecily wondered what role they would play. She only wished Walter Venables were seated beside her to whisper counsel and good advice. However, the King had been most insistent: 'No henchman, dearest Mother. If you bring yours, my darling brothers will bring theirs.'

Edward was still staring down the table as if fascinated by the blue-and-white shield fixed on the wall above the oak-panelled wainscoting. Cecily glared across at her two other sons. Richard she could never understand; he was merely his eldest brother's shadow. If Edward said Monday was Sunday, Richard would believe. Secretive and withdrawn! Cecily regretted her epithet, "the runt of the litter"; he'd never forget that! Impetuous and very proud! Richard's green eyes came up and caught his mother's glance and gave her that lopsided smile as if he could read her thoughts. Beside him Clarence was pretending to be asleep. Beneath the table Cecily squeezed the knotted handkerchief. Clarence was very dangerous, a truly unstable young man. He had fought for York but also for the other side, allying himself with traitors. Yet Clarence had all the cunning of a cat: He knew when to spring and deftly change sides. Did Clarence know of her fears? Had he whispered them to young Richard, whom he'd always tried to seduce with his golden locks and false bonhomie?

Cecily of York stared at the picture of her husband on the far wall: He had been a broad-faced, golden-haired man. The artist had been flattering. Cecily had not really loved her husband, but she had supported his cause and shared his triumphs as well as eaten the bitter ashes of defeat: flight, penury, and exile. And disgrace? Cecily shuddered at the thought. Yet she must not panic. The game was afoot: That old spider, King Louis, in his turreted fortress, had spun his web to see what flies he could catch. A spy lurked here. The King was reluctant to believe it, but Cecily was convinced. Venables had hinted as much, just the odd whisper, the comment. She had put all her trust in that Irishman, Padraig Mafiach, and only hoped he could bring news which would reveal the traitor and send him to the scaffold, his mouth sealed once and for all. If only the Blessed Roger had lived! He could have given her ghostly advice; sitting on the shriving pew, she would turn her ear and listen to his counsel, the fruit of prayer, penance, and fasting. But Roger was gone. Perhaps if she supported his cause, saw him hallowed in the Court of Heaven . . . ? She glared across at old Bourchier. He'd never liked her! From the very start he had placed one obstacle in front of another. Spineri, the papal legate, was hers both body and soul. She had wanted one of the court physicians, but Bourchier had objected, instead appointing some woman, an apothecary from the city. Well, she'd soon take care of her, or at least Venables would.

'Padraig Mafiach is dead.'

The knotted kerchief fell from Cecily's nerveless fingers.

The King held up a piece of parchment. 'He was murdered in a chamber at the Falstaff Inn.'

'You said he'd be safe!' Cecily snapped.

She could have bitten her lip as her two other sons' heads came up, like hunting mastiffs who had scented their quarry.

'You said he would be safe!' she repeated, trying to keep her voice level. 'He was from my household.'

'Madam'—Edward smiled—'he was also paid for with my gold. The man was a fool. He arrived, still hiding under his disguise of Robin Goodfellow.'

'How did he die?' Clarence asked languidly.

'His brains beaten out with a battle-club.'

'And his killer is under arrest?' Gloucester's voice was mocking.

'There is no sign of an assassin. Colum Murtagh, Master of the Royal Horse, has the matter in hand.'

Cecily, to hide her consternation, picked up the fallen kerchief. She didn't like the way Bourchier was staring at her, but she felt her tension ease. Murtagh the Irishman was one of her late husband's henchmen, one of those few men who could not be bought and sold for a bag of coins.

'And the message?' Bourchier asked. 'Mafiach brought a message, yes?'

'A passage from the prophet Zephaniah in both Latin and English, with some observations written beneath. My clerks of the chamber tell me it's in cipher, but they cannot understand it. I have sent it to the House of Secrets in London.'

'Will it contain the name of the traitor?' Hastings, Edward's leading general, drank the wine cup he had insisted on bringing into the Council meeting. 'I mean, if it contains a name, we have a case. And if we have a case, we will have a trial.' He paused. 'Someone's head will adorn London Bridge.'

'But that's the problem.' Edward leaned back in his chair. 'The cipher, you might say, contains the letters of everyone at this Council meeting.'

'What?' Lovell demanded.

'So my cipher clerks tell me.' Edward spread his hands. He picked up a piece of parchment and tapped the table. 'And I've more news. Our sweet brother, Louis of France, wishes to show us great amity and friendship. The Vicomte de Sanglier is already at sea. He will land at Dover tomorrow and be at Islip within days.'

'Why?' Cecily asked harshly. 'To exchange the kiss of peace?'

'I don't think so.' Bourchier's vein-streaked face broke into a smile. 'I think he's here to see what damage can be done. When the bowl cracks and the milk splatters, the cat always appears.'

'Elaborate, Your Eminence.' Clarence leaned across the table, fingers beating against his lower lip.

'We all fear Louis,' Bourchier replied. 'He has a spy in both the Royal Household and in Canterbury. I think that spy killed Mafiach. Who, apart from us and Murtagh, knew he was coming? Who would have been waiting?' He sat back at the exclamations of protest. 'You can shout and shout,' Bourchier continued, 'but

I deal with facts. Mafiach was murdered, and according to Murtagh, who brought me that parchment, his psalter was stolen. Only Mafiach knew how to break that code. He chose it and has taken the secret with him to the grave.'

'De Sanglier'—Gloucester's voice was barely above a whisper—'could have sent agents in pursuit?'

'True,' Bourchier murmured. 'But my hypothesis is more logical. I suspect it's going to get worse before it gets better.' His eyes now held those of Duchess Cecily. 'Your confessor, Madam, Roger Atworth. Tomorrow, the hour after noon, his corpse is to be exhumed in the cause of his beatification.'

Bourchier ignored Clarence's bark of sneering laughter.

'And what has that to do with Mafiach?' Edward asked crossly.

'Perhaps I am mistaken'—Bourchier joined his hands before him as if in prayer—'but Atworth, like the late, lamented Mafiach, knew too many secrets. Madam, I hesitate to say this, but I wonder if Blessed Roger died of natural causes?'

Protests and demands rose to clarify his remarks. Bourchier shook his head and hitched the thick robe closer about his shoulders, his eyes never leaving those of Duchess Cecily.

'Something was mysterious about Atworth's death,' the Archbishop continued. 'Madam, I understand he should have written to you and did not? His withdrawal from community life just before he died, all these strange phenomena . . .'

'The manifestation of God's will!' Cecily snapped. 'Atworth was a holy man!'

'Aye, Madam, but he was also a sinner, as we all are in the eyes of God.'

Cecily felt herself go ice-cold, as if some mysterious hand had withdrawn the warmth from this scented chamber and allowed the cold night air to drift in. *You old fox,* Cecily thought, *you know about me!* She glanced down the table, allowing the babble of conversation which had broken out to wash over her as the others questioned Bourchier. Cecily kept her face impassive, but she was taken back in time, long before these sons of hers had ever seen the light of day. She and her husband were in Calais as the French forces drew closer and England's great empire in France crumbled and broke—tempestuous, hot-blooded days! She glanced up. Edward was staring at her strangely.

'Madam,' he whispered. 'What is it?'

Bourchier was now involved in answering some question posed by Clarence, but he was still watching her from the corner of his eyes.

'Your Eminence,' she called out, 'Blessed Roger Atworth was my confessor. Do you know who, in the community, was *his*?'

'Why, Madam, he had none there.'

'But he must have been shriven? He was, as you say, a sinner like us all in the eyes of God.'

'Of course, Madam, but didn't he ever tell you?' Bourchier clasped his hands together. 'I performed that service for him.'

Cecily of York gripped the table to steady herself. *You are lying,* she thought. *You must be lying!* Everything she held secure was now crumbling, breaking down. All she could think of was Atworth. The Duchess started as the King banged the table with the pommel of his dagger.

'You have heard what I know. The hour grows late; there is little more we can do.' Edward held up his hand at the murmur of voices. 'We must prepare for the arrival of the Vicomte de Sanglier,' he added silkily. 'The night goes on, and the ladies await us.'

A chorus of laughter greeted his words. Bourchier got to his feet, bowed, and waddled out. The others rose and drifted away. Edward tapped his mother's toe with his soft-booted foot, a sign for her to stay. Once the chamber was empty, Edward stretched and got to his feet. He opened the door and said something to the captain of the guard; he closed and locked the door, then re-took his seat.

'Mother, you are perturbed?'

'Son, I am not.'

'Mother, you are lying. What is this Atworth to you? A mouldy old friar who listened to your petty sins and shrived you? Oh, I know, I know'—he raised a be-ringed hand—'you knew him in France.'

'He was valet to my chamber.' Cecily moved in a rustle of taffeta to face her son squarely. 'I was young.' She smiled. 'Your father and I, we had gone to France to see if we could turn back the tide, but the Dauphin's men believed in "La Pucelle," the Maid of Orleans, Jeanne d'Arc. They maintained God had showed his hand. I don't know if he had,' she added drily, 'but he certainly wasn't with us. The English army broke and fled; your father and I sheltered in Calais.'

'And what happened?' Edward insisted.

'I committed a murder; that's all I'll tell you, my son. I killed a man. He threatened both me and your father.'

'But I have killed.' Edward leaned forward, resting his arms on the table, searching his mother's face as if he could find the truth there. 'We've all killed, Mother. Those who wear the Crown, or who want to wear it, wade through a sea of blood to the throne.' He paused. 'You've got nothing to fear. Who was this man?'

'He was an enemy; he could have wreaked destruction.'

'And you cannot tell me his name or why?'

'No.' Cecily kept her voice steady. 'But the incident weighs on my conscience.'

'But how can he threaten you now?'

'I don't know,' Cecily whispered, 'but I have a feeling it matters.' She kissed her fingers and pressed them against her beloved son's lips. 'And that, my golden boy,' she whispered, 'is all I will say!'

In the woods to the north of Canterbury, the woman calling herself Blanche Southgate gingerly dismounted from the palfrey she had bought in the small horse market outside Queningate. As instructed, she led her horse along the narrow trackway. At any other time Blanche would have been nervous, but tonight she felt confident. The merchant had promised that she would be safe, as well as rich, and Blanche revelled in the idea of her new-found wealth. The palfrey, as well as its harness and saddle, must have cost a pretty penny, and the same for the dress, kirtle, and cloak she now wore. She had proper shoes on her feet, whilst her hair had been washed and dressed like the rest of her to be comely and sweet-smelling.

All around echoed the sounds of the night, the rustle in the undergrowth, the lonely hoot of a hunting owl. Blanche gulped to hide her nervousness. In the saddle-bags she carried a dagger, but the woods were safe. No outlaws prowled there. The city watch had been most vigilant; and Royal Household troops, only a mile away at Islip, had hunted these lonely copses, cleaning out the beggars and tinkers, the men who lived in the shadows well away from the light of the law.

Blanche prided herself that she knew these things. She was not an ignorant girl but had been part of a travelling troupe who had fallen on hard times in London. Blanche had seen the world. She had played in the households of the great ones of the land. She had entertained powerful merchants and sold her favours for no less than a silver piece. She only wished the man who had hired her could have kept her, had not insisted that she leave a comfortable bed and meet him here, well past the hour of midnight, under the starlit sky. The palfrey stopped in its tracks and whinnied, head turning as if attracted by a sound. Blanche, holding the halter, stared into the darkness. She could make out the trees, the glint of the moonlight on a small mere.

'What is it?' she asked, patting the palfrey's neck.

The horse, snickering, let itself be led on. A small animal raced across their path. Blanche started, and the horse whinnied and backed, but it was well-trained, and Blanche had nothing to fear. Clicking her tongue, she led it on as she used to the pack ponies of her travelling troupe. At last she reached the clearing awash with moonlight. She smelt the dampness of the wood and the faint tendrils of wood-smoke, probably from some poacher's fire. Blanche was quite determined. At the slightest hint of danger, she'd mount this palfrey and ride like the wind back to the comfort and security of the city walls. She glimpsed the disused charcoal-burner's cottage, its roof long gone, the wattled walls open to the elements. She led the palfrey across and paused.

'Good evening, Blanche.'

She whirled round. The man dressed like a friar had appeared as if out of nowhere. Blanche wasn't sure. Was this the merchant?

'I am sorry I'm late,' she stammered. 'But'—she laughed nervously—'better late than never!'

'Yes, Blanche, better late than never.'

She recognised the voice and relaxed.

'Come, I'll take the horse.'

She went across and handed him the reins, so pleased the knife the man thrust deep into her stomach, twisting and turning, was hardly glimpsed. Blanche staggered away as the cowled face watched her, already steadying the horse against the sudden smell of blood.

Kathryn sat at the kitchen table. Thomasina, head-dress billowing out like the sail of a great cog, her fat face red and sweaty, was raking out the coals from the bread oven beside the hearth.

'I will be well prepared for Purgatory,' Thomasina muttered, 'but, Kathryn, the bread's baked.' She looked up at the basket pulled up to the rafters against foraging mice. 'The little thieves won't get it, will they? Where's that Wulf?'

'He's out in the garden,' Kathryn replied absent-mindedly.

'You've been busy.'

Thomasina stood, hands on her hips. Kathryn agreed, again absent-mindedly. There'd been a stream of customers all morning to her shop at the front of the house. The council had not allowed her to have a stall; instead the customers came to her house to buy their herbs and spices: goat's beard, tarragon, thyme, basil, nipplewort, black poplar, white clover. There had even been a few requests for those phials and small jars of poisons locked away in her strong-box, the malevolent mushroom or the ground leaves and bark of the boxwood plant. Kathryn wrote such purchases down in the great ledger. She knew the reason for such sales. Everyone was complaining about the infestation of rodents and demanding poisons to clear them out.

The usual patients had arrived: Molkyn the miller complaining about his stomach; Edith and Eadwig, the daughters of Fulke the tanner, who had begun their monthly courses; a pedlar with a gum infection; a woman with a boil on her breast. Kathryn had examined this carefully. She always kept an eye on such matters. If there was something she didn't understand, some evil contagion or malignant tumour, she would always direct such people to Father Cuthbert at the Old Priests' Hospital. Thomasina was always ready to take people there. Kathryn glanced up. Thomasina fulfilled all the roles of maid, mother, and shop-keeper, and, above all, close friend. She liked nothing better than stomping round the house, but she always leapt at a chance to visit the Old Priests' Hospital. Many times widowed, Thomasina, as a young girl, had carried a fervent flame for the young, handsome Father Cuthbert, who, like Kathryn's father, had studied physic and medicine at Salerno and Montpellier.

'When will that Agnes be back?' Thomasina gripped her knife like an executioner and advanced towards a piece of ham.

'You know where she is,' Kathryn replied, staring down at the scrap of manuscript. 'She has gone to the Butter Market. Wulf's in the garden.'

'And Colum?'

'He has ridden hastily out to Kingsmead. He's going to leave matters with Holbech, his serjeant.'

'And he's coming back to marry you?'

'No, Thomasina, he's coming back to take me to the Friars of the Sack.'

'Another coven of time-wasters,' Thomasina muttered. 'Can't stand monks, can't stand friars, can't stand Irishmen with hot eyes and greedy fingers.'

'You like Colum,' Kathryn replied, as if reciting a psalm. 'Colum likes you. I love Colum. Colum loves me. I told you, if Monksbane finds the truth, Colum and I will be handfast at St. Mildred's Church. You and Father Cuthbert can dance on the green.'

'I can't dance!' Thomasina blustered and disappeared into the buttery.

Kathryn lowered her head. Colum had made a very swift copy of what they had found in Padraig Mafiach's chamber at the Falstaff. They had not returned home until just before midnight. Kathryn had retired immediately, but they had all risen early before dawn and broken their fasts here in the kitchen. Kathryn had told everyone what had happened the day before, to the round-eyed glances of Agnes the maid, the "Oohs" and "Ahs" of Wulf, and the muttered commentary of Thomasina.

Kathryn cupped her chin in her hand and nibbled at her fingernail. Much as she tried to figure it out, Mafiach's murder was a total mystery, as was the message he had copied out and placed in that crucifix. She had taken down the family Bible her father had bought in Cheapside and traced the Latin extract from the prophet Zephaniah. She looked at it again.

Regis regum rectissimi prope est dies domini
dies irae et vindictae tenebrarum et nebulae
diesque mirabilium tonitruorum fortium
dies quoque angustiae meroris ac tristitiae
in quo cessabit mulierum amor ac desiderium
hominumque contentio mundi huius et cupide.

The day of the Lord,
The Kings of Kings most righteous, is at hand:
A day of wrath and vengeance, of darkness and cloud:
A day of wondrous mighty thunderings,
A day of trouble also, of grief and sadness,
In which shall cease the love and desire of women
And the strife of men and the lust of this world.

And the strange message on the bottom: 'Recto et Verso' (Front and Back)? Yet there was nothing on the back! Was there something missing? And the strange scrawl in Latin at the end: 'Veritas continet Veritatem'? A doggerel phrase translated 'The truth contains the truth.' What on earth did that mean?

'Mafiach was a scholar,' Colum had declared proudly, 'and he loved nothing better than a cipher; but this time he's been too clever for his own good.'

Colum had sent the original to Islip by a courier who lived two alleyways down and often carried out such errands for Kathryn and Colum.

Where did the truth lie, Kathryn wondered, in the Latin text or the translation? Colum had begun to quote Chaucer's poetry.

'That's what I'd use,' he said. 'I wonder why Padraig chose Zephaniah?'

Kathryn took up her quill and pulled across the writing tray. She tried to make sense of the cipher but was unable to make out any pattern, discover any reason. She started at a pounding on the front door.

Thomasina, fast as a swallow, disappeared down the passageway. The door opened, and Kathryn heard a gruff voice demanding to see her. Thomasina sweetly objected, but the stranger's voice was loud and insistent. Thomasina came back. The burly individual behind her scooped off his leather cap and stood in the kitchen doorway; it was a tall, thickset man with a red drinker's face marred by warts and pox marks, a balding head, and quick, darting eyes.

At first he seemed more interested in the chamber than Kathryn and glanced round quickly as if assessing its worth. He was dressed completely in leather: a dark-brown jerkin tied with cord down the middle and hose of the same texture and colour, with hard-boiled leather boots on his feet. He wore no war-belt, but a great strap running across one shoulder buckled at the front; this carried a number of strange implements in small sheaths: keys, rods, little knives.

'Are you Kathryn Swinbrooke?'

'No, she's the Queen of England!' Thomasina declared, pushing her way back into the kitchen to confront this stranger.

'I am Mistress Swinbrooke.' Kathryn got to her feet. 'And you, sir . . . ?'

The fellow advanced, big chapped hands extended. 'Malachi Smallbones, rat-catcher, formerly holder of such a position in the King's town of Oxford. Now hired by the Mayor and Council of Canterbury for the extirpation and ruination of all such vermin.'

'Four-legged or two?' Thomasina interjected.

Kathryn kept her face straight. Malachi was like many such individuals, full of his own importance and status. His eyes had the sharp, humourous glint of a cunning man. She knew he was the sort of pedlar or trader, relic seller or conjuror, who swarmed into Canterbury for rich pickings from the pilgrims.

'You'd best sit down, Master Smallbones,' Kathryn said.

The man would have taken Colum's chair at the end of the table, but Thomasina almost pushed him onto a bench at the side.

'You want some ale?'

The man smacked his lips. Thomasina served two black jacks, Kathryn's brimming to the top, Malachi's only half-full. Kathryn smiled apologetically and exchanged the tankards. She raised hers in salutation.

'Good fortune to your work, Master Malachi.'

'I am here at the bidding of Luberon, the city clerk.' Malachi took another gulp, watery brown eyes glaring at Kathryn over the tankard. 'He said I would have to deal with you, keep you informed of what I was doing.'

'And what are you doing?'

'Well, it's started already.' Malachi stared into the tankard. 'The number of scavengers has been doubled, and the clerks are all out. Proclamations are going up on church doors about the dumping of refuse. Master Luberon wanted all stray cats and dogs killed, but I told him not to. Such animals can kill rats, and we need all the help God sends us.'

Malachi raised his eyes intercedingly as if in prayer. Kathryn studied him closely. At first Smallbones had seemed slightly oafish, but the more he spoke, the less certain of that Kathryn became. Malachi was a man acting a part, the rough, clumsy rat-catcher. Yet the way he drank, the use of words like *extirpation,* the amused, detached look in his eyes belied this. The ring he wore in one ear-lobe appeared to be made of pure gold, and the bracelet on his left wrist looked costly enough. His leather jacket was of good quality, as was the belt and the strange implements it bore. Malachi followed her gaze.

'Rods and traps,' he explained, 'for our enemy, the vermin: pouches of poison and tinders. Two things rats hate: poison and fire. Well, Mistress, will you advise me?'

'Do you really want my advice, Master Smallbones? Aren't you skilled enough? Where are you from?' She'd caught the burr in his voice.

'Helston in Cornwall.' The rat-catcher became slightly defensive.

'And where do you work?'

'Up and down the kingdom. My last indenture was with the city of Oxford, where I cleared the vermin from the streets and cellars.'

'You are a wealthy man, Master Smallbones?'

'I take lodgings in the Mercery, but my house is in London: a small tenement near St. Giles Cripplegate.'

'Ah yes,' Kathryn agreed, as if she knew the capital like the back of her hand. 'And this infestation, Master Smallbones?'

'Oh, it's common at this time of the year.'

'And what do you think is the cause?'

Malachi undid the belt round his chest and gently lowered it to the floor.

'Probably a swarm, Mistress. Rats do swarm. As I journeyed into Canterbury, I saw that there are a number of derelict villages. Like humans, rats live in colonies. Only the devil knows the reason, but sometimes they move.'

'You will be paid well,' Kathryn declared.

'Aye, Mistress, and I'll work hard.'

'How did you resolve the problem in Oxford?'

'Well, it's smaller than Canterbury, Mistress, so it was easier to work there. Cesspits and sewers were cleaned. Scavengers removed all refuse from the streets and lanes; but in Oxford, there are ruins, underground cellars, and streams. As I said, fire is a great cleanser!'

'You will not do the same here,' Kathryn warned, fearful for the close-packed houses, many of them built of wood and plaster.

'No, Mistress, we'll try poison first, and we'll see how it goes. But that's the problem.' He scratched his head. 'Poisons cost money. What can you recommend, Mistress?'

Kathryn pursed her lips. *If the truth be known,* she thought, *I have no solution.* The rat-catcher was correct: Poisons cost good silver. They would have to find something common as well as alert householders to the dangers it posed.

'I will consider that, Master Smallbones.'

'Well, I must go.'

Malachi got to his feet and picked up the belt. Kathryn had the impression he had come just to introduce himself rather than seek her advice.

'Master Smallbones, do you have a map of Canterbury?'

'Master Luberon has supplied one.'

'Is every ward infested?'

'No, not yet.'

'So what will you do?'

'I am going down to the Cathedral close. I have had bills posted, proclamations made at the Market Cross. I am hiring men. We'll go through each ward; some will have cats, but they are fairly useless. We'll just seek out the vermin and kill them.' He moved to the doorway. 'Mistress, if you could think of anything, I am lodged at the Standard in the Mercery. I'll always be there just after vespers.'

Thomasina showed him out.

'What do you think?' Thomasina asked, coming back into the kitchen.

'I don't know.'

Kathryn sat down at the table and folded the piece of parchment. She put this carefully in her writing satchel along with her ink-horn, quills, pumice, and sharpening knife. She checked the strap to make sure it was still good and strong and, ignoring Thomasina's chatter, went along to her writing office. She stared at the piece of polished steel which served as a mirror.

'I am ready for the Friars of the Sack,' she whispered, staring at her reflection. In fact, Thomasina said she looked like a nun in her light-blue wimple and fringed gown of the same colour. Kathryn had not painted her face; she noticed the lines beneath her eyes.

'Medice sane te ipsam: Doctor, heal thyself,' she whispered.

Colum would be home soon. Despite all the excitement of the night before, Kathryn couldn't forget Monksbane sitting so assuredly in that tavern room. She heard the bells of St. Mildred's toll the mid-day angelus. A short while later Colum returned, 'smelling to high heaven,' as Thomasina put it, 'of horse and meadow.' He quickly washed, ate, and drank whilst Kathryn told him what had happened. The Irishman, sitting on a stool, changing his boots, nodded, interrupting now and again with the occasional question.

'I've been thinking about Mafiach. I must ask Father Cuthbert to say a Requiem Mass. Serjeant Holbech was sad. He fought with Macfiach in France, both outside Calais and in the Narrow Seas. I also told Holbech about the rats.' He grinned at Kathryn. 'Have you ever heard of a poem called *Beowulf?*'

'Yes,' Kathryn answered. 'About a warrior in ancient times who fought a great monster: I've read the tale.'

'Well, Holbech surprised me; so has my valiant lieutenant out at Kingsmead. In *Beowulf* the hero claims that every man has a fear within him. Holbech confessed that his was rats. He hails from one of the southern ports, Rye or Winchelsea. Anyway, years ago, French privateers landed. They brought fire and sword. Holbech's parents were killed. He sheltered in the sewers, where the rats were as thick as flies on a rubbish heap. Strange, isn't it? Holbech confessed that he preferred to face a mounted knight, armed only with a horn spoon, than wade through a cellar half full of water and teeming with rats. He's studied them. Holbech claims that, because rats eat such putrid waste, what would kill a man scarcely touches them.'

Kathryn, interested, pulled across a stool and sat opposite.

'And so what does he recommend?'

'He claims poison would cost a fortune and be very dangerous. He also said a strange thing. He's heard all the gossip and chatter of the taverns. He says this infestation is very peculiar. Some parts of Canterbury haven't seen any . . .'

'Whilst other parts have them a-plenty.' Kathryn finished his sentence.

'Yes.' Colum got to his feet and clapped his war-belt on. 'Holbech is all a-feared. He says he won't go where the rats are. Apparently they are thick in Westgate, along the high street and near the Cathedral; that's what the scavengers have told him. Anyway, enough of our four-legged friends, "our little nightmares in black velvet," as Holbech calls them. Now for the Friars of the Sack. Thomasina,' he turned, 'whilst we are gone, you will not entertain young men? I have spies, you know.'

'Aye, and so have I about bog-trotting Irishmen!'

Colum laughed, helped Kathryn put on her cloak, and taking her gently by the elbow, led her down the passageway.

Ottemelle Lane was quiet, but as soon as they turned into Hethenman's Lane, they met the crowds surging up to the market place. They reached the high street where the crowds pushed busily amongst the caparisoned stalls. The cookshops and taverns were doing a roaring trade, the air sweet with their spices and sauces. Pilgrims, round-eyed and rather lost, made their way through, grasping their staffs with one hand, the other on their wallets and purses. At every corner city officials shouted warnings about pickpockets and thieves. The beggars, too, were waiting. The blind were holding each other's hands, crying out for alms. Packmen and journeymen, who had no licence to trade from the council, offered their wares and shouted raucously for custom, one eye on making a profit, the other on the market beadles ever ready to place them summarily in the stocks around the Market Cross. Kathryn gripped her writing satchel, which hung over one shoulder. The day was surprisingly fine, and the weather had turned hot. The noise and shouting, the sea of shifting colour, made her journey difficult.

On either side rose the great timbered houses of the wealthy merchants and aldermen, their mullioned glass windows shimmering in the sunlight. A monkey raced across the street, a little yellow cap on its head, followed in hot pursuit by two dogs and a screaming child. A felon caught stealing from the stalls for the second time was being nailed by one ear to a pillory; his screams rent the air, but people had little time or compassion for him. Chanteurs and preachers tried to catch the attention of the crowd with stories or fiery sermons. A packman offered to sell them pilgrim medals. An apprentice darted out with a piece of cloth over his arm.

'Madam, this will suit you, and if you lack anything . . .' He gestured back at the stall guarded by his master.

Kathryn shook her head. The apprentice grew insistent and only retreated when Colum glowered. Here and there Kathryn could see the effects of Malachi's work: the huge-sided scavengers' carts clearing sewers and runnels, the annoyance of traders who claimed that the smell and the chaos drove away custom.

Kathryn was pleased to turn down an alleyway. It was shady here, and the beggars were as many but not as raucous. They crossed a piece of wasteland and went in under the shadow of the great gate-house of the Friars of the Sack. A lay brother let them through a postern door. Kathryn closed her eyes in welcome relief. The cobbled stable-yard was silent, the din of the city only a faint echo. Colum explained who they were and why they were here. The lay brother nodded. They went through cool, shadow-filled cloisters, where fountains splashed and wild roses throve, and along paved, stone-vaulted passageways. The silence was only broken by the faint singing from the soaring chapel or the murmur of the brown-garbed friars in their offices and chambers. They crossed a small garden and went through a porticoed door.

'This is the Prior's parlour,' the lay brother whispered as they entered this Holy of Holies. 'I believe Father Anselm and the others are waiting for you.'

The lay brother tapped on the door, pushed it open, and gently ushered them in.

Chapter 5

'The clothered blood, for any leechcraft,
Corrupteth, and is in his bouk ylaft.'
—Chaucer, 'The Knight's Tale,'
The Canterbury Tales

M istress Swinbrooke.'

Venables, in a costly velvet cote-hardie loosened at the collar, made the introductions in the friars' parlour.

'This is Brother Jonquil, the late Roger's lay brother and man-servant; Brother Gervase, the sub-prior; Brother Simon, the infirmarian; and Prior Anselm. Reverend Fathers, this is Colum Murtagh, the keeper of the royal stables at Kingsmead.'

The introductions were completed, people shuffling backwards and forwards, and only Venables seemed to have any poise. Prior Anselm, smiling with his watery eyes, waved them to seats round the polished walnut table whilst Jonquil served them white wine and a dish piled high with sugared comfits. Kathryn placed her writing satchel over the back of the high ornate chair and took her seat. She had been to the Friary of the Sack once as a child and had never returned. It was a wealthy house, as the parlour demonstrated with its dark, wooden panelling, the cream-washed walls above decorated with coloured cloths and small pictures depicting the life of Christ. The fire in the large hearth had not been lit, but the room was warm and comfortable; rugs lay on the floor, whose tiles were specially carved in the shape of lozenges, as were the small, mullioned panes in the windows.

Prior Anselm gestured at Jonquil to take his seat and shuffled certain papers about on the table in front of him. A tall, angular man with high cheekbones and sunken cheeks, Anselm had hair reduced to mere white tufts. A careful, considerate man, Kathryn judged, eager to please and highly nervous. Sub-prior Gervase was rather sombre-looking with bushy eyebrows and red-veined cheeks; with his snub nose, pouting mouth, and protuberant belly, he reminded Kathryn of a piglet Thomasina had once kept. Simon the infirmarian was young-looking, smooth-faced, olive-skinned, his tonsure perfectly cut, not a speck on his brown gown; the white, knotted cord was pulled correctly across his slim waist; the cowl and hood were neatly folded back behind his head.

Brother Simon had beautiful white hands with long, womanish fingers. A rather shy man, every time he caught Kathryn's gaze, he coloured slightly and glanced away. Brother Jonquil looked like a farm boy with his blonde hair, red cheeks, and protuberant blue eyes. He sat, mouth slightly gaping, a youngish man Kathryn judged to be not yet thirty. Kathryn secretly wondered if he had all his wits about him. Prior Anselm sat at one end of the table, and Venables slouched in the chair at the other. The Queen Mother's henchman looked as if he had slept badly and sat tapping his fingers quietly on the rim of the table. Beside her Colum pushed his chair back and crossed his arms as if he wished to observe but not participate in what was about to happen. Brother Anselm seemed fascinated by the candelabra standing on a flat bronze dish to catch the wax.

'Father Prior!' Brother Gervase sat up straight in his chair. 'I think we'd best begin.'

'Yes, yes, we ought.' Prior Anselm picked up a scroll and tapped it on the table. 'I . . . I do,' he stammered, 'I do welcome you here. Er . . .' He glanced despairingly at the sub-prior, who just glared back. 'I really don't know where to begin, but well, we'll begin at the beginning, yes? Erm . . .'

'Ten days ago,' Simon the infirmarian intervened, 'Brother Roger Atworth was buried before the Lady Chapel in our Conventual Church. He was a holy man, whatever his past life. He died in the odour of sanctity, both literally and figuratively.' He laughed sharply at his own joke. 'Since then Brother Jonquil here has experienced a vision above his tomb whilst certain miracles have taken place.'

'You are gathering the recipients of these miracles together?' Venables spoke up.

'Oh yes.' The infirmarian nodded quickly. 'They'll assemble here tomorrow.'

'Continue,' Venables ordered.

Prior Anselm, his agitation now under control, cleared his throat. 'We've had the vision; we've had the miracles.'

'So-called miracles,' Gervase declared.

'And we've had the interest of the Queen Mother and Cardinal Spineri. His Eminence is already in the church.'

'Then I think we should go there.'

Anselm looked as if he wished to continue: Kathryn could sense the agitation of these friars but was unsure of its source.

'Everything depends on the exhumation,' Brother Jonquil leaned across the table and whispered to her. 'If that goes well, Brother Roger will be a saint, won't he?'

Kathryn just smiled in return. The Prior, all a-fluster, led them out of the parlour, along passageways, out through a porticoed entrance, and across a small courtyard into the church. They entered through the Galilee porch. Kathryn was immediately aware of how imposing and sombre the church was. Sculptured statues, faces carved in images of serenity, stood cheek by jowl with the most grotesque and ugly gargoyles, the faces of demons and monkeys, hares with protuberant eyes, griffins and dragons. Inside, the church was grand, with a long nave and small oval windows high in the walls; a black-beamed roof supported by squat pillars guarded shadowy transepts. The floor was made of paving-stones, neatly laid and carefully scrubbed; these caught all sound and made it echo.

'Truly a place for a vision,' Colum whispered.

They walked up the centre of the nave towards the rood screen, a great carved, wooden barrier placed across the entrance to the sanctuary; this was ablaze with candlelight, as was the recess to the left, where a group of lay brothers armed with picks, bars, and poles clustered round a paving-stone. Kathryn glimpsed Spineri, who, to keep his dignity, had persuaded someone to bring one of the throne-like chairs from the sanctuary. The Cardinal now sat like a judge come to judgement.

Led by Prior Anselm, they all genuflected at the entrance to the rood screen. Kathryn glimpsed the high altar, its tall candles lit, and on either side, the polished wooden choir stalls of the community. The Lady Chapel was just as grand, a small church in itself with its tiled floor and paintings on either side depicting scenes from the Virgin's life. There was a small altar and, above that, a black, ancient statue of the Virgin Mary depicted as a queen sat embracing the Child Jesus. A gorgeous oriel window full of brilliantly painted glass provided light. Before the shrine rose iron stands, carrying small, blue oil lamps, which the faithful could light after placing a coin in the strongbox bolted to the floor beside the red-quilted prie-dieus.

Kathryn wandered off to look at this hallowed place before coming over to join the rest. Spineri was on his feet, extending his hand so Colum could kiss the episcopal ring; he then did the same to Kathryn. Spineri's hand was soft, warm, and heavily perfumed, and the garnet ring caught the light and dazzled her eyes. For a while all was confusion. Jonquil wanted to tell everyone where he was kneeling when the vision took place. Anselm was trying to impose order amongst the lay brothers, who kept milling about, uncertain as to what to do. At last order was imposed. Chairs and stools were brought for Kathryn, Prior Anselm, and his guests. Kathryn inspected the paving stone on which Atworth's inscription had been carved. She and Spineri pronounced themselves satisfied. The stone was lifted, and the exhumation began. Loose soil and rubble were cleared, and the burial pit was exposed. At this point Cardinal Spineri insisted on prayer and led the brothers in singing the 'Veni Creator Spiritus.' The grave was then sprinkled with holy water, and one of the lay brothers was gingerly lowered down to attach cords to the grip handles on either side of the coffin. Even as he did this, Kathryn was aware of muttering amongst the friars. She got up and walked across. At first she wasn't sure, but then she caught the most delicious fragrant smell, like that of sweet crushed roses but thicker, heavier, like the perfume of some high-born lady.

'Is it myrrh, frankincense?' Kathryn murmured.

'I can smell it, too!' Venables exclaimed.

Colum, his curiosity aroused, also came over. Kathryn swiftly looked round.

'What is it?' Spineri, plump hands folded as if in prayer, leapt to his feet.

'I can smell the strongest perfume,' Kathryn replied drily. 'I am searching for its source.' She stared around.

'But that's impossible!' Simon the infirmarian spoke up. 'There are no flowers in the Lady Chapel. No baskets. I tell you, it comes from the grave itself!'

Kathryn was forced to agree and withdrew. Slowly and surely the coffin, scraping and creaking, was raised to the top, where wooden boards were swiftly placed across the opening. The coffin, of the finest wood, was covered in dust and dirt, its silver-encrusted handles dull and dingy. The smell of perfume, however, had grown stronger, as if a jar of the precious stuff had been shattered on the hard, paved floor. The lay brothers raised the coffin and placed it on the trestle table brought specially in; their task finished, they were then ordered to withdraw.

Kathryn and Spineri were invited to inspect the casket. Spineri simply walked round. Kathryn, however, took the small knife from her writing satchel and carefully checked the casket lid. The smell of perfume was now very strong. She tapped the wood, but the clasps held tight, and Kathryn could see they had not been loosened or interfered with. At her request Colum and Venables put on their gloves and began to unscrew these. Outside the sunshine faded. The transept grew darker, gloomier. Candles were brought.

'They are all loosened.' Colum stood back.

He looked rather fearful, uncomfortable. A true Irishman, Kathryn reflected, winking at him: Colum was a man of this world with a healthy respect for anything which might lie beyond the veil.

The coffin lid was removed. Kathryn expected a foul smell, the usual gases and bad humours which any corpse would exude, but she could detect nothing except a pervasive fragrance. The corpse itself was hidden by linen sheets, and when she was removing these, Kathryn noticed how they were coated with a fine red dust, as were the white satin cushions around the edges. At last the cadaver of the Blessed Roger was exposed to gasps and cries of exclamation.

Kathryn herself stood astonished. Atworth had been buried in the brown robe, white girdle, and open leather sandals of the Friars of the Sack. He had been dead for days, but though his lined cheeks were slightly sunken and slight hair had grown round his mouth and chin, he looked as if he had only died in the last few hours. His body had a white, waxen appearance like that of some effigy Kathryn had seen in funeral processions. The dead friar's hands were clasped before him. A crucifix had been lashed to the fingers and had slipped slightly to one side. Kathryn peered into the coffin; ignoring the pious ejaculations, she stared hard at this would-be saint. Atworth had a severe face, like that of a hunting falcon: strong chin, the lips now bloodless, a beaky nose, and deep-set eyes. The skin was old, wrinkled, the hair round the makeshift tonsure mere wisps; but in her mind's eye, Kathryn could imagine this man with a war helm on, eyes glinting, or indeed, as a saint kneeling before the altar staring in a mystic trance at a crucifix or statue. She felt the skin of the corpse's face, hands, and neck; it was like touching cold, soft wax. She smelt the perfume but was more curious at the bittersweet smell of his skin. Was it corruption? Kathryn felt the legs and arms, which were spongey but slightly stiff. She drew her hand along the satin-covered side of the coffin and noticed the red powdery dust on her fingers.

Could it be? She stepped back, hastily wiping her hands on her dress. She remembered one of her father's lectures and a memory from the past: St. Mildred's churchyard one rain-swept afternoon in October, seven or eight years ago. The King's coroner, the dirt of a grave piled high, the wooden casket of an exhumed coffin, the lid being taken off. Her father later studied the corpse in the nearby charnel-house, made all the more sombre and ghoulish by the flickering light of a fat tallow candle. What was the woman's name? Margotta, that was it! She had been dressed in a crumbling shift, her face still recognisable.

Venables stretched out his hand to touch the corpse.

'Don't!' Kathryn exclaimed.

Venables hastily withdrew. The rest stared owlishly at her.

'Prior Anselm, I want bowls of hot water and clean napkins. Quickly! No one is to touch the coffin. If they do, they must wash their hands very carefully.'

The Prior stared fearfully back.

'Why? What is the matter?'

'I am not sure,' Kathryn replied. 'I may be wrong. I must consult my manuscripts. However, I believe Roger Atworth'—she continued in a rush—'may not have died of natural causes but of a heavy infusion of red arsenic, a deadly poison.'

'What?' Brother Simon came forward, hands extended. 'What are you saying, Mistress Swinbrooke? That Blessed Roger was poisoned? You are mistaken, you foolish woman!'

'Watch your tongue, Friar!'

Colum broke from his reverie and came to stand beside Kathryn, who stared quickly around. Anselm stood like a frightened boy, fingers to his lips. Jonquil couldn't understand what was happening. Gervase was smirking as if relishing some secret joke.

'I apologise.' The infirmarian lowered his hand and stepped back.

'Will you do what Mistress Swinbrooke demanded?' Colum insisted.

Simon snapped his fingers at Jonquil. 'Go on!' he urged. 'Bring the water!'

Now Kathryn, not the corpse, was the centre of attention. Venables had turned his back on her. Kathryn wondered if it was to hide his surprise or to study the corpse more carefully. Kathryn walked back to the nave and sat at the foot of the steps leading up to the sanctuary. The rest gathered around.

Kathryn kept looking at her hands. 'I urge you not to touch the corpse and eat with polluted fingers. Prior Anselm, you have a library here, manuscripts? A pharmacopeia?'

The Prior nodded.

Kathryn kept her hands resting in her lap. She was relieved when Jonquil came hurrying back: he had had the presence of mind to bring water and a small tablet of expensive Castilian soap. Kathryn rose, washed her hands vigorously, and cleaned them on the napkin provided.

'Arsenic,' Kathryn said, now more composed, 'is one of nature's deadly poisons; there are two main types, red and white. Both are noxious substances. If taken in considerable quantity, they will cause sudden death.'

Simon the infirmarian had lost his poise and was chewing his lip nervously.

'Arsenic is a well-known poison,' Kathryn explained. 'Any book on herbs or substances will tell you this. Arsenic interferes with the humours of the body, and a victim will retain the poison long after death. It can halt, even prevent, decomposition and decay. I must examine the corpse further,' she added hastily, 'but in my view, this is the reason for the state of the corpse and why the shroud, as well as the satin covering around the edge of the coffin, is covered in a fine red dust: that is the effect of the arsenic. So if that coffin and whatever it contains are touched, I urge you to wear gloves and wash your hands and face carefully of any of that dust. Brother Simon, wouldn't you agree?'

'It has been known.' The infirmarian didn't raise his head.

'I remember a similar case in Canterbury,' Kathryn continued. 'It was after Michaelmas, seven or eight years ago. The children of a woman named Margotta Arrowsmith informed the city coroner that their mother had been poisoned by her second husband. Eventually their petition was accepted by the Church, and an exhumation was ordered. My father found Margotta's corpse in a similar condition to the Blessed Roger's. The murderer later confessed, when he was confronted with the evidence, that he had travelled to Dover and London and spent considerable amounts purchasing large quantities of arsenic.'

'But what about the stigmata?' Prior Anselm exclaimed.

Kathryn drew her writing satchel closer, opened it, and put on her rather expensive calfskin gloves. She told the rest to stay, went across, and stood over the corpse. The cowl had been pulled up, and a fringe of hair hung down over the white forehead. When she pushed this back, Kathryn could see red marks as if a crown of brambles might have been placed there, though the cuts had faded in the days since the burial. She then looked down at the wrists and realised these had been bound with strips of brown fabric very similar to the habit Atworth had been buried in. Kathryn, using a small knife, cut these and saw the dull red wounds on the inside of each wrist. Both wounds were just under an inch long and about half an inch across. On the back of the wrist the wound was more like a small, red puncture mark; any blood flow had been congealed by death as well as the corpse's stay in the casket. She then removed the sandals and the strips of fabric and examined each instep just above the ankle. She probed with her finger and could feel the wounds in the gaps between the bones. The wounds were very similar to those of the wrists, with a small, red hole on the back of each leg just above the shin.

Kathryn ignored the exclamations and cries of the brothers as she now turned the corpse over to undo the cord. She pulled up the brown robe and the shift beneath, exposing the white, vein-streaked flesh. The stomach was slightly distended, but Kathryn realised that, when the corpse had been prepared for burial, the innards had probably been drained. The wound to the left side, just under the rib cage, was long and thin, as if a sword had pierced it; it left a dullish, red gape in the white, waxy flesh. Kathryn noticed how the perfume had now faded and the odours of the corpse were more apparent. She shook her head and stepped back.

'I see the wounds,' she called across. 'Prior Anselm, I must insist—and I mean no disrespect—that the corpse be removed to the charnel-house, where it should be stripped and carefully washed.'

'That can't . . .'

'It *will* be done,' Kathryn insisted. 'The robes.' She held up one of the brown bandages. 'Everything else must be burnt.'

Kathryn's mind was all a jumble, scraps of information, memories, images. After the exertion of examining the corpse, she felt slightly faint and wished she had eaten more before she had left Ottemelle Lane.

'I would like to reflect'—she smiled thinly—'I am not as expert as I appear.'

'And I am a busy man.' Spineri had lost his bonhomie. He now played with the tassel of his black cape, impatient to be gone. Kathryn knew that, within the hour, he would be at Islip telling everything to the Queen Mother. Perhaps it was best if he went before more was discovered? Kathryn could tell from the friars' faces, their guilty glances, and the way Brother Simon kept licking his dry lips that the good brothers knew more about the Blessed Roger's death than they'd confessed.

'Prior Anselm, is it possible I could have something to eat?'

'I'll see to that,' Colum offered.

He grasped Kathryn by the elbow, picked up her cloak and writing satchel, and, followed by the rest, walked out of the nave through the porch onto the small, grassy enclave. Kathryn sat on a stone bench. Anselm insisted that he wanted to know more. Kathryn suggested that, after she had reflected, perhaps they could meet again in the parlour. Venables was now making hushed farewells to Spineri, who announced his departure as if he had an urgent appointment with the Holy Father. He left, absentmindedly sketching a blessing in the air. The others drifted off, Murtagh hurrying across to the kitchen.

Kathryn moved on the stone bench and studied the yellow roses on their rambling bush. The buds had recently broken, and the flowers were young and fresh, the petals still tightly coiled as they searched for the strengthening sun. Behind her Kathryn heard the lay brothers, shepherded by the infirmarian, enter the church to remove Atworth's corpse to the charnel-house.

Kathryn decided not to consult any text but tried to remember everything she knew about arsenic, its deadly effects and temperamental nature. A mineral extract, her father had defined it. What else had he said? Ah, yes! How, after the person had died, the corpse gave off the very signs of poisoning so expertly hidden in life. 'The Judgement of God,' her father had called it. He had been unable to explain the reasons why, as had the authorities, but the signs always emerged after death. Nevertheless, Atworth's corpse certainly bore all the traces of arsenic poisoning: that waxen appearance, the smoothness of the skin, the red dust, and the slowness of corruption. He must have taken a powerful infusion. Or was it something else? She heard footsteps and glanced up. Colum had returned with a lay brother bearing a tray with some dried meat diced into small portions and covered with a light herbal sauce, a small white loaf, and a cup of wine. He'd also brought fresh water and a napkin. Kathryn cleaned her hands. She thanked the lay brother, refused the wine, but took the bowl and ate carefully with the horn spoon from her own wallet. Colum wandered off as if fascinated by the rose bush.

'I watched them serve it,' he called out over his shoulder. 'If you are correct, Kathryn, you must be careful what you eat and drink here.'

'Oh, I don't think we are in any danger,' she replied. 'At least not yet.'

'So Atworth was poisoned?'

'Undoubtedly! What we have to decide is how.' Kathryn put down the bowl on the stone seat. 'But come, we can't keep the others waiting.'

She and Colum returned to the parlour. The four friars and Venables were present. The only person who looked pleased was Brother Gervase. Kathryn took a seat at the top of the table.

'The corpse has been removed,' Prior Anselm declared, 'to the charnel-house. I have ordered the robe and cloths to be burnt, as well as the coffin.'

'But that's the only proof you have,' Gervase drawled, almost hugging himself with pleasure. 'They will be destroyed, Father Prior. I mean, we don't want relics being kept.'

'Brother Gervase,' Kathryn asked, 'why are you so pleased?'

'I never liked Atworth.' The sub-prior seemed totally at ease. 'I wouldn't call my late departed brother a liar, but he was a charade, a counterfeit, a cunning man.'

'Do you have proof of that?' Jonquil, flushed with anger, demanded.

'He wanted to flee the world'—Gervase blew his cheeks out— 'and yet he remained as confessor to the Queen Mother, meeting important people. He accepted her letters, not to mention the gifts she and others sent.'

'That's unfair.' Prior Anselm rapped the table with his knuckles. 'Brother Roger always shared what he had with the poor; he kept nothing for himself.'

Kathryn studied Gervase: his fat face, the vein-streaked cheeks, the cod-like mouth, and the cynical smile. He was a man who had gone through life, she concluded, with bounding ambition but not the talent to match. Gervase was probably jealous of Atworth and the patronage he enjoyed.

'You should be careful, Gervase,' the infirmarian warned.

'No, no.' The sub-prior held his hand up. 'I'll have my say. The Blessed Thomas à Becket may be a saint and martyr, and our founder St. Francis undoubtedly is. But Atworth? A soldier, a merchant, a man who ate, drank, and did what he wanted until it turned to ashes in his mouth!' Gervase made a rude sound with his lips.

'You were very interested in him,' Jonquil almost shouted, 'ever solicitous! Did you tell him you were so two-faced?'

'Did he ever tell you,' Kathryn intervened quietly, 'that he was poisoning himself?'

'What!'

Anselm held his hands up as if Kathryn had announced the Second Coming.

'It's common enough,' Kathryn continued. 'Let me see, Brother Simon, you are infirmarian; you keep a careful ledger of powders dispensed to your community?'

The infirmarian, clearly embarrassed, simply nodded, his face flushed.

'And you have arsenic?'

'Well, why yes,' he stammered.

'And like many physicians, you prescribe it in minute grains for stomach upsets—that includes the Blessed Atworth's?'

The infirmarian reluctantly agreed. 'He complained of stomach cramps, colic, retching, and diarrhea for as long as he was here. The infirmarian before me had prescribed it, so I continued: They were the minutest grains, not enough to kill a sparrow. What are you saying? That I increased the dosage? You can scrutinise my ledger. . . .'

'You could have told me this earlier,' Kathryn declared sweetly; it was obvious Anselm and Jonquil had also known of it. Gervase was quietly chuckling, shoulders shaking with glee.

'I mentioned arsenic in the church,' Kathryn continued, 'and you said nothing! Brother Simon, please don't act the innocent with me. You know full well the properties of arsenic. You may have even suspected what the exhumed body might look like and shared such knowledge with your colleagues!'

'It was only the minutest dose,' Jonquil stammered. 'It could still be God's work. . . .'

'Is this arsenic kept safe?' Kathryn snapped.

'Oh yes, like yours, Mistress Swinbrooke,' Brother Simon replied spitefully, 'in a coffer bound by three locks; only I and one of the helpers hold the keys. It can never be opened by one person or, indeed, by anyone else but us.'

'You have a library?' Kathryn asked. 'A pharmacopeia?'

'Oh yes, the works of the great masters: Hippocrates, Galen. Do you wish to see them?'

'They won't be necessary,' Kathryn said. 'I quote from a treatise my father brought from Salerno: "Arsenic, in minute proportions, is sometimes used for stomach ailments." That is not uncommon for such powders: Belladonna is sometimes used as a cosmetic, foxglove for ailments of the heart. Now some potions are washed out of the body. According to my father and others, arsenic is different; being a mineral, it becomes part of the body's humours, its fluids and flesh. It may help the stomach, but over a period of months, even years, its noxious effect accumulates.'

'So why didn't Blessed Roger die earlier?' Anselm asked.

Kathryn looked at Venables, who was listening intently, his head slightly turned as if he was hard of hearing.

'Arsenic is a mystery,' Kathryn confessed, 'a two-edged sword; at one extreme it can heal, or so they say, but eventually it will kill. Indeed, taken often and long enough, arsenic even has the property to make the recipient more resistant to it.'

'I don't understand,' Venables spoke up. 'Mistress Swinbrooke, I have no knowledge of physic.'

'I do,' Colum intervened. 'It's like training a war-horse. At first you expose him slightly to the smell of blood, and his fear subsides. You then take it forward by steps. I have known those who train war-horses to finally put the bloodied corpse of a sheep in a stable.'

'Yes,' Kathryn agreed, 'something like that. So it is with the bodily humours. They harbour this strange guest; they may draw strength from it. Only over time does it overcome their defences. Brother Simon, surely you knew this, as well as the important fact that the presence of arsenic in the body only reveals itself after death, though God knows why?'

'I have heard of it,' he confessed. 'But the grains were so small. Anyway, why would Brother Roger die now?'

'Like a key turning in a lock,' Kathryn replied. 'He said he was ill, yes?'

'Yes, he had the rheums, a chesty cough.'

'His heart could have been weakened,' Kathryn pointed out, 'his body depleted, and so he died in his sleep.'

'What did he eat and drink?' Venables asked.

'I served him his food,' Brother Jonquil declared. 'In the week before his death it was meagre; the kitchen will affirm this. Watercress soup with small pieces of meat, fragments of bread, and a little honey and watered ale. Brother Atworth ate like a sparrow.'

'Yes, I am interested in that,' Kathryn declared. 'Brother Roger died on the morning of the Feast of the Annunciation, or at least that's when he was found dead. For the previous two days he had been confined to his chamber?'

'Yes,' Prior Anselm confirmed, rolling back the cuffs of his brown gown. 'Brother Roger kept to himself. Some of the brothers could be curious. He always kept his chamber locked and bolted. The only people who could approach him were those seated here before you—in particular, Brother Jonquil.'

'And no one else saw him?' Kathryn demanded.

'No.' Prior Anselm held her gaze.

'But he had promised to correspond with the Queen Mother?'

'He had grown weak; he was out of sorts.'

'These letters,' Venables interjected, 'which the Queen Mother sent him? Where are they now?'

'He kept them in a wallet on his girdle. Where he went, so did they.'

'But now they've gone,' Venables declared crossly. 'Her Grace the Duchess would like them returned.'

'Perhaps Brother Roger destroyed them,' the Prior retorted. 'He had a brazier in his room. He was a man who kept to himself: He knew his days were numbered and wished to destroy everything that was his before he died. He was a holy man who may have experienced a premonition that he was not long for this vale of tears.'

Gervase chuckled noisily.

'It's true,' Jonquil interjected. 'He wouldn't answer the door the night before. When silence greeted me the next morning, I alerted Father Prior. We broke in, and the brazier was full of ash. You could see he had been burning something.'

'What things?' Kathryn asked.

'Oh, his ave beads were gone, and so were the little items he kept: a wooden crucifix, a triptych of the passion.'

'What is important,' Prior Anselm spoke up, 'is what Mistress Swinbrooke is implying. I do not think,' he added softly, 'the Blessed Roger was deliberately poisoned.'

Kathryn did not answer.

'He just died in his sleep,' the Prior continued. 'Perhaps he had a spasm and realised his hours were numbered. He did live in the true spirit of poverty. He may have got up and burnt all his possessions, including the letters. Now'—he waved a hand—'the arsenic may be the reason for his body being preserved, but the other phenomena?'

'I'll investigate those.' Kathryn pushed back her chair. 'I must also re-examine the corpse. Now, however, I would like to see Atworth's chamber.'

'It's not far, just above the stairs,' Anselm replied. 'There are three chambers: my own, Jonquil's, and Brother Roger's.'

'Why didn't he live with the rest?' Kathryn asked.

'Because he was a saint.' Gervase raised his eyes to heaven and joined his hands in mock prayer.

The rest ignored him. They left the parlour and went up the wooden staircase, which stood across the small hallway. Kathryn was aware of how serene these lodgings were, except for their many wall paintings. These depicted harrowing scenes of martyrdom and suffering portrayed in dark colours. What the artist lacked in skill, he compensated for with crude vigour: St. Sebastian, pierced by arrows; Appollonia having her teeth removed by pincers; St. Lawrence, slowly grilled to death over a roaring fire. Colum paused and stared at these.

'Everything but the horrors of hell,' he whispered.

The gallery above was clean, its walls washed in a light-green shade. Small, oriel windows overlooked a garden, and on the other side stood three chambers.

'Atworth's was at the end,' the Prior explained. 'It was really a store-room, but he claimed it would be good enough for him.'

The door was off the latch. Anselm pushed it open, and they entered. It was nothing more than a small, white-washed box with a black-timbered ceiling, a small, shuttered window high in the wall, and beneath that a table, a stool, a bench, and an empty coffer with its lid thrown back. A stark, black wooden crucifix hung on the far wall. Just within the doorway stood a narrow cot-bed stripped of all its sheets and blankets; only the thin, straw-filled mattress remained. A lantern on a chain hung from one of the beams, but its candle had been removed. Jonquil opened the shutters. Kathryn realised the room had been stripped of candlesticks and every possible ornament. She had never seen a room so stark, so bleak. She examined the door where it had been broken down and knelt beside the bed. She sniffed at the mattress and smelt a faint perfume mingled with body odours.

'So you broke the door down? And where was Brother Roger?' Jonquil gestured. 'Lying as if asleep, hands crossed above his lap.'

'Show me.'

Jonquil obeyed. Rather self-consciously he spread himself out on the mattress and turned his head slightly to one side, crossing his hands over his groin.

'It was like that?' Kathryn turned to the others.

'Oh yes,' Anselm assured her.

'But the blankets?' Colum asked. 'Wouldn't he be prepared for bed?'

'Oh no'—Jonquil got up—'it seems he just lay down on the bed and died.'

'And where was the brazier?'

Anselm pointed to the far corner.

'Over there. It was dead, full of ash. He also had a candelabra of bronze; all three candles had burnt down. Everything's now been cleared away.'

Colum was about to ask another question, but Kathryn warned him with her eyes, so he fell silent.

'Well, well, well.' Venables went and perched himself on the edge of the table. 'Her Grace the Duchess is going to be interested.'

'As I am.' Kathryn was now intrigued. 'Tell me, what did Roger do here, apart from praying, fasting, and corresponding with the Duchess?'

'He had good eyesight,' the Prior declared. 'The library contains a book of his prayers. He often liked to illuminate the capital letters. But apart from that, as you say, prayer, good works, fasting.'

'Did he have enemies?' Colum asked, staring at Gervase.

'None that I know of,' the sub-prior answered curtly. 'Had his eyes not on this world but the next, did Brother Roger.'

'He liked walking,' Jonquil added. 'He often strolled in Gethsemane; it's a garden at the far end of the priory. It has a lush green lawn fringed by trees near the curtain wall. Brother Roger claimed Gethsemane had the best of both worlds: It was serene and quiet, but he could still listen to the bustle of the city. The wall is high; there's no postern gate. . . .'

He was about to continue when Kathryn noticed how the Prior gestured with his hand for silence.

'Can I wander here?' Kathryn asked.

The Prior looked surprised but agreed.

'To your heart's content, Mistress.'

Colum came and stood beside her, and Kathryn tapped his boot with her own.

'I also want to stay tonight in your guest-house. It would save me going backwards and forwards. Tomorrow I have to investigate the miracles of Brother Roger.'

'Do you doubt them?'

'I didn't say that.' Kathryn smiled tactfully. 'However, I would now like a word with Master Murtagh alone.'

Venables made his excuses and left. He shouted from the gallery that he was returning to Islip but might come back on the morrow. Colum closed the door.

'What's the matter, Kathryn?'

She walked over, opened the door, glanced down the now empty gallery, and then closed the door.

'Everything is wrong,' she murmured. 'I really do doubt if Brother Roger died in his sleep.'

'What makes you say that?' Colum took her by the hand; they went and sat on the edge of the bed.

'Do you remember the way Jonquil lay down?' Kathryn patted the mattress. 'I have seen many a corpse, Colum, including those who've died in their sleep. I've never heard of that: feet together, hands clasped over the groin, face serene.'

'They could be lying.' Colum picked at a burr on his hose. 'These friars want Brother Roger to be a saint. They have to depict him as dying in the odour of sanctity.'

'But isn't it curious, Colum? Here's a man who thinks he is going to die. He even burns his possessions on the brazier, a leather wallet full of letters, other bric-à-brac, tawdry items.' She paused. 'Have you read the lives of the great Franciscans, Colum? One thing about the Order of St. Francis and its great founders, such as the notable Anthony of Padua: They always wanted to die in church before the altar. Why didn't Roger do this? Why didn't he send for Jonquil and ask to be carried down to lie before the high altar? This great saint who, according to the evidence, bore the stigmata as did Francis of Assisi refused to follow his great master?' Kathryn shook her head. 'Atworth seemed more concerned with burning things than anything else. He makes no farewells, writes no letters, but dies quietly in the odour of sanctity.' She spread her hands. 'Nevertheless, these phenomena, the stigmata, the beautiful fragrance, the vision, the incorruptible corpse . . .'

'Which you now think is due to arsenic?'

'I know it is,' Kathryn affirmed.

'Could he have been deliberately poisoned?'

'Possibly, yet we know that he was taking small doses.'

'There's something else as well'—Colum got to his feet—'and one matter you must probe, Kathryn. Was there any mysterious visitors to this house? Any connection between the Friars of the Sack and the Court of France?' He leaned down and kissed her on the brow. 'But be careful,' he warned her, 'hallowed precincts are no defence against sudden death!'

Chapter 6

'Radix malorum est Cupiditas.'
—Chaucer, 'The Pardoner's Tale,'
The Canterbury Tales

Brother Timothy, one of the ancient ones at the Friary of the Sack, had very few occupations in life except prayer and staring through a small window which overlooked the green expanse of Gethsemane Garden. Brother Timothy loved this place; the pebble-dashed pathways beneath were always quiet. He loved to study the great lawn which stretched out towards the high curtain wall, as well as the trees which thronged the lawn in the shape of a horse-shoe. Gethsemane would change according to the seasons: Bright frost on a winter's morning or thick, heavy snow could transform the place into the white courtyard of one of Heaven's palaces: above all, the gentle touch of spring as the grass grew long and lovely, the birds swooped, the flower-buds broke, and, like the risen Lord, resurrected once again was breathtaking. Brother Timothy had been the friars' gardener: he knew every inch of Gethsemane. He was particularly fascinated by a colony of stoats which nested in the curtain wall and often foraged across the lawn.

'Pity,' he murmured, 'about the rabbits.'

The stoats had settled bloody accounts with them, but that was life! Brother Timothy was well past his eightieth year. He had fought as a boy archer in the great Henry's Battle of Agincourt. He had witnessed the execution of helpless prisoners of war. He had returned home sickened by it, determined to commit himself to a life of prayer and reparation. Brother Timothy scarcely moved from his chamber. He kept a faithful account of what he saw. Sometimes he drew the different birds and animals in the parchment folio the Master of the Scriptorium had given him. The friary was such a busy place, but Gethsemane Garden was scarcely frequented. It was like a lost island of dreams in the busy routine of the friary, except for the Blessed Roger!

Brother Timothy chomped on his toothless gums and wiped away a trickle of saliva from his lips on the back of his hand. Brother Timothy regarded himself as the guardian of Gethsemane. He knew which friars walked there—sometimes Anselm, the busy-eyed Prior, and, of course, Gervase the sub-prior, who had direct responsibility for the friary precincts. Finally, there was Brother Roger Atworth with that moon-eyed lay brother, his constant companion and shadow. Atworth often walked in the garden; he'd even go to the far corner. Brother Timothy clutched the windowsill. Ah yes, the far corner behind the great hawthorn bush, that stone enclave built against the wall, the small prison of the Accursed. Ah well! Brother Timothy bowed his head.

'Jesu miserere!' The old friar whispered a prayer for the woman imprisoned there. He glanced up. The day was dying. He had heard about all the excitement—how Brother Roger Atworth had been found dead and the eerie phenomena which surrounded his death, the vision in the chapel. Brother Timothy grinned mirthlessly. He was in his eighty-fifth summer; he didn't believe in visions. The good Lord was too busy to care about Canterbury, which was already well looked after by the sainted Becket's bones. One of the lay brothers had also talked about the arrival of important men, people from the Court. But whose Court? Sometimes Brother Timothy was confused. All that struggle, those bloody battles, armies marching backwards and forwards. There was even a female physician present! Brother Timothy's legs were beginning to ache, so he sat down in the high-backed chair. Someone said it was Swinbrooke's daughter. The old friar's eyes crinkled in amusement. He had liked Mistress Swinbrooke. The physician had come here during the pestilence, and wasn't there a bright-eyed, red-haired, plump woman with him? What was her name? Aminsa? Thomasina? Anyway, according to that gossip Brother Eadwig, who always brought his meal, the woman physician was staying the night.

Brother Timothy might be old, but he prided himself on his hearing and his sight. He heard the pebbled path crunch. Pert as a sparrow, the Ancient One returned to his perch and stared out of the window.

'Ah!' It was Sub-Prior Gervase. He could tell that by the white ermine fur which edged his cowl. Timothy watched Gervase walk across the lawn and into the fringe of trees and bushes on the far side. Why did he do that? Hadn't he been there earlier in the afternoon? Brother Timothy shook his head. Gervase's conduct over the last few months had grown rather strange. Perhaps he was visiting the Accursed? Timothy watched the sub-prior disappear. If he was agile enough, Timothy would have gone out and discovered what was so interesting at the far side of Gethsemane.

The priory bells began to toll, a signal that, within a quarter of an hour, the brothers would gather in church to sing divine office, so Gervase wouldn't be there long. Brother Timothy kept his vigil. He saw a small, shadowy form creep out from beneath a bush and scuttle across the grass. Timothy, distracted, stared at it. Wasn't it one of those damnable rats? A few weeks ago Timothy had noticed the first of these, bold as brass, daring to forage out on the lawn; then they had disappeared. Timothy had consulted a book in the library and recognised the bloody handiwork of his old friends the stoats. Brother Timothy had asked Eadwig about the infestation. Eadwig had even trapped and killed one so he could draw it in his sketchbook. Timothy had taken one look at the bloody, rather charred corpse and thought otherwise.

'An ugly, devil-made beast!' he'd exclaimed, but he had drawn the creature from memory. He turned and went back to his table and picked up the folio; the pages crackled. Ah, there it was, with its black forehead and long, evil snout, black gleaming eyes, devil-like tail.

'Did you burn it?' he'd asked Eadwig, remembering the charred fur.

'I don't know what you are talking about,' the lay brother had replied. 'I was in one of the outhouses. One of the brutes appeared, so I hit it with a log.'

Brother Timothy remembered his vigil and went across to the window. The shadows across the lawn were growing longer, and the bell tolled for divine office, but Brother Gervase hadn't reappeared. Timothy felt a prickle of cold between his shoulder blades. What was wrong? Why would Gervase stay there? Timothy racked his brains. Of course, the ruins! Buildings had stood here before the friary was ever built: A merchant house had been turned over to the order some 250 years earlier; its foundations and cellars still lay behind those bushes, nothing more than dank pits. Brother Timothy remembered the brass-studded door at the foot of the crumbling steps. Alcuin, the old librarian, had told him about them. Once upon a time, before the Franciscans ever arrived in Canterbury, this had been a park owned by a great nobleman who, in turn, had built on even more ancient dwellings. Gethsemane had been his own private garden: His house once stood where the monks' store-rooms were built. Perhaps Gervase was involved in some business over there?

Brother Timothy sat down on his cushioned chair brought specially over to the window so he could take rest during his vigils. He knew so much about this place. He dozed for a while. What if Brother Gervase returned? He got up and opened the little, latticed door-window. The evening air was turning cold but was still sweet with the smell of flowers and trees; it even carried the distant bustle of the city. Another bell tolled. Brother Timothy heard a sound. He got to his feet and, clutching the windowsill, peered out. Gervase was standing next to the large hawthorn bush, cowl pulled up, arms up the sleeves of his gown. He just stood as if lost in contemplation. Brother Timothy blinked and stared again. Was that a tendril of smoke? He gaped in horror. One moment Gervase was just standing there; the next, it was as if the earth had opened up and spat out a spume of fire.

'Gervase!' he screamed.

Old Timothy's heart beat faster. He watched in absolute terror as the sub-prior was suddenly engulfed in a tongue of fire which roared up to the sky. Brother Timothy dug his fingernails into the palms of his hands. He tried to shout, but he couldn't. The sub-prior was still standing, the flames roaring all about him. Brother Timothy staggered away, battling for breath; he picked up the hand-bell from the table, fell to his knees, and began to ring it vigorously.

Kathryn was in her chamber in the guest-house when the tocsin began to boom; she had been given pleasant lodgings consisting of a spacious chamber, clean and well swept, with a comfortable bed, chair, table, and a narrow window overlooking the friary gardens. Colum had left, promising that he or Thomasina would return with a change of clothing and other things Kathryn needed. She was sitting at the table laying out her writing satchel when the strident tones of the bell alarmed her. She was reluctant to act, as she was only a guest and anxious not to interfere with the smooth running of the friary. Footsteps pounded along the gallery, followed by a hasty knocking at the door. Brother Jonquil burst in, white-faced, round-eyed.

'Mistress Swinbrooke, you'd best come! It's hideous, you . . .'

'What?' Kathryn jumped to her feet, quickly slipping on her sandals. She hitched her dress to fasten the clasps and caught Brother Jonquil's embarrassed gaze. 'Don't worry, Brother,' she teased, 'they're only my ankles. What is the matter?'

'Gervase . . . Gervase, he's all a-fire!'

Kathryn could make no sense of it but followed Jonquil down the stairs and out of the guest-house. Jonquil was walking fast, striding ahead along narrow passageways, out of the friary buildings onto a pebble-dashed path, flanked on one side by the friary and on the other by the curtain wall. Other members of the community were hurrying in the same direction, hitching up their robes, anxious-eyed, worried-faced; a few threaded ave beads through bony fingers. They rounded a corner: friary buildings with small bay windows, jutting cornices, and buttresses lay to Kathryn's immediate left. On her right, across a broad, white-pebbled path, lay a beautiful, expansive lawn shaped in the form of a *U* which stretched out to a fringe of trees and bushes. At the far side of the lawn a group of friars had assembled. Billowing clouds of black smoke carried across the sickening stench of burning flesh.

'In God's name!' Kathryn whispered.

That smoke, that terrible odour shattered the garden's beautiful serenity. Anselm was there beckoning her over, gesturing with his hand. She hurried across the lawn. The group of monks parted to reveal a broad, dark canvas cloth which covered remains of the fire. Spirals of smoke still curled out from under its edges, and the air was sickly-sweet with that dreadful odour.

Anselm looked as if he had lost his wits; his face had a strange pallor. He grasped Kathryn's hand, swallowing hard. 'God forgive me, Mistress, I don't feel well. I'm going to be sick.'

Kathryn took him by the arm and led him away. 'Kneel down,' she ordered.

The Prior obeyed, coughing and retching, covering his mouth with his hand.

'Jonquil,' she ordered, 'look after Father Prior!'

Kathryn went back to the small group. She recognised Simon but not the others; the infirmarian looked ashen, hands shaking.

'God forgive us, Mistress, but Brother Gervase . . . !'

Kathryn waited no longer. She pulled back the sheet. If the infirmarian hadn't told her, Kathryn would not have recognised the corpse. It consisted of nothing but lumps of charred flesh clinging to cracked, yellowing bone. The head and face were unrecognisable, shrivelled flesh, made all the more grotesque by the jutting teeth and the empty black sockets where the eyes had been.

'It is Gervase?' she asked.

She noticed how all items of clothing or footwear had disappeared, leaving only a grisly parody of a human being. Kathryn had seen similar corpses dragged out from burning buildings, unrecognisable, nothing more than charred bones to which lumps of black flesh still hung.

'He wore a steel chain round his neck,' Simon confided, 'with the Cross of Lorraine on it, whilst one of the ancient ones saw him walk over here.'

Kathryn bent down, recalling the advice of her father: 'Do not think, do not reflect, don't let your humours cloud your mind or sicken it with images.' Kathryn swallowed hard. She asked the infirmarian to bring her a stick. He hurried off and returned with a branch pruned of twigs and leaves. Kathryn turned the charred remains over, pinching her nostrils at the foul smell.

'Remember, Brother,' she whispered, 'this is the corpse of a man consumed by fire: It burnt his outer robes, under-garments, hose, and any footwear he was wearing. The fire also has removed most of the flesh, burning out the blood and the vital organs. Like the eyes, most of them would turn to liquid.' She stared at the large stain on the grass around the corpse. 'He was burnt here?'

'No, no, he was brought here.'

Kathryn, only too pleased to leave the smouldering remains, followed the infirmarian into the clump of trees and bushes which separated the lawn from the high curtain wall of the friary. It was a dark, shadowy place, more like a copse with its brambles and bushes and different trees of sycamore, ash, and oak. Simon stopped to push aside a hawthorn bush. Kathryn noticed how the greater part of this, as well as the ground beside it, was also charred black, an area of two yards wide the same across. The smell of burning smothered any garden fragrance. Kathryn crouched down and stared at the ground; the grass and under-growth were shrivelled black ash which crunched under her feet. She got up and examined the hawthorn bush, part of which had also been consumed by the fire. Feathery ash still floated in the evening breeze.

'What is this place?' she asked.

Brother Simon pointed across the lawn, now dappled in shad-ows by the setting sun, which shimmered in the mullioned glass of the bay-windows.

'This is Gethsemane, Mistress Swinbrooke—a small park or pleasaunce where the brothers can walk. The noble who once owned this place only granted it to our friary on condition this part never be built upon. He called it his Gethsemane.'

Kathryn nodded. Gethsemane was a serene, gentle place, full of the joys of nature but now marred by those grotesque, stinking remains, the dreadful black patch on the lawn, and the pervasive smell of burning and destruction. Other members of the commu-nity stood in watchful silence across the lawn. Those with a weak stomach had taken one glance and walked away to sit on the stone benches along the pebble-dashed path. Prior Anselm had regained his composure; he now stood, supported by Brother Jonquil, gaz-ing in horror at this hideous scene.

Kathryn walked deeper into the trees. She felt queasy herself and, as she brought her hand up to her mouth, almost retched at the smell of burning. She lowered her hand and took deep breaths.

'Are you all right, Mistress?'

Kathryn kept her back turned. She stretched out and leaned against a tree.

'Mistress, is there anything wrong?'

Kathryn shook her head and gestured with her other hand. She stood for a while listening to the distant sounds of the city beyond the wall.

'Isn't it strange?' she murmured. 'This must be a place of birdsong, yet how silent it has become.'

'What are we to do?' Prior Anselm's wail cut the air.

Kathryn walked back.

'Brother Simon,' she grasped the infirmarian by the elbow, 'have the remains sheeted and taken to the charnel-house. Tell your community to leave this place.'

'Shall I bring out vats of water,' the infirmarian offered, 'for the grass to be cleaned?'

'No, no.' Kathryn walked back onto the lawn. She kept her eyes on the friary buildings, unwilling to stare at the remains now being covered up by the brothers. 'Have them taken away!' she said quickly. 'Prior Anselm, Brother Simon!' she called out; the two friars followed her across the grass.

The rest of the community were now being shooed gently away. Kathryn sat down on one of the stone benches, closed her eyes, and fought to retain her composure. Anselm, Simon, and Jonquil walked away and stood whispering together. Kathryn felt her knee being lightly touched and opened her eyes.

'My name is Eadwig.' The kindly eyes of the lay brother smiled at her. He offered her a goblet of wine. 'Slightly spiced,' he explained. 'I am serving the same to the rest of the brothers. It will give you strength.'

Kathryn grasped the pewter goblet. The wine was rich Bordeaux, juicy and fresh: it washed away the foul taste in her mouth. She sipped carefully; Eadwig crouched before her, watching intently.

'He saw it, you know.' He gestured with the tip of his finger up at the sky.

'God sees everything, Brother.'

'No, no.' Eadwig's thin face broke into a smile. 'Not God but someone almost as old as him: Brother Timothy. He was the one who raised the alarm.'

Kathryn pulled herself up in the seat. She felt better, even though Gervase was dead, his soul gone to God, his body consumed by that hideous fire. There was nothing she could do for him except pray and find out what had really happened. Eadwig sat beside her. Kathryn stared across the lawn. Gervase's corpse, now rolled up in the canvas sheeting, was being carried off on a makeshift stretcher. All that remained of his brutal death was that dreadful stain on the grass, the faint lingering odour, and wisps of smoke moving like the shades of lost souls above the grass.

'It's terrible, isn't it?' Eadwig confided. 'Such a contrast. Green grass, a fresh spring evening, setting sun, and death strikes: Like an arrow to the heart, eh Mistress?'

'What was Gervase doing over there?' Kathryn asked.

'No one knows.'

Anselm and the other two joined them.

'What's the matter?' Anselm demanded crossly, glaring at Eadwig. 'Why are you chattering?'

'Father Prior, I am only trying to help.' Eadwig got to his feet. 'I told you already; I raised the alarm. Brother Timothy saw everything.'

'Who is this Brother Timothy?' Kathryn glanced at the Prior. 'Can he come down here? I would like to speak to him.'

'Mistress,' Prior Anselm retorted, eager to reinforce his status, 'you have no authority here.'

'I have every authority.' Kathryn sighed. 'If you want, Prior, I'll go to the city and obtain confirmation of that. I came here to investigate Blessed Roger Atworth's death. Now your sub-prior dies, consumed by a mysterious fire. Please bring Brother Timothy down.'

The Prior reluctantly gave in. Kathryn sat and finished the wine. A small wicker chair was brought and placed before her, and a few minutes later Brother Timothy came hobbling out. He eased himself down in the chair, bony, vein-streaked hands clutching a cane. Bright, pert eyes smiled at Kathryn as he patted his bald head.

'All gone.' He chomped on his gums. 'I know I've a skull-like face, but my eyes and ears are sound. I remember your father.' He leaned closer. 'You're rather like him and that nurse or maid, Camasina?'

111

'Thomasina.'

'Ah, that's right.'

'Brother,' Kathryn sat on the edge of the seat, 'tell me what you saw this evening.'

Brother Timothy had recovered from the shock and succinctly described what had happened. Prior Anselm, Jonquil, and Simon brought across a bench and sat alongside them.

'Why would Gervase walk over there?' Kathryn asked.

Anselm shrugged. 'This is Gethsemane, the friary gardens.'

'But why go into those bushes?'

'The friary grounds were his responsibility.'

'He may have been going to see the Accursed,' Prior Anselm murmured.

'The what?' Kathryn demanded.

'Mathilda Chandler.'

'I've heard that name.'

'Once upon a time everyone did,' the infirmarian intervened. 'Mathilda Chandler was married to Robert the candle-maker in Honeypot Lane. Twenty-three years ago, on the eve of the birth of John the Baptist, the bailiffs were called to Robert's house. They found him with his throat cut and their four children, the eldest being no more than six, all dead!'

Kathryn stared at the sombre line of trees and wondered at the terrible secrets they protected.

'Sweet God in Heaven!' she murmured. 'She should have been hanged!'

'That's what the royal justices said. But Mathilda was witless in court. More than that, she escaped her guards and claimed sanctuary here in the friary. "Deranged and moon-struck," "possessed by a demon," that's how the friary chronicle described her. The Sheriff received orders from the Archbishop: If Mathilda Chandler had asked for sanctuary, then sanctuary she would have. A small cell was built in the corner of the friary wall, about six feet high and three yards across. Mathilda was imprisoned within; there's a gap for her to receive air, light, and other items of sustenance.'

'Is she ever let out?'

'There's a small door in the cell, but that's protected by a steel plate. Every so often,' Simon conceded, 'the poor woman is taken out and the place cleaned. Brother Gervase was responsible. He might have been visiting her.'

'Is she still witless?' Kathryn asked.

'Oh no, lucid as a spring pool,' Simon declared. 'Brother Roger Atworth also visited her. They talked about many things. Roger felt sorry for her. He once confided in me'— Prior Anselm played with the tassel of his cord—'that he would try and get her a pardon, some release from her pain.'

Kathryn stared across the lawn. A wood pigeon had come strutting out as if the advance guard for the rest of the birds, to spy out and check that the harmony of this hallowed place had now been restored. The sun was sinking, flashes of red across the sky. The shadows of the trees stretched like black fingers over the lawn as the evening breeze strengthened.

'Tell me again, Brother Timothy.'

The old man turned in his chair and pointed across.

'Brother Gervase came out of the line of trees, hands up the sleeves of his gown. He must have stood for a short while. I saw a tendril of smoke, then his whole body was sheathed in flames.'

'Did he cry out? Did he run forward?'

'I don't know, Mistress. I looked away. When I glanced back, he had collapsed to the ground, burning from head to toe.' Brother Timothy turned to the Prior, chin jutting out aggressively. 'Gervase wasn't a bad friar. I've heard what the brothers say, how he died because he didn't believe in the Blessed Roger Atworth.'

'That's nonsense!' the Prior snapped, getting to his feet. 'Mistress Swinbrooke?'

Kathryn held up her hand. 'Brother Timothy, I thank you. Father Prior, I would like to stay here. I want to go back across the lawn.'

'It's getting dark,' the infirmarian warned.

'It's still light enough to see.' Kathryn got up and kissed the Ancient One on the brow. 'But first I must visit your kitchens.'

She thanked them and walked away. A lay brother gave her directions. Kathryn entered the great stone-flagged kitchen; the friar in charge came bustling over, pot-belly covered by a snowy white apron. He listened to what Kathryn wanted.

'Of course, of course. And you will eat in your own chamber?'

'In a while,' Kathryn said. 'But if I could have what I wanted?'

The lay brother handed over a small wineskin, strips of meat, cut bread, a small pot of honey, and some marchpane, all wrapped in clean linen cloths. He placed these in a small leather sack. Kathryn looped this round her wrist and returned to Gethsemane. Apart from the infirmarian, who was wearing a stole and blessing the spot where Gervase had died with asperges rod and bucket, Gethsemane was deserted. Kathryn nodded at Brother Simon, who continued the ritual, and entered the line of trees. She stopped next to the hawthorn bush and stared back at the friary. She saw a blur, a face pressed against the window on the second floor, and raised her hand. Old Brother Timothy raised his in return.

'So you did see everything,' Kathryn murmured.

She placed the leather bag behind her and stood as Gervase must have done, arms folded. She crouched down and sniffed, smelling a slight, lingering perfume. What was it? Soap? Something more acrid? She walked deeper into a small copse. Through the tangle of bushes she glimpsed the far wall of the friary; narrow, manmade tracks led off in every direction.

'If anyone wished to make an assignation,' she murmured, 'some friar who wanted to meet his leman, this would be an ideal place.'

She noticed how the grass was scuffed, and here and there the tangle of briars snapped. The undergrowth ended, and she entered a small clearing, the ground covered by dead leaves and bits of branches. She tapped with her foot; the thin coating of soil covered hard stone, and a short distance away lay a raised wall with steps leading down. Kathryn walked to the top of these. The crumbling, stone steps were manmade. The walls on either side were red, of fire-burnt brick. Kathryn realised she must be standing on the site of the old manor house and all that remained was this wine cellar. She carefully made her way down. The stones were slippery. She recalled the plague of rats and quietly prayed she would meet none of those devil's minions.

The door at the bottom was on a latch, no padlock. She lifted this up, pushed the door open, and made her way in, sliding her feet. She felt the side of the wall and grasped a thick, half-burnt tallow candle; beside it lay a tinder. After a great deal of scraping, the candle was lit, and its wick flared fiercely. Kathryn held it out.

The chamber was long and dark; two more steps led down to an earth-beaten floor. The ceiling was of brick, as were the walls; the plaster surface had long crumbled. At the far end were two wooden pillars, and in between them stood a table. Kathryn searched around. She noticed the barrels in the far corner and went and lifted their lids. One was full of old rope; the other had some chains and scraps of metal, rusted and gnarled. Kathryn checked the cellar carefully. Satisfied, she blew the candle out and went back up the steps. Only then did she realise how she had left the door off the latch, and she cursed her own stupidity. She would not return to a place like that without Colum or someone to protect her.

The light was now fading, but she examined the ground carefully. Someone had been here. She could make out the imprint of sandals. Was it Gervase or someone else? She started as a small, brown, furry body raced across the ground in front of her. At first she thought it was a rat, but then she recalled the white-tipped tail and recognised it must be a stoat. She collected the food and went towards the curtain wall, using it as a guide. The wall was of hard, blackened brick, very ancient but sturdy and thick, about three yards high with a crennelated top. She paused. Distant sounds were audible. She tried to remember the outline of the friary and realised an alleyway must run across the other side. Kathryn continued walking.

'Who's there?' the voice seemed to come out of nowhere.

'Who's there?' the woman's voice repeated. 'You are not a friar. I can smell your perfume. One of my own kind.'

Kathryn moved aside the branch of a bush. She had reached the far corner. The anchorite's cell jutted out, a large rectangle of stone with a broad slit high in the wall. Kathryn saw dirty fingers and bright eyes.

'Who are you?' The voice was softer.

'My name is Kathryn Swinbrooke, physician in the city. I'm a visitor here.'

'A visitor?' The woman's voice was soft. 'But you know about me?'

'I know all about you, Mathilda Chandler.'

'Do you now?' the voice taunted. 'That's an arrogant thing to say, Mistress, about someone you've never met.'

Kathryn smiled in apology.

'You have a strong, good face, Mistress, though you look tired. I'd be wary of some of these friars, with your swelling breasts, long legs, and slim waist. But what are grey hairs doing on a young woman like you? You say you know me. Do I know you? There was a physician once, Swinbrooke; he lived in Ottemelle Lane.'

'I am his daughter.'

'Well, well, well, how this busy world turns. A woman physician!'

Kathryn walked closer and undid the leather bag. The fetid smell of the cell tickled her nostrils.

'Are you ever released?' Kathryn asked.

'Once every fourteen days, but I wear the chains—or used to. The good brothers clean my cell and take the rubbish away.'

'I have some food for you.'

'Come closer. I won't hurt.'

'Stand back,' Kathryn ordered.

She heard a rustling and went up against the slit and peered in. The smell was stale rather than offensive. The cell inside looked clean. Fresh rushes lay on the floor. It contained a table, a stool, and a cot bed, a shelf bearing earthenware pots, a small brazier, and, in the far corner, a jakes pot covered with a leather cloth. Two candles glowed in bronze dishes on the table. Kathryn even saw a small, calfskin-bound book lying on a stool.

'Much more comfortable than the castle dungeons,' the voice declared.

Kathryn placed the linen cloths onto the ledge and started at the face which suddenly appeared. Chandler's eyes were dark-blue, her skin surprisingly brown though pitted around the eyes and forehead. Kathryn felt Mathilda's fingers pressing hers.

'I won't hurt you, Mistress. I thank you for the food.'

The linen cloths disappeared. Kathryn heard the sound of eating; then Mathilda came back.

'Marchpane,' she whispered. 'It cleanses the mouth, doesn't it? It's wonderful to eat something sweet.'

Kathryn stayed her ground. She had dealt with enough mad people to recognise the signs, but she felt no danger from Mathilda Chandler.

'The friars treat you well?'

'Oh, it varies from season to season. I am sorry Brother Atworth is dead. He made me more comfortable. Thanks to him I have rushes on the floor and more food every day. He called me "Unfortunate," her eyes blinked, 'whereas the rest call me "Accursed." '

'And are you?'

'Once I was; now I have atoned. You've heard my crime?'

'You murdered your husband and four children.'

'Ah, the same old story. I've told it once, I've told it again, but no one listens. Yes, I killed my husband. Cut his throat when he was in a drunken stupour. Do you know why, Mistress Swinbrooke? He killed my little ones. Drunk he was, sottish and wicked. He was a candle-maker by trade but drank the profits. I was reduced to taking what he did make and selling them from a tray in the Mercery.' The eyes behind the slit watched Kathryn intently. 'I came home one night, a beautiful June evening. The house was quiet. I pushed open the door. My first child lay within, his little head cracked like an egg.' The woman began to sob.

Kathryn waited by the slit. Around her was the noise of the copse, the muted evening song of the birds as they prepared for the night, the rustle in the undergrowth; she heard the distant toll of a friary bell echoing those being rung in the city for the hour of vespers. A cart in the lane on the far side of the wall clinked as it trundled by.

'Do you listen for such sounds?' Kathryn asked.

'They keep me sane.' Mathilda was now back at the slit, eyes wet with tears. 'I tell you, Mistress, I found my other bairns killed just as violently. Robert lay fast asleep, drunk as a pig on our bed. I took a knife and slit his throat. When the bailiffs came, I tried to tell them. I suppose the rest you know.'

'Didn't you protest?'

'Who would believe me?'

'Did Roger Atworth?'

'Yes, he did. He used to hear my confession. I told him about the murder, and he told me about some of the hideous crimes he had perpetrated. Believe me, Mistress, in many ways he was a terrible man: women raped, children killed, men hanged above their own doorways, entire villages burnt and ravaged. I'd confessed to him, and he'd confess to me. He told me how once he had been cursed by a witch to die a violent death; the only thing he could do was prepare for it. He would console me, say that I would go to Heaven whilst he expected to suffer, for millions of years, the agonies of Purgatory. He used to stand where you do, Mistress Swinbrooke, and cry like a child.'

'What was he like?' Kathryn asked.

'A broken, fearful man who believed the demons were not very far away.'

'Did he ever talk about Duchess Cecily?'

'Oh yes. He said we all had secrets and that included the greatest in the kingdom.'

'Was he a great saint?'

Kathryn waited.

'No, Mistress, a great sinner who wanted to atone.'

'What did he say to you?'

'I can't tell you. It's wrong to break the seal of confession, but he talked of murder, of snuffing mens' lives out like you or I would crush a fly. He said that in Gethsemane the dead sometimes thronged all about him: all his victims, scores and scores of people staring hollow-eyed.'

'Did he walk here often?'

'Oh yes. He found the company of the other brothers onerous; their lives only reminded him of his sins.'

'And Brother Jonquil?'

'A cross'—Mathilda laughed sharply—'he had to bear.'

'What did he mean?'

'Jonquil is a strange one. He acts the fool, but I don't think he is. He's not a friar. He came here some months ago. He hasn't taken solemn vows, just simple ones.' Again Mathilda laughed. 'As is fitting for a simpleton. Roger Atworth claimed Jonquil was his guardian angel and would say no more.'

'And the other brothers?'

'They vary. Some are kind, most ignore me, a few are cruel.'

'And Gervase?'

'Ah, I have heard of his death. He never spoke to me, never looked me in the eye. He'd bring me food, stand and feed me as if I were a dog.'

'You didn't like him?'

'I didn't know him, Mistress; perhaps that was the greatest cruelty, to be regarded as nothing. He'd even belch and break wind as if he was by himself. A man of secrets, Gervase.'

'You could tell me more, couldn't you?' Kathryn asked.

'Mistress, I can only tell you what I see and hear.'

'Atworth's death?'

'Jonquil came and told me. I cried for a while and said a prayer.'

'Do you think he was murdered?'

'I have been immured here for over twenty years, Mistress. I don't have visions, and no angel of light has ever visited me. I cried for a while when I learnt of Atworth's death and said the requiem. Perhaps he will find some peace. He did complain of stomach pains, savage gripes, but claimed he had some potion to ease the pain.'

'And this evening?' Kathryn asked. She started at a rustling close to her.

'Oh, don't be nervous, Mistress. It's only my friends the stoats. They like the wall. They build their nests there and play bloody havoc amongst the rabbits and rats.'

'Rats?' Kathryn asked, distracted.

'Oh yes. One day they weren't here; the next day they were, impudent and ravenous.' She tapped the ledge. 'I leave some small crumbs here for the birds; they are my messengers. I pray to them. I hope they take my words to my little ones.' The eyes behind the slit smiled. 'One morning I awoke and saw a rat, like some black-garbed varlet; it had crept to the wall and was eating the crumbs, wedging itself on the ledge here, so intent.' The eyes disappeared then came back. Kathryn saw a small club being raised. 'I hit it on its snout. Brother Atworth found the corpse, said it had been burnt by fire. He buried it over there.'

'And the other rats?' Kathryn asked.

'I heard the news. Brother Atworth used to tell me gossip from the city. He claimed the rats could not live in such a hallowed place and had fled the friary. I replied if that was the case, why did other strange creatures come here at night?'

Kathryn shivered, a prickle of fear along her spine.

'Creatures?' she asked.

'This is not a hallowed place, Mistress.' Mathilda's voice had fallen to a hoarse whisper. 'All forms of devilment take place!'

Chapter 7

'His deeth saugh I by revelatioun . . .'
—Chaucer, 'The Summoner's Tale,'
The Canterbury Tales

Kathryn looked back through the bushes. Chandler's cell was virtually cut off, though Kathryn could make out the buttresses and cornices, the glint of windows in the friary. Above her the sky was growing darker. She wanted to return to her chamber, yet Chandler's mysterious references intrigued her.

'You heard what I said, Mistress. I am not the Accursed. I am a poor woman locked in this chamber for murders I did not commit. My world is what I can see and hear, and believe me, appearances lie. You'd think this line of trees and bushes,' her voice continued matter-of-factly, 'was desolate, the nesting place of birds, the hunting ground of stoats?'

'What have you heard?' Kathryn asked. 'What have you seen? Besides Brother Atworth?'

'Gervase often came over here, not just to tend to me as he would a dog in a kennel. I think he met someone.'

'Who?'

'Another friar.'

Kathryn recalled the scandal and gossip of the tap-room which Thomasina loved to repeat.

'Are you talking of an illicit relationship?'

'I'm no man's judge, Mistress Swinbrooke. I have seen two figures in the brown habit of the friars: one of them was definitely Gervase; the other had his face masked.'

'How many times?' Kathryn asked.

'In the last few months, five or six. Gervase apparently came across this evening, but I didn't see him then.'

'What?' Kathryn exclaimed.

'I saw the flames, heard the crackle, and smelt the smoke,' Chandler replied. 'But, talking to you, I am curious. Gervase came across here hours earlier than that.'

'Are you sure?' Kathryn demanded.

'I have told you, Mistress . . .'

'Please call me Kathryn.'

'Thank you, I will. Gervase usually came across here to meet the stranger about three o'clock, when the friary is at its quietest. Brother Timothy has his sleep, and Atworth did the same. I'd glimpsed him coming in through the bushes. On one occasion I heard voices, one raised as if in anger; that was two weeks ago.'

'Did you ever question Gervase?'

'Kathryn, I am no fool: What I know and what I tell are two different things.'

'And you saw Gervase come much earlier this afternoon?'

'Yes.'

'But not leave or return just before he was engulfed by fire?'

'No.'

'Did you see or hear anyone else?'

'No one but Gervase!'

Kathryn stepped back. 'I will return tomorrow,' she declared. 'Is there anything you want?'

'My freedom.'

It was on the tip of Kathryn's tongue to promise something. She could approach the Archbishop and Luberon, whilst it was not unknown for Royal Servants like Colum to seek a pardon from the Crown.

'Be of good faith,' Kathryn replied. 'I shall return tomorrow.'

Kathryn walked back to the bushes, pushing aside the tangled undergrowth. She kept her hand on the curtain wall. This was the deepest part of the copse, completely obscured from the friary. Near to the buttress she noticed how scuffed the ground was. She crouched down: It was damp. She sniffed at her fingers: blood, water? She couldn't decide. Kathryn looked up the wall; the buttress provided a natural ladder, and carefully she began to climb. She laughed to herself; it reminded her of the days when, as a child, she'd invaded Goodman Proutler's orchard. She bruised her fingers and cut her knee, but she reached the top and peered over. The alleyway below was mud and cobbles and stank of rotting vegetables—a lonely spot, the other side being the garden wall of a large merchant's house, certainly a place to avoid in the dark. She glanced quickly down the outside wall, arms aching with the strain, and noticed the gaps in the crumbling bricks, a good foothold for anyone who wished to climb over. She gingerly climbed down, brushed herself off, and looked over her shoulder. Chandler's cell was now hidden. She walked back onto the lawn. It was dusk. Kathryn felt cold and tired, though still intrigued by Gervase's visit earlier in the afternoon. She returned to the friary and went immediately to Prior Anselm's chamber. Vespers had been sung, and the rest of the brothers were in the refectory, but Anselm and his two companions were gathered in the parlour eating a meal, apparently in deep discussion by their look of annoyance as Kathryn knocked and came in.

'What is it?' Anselm demanded.

'Brother Gervase's remains have been removed?' Kathryn asked.

'Of course.'

'Have you searched his chamber?'

'Why no, that will happen tomorrow.'

'I would like to go there now.'

'But, Mistress, this is . . .'

'Please!'

Anselm sighed, threw his napkin on the table, and picked up a bunch of keys from the desk. With the infirmarian and Jonquil accompanying him, he led Kathryn out across a small cobbled yard and through a side entrance up some stairs. The gallery above was very similar to Prior Anselm's; Gervase's chamber stood immediately at the top.

'God knows where Gervase's key is!' Anselm exclaimed, as he turned the key in the lock. 'Perhaps it was burnt with him?'

'I don't think so,' Kathryn declared, remembering the grisly remains she had examined.

The door swung open, and Jonquil pulled back the shutters and lit a candle. The room was fragrant with incense and beeswax polish; rather opulent, dark-blue, gold-edged cloths hung against the walls; blood-red curtains with purple tassels shrouded a four-poster bed. The silver crucifix on the table stood beside matching candlesticks. There were small coffers and chests, shelves of books. Kathryn was immediately impressed by how tidy everything was.

'I would like to search Gervase's possessions. Please, Prior, don't object. The human body doesn't generally burst into flames. Gervase was murdered; I am sure of that.'

'But how?' the infirmarian asked. 'He was seen walking across there.'

'And what was he doing beforehand? Did anyone see Gervase during the afternoon? Do you know he crossed Gethsemane about three o'clock?'

Anselm looked sheepishly at the infirmarian. Kathryn stepped closer. 'You know something, don't you?'

'We were just discussing that,' Anselm confessed. 'Apparently, Mistress Swinbrooke, Gervase could not be found just after we met you. He seemed to have disappeared, at least until Brother Timothy saw him walking across Gethsemane.'

'Look around you,' Kathryn urged. 'Don't you think there is something strange, Father Prior? How tidy and clean everything is?'

'Gervase was a precise man.'

'Not to this extent.' Kathryn walked across to the table. 'It's almost as if Gervase tidied up and left as if he wasn't returning.'

'Oh, that's nonsense! Only he and I have a key to this chamber.'

'Did he have other keys?' Kathryn questioned.

'Of course, look at the desk. The work of a craftsman, each of its drawers can be locked.'

Kathryn crouched down. She would love a desk like this with its fine oak top and cleverly contrived drawers, the work of some master carpenter either here or in the city. She pulled at a drawer but it remained locked; the same for the coffers around the room.

'Gervase always carried his keys with him,' Simon the infirmarian explained.

'But when he was found dead?' Kathryn got to her feet. 'I don't recall seeing any keys, and neither did those who took him to the charnel-house.'

'I agree.' The infirmarian walked to the window and stared out. 'What are you saying, Mistress?'

'I want these drawers and coffers to be forced. You must do it,' she urged. 'Whatever keys Gervase held are now gone whilst these seem to be replacements.'

Anselm clapped his hands together as if he wanted to pray for guidance.

'It must be done,' Kathryn repeated.

Simon agreed. Jonquil left and returned with a mallet and a chisel and, much as it pained her, Kathryn watched the beautifully carved drawers being forced and the coffer padlocks broken. They must have stayed an hour rummaging through the contents, but they found nothing, only letters, bills, rolls of accounts, ave beads, a psalter, personal mementos, and possessions. Prior Anselm's irritation grew; on one occasion he accused Kathryn of prying.

'Of course I am!' she snapped. 'But who can object? Gervase? He's gone to God. Don't you think it strange, Father Prior? Here is a friar who had secret assignations near the curtain wall overlooking Gethsemane, yet there's nothing amiss amongst his possessions?'

'What assignations?' the Prior demanded. 'That's the first I've ever heard of them.'

'Well, if they were secret, you wouldn't have heard of them!'

Kathryn explained what she had learnt; as she did so, the three friars grew agitated.

'Did Gervase lead a good life?' she asked.

'Not a whisper of scandal. Oh, he could be overbearing and cynical, but he kept to his vows. He was a good administrator, a faithful priest.'

Kathryn told all three to sit down and closed the door.

'Listen,' she began, pulling up a stool, 'Gervase definitely met someone from the city there or a member of this community. What they discussed must have been highly confidential: That's why Gervase chose the time and the place. I would hazard a guess, though I have no evidence, that such meetings were connected with Brother Roger Atworth. I don't know why'—she held up a hand—'I just do. Atworth has died; now Gervase is murdered.'

Kathryn then explained about the murder of Padraig Mafiach at the Falstaff Inn. As she studied the three friars, her suspicions deepened; she realized that most of what she had seen and been told here was based on a lie. The infirmarian was calmer, and Jonquil hid behind a solemn expression; but Prior Anselm was more apparent, constantly scratching his cheek, blinking, refusing to meet her eye.

'What are you implying, Mistress?' the infirmarian demanded.

'Brother Roger Atworth,' Kathryn replied, 'was Duchess Cecily's confessor. He would therefore know her secrets, as would any priest who shrives the high and mighty. Atworth was once held prisoner by the Vicomte de Sanglier, who now controls the King of France's legion of spies. Now there are spies at Court, close to the King's Council'—Kathryn paused—'I tell you this in confidence; you must not repeat it. There is also the possibility of a French spy here at the Friary of the Sack. It may have been Atworth himself; Duchess Cecily would chatter, and your dead companion was probably better acquainted with the dealings at Court than even our Archbishop.'

'I agree, I agree,' Prior Anselm broke in. 'When Duchess Cecily came here, sometimes she would spend a day or many days. She and Atworth would walk round and round Gethsemane, arms linked like brother and sister. But Atworth being a spy! He was old and frail. He never left this house. He hardly ever met anyone else.'

'True,' Kathryn answered, 'but he did go for walks in Gethsemane. He may have met someone, passed messages on. A second possibility is that someone here, amongst his brethren, spied on him.'

'We are Franciscans,' Simon the infirmarian broke in, 'dedicated to poverty, prayer, and chastity.'

'Aye, Brother, but in every barrel not every apple is wholesome! I ask you, is there anyone in this friary, however tenuous the link, connected with the Court of France? Have you had recent visitors, French merchants, pilgrims?'

'The occasional guest,' Jonquil volunteered. 'But no one Brother Roger met. Mistress Swinbrooke, we are all English, and our loyalty is to God and to the King. What profit is there for any of us to spy or become involved in treason? Visit our cells. True, we have a measure of comfort, but how can betraying Crown secrets advance any of us?'

'Sharply said, Brother.'

Kathryn stared at this young lay brother. *I must remember,* she reflected, *you are not as witless as you pretend.*

'Is there anything,' she asked, getting to her feet, 'you can tell me about Atworth's death?'

'It is as we have said,' the Prior replied. 'Atworth was a good friar, a man of holy life. Whatever he did in his youth. He became ill and died. I have been down to the infirmary and scrutinised the account. You're correct, Mistress. Brother Simon here will go on oath: Atworth suffered prolonged ailments of the stomach and often took minute grains of arsenic.' He got up and sniffed loudly. 'Mistress, how long will you stay here?'

Kathryn smiled at the exasperation in his voice.

'Why, Father Prior, I can't say. I have a number of tasks.' She ticked them off on her fingers. 'I wish to examine the corpses of both Atworth and Gervase. I must interrogate the benefactors of these so-called miracles. I need to talk to you, Brother Jonquil, about your vision in the Lady Chapel. I would like the psalter Brother Roger wrote and illuminated sent to my chamber. But'— Kathryn played with the bracelets on her wrist—'I must also drink, eat, and rest. Brother Jonquil, if you would show me to my chamber?'

Kathryn left the Prior and infirmarian nonplussed.

Jonquil led her out along a maze of corridors and porticoed passageways back to the guest-house. He explained there'd been only two other visitors: an English merchant from Southampton and a prioress on her way to Becket's shrine. Kathryn took the key out of her pouch and unlocked the chamber door. She stared around. Nothing seemed disturbed, yet she was suspicious; the rug on the floor had been moved, whilst the bed coverlet looked disturbed, as if someone had been there.

'Is everything all right?' Jonquil asked, lighting the candles. 'I will have food sent across from the refectory.'

'Ask Brother Eadwig to bring it. You know'—Kathryn smiled—'the one who serves Brother Timothy.'

Jonquil agreed and left. Kathryn took off her shoes and loosened her dress. She washed her hands and face in the lavarium. By the time she had finished, Eadwig came clattering up, bearing a tray with a small jug of wine, an earthenware goblet, and a bowl.

'Beef'—he grinned—'it's fresh! Diced in a mushroom sauce.' He pointed to the next bowl. 'And some vegetables straight from our garden. The bread is from tomorrow's batch, so it's soft and hot.' He placed it on the table. 'Is there anything else, Mistress?'

'Just one thing.' Kathryn opened her purse and slipped a coin into Eadwig's hand. 'No, keep it,' Kathryn urged when Eadwig objected. 'Please ask Brother Timothy at what hour he saw Gervase and if there was anything strange about him.'

Eadwig looked surprised but agreed and left. Kathryn washed her horn spoon and sat down at the table. She filled the wine goblet and stared at the jug. It reminded her of that chamber at the Falstaff Inn. What had she heard that was out of place? Something troubled her. She tasted the wine. The friars had been generous; it was not the common stuff but the best Bordeaux. The food was equally delicious. Kathryn ate hungrily. Eadwig returned, clattering like a boy into the room.

'About six o'clock!' he shouted from the doorway.

'And anything strange?'

'No. Gervase walked across. He had his cowl up; that's all Timothy can say. Don't forget, Mistress, he is the Ancient One.'

The lay brother made to leave.

'Tell me, Eadwig,' Kathryn asked over her shoulder, 'you saw the sub-prior walk around the friary?'

'Oh yes.'

'Did he ever have his cowl up?'

'Oh no! We only do that as we process into church or if the weather is particularly cold.'

'Thank you.'

She bade Eadwig good-night, and he left, closing the door behind him. Kathryn refilled the wine goblet and stood by the window. Night was falling. She wondered how matters were in Ottemelle Lane. Thomasina would be protesting, but she would keep everything tight and secure. . . .

'Are you never coming home?'

Kathryn nearly dropped the wine cup as she whirled round.

Colum stood in the doorway, saddle-bags over his shoulder.

'I am not supposed to be here.' He grinned. 'The guest master said no more than half an hour. Men and women are not supposed to share a chamber.'

Kathryn came across. 'Then what you have to do,' she said playfully, 'do quickly.'

Colum put the saddle-bags on the floor and pulled her to him, kicking the door closed behind him. He kissed her roundly on the lips and cheeks. Kathryn, alarmed at a footfall on the stairs, pulled away.

'I understand there has been a death,' Colum said, backing away from her.

Colum took up the saddle-bags and moved to the chair Kathryn offered. She told him what had happened. Colum whistled under his breath.

'I have heard rumours in the Mercery. People are talking about it.'

'Is everything well at Ottemelle Lane?' Kathryn demanded.

'Of course. Of course. Thomasina was upset at you not returning. Why can't you, Kathryn? It's only a walk away.'

'No, no, I want to know this place.'

'You could be in danger.'

'The same is true of any alleyways in Canterbury. Any news of Monksbane?'

Colum shook his head. 'Too soon. Too soon.'

Kathryn went over and kissed Colum on the brow, patting him on the shoulder.

'Very well. Listen to what I have to say. Oh, by the way, why are you late?'

'Trouble at Kingsmead—the Court wants more horses—but go on!'

'When my father was confronted by a patient with mysterious ailments,' she began, 'he created a hypothesis, a theory, then looked for evidence; that's what I'm doing now, Colum. We all know about Atworth, a former soldier, a cruel Ecorcheur who repented and became a friar. For some unknown reason Duchess Cecily of York chose him as her confessor. They communicated, and she often visited him. Now there's no doubt Duchess Cecily has her secrets, but does that have anything to do with Atworth's death?'

'Could he have been murdered,' Colum asked, 'to silence him?'

'In which case Duchess Cecily is the murderess or someone she, or Atworth, communicated the secrets to, someone who would be equally damaged by public revelations.'

Kathryn sat down on the chair and went on. 'But that's ridiculous. Atworth, in his later years, was a saint; he tried to be a good man, a holy priest. He would never dream of revealing anyone's confession, let alone someone like Duchess Cecily's.'

'But the arsenic?'

'An accident, Colum. I treat many patients in Canterbury. A great deal of ill health, even death, is caused by people treating themselves or buying a cure from some cunning man. Do you remember that poor carpenter poisoned by his wife? Forced to drink Holy Water which was as putrid as that from any horse trough?' Kathryn sighed. 'I also believe God manifests himself, but apparitions, fragrant perfumes?'

'You talk about a hypothesis?' Colum teased.

'I don't know whether I am looking at the right symptoms. Something very strange happened to Atworth. Then we have the other business, the traitor close to the English Court, Padraig Mafiach's murder.'

'Could there be a connection?'

'To all appearances'—Kathryn shook her head—'no.' She patted her stomach. 'But as one of my old patients, a Yorkshireman, would say: "In my water I feel there is." '

'And so we come to Gervase's death.'

'Yes, my wild-haired Irishman; I think that is the clasp. Someone doesn't want Atworth's death fully investigated. Gervase may have known something.'

Kathryn paused at a knock on the door.

'Come in!'

Eadwig shuffled anxiously into the chamber. 'Mistress Swinbrooke, I am sorry, but the guest master . . .'

Colum, looking as fierce as possible, got to his feet, hand falling to his war-belt, but the lay brother stood his ground.

'Don't you bully me, Colum Murtagh. I know you. I served as an archer in the Duke of York's retinue. I was then known as Edmund Appletree.'

'So you were.' Colum's face broke into a smile. He stretched out his hand. 'Nimble as a cricket you were. What are you doing hiding here?'

'After St. Albans—Do you remember, you were only a stripling?' Eadwig said—'a group of Lancastrians caught me. They had one end of a rope round my neck, the other over the branch of a tree. I took a great oath to my patron saint, Anthony of Padua, that if I was spared, I would dedicate myself to God.'

'And they let you go?'

'Oh no,' Eadwig chortled. 'They hanged me!'

Colum looked at the lay brother from head to toe.

'You're a sprightly enough ghost!'

'The branch snapped.' Eadwig beamed at Kathryn. 'The Lancastrians thought it was a sign from God. They gave me my warbelt and a penny and told me to go and fulfil my vow.' He tapped his foot on the floor. 'Old Colum Murtagh trying to look fierce! You were nearly hanged once, weren't you?'

'As a boy, in my wild days.'

'Tell me'—Kathryn was bemused by this chattering lay brother—'you fought with the Duke of York, Eadwig?'

'He was a grand man, Mistress. Colum will tell you: arrogant, vain as a peacock, but a good fighter. He was always kind to "the Earthworms," as he called us.'

'So you must have known Atworth?'

'Oh yes, but I never told him.'

Kathryn got up and closed the door.

'Let the guest master wait,' she whispered, 'or his feverish imagination run riot. Why didn't you tell people you knew Atworth?'

'Mistress, we take vows when we come here. We give up the world and therefore the past. It wasn't my duty to come up to Brother Roger and say, "I knew you. Do you remember so and so?" '

'And what was he like? Come on, tell me.'

'A killer, born and bred, Mistress. Certainly in his soldiering days.'

'Did he like killing?'

'Not when he came back to England; he was beginning to change. He was a henchman; Master Murtagh knows what I mean. If the Duke said, "Do this," Atworth would have done it. I only knew him for a short while; then we went our separate ways. I joined the monastery first. I nearly fell out of my stall when I saw him for the first time. He had changed. He was a great sinner trying to be a great saint: That's why Duchess Cecily chose him as her confessor.'

'What did he do?' Kathryn asked.

'Kept to himself. The Prior and Brother Simon looked after him, oh and that Jonquil.'

'You don't think much of him?' Colum asked.

'No, I don't. Brother Atworth called him his Guardian Angel. I think he was put here.'

'Put here?' Kathryn grasped Eadwig's hand. 'You are a veritable source of stories, Brother Eadwig.'

Eadwig tapped the side of his nose. 'I watch and listen.' He squeezed Kathryn's fingers. 'To put it bluntly, Mistress, I would have told you this anyway. I don't like Anselm, and I think Jonquil is a spy.'

'For whom?' Kathryn asked.

'Why, Mistress, the Duchess.'

'To spy on her own confessor?'

'Well, to keep an eye on him, though for what reason, I don't know.'

'How long has he been here?'

'Oh for some months. After the Yorkist ascendancy, he turned up at the friary gate with letters of accreditation from some merchant in London. At first I thought he was a pleasant lad, rather simple, until I noticed he used to leave the friary and slip back in the early hours.'

'Is that common?' Colum asked.

'No, the brothers here are fairly faithful to their vows; their sins are gluttony and overtippling rather than the pleasures of the flesh. You see, Mistress, I like the Ancient One. Brother Timothy's a great storyteller. He's wonderful to listen to as long as you don't believe half of what he tells you. I put the old one to sleep. I then hide in his room, well away from the others, who are constantly saying, "Eadwig, go and get this," "Eadwig, go and get that." It's wonderful what you can see from his window.'

'So Jonquil crosses Gethsemane?'

'As fast as a squirrel to a tree into the bushes he goes. I wager he's touched that wall so much the very stones would cry out and recognise him.'

'And where do you think he goes?'

'He doffs his robe. If he's dressed in a jerkin, hose, and boots and keeps well away from certain places, he's as free as a bird.'

'So Jonquil is used for errands in the city?'

'Of course, Mistress! I think to myself, why doesn't Jonquil just leave? He hasn't taken any vows yet. He acts like a fish out of water. He followed Brother Roger everywhere; the only reason that he is in the Friary of the Sack was Brother Roger. I wager a jug of wine to a jug of ale, Brother Jonquil is gone by Michaelmas.'

'And you tell no one,' Colum asked, 'what you see or suspect?'

'I am not stupid, Irishman. I know my place in the scheme of things.'

'Will you help me?' Kathryn asked.

'If I can, Mistress, but . . .'

'Brother Eadwig!' The voice boomed like a bell from outside.

'Ah, my master has summoned me. Irishman, I think you should go.' The lay brother opened the door. 'I'll wait for you outside. You'd best make it quick.'

As soon as he was gone, Kathryn and Colum embraced. He held her fiercely, kissing her on the cheeks and brow.

'Be careful,' Colum whispered. 'I trust Eadwig. If anything happens, send him to me!' He backed away. 'How long will you stay?'

'Until I have the measure of this place.' Kathryn stood on tiptoe and kissed him on the chin. 'Now you'd best go before being excommunicated by bell, book, and candle.'

Colum winked, caressed her face with his hand, and slipped through the door. Kathryn felt sad listening to Colum's laugh as he went down the stairs with Eadwig, his profuse apologies to the guest master, the retreating footsteps, the door being opened and closed. Kathryn shivered and looked down at her feet. She was tempted to follow him, collect her possessions, and leave this place. She walked to the window. Lights glowed here and there, but the friary lay silent. Kathryn felt uneasy and went back to the door, pushed the bolts across, and turned the key in the lock. For a while she lay on her bed but was restless. She got up and lit more candles and placed them on the writing-desk. Her mind teemed with the events of the day: Malachi sitting insolently in her kitchen; the whispered confessions of Mathilda Chandler; the wax-like corpse of Brother Atworth; those hideous, smouldering remains.

'I'll make sense of it yet,' Kathryn murmured.

She took a piece of parchment. 'Quid novi?' She scribbled the Latin tag: 'What is new?' She wrote down the title. 'On the matter of rats.' Kathryn dipped her quill into the small jar of black ink. Father had taught her how to write, not in a cipher but with abbreviations as a clerk would do. She marshalled her thoughts. The infestation was sudden, obvious in some parts of the city but not others. Here in the friary, the corpses of two rats had been described as singed. 'Had there been a fire here?' she continued writing, 'or in another part of the city?' Kathryn couldn't recall any conflagration being reported. Why had the rats disappeared from here? Who'd mentioned stoats? Ah yes, Mathilda Chandler! Kathryn recalled Bourchier's and Luberon's insistence that she liaise with Malachi Smallbones, but what could she advise?

'Poison,' she wrote. 'But what potion? How is it to be administered safely?' Kathryn sighed and drew a line. She started her second column: 'On the death of Padraig Mafiach.' Kathryn breathed in deeply. Colum hid it well, but he was worried. He had been appointed to meet Mafiach, but the agent had been murdered. How? Kathryn paused, quill poised. What could she write about that grisly killing? How could a man like Mafiach be slain and his assassin so easily escape? She wrote down the question: "What does the cipher mean?" And there was something else. What had she seen or heard in that chamber? Was it something the taverner had said? Kathryn threw the quill down in exasperation. She went and knelt on the prie-dieu.

'Oh, Lord,' she whispered, 'what a tangled mess!'

And that was before she ever came to Brother Roger! Kathryn was convinced that Atworth's death was due to self-poisoning, but the other phenomena? And Gervase? Why had he been murdered in such a barbarous fashion? And what was Jonquil doing here spying on Atworth? Was it for the Duchess? Or someone else?

Kathryn rose. She walked up and down the chamber. Only then did she notice the piece of parchment stuck under the door; it was jagged and rather dirty. Her heart skipped a beat. She went across and picked the paper up. The message was scrawled in an untidy hand. 'Meet me now at the Blessed Roger's grave.'

Kathryn noticed how both the words 'meet' and 'blessed' had been mis-spelt; written as 'mete' and 'blesed'; the scrawl could have been in anyone's hand. Underneath was a further message, a quotation from the Book of the Dead: 'And the grave will give up its secrets.' Kathryn hurriedly put on her boots and grabbed her cloak. She was about to draw back the bolts when she saw that the ring handle of the door had been moved. It had been swung to one side. Kathryn drew back the first bolt and bent down to draw the bottom one when she heard a faint shuffling. She stood back in a spasm of cold fear.

'Stupid hussy!' she whispered.

She looked at the message. Whoever had put that under her door was just beyond it. Kathryn recalled the shadowy stairwell outside. The guest-house was fairly deserted. Anyone could have written that message or had it written for them.

Kathryn went across to her panniers; fingers trembling, she undid the buckles. She was aware of a cold sweat on the nape of her neck. She drew the dagger out, casting away its velvet sheath—a present from Colum—and stood staring at the door. She went quickly to the window. The small, latticed door was clasped securely. She pulled across the shutter, lowered the bar, turned, and stared at the door.

I am safe, she reflected, *as long as I don't open that door and step out into the darkness.* She wanted to scream. On the one hand she was frightened of what was waiting for her, but on the other, she realised a piece of wood might separate her from the solution to some of the mysteries which cloaked this place. Who could it be? Jonquil? A hired assassin? Kathryn breathed in deeply. The dagger felt slippery in her sweaty hand. She moved across to the door and pressed her ear against the wood. She stood holding her breath, ears strained for any sound, trying to curb both her panic and her imagination. She heard it again, a slight movement, a creak which, at any other time, she would neither have heard nor bothered about. Kathryn stepped back. This cat-and-mouse game could go on for hours unless one of the brothers came to see that all was well. Even then, whom could she trust? Kathryn remained rooted to the spot, staring at the door, and jumped at the loud knock.

'Who is it?' she called out.

No answer.

'Who is it?' she repeated.

'Mistress, open the door, please! I bear mesaages!'

The voice was disguised. The thickness of the door, that hollow stairwell; the voice had a twang to it. If only . . . ? Kathryn gripped the dagger and cursed her own impetuosity. She could have asked for Colum to stay in a separate chamber, demanded some sort of protection. She was here alone. Many friars would never dream of entering a guest-house in which a woman was present or come knocking at her door in the late hours. Again came the knock, the whispered voice. Kathryn found it hard to control her panic.

'I will not open!' she shouted. 'Identify yourself! What do you want?'

Who else was in the guest-house, she wondered? Some visiting merchant? Kathryn heard the door creak. She glanced at the leather hinges. Was her would-be assassin trying to force the door a little further in? Would he fix on its weakest point, the stiff leather hinges? Kathryn's mouth went dry. The window was too small to climb through, yet it was her only security. She raced across, pulled back the shutters, and pushed open the latticed door. The ground below was shrouded in darkness. Kathryn looked around. What could she use? Her eye caught the pieces of parchment on the table. She took one up and held it above the candle flame, watching the fire turn it black as the flame began to lick. Grasping it, Kathryn hurried to the window and shouted for help, waving the parchment for as long as she could. The flame grew stronger, fanned by the breeze, and the heat scorched her fingers, so she had to let it go. She was now shouting at the top of her voice. She grabbed another piece of parchment and lit this, all the time aware of the crashing against the door. Kathryn's throat hurt from shouting so loudly. She heard a cry from below, and then there was silence on the stairwell outside. She stood fighting for breath and grasped the dagger where she had dropped it on the floor. She heard footsteps, a loud knocking.

'Mistress, Mistress Swinbrooke!'

She recognised Eadwig's voice.

'Identify yourself!'

'Mistress, you know me.'

'What are you doing?' Kathryn demanded. 'Why were you near the guest-house so late at night?'

'Mistress, Master Murtagh asked me to come.'

Kathryn pushed at the door, wiping the sweat from her brow on her gown. She was so tense that what she had eaten earlier felt like a ball of lead in her stomach. She stood by the door.

'Eadwig'—she fought to keep her voice level—'is that you?'

'Mistress, I saw the parchment, the fire.'

'The guest-house,' Kathryn asked, 'is it deserted?'

'Yes, Mistress, the merchant left two hours ago. I found the entrance door slightly off the latch.'

'Is there anyone else there?' Kathryn insisted as other footsteps echoed on the stairs. She heard Prior Anselm's high-pitched voice and the infirmarian demanding what Eadwig was doing there. Kathryn sighed with relief, pulled back the bolts, and turned the key. Eadwig almost fell into the room, followed by the Prior and Brother Simon. Kathryn went and sat on the edge of the bed, her legs still trembling.

'In God's name,' Simon came and crouched beside her, 'Mistress, you look as if you've seen a ghost!' He prised her fingers gently from her face.

'Someone was out there.'

'Mistress, there was no one.'

'Then what's that?' Kathryn demanded, pointing to the piece of parchment on the floor.

The friar picked it up. 'This could have been written by anyone.'

'No, Father Prior, it was not written by just anyone,' Kathryn retorted. 'It was put under my door not so long ago. And, like a fool, I nearly drew the bolts, unlocked the door, and went out. No one was waiting for me at Roger Atworth's grave; there was only a killer wanting to put me in mine, sword, dagger, axe, or garrotte string!' Kathryn felt the anger welling within her.

The Prior and the infirmarian didn't look so comforting now but more like very worried men.

'Mistress, this is a friary.'

'No, sirs, it's a place of mystery and sudden death. I am in your care. And how did you know I . . . ?'

'I alerted them,' Brother Eadwig replied. 'I heard your shouts and saw the fiery pieces of parchment being dropped as I approached. I hurried to the Prior's chamber, then ran across here. Mistress, there was no one.'

'Oh yes, there was,' Kathryn declared, 'and I want to make sure that he doesn't return.' She fought back tears, got to her feet, and turned her back on them. 'As I said, Father Prior, this is a place of murder and mystery. But I will find the truth, and you shall help me!'

Chapter 8

'Somme hadden salves, and somme hadden charmes;
Fermacies of herbes, and eke save . . .'
—Chaucer, 'The Knight's Tale,'
The Canterbury Tales

P er ipsum et cum ipso . . . Through Him and with Him, in the unity of the Holy Ghost, all honour and glory are yours All Mighty Father, world without end . . .'

'Amen,' Kathryn intoned.

She was sitting before the Lady Altar and watching the priest, his back to her, raise the chalice and host to the tortured figure of Christ on the cross. Kathryn ignored the incongruity of the open tomb of Brother Roger, which lay to her right: the raised slab stones, the mound of loose earth, the yawning gap in the transept floor. She still smelt the faint perfume, and distracted from the Mass, wondered once again about its source.

'May the body and blood of Christ,' the priest intoned, 'be not to my damnation.'

Aye, Kathryn thought. From the other side chapels, she could hear similar whispered words of the mass. Was one of these Friars of the Sack committing sacrilege and blasphemy? Did they include the assassin who had so barbarously killed Brother Gervase and been waiting for her on that darkened stairwell the night before? She stared up at the gargoyle in one of the pillars separating the altar from the main sanctuary—a macabre, devilish face. Kathryn couldn't make her mind up whether it was demon or human, with its popping eyes and twisted mouth.

Brother Eadwig picked up the hand-bell and rang it, the sign of the priest's communion. Kathryn glanced at the altar and flinched, shielding her eyes at the blaze of sunlight which came pouring through the rose-tinted oriel window above the Lady Altar. It was so piercing, so brilliant, that Kathryn had to look away. At first she thought it was some phenomenon, but of course the altar faced east: Outside the sun was rising full and strong in the clear April skies. Black motes danced before her eyes. Kathryn shook her head and tried to compose herself. She had to move on the bench and peered up at the altar out of the corner of her eye. The old friar celebrating his dawn mass had turned and come to the edge of the steps; he was waiting, a small host between his fingers. Kathryn smiled apologetically, went up, and knelt before him. She tilted back her head, and the silver paten Eadwig held gently grazed her chin to catch any of the sacred species which might fall.

'Ecce Corpus Christi! Behold the Body of Christ!'

'Amen,' Kathryn replied.

She took the wafer of bread and let it dissolve in her mouth. The priest returned to the altar as Kathryn went back to her bench and sat, head bowed. She ignored all distractions, closed her eyes, and prayed earnestly for Colum, Thomasina, Agnes, and Wulf. She said the 'Miserere' for the souls of her dead parents and asked for guidance and safety in solving this bloody tangle of murder. Kathryn glanced quickly at the statue of the Virgin and prayed that Monksbane would return with good news. The mass ended. The priest left the side altar. Eadwig came and sat beside her. She crossed herself, a sign that her thanksgiving was over.

'Well?' Eadwig shifted along the bench. 'Mistress Swinbrooke, I am now your guardian angel. Where you go, I follow. I'll sleep outside your chamber. I'll watch your every step.'

Kathryn smiled at his unshaven, grizzled face, the friendly brown eyes.

'I am sorry I lost my temper last night, but I didn't imagine it.'

'I don't think you did,' Eadwig agreed. 'I've never seen anyone in such a state. Anselm should have been more careful. If anything had happened to you, Colum Murtagh would have sacked this place.' Eadwig chuckled at his own pun. 'Now come, you've fed the spirit, so feed the body.'

'No, wait a minute.'

Kathryn got up and inspected the raised slabs. She picked up the soil and ran it through her fingers. She couldn't trace the origin of the perfume, but it was still there, a subtle lingering fragrance which teased both her palate and her memory.

'Do you think this perfume has a spiritual origin?' she demanded.

'Are you saying God can't afford perfume for his saints?' Eadwig teased her.

Kathryn shook her head and followed Eadwig out through the corpse door into the over-grown cemetery. The tombstones were almost hidden by the sprouting grass and wild flowers; this was a peaceful, sun-dappled place echoing with the liquid song of the blackbirds in the gnarled yew trees, their branches spread out like the arms of some monster.

'My last resting place,' Eadwig murmured. 'Now that spring's come, we'll have to have it cut. We allow the grass to grow very long; it provides good fodder after the winter. Mistress, you'll break your fast?'

Eadwig was extremely curious about this young woman with such an old head upon her shoulders. How many years, Eadwig reflected, was it since he had last kissed a woman? Twenty? Twenty-five? Mistress Swinbrooke was definitely attractive, with large, dark eyes and the creamy smooth colour of her face. She had a serene, calm appearance, which, as he'd learnt the previous evening, masked a fiery temper. Now she stood as sedately as any prioress in her dark-blue dress tied chastely and fringed, at cuff and collar, with white bands. A dark-blue wimple hid most of her hair. Eadwig could see why Colum was so attracted to her: She was a subtle mixture of the comely and the alluring. Eadwig clutched his belly as his stomach rumbled.

'Mistress, you'll break your fast?'

'Has Father Prior assembled those who experienced the miracles at Atworth's tomb?' Kathryn asked over her shoulder. She had been thinking about what wild herbs must grow here, quietly promising herself that, one day, she would return: in these wild, over-grown areas rare plants and herbs could often be found.

'They will all be assembled by noon,' Eadwig replied.

Kathryn turned to face him. 'And you are going to follow me everywhere?'

Eadwig grasped the staff he had left in the porch before mass.

' "One thousand may fall on your left hand," ' he quoted from the Psalms, ' "ten thousand on your right, but the Terror which stalks at mid-day shall not approach you." '

Kathryn's serenity disappeared, her burst of laughter transforming her face. Eadwig's heart warmed to her.

'You'll be safe, Mistress.'

'But will you be?' Kathryn teased. She patted her writing satchel, its leather strap over one shoulder. 'Are you used to corpses, Eadwig?'

'At St. Albans, Mistress, they sprawled knee-high, eyes gouged, limbs missing, the blood ankle deep.'

'Very well,' Kathryn breathed. 'In which case we should visit the charnel-house for one final look at the corpses of Atworth and Gervase. I would like you with me.'

The smile disappeared from Eadwig's face.

'I think it best,' Kathryn declared, 'that we examine such grisly remains before we eat.'

Eadwig swallowed hard and agreed. He led her round the church and across to the infirmary. The charnel-house stood in a small courtyard behind this: a low, one-storied chamber, its ceilings were supported by black pillars, the walls thickly coated with lime against flies and other insects. The floors had been similarly treated. The lay brother who let them in was only too happy to stand outside and, as he put it, "catch God's air." Three corpses lay under the canvas sheets. Eadwig explained how the first was a poor beggar who had been found dead in an alleyway outside. The second was Atworth's. Eadwig removed the sheet, and Kathryn began a careful examination. She noticed how exposure to the air had increased putrefaction and decay. The corpse was beginning to lose that waxen feel, the stomach was starting to bloat, and surprisingly, the left eye was slightly open.

'A bad sign,' Eadwig muttered behind his hand. 'It means that someone else is to die.'

Kathryn, however, was immersed in her scrutiny. She studied every inch of the corpse, front and back, but could find, in the circumstances, nothing untoward. Old scars from Atworth's fighting days marked the arms, shoulders, and back; the right arm must have been broken, but had been expertly fixed by some leech or physician. She turned her attention to the so-called stigmata on

141

the wrists and ankles: large puncture wounds on the inside with some break in the skin on the back of both wrists and ankles; they were faintly scored as if something had been tied round them. Kathryn recalled how these wounds had been bound very tightly before Atworth had been buried. She could still detect a faint perfume but nothing else. Satisfied, she moved on to Gervase's corpse; because it was now nothing but blackened ash, it was difficult to realise that, only the previous day, this had been a vibrant human being, an important friar, a leader in this community. Now his features, hair, and limbs had all been horribly scorched, shrunken by that fearsome blaze.

'If we didn't have Brother Timothy's testimony,' she whispered, 'this corpse could be anyone's. But why? What was he like, Eadwig?'

'Gervase was a good brother. It's against our rule to curl our lip, lift our hand against another, or speak ill of any member of our community,' the lay brother chattered on. 'In his own way Gervase was kindly enough, but he had his weaknesses.'

'Such as?' Kathryn asked.

'Oh, not wine and women. He was the treasurer of the friary. He always liked to see gold and silver pour into our coffers. Mistress.' Eadwig pulled a face. 'Must we talk here?'

Kathryn agreed. They went out and washed their hands at a nearby well. Kathryn shook her hands dry.

'Well,' she asked, 'did Gervase respect Brother Atworth?'

'Mistress, you know he didn't. Yet on one occasion, about eight months ago, just as autumn began, Gervase offered to write Atworth's life story. Brother Roger refused. Gervase was deeply offended.'

Kathryn stared up at the spire of the church: the blue sky around it was cloud free, and the day promised to be warm. Only a few friars walked about; others were in the refectory or the Chapter House.

'The brothers were saying,' Eadwig chattered on, 'that Gervase was consumed by a heavenly fire.'

'Nonsense!' Kathryn retorted, wiping her hands on the side of her gown. 'Gervase was murdered.'

Eadwig gaped. 'Murdered? Well, why not just have his throat cut? Or a knife between his shoulder-blades?'

'I've been thinking of that,' Kathryn replied. 'Come, I'll show you.'

She picked up her writing satchel, stared once more at the door of the charnel-house, and led Eadwig back to Gethsemane. In the morning sunlight this was a paradise: The broad expanse of green lawn was fringed by the great trees; the air was sweet with the smell of grass and all things fresh. Of course, they had to wave a hand at Brother Timothy, who'd opened the casement window and was staring down at them. He reminded Kathryn of an old bird peering from its nest.

'I've seen nothing untoward!' the Ancient One shouted. 'I've been watching where Brother Gervase died; I have glimpsed nothing.'

Eadwig thanked him, and with his benediction ringing in their ears, they crossed the grass. Kathryn paused at the great, dark stain where Gervase's corpse had lain, then walked towards the hawthorn bush. The ground was still grey with feathery ash.

Kathryn crouched down. She tried to remember what she had seen the night before. 'Someone has been here.' She picked up a rotting branch and sifted amongst the ash.

'Well, of course they have,' Eadwig retorted. 'Brothers came out here this morning: The whole community is talking about Gervase's murder.'

'I suspect the assassin may have returned to check his handiwork.'

Kathryn went deeper into the bushes. From behind the wall rose the sound of a hand-cart being wheeled along the alleyway.

'What are you implying, Mistress?'

Kathryn grabbed Eadwig by his bony shoulder and stared into his eyes. 'Eadwig, I am going to tell you! I lay on my bed last night puzzled. Why should Gervase suddenly be engulfed in flame? And, no, I do not think the fires burst from heaven or hell. The Ancient One, Brother Timothy, informed me how Gervase used to come across here, ostensibly to visit Mistress Chandler.'

'Ah yes, the Accursed!'

'Let's call her the widow woman,' Kathryn replied. 'I have also spoken to her. Gervase treated her as he would a pet dog. However, he didn't come over here yesterday,' she continued, 'out of concern for her, but because he was meeting someone. Who, I don't know. Why?' She shook her head.

Eadwig's eyes rounded.

'Now, this is only a surmise,' Kathryn continued. 'But I believe Gervase chose this spot because, possibly in all the friary, it's the safest place to meet, yes?'

Eadwig nodded.

'After all,' Kathryn added, 'this is where young Jonquil leaves the friary for his own nefarious purposes.'

'Could he be the assassin?'

'Anyone could be. I suspect Gervase's death is linked to my arrival here. Early yesterday afternoon Gervase met his assassin in this secret place and was murdered.'

'Impossible!' Eadwig scoffed. 'I may not be a scholar or learned man'—a bony finger tapped his temple—'but I've got keen wits. Gervase died in the early evening.'

'No, he didn't.' Kathryn led him deeper into the bushes. 'This is what happened: Gervase came here in the early afternoon and met his killer. Only God knows what happened then, but his murder was sudden and silent.'

'How do you know that? Chandler?'

Kathryn pointed further along the wall.

'The widow woman wouldn't have heard any disturbance. Gervase was surprised: a swift knife thrust to the back or his throat cut.'

'And?'

'The killer knew then that he couldn't just leave the corpse; it would be too suspicious. He also needed time. Dressed as Brother Gervase—or, if he was a member of this community—in a simple friar's habit, he took the sub-prior's keys and went to his chamber.'

'Why?' Eadwig stared at this young woman. Her theory behind the sub-prior's death was not as mysterious as those discussed in the refectory, but it made more sense.

'I don't really know'—Kathryn paused—'except that the killer wished to go through Gervase's possessions. In the afternoon the friary is fairly quiet. Everyone is going about their duties, yes?'

Eadwig agreed.

'Hooded and cowled, the killer slips into the sub-prior's chambers. He has the keys he needs and all the time.'

'Someone may have disturbed him.'

'Oh, they could knock and tap on the door, but the killer would have remained silent. He gets what he wants, puts everything neatly back, tidies the room, and returns here.'

'But he could have been noticed.'

'Oh, come.' Kathryn smiled. 'If a friar walks across the lawn, would you give him a second thought?'

Eadwig joined his hands together. 'I stand rebuked, Mistress.'

'I believe,' Kathryn pointed back to the hawthorn bush, 'the killer returned here with a wineskin full of oil. You've served as a soldier, Eadwig, or seen accidents in cookshops. I certainly have. A scullion, his apron soaked in oil, too close to a naked flame?'

'Oh, it's happened to me,' Eadwig agreed.

'Gervase's corpse is doused in oil from head to toe, totally soaked. Who knows, grains of saltpetre or some inflammable mixture may have been added.'

'Why not just burn it out in the copse?'

'The Ancient One definitely said Gervase was standing by the hawthorn bush. Look around you,' Kathryn offered. 'Find me a stout pole, a branch.'

Eadwig shrugged but did as Kathryn said. He went off into the undergrowth and came back.

'Now, I may be wrong, but Eadwig, you can pretend to be a corpse.' Kathryn turned the lay brother round and pushed him towards the hawthorn bush. 'All Brother Timothy saw was Gervase standing here.'

Kathryn grasped the long branch, dug one end into the ground, and propped the other against Eadwig's back between his shoulder-blades.

'His hands were up his sleeves!' Eadwig protested over his shoulder.

'Wrists can be loosely tied.' Kathryn answered. 'His cowl was pulled up. Now we have a corpse standing, propped up, staring across at the friary. The killer is hidden by the bush as well as by Gervase's corpse.'

'And how was the fire lit?'

'A slow fuse,' Kathryn declared, dropping the stout pole.

Eadwig turned round.

'A piece of string or rope soaked in oil and fastened to the back of Gervase's robe. Again, Brother Timothy wouldn't see this in the sunlight. The flame runs along it, and Gervase becomes a human torch. Now,' she spread her hands, 'I've expressed it clumsily. Perhaps there was no pole? Perhaps Gervase was held up by the branches of the hawthorn? Come.' She walked to the other side of the bush untouched by the fire, its branches stout and firm.

'For a while they'd support a man propped up.'

'You are right, Mistress. I have heard similar stories about soldiers attacking a castle. The defenders soak them with oil and drop firebrands on them.'

'Colum Murtagh would say the same,' Kathryn replied, staring at the sky. 'The fire is ravenous. It can't be put out. By the time anyone arrives, poor Gervase's remains are nothing but charred cinders, unrecognisable.'

'And the killer?'

'He has prepared everything well. The oilskin is thrown over the wall, the ground is cleared of blood stains, and any trace of what truly happened has disappeared.'

'But why?' Eadwig insisted.

'As I have said, to give the killer time to search the sub-prior's possessions, as well as create an illusion—which your community fastened on—that Gervase's death was linked to doubts about the Blessed Roger Atworth. Illusion often hides the truth.'

'And the killer?'

'God knows.' Kathryn went and picked up her writing satchel. 'The killer probably studied every inch of this ground. He has covered up his tracks. He may have been elsewhere by the time the fire fully caught hold. Look around you, Brother. The trees stretch on every side, the curtain wall, the deserted alleyway beyond. A coven of outlaws could hide here for hours without being traced.'

'Gervase could have met this person in his chamber?' Eadwig, immediately regretting his question, grinned apologetically. 'In an enclosed community!' he exclaimed.

'Precisely,' Kathryn agreed. 'In a place like the friary, the walls have eyes as well as ears. Anyway, let me prove my theory is correct.'

Kathryn positioned Eadwig next to the scorched hawthorn bush and walked back across the lawn. She turned.

'Bring your cowl up!' she called. 'Put your hands up your sleeves!' Eadwig obeyed. Kathryn walked to the bench she'd sat on the previous evening.

'Of course!' she murmured.

Eadwig, motionless, looked like any other friar, whilst what might lie behind him was hidden. A whole horde of killers could have lurked there. The bushes and vegetation were densely packed to conceal any movement. Kathryn imagined the figure pushing the corpse forward, almost walking behind it. Indeed, because of the high grass which fringed the lawn, not to mention the scrub and brambles, Eadwig's feet couldn't be seen. Kathryn remembered what Brother Timothy had told her: "I glanced up, and he was just standing there."

'Mistress!' Eadwig called plaintively.

Kathryn walked across. 'Thank you. Now let's visit Mistress Chandler. I wish I had brought some food. Brother, you'll be a kindly soul to her, won't you?'

'Oh, of course! Last night, after we met you, Prior Anselm said someone must take over looking after her.' He beamed a smile. 'Perhaps I'll volunteer?'

They left the lawn and went deeper into the trees. In the full light of day Kathryn appreciated what a suitable secret meeting place this was. Chandler heard them, and Kathryn was relieved when she called out a salutation.

'I must see Colum about her.' Kathryn paused.

'Why?' Eadwig asked.

'I keep thinking of my midnight visitor. If I am going to ask Mistress Chandler about anything suspicious, the same thought must have crossed the assassin's mind.'

'She's fairly safe in there,' Eadwig replied.

'Except for the aperture,' Kathryn declared. 'Tell me, what if something happened, if our killer poured oil through that slit?'

Eadwig pulled a face. 'A steel plate guards the door. She wouldn't be able to get out.'

'What are you chattering about?' Chandler's voice was strong. 'Mistress, have you brought food?'

Kathryn walked up to the small Judas squint and peered through.

'Stand back!' she ordered. 'I want to see your face.'

Mathilda obeyed. Kathryn could make out a lined, rather dark face, a mass of iron-grey hair, bright eyes.

'Are you well, Mistress Swinbrooke?'

'Of course,' Kathryn replied, 'but I am concerned about you. You've seen and heard things, haven't you, Mistress? Gervase was murdered. I don't want to alarm you, but the killer may have his eye on you.'

'I'll go when God calls me.' Chandler returned to the Judas squint and peered through.

'It's more about how that call will come,' Kathryn replied. 'Mistress Chandler, I am going to trust you. I am going to take it upon myself to order Eadwig here . . .'

'Oh, I know him. He's always scurrying about after Brother Timothy, isn't he?'

'The same,' Eadwig cheerfully called back, but when he glanced at Kathryn, his eyes were troubled.

'I know.' Kathryn spoke his thoughts. 'The law ruled she is to be confined, but the law also adds that she is to be kept safe. Mistress Chandler, I am going to have the iron steel plate removed so that, if you are in danger, or even if you wish to walk, feel the sun, take God's air, you can do so.'

Mathilda stepped back, shaking her head.

'No, no, they'll punish me for that. I'd be taken down to the stocks and whipped.'

'No one will punish you,' Kathryn assured. 'What's more, I'll bring you food and wine. Brother Eadwig will help.'

They moved round the stone cell. Kathryn crouched down and, with Eadwig's help, pulled the rusty steel plate from between the wooden slats which kept it up against the wooden door.

'Mistress,' he whispered, 'she's not the only one who will be in trouble.'

'Murtagh will take care of everything. Now look, Brother, I want you to go across to the kitchens. We'll break our fast in the open air. I also want you to get a knife, sharp and pointed; I am going to give it to Mistress Chandler to protect herself.'

Eadwig looked as if he was about to refuse. Kathryn grasped him by the hand. 'Brother, I don't want her blood on my hands. It's only a matter of time.'

'Then she should be removed to the castle prison.'

'Perhaps! But for now, please do what I ask.'

Eadwig crossed himself and hurried off. Kathryn stared at the wooden door. The steel plate was no more than a foot square, fastened between two wooden slats to prevent the door from being opened from the inside. Kathryn noticed how the door had been freshly painted and re-hung.

'Mathilda,' she opened the door. 'If you wish to leave, you can do so.'

Kathryn stepped back. At first there was silence, then she heard a faint sobbing. She was tempted to lead the poor woman out. Instead, Kathryn went, sat on a fallen tree, and waited. At last the door was pushed open. Mathilda Chandler crept out. She shielded her eyes against the light and, for a while, leaned against the wall of her prison. Kathryn reckoned that she was well past her forty-fifth summer: She was comely enough, small, her shoulders rather hunched, her face ravaged by the pain of her long imprisonment.

'Over here, Mathilda!'

The woman got up and walked across. She paused and stared up at a branch. She came and sat by Kathryn, head down, hands resting in her lap.

'You've shown me a great mercy, Mistress, and for that I am truly grateful.'

'How often are you released?' Kathryn asked curiously.

'Two, perhaps three times a year, for no more than an hour, around the great feasts of Easter, Christmas, and Michaelmas. It's good, isn't it, to stand under God's sky?'

Kathryn grasped her hand; the skin was calloused; Mathilda's nails were bitten to the quick.

'I will do what I can for you,' Kathryn promised. 'But Mistress Chandler, time is short. I will take you into my confidence.'

Kathryn quickly described what had happened to Gervase and how the assassin had struck; she even mentioned Jonquil.

'I can only speak of what I see and hear,' Chandler replied. 'Now and again I hear footsteps, or what I think are footsteps, a twig snapping, sounds as if someone is climbing the wall. On one occasion a muttered curse. But don't forget, Mistress Kathryn, everyone knows I am here. My little window on the world is narrow and blocked, and many times I sleep or doze.'

'Did Gervase ever speak to you?' Kathryn asked.

'On a few occasions.'

'And Jonquil?'

'Oh, I saw him with Brother Atworth. On one occasion I glimpsed him by himself, but I could not go on oath.'

'And Gervase?' Kathryn insisted. She was confident that this woman knew more than she was saying.

'He used to come over.' Mathilda's fingers laced together. 'On one occasion I heard voices raised in argument. Also the clink of coins.'

'Coins?' Kathryn asked.

'It was a very clear day, just after noon; the friary was silent, and certain sounds carry. Gervase was amongst the trees: I heard the clink of coins, but don't forget, Mistress, in a court of law they would say I am fey.'

'What else do you know?'

Mathilda sat, head down. Eadwig returned, bearing a platter, three bowls of steaming oatmeal, bread wrapped in a linen cloth, a small jar of butter, and a pot of honey, three horn spoons, and a wicked-looking meat knife. He was about to join them, but Kathryn indicated with her eyes that he should take his food elsewhere. Eadwig picked up a bowl, took a horn spoon, and walked out of earshot. Kathryn persuaded Chandler to eat.

'I couldn't get any ale!' Eadwig called out. 'The kitchen was too busy, and a new cask had to be broached.'

'I have a small cask myself,' Mathilda muttered. 'Mistress, this is good.'

She took the honey, poured some of it over the oatmeal, and began to eat hungrily. Kathryn followed suit. The oatmeal was hot and delicious, very similar to what Thomasina would make. She waited until Chandler had finished the bowl and put it back. The woman snatched one of the small, white loaves, using the meat knife to smear it with butter and the remains of the honey.

'Oh, God!' Mathilda whispered, 'this is heaven!' She turned, eyes filled with tears. 'The simple things of life, eh, Mistress?'

'Tell me what you know,' Kathryn urged.

Mathilda took another mouthful. 'I told you there are comings and goings.'

'The truth,' Kathryn insisted.

'Atworth was a very frightened man,' Chandler began. 'He

claimed how his past sins haunted him. I told him to put his trust in God. He replied with a story about how in France he'd raped a young woman and hanged an old crone who had objected. She'd prophesied Atworth would die a violent death.'

'But he didn't,' Kathryn broke in. 'He died in his bed, in something akin to the odour of sanctity.'

'Did he?' Chandler looked mischievously out of the corner of her eye. 'Atworth told me other things, not in great detail; he held secrets about the Great Ones. I suspect he was talking about the Duchess, and he linked these secrets to his fears.'

Kathryn glanced to where Eadwig was sitting, his back to a tree, happily eating. The morning seemed to have lost its brightness. Kathryn felt afraid, not only for herself but for this woman.

'Continue,' Kathryn urged.

'Atworth said that others would love to know his secrets.'

'Who? Did he mention the French?'

'Oh, he told me about his imprisonment in France. Someone called de San . . . San . . . ?'

'De Sanglier?' Kathryn offered.

'That's it. How the man had treated him most cruelly. How burning irons had been placed against his flesh.'

'Was the holy Atworth frightened of death?'

Chandler laughed abruptly, a short bark.

'I asked him that myself. Sometimes, Mistress, when I am walled up in there,' she gestured with her hand, 'death loses some of its horror: it becomes more like an old friend eager to visit. Atworth was the same: He said if it wasn't such a great sin, he would take his own life.'

'So what was he frightened of?'

'That they would come for him, those who wanted to know his secrets.'

Kathryn closed her eyes and smiled. She had found it! There must be a link between Atworth and the murder of Mafiach.

'He didn't say who they were. When I questioned him,' Chandler chose her words carefully, 'he just said those who had power. He claimed to have murdered a man.'

'But didn't he murder many?'

'Ah yes, Mistress, but this was one murder which seemed to haunt his soul.'

'Did he fear vengeance for that?'

'No, he said he was suffering for what he had done.'

'Are you all right?' Eadwig called.

'Oh, yes.'

Kathryn put her arm round Chandler's shoulder. Up close the woman didn't smell pleasant, and the gown she wore was threadbare and stained. Kathryn felt a pang of compassion at seeing her bony, stooped shoulders.

'Isn't it strange?' Chandler looked up, and her hand crept across and rested softly against Kathryn's thigh like a child's would against her mother's. 'Here was Atworth, the holy one, the confessor of the Duchess and God knows who else, confiding in Mathilda Chandler. Do you know, Mistress Swinbrooke, when he talked to me that day, he was truly frightened. Only heaven knows what secrets he carried! I asked him to share these. He shook his head and loudly proclaimed that when he talked to me he was hearing my confession; he always pretended to give me absolution, sketching a sign of the cross in the air. On a number of occasions he even brought me the viaticum. He swore me to secrecy. I am breaking that vow now because I think he would have liked you.'

Kathryn strove to curb her excitement.

'You want to know the secrets?' Mathilda's eyes held a shrewd and calculating glance. 'As God is my witness, Atworth never told me. He said that if he did, and others learnt, I would be marked down for death; that could easily be arranged. The sentence passed against me is that if I leave the Friary of the Sack, I can be killed on sight.'

Kathryn brushed the crumbs from her gown.

'Did Atworth ever return to this matter?'

'No, but I noticed that this year, certainly in the last few months before he died, Atworth's serenity was shattered; he was ill-at-ease and nervous. He complained how the pains in his stomach were growing more intense.'

'And his death?' Kathryn prodded.

'As I have told you, I was informed.'

'He died on the Feast of the Annunciation?' Kathryn asked.

'According to common report. Now something very strange happened the night before.' Chandler had apparently decided to tell Kathryn everything. 'Those two days before the Blessed

Roger's death were very strange! You talk about people coming and going through this small wood. During those two days I heard more movement than at any other time. I heard a creak as if a door was being opened, groans as if someone was in pain. I remember the evening of the Annunciation well because, it being a feast day, Gervase brought across some sweetmeats, a delicacy for me.' Chandler screwed her eyes up and stared across at the open door to her cell. 'You'll leave the steel plate off?' she asked.

'It will stay off,' Kathryn replied.

'And the knife?' Mathilda picked this up from the tray. 'Eadwig won't miss this when he returns to the kitchens?'

Kathryn only smiled.

'On that night,' Chandler continued, 'I definitely heard Anselm and Jonquil and one other; they were over there screened by the bushes.'

'Any words?' Kathryn asked.

'No, Mistress, but Anselm had a high-pitched voice, especially when he was querulous. He'd visited me on a few occasions. On that particular evening he was agitated. They then left. I ate and I drank. I said my ave beads. When darkness fell, and I am sure of this, Mistress, more than one person returned here. They carried no lanterns or torches so they stumbled about.'

'For what?' Kathryn asked.

'I don't know. It lasted for a while.'

'Did they go over the wall?'

'No, I am sure they came from the friary and returned there.'

Mathilda opened the small, battered purse she carried on the simple cord round her waist. She took out her ave beads and held them in one hand as well as what looked like a piece of membrane, thin and clear, which she began to stretch backwards and forwards.

'It's animal skin.' She smiled at Kathryn. 'It's worn thin over the years. I play with it often when I am agitated.' She rolled the piece of membrane up in her fingers and lifted the ave beads. 'Atworth gave me these.'

Kathryn examined the battered rosary: its chain was now slightly rusting, whilst the black, hardened beads were chipped and cut.

'He said it was a present. Mistress, that's all I can tell you.'

Chandler got to her feet and stretched. Kathryn noticed that the knife had disappeared, hidden in the folds of the woman's dress.

'I'd best go back in.' She walked across then turned. 'You are frightened, aren't you, Mistress?'

Kathryn nodded.

'For me as well as for yourself?'

'God save us, yes.'

Chandler, however, almost as if she hadn't heard, entered her cell, slamming the door shut behind her. Eadwig came wandering over.

'The hour is passing, Mistress. The Prior has summoned the miracle seekers.'

'Oh yes.' Kathryn got to her feet and gestured at the tray. 'Don't tell anyone what you saw and heard this morning. Brother, will you return these to the kitchens?'

Eadwig picked up the tray. He threw the crumbs onto the ground; they crossed the lawn just as the friary bell began to toll for the mid-morning divine office.

Eadwig began asking questions about Chandler. Kathryn replied absent-mindedly. What could she do? She felt a slight resentment at Bourchier and Luberon; surely they could have told her more? Kathryn was also convinced that Mafiach's and Atworth's deaths were linked. The more she investigated, especially in this so-called cloistered, hallowed place, the more certain she became that Atworth's death was not due to natural causes: it was shrouded in lies and half-truths, trickery and illusion. Kathryn recalled the old proverb about sleeping dogs and the hideous dangers which might confront her if these savage dogs, whoever they might be, were roused.

Chapter 9

'And somme seyen that we loven best
For to be free, and do right as us lest ...'
—Chaucer, 'The Wife of Bath's Tale,'
The Canterbury Tales

Kathryn sat at a desk in the beautifully polished library of the Friary of the Sack. It was a long, church-like room under its raftered ceiling, its coloured windows high in the wall illuminated by the streaming sunlight. Kathryn vaguely remembered coming here as a child, holding her father's hand as he consulted with the librarian of the day on one of the great works of medicine by the masters. Kathryn gazed around: The same fragrant smell of calf-skin, leather, and ink pervaded the room, what her father had called 'the perfume of books.' The library was certainly well endowed with rows of shelves with manuscripts, tomes, ledgers, and folios divided into sections: Theology, Philosophy, History, Chronicles, works of devotion. Usually the library was busy, but the events of the previous day had shattered the harmony of the brothers' routine. The librarian now sat at his high desk at the end of the gallery, peering at a manuscript, talking to himself under his breath. He raised his head. Kathryn couldn't make out his face because of the sunlight streaming behind him.

'Are you well, Mistress Swinbrooke? You have all you need? Brother Eadwig said he would be back soon.'

Kathryn lifted a hand to indicate that all was well, then stared down at the small calf-skin tome studded with imitation jewels. She opened the crackling pages, making full use of the light lancing through the window above her. On the first folio were Atworth's name and the date, written some two years previously. Kathryn leafed through it quickly. It was nothing more than a collection of prayers: the 'Anima Christi,' 'De Profundis,' 'The Lord's Prayer,' and the 'Ave Maria.' Kathryn noticed how Brother Atworth seemed very fond of Psalm 51:

> Have mercy on me, oh God, have mercy on me.
> And, in your great compassion, blot out my offence.
> Truly my sins I know. They are always before you. . . .

Kathryn marked how this verse was constantly repeated throughout the psalter, whilst the phrase 'Truly my sins I know' was underscored time and time again. Kathryn's attention, however, was drawn to the crude miniature paintings which often prefaced the prayers. In the opening words of Psalm 51; 'Have mercy on me,' the *H* was enlarged to include a painting in the top and bottom loops of the letter, both done in red, green, and black. Kathryn had seen better in many a Book of Hours, though these paintings had a vibrancy, a vigour all their own. She picked up the magnifying glass the librarian had provided and studied them more closely. The first was of a woman lying in a bed, a man beside her. In the second painting the woman was lying by herself. Kathryn looked for any insignia, livery, or heraldic device, the common trick of illuminators to signify whom they were describing, yet she could find none. She cradled the glass, tapping her fingers on the polished desk. Was this a scene from the Old Testament? Or perhaps a fable? Kathryn racked her brains. She turned the page over, and her eye caught the beginning of the 'De Profundis': 'Out of the depths have I cried to ye, O Lord.' Kathryn again studied the painting. This time there was no woman but a man, a king—or was it a duke?—sitting at a table surrounded by his knights. Kathryn immediately thought of the legend of Arthur. She noticed how the king's standard bore the red, blue, and gold livery of England, whilst his livery was emblazoned with the Suns of York. Kathryn, now intrigued, turned the pages over.

'It's not from the Bible,' she whispered.

Kathryn recognised the legends of Arthur. One painting had the Green Knight appearing at Arthur's court. At last the significance dawned on her. Atworth, in his own shrewd way, had been paying homage to his patron, the Duke of York, symbolising him as Arthur. The series of paintings, however, abruptly ended: There were no more references to York or Arthur, but two knights, one killing the other, stabbing him in the back. Kathryn couldn't recall anything like this from the Arthurian legend and wondered if Atworth had decided to include the story of Cain and Abel. Or was this the killing, the sin over which Atworth constantly grieved? Kathryn heard a door close and looked down the room. The librarian had gone.

'Hello!' Kathryn called. She got to her feet. 'Hello!'

She walked down the library, looking in the different carrels, but all were deserted. She turned and went back, slightly alarmed. The library was empty; she was alone! Kathryn returned to her seat. The shelves of the library jutted out at right angles to the walls, but from where she sat, she had a good view of the librarian's desk and the door beyond. She could see anyone come or go. Yet she was reluctant to continue her studies; a feeling of danger—a cold prickling of sweat on the nape of her neck—alarmed her. To all appearances this place was deserted; Kathryn tried to remember the different sounds she'd absent-mindedly heard. The librarian left, but hadn't she heard the door open and close again? Had someone else slipped in? Kathryn clutched Atworth's small psalter, and as she did so, her middle finger was pricked by something sharp. Forgetting her fears, she opened the book and realised, only on close inspection, how certain pages had been expertly removed with a razor-sharp paper-knife, cut so close to the binding that their absence would not normally be missed.

So this book did contain some truth. Someone had already tampered with it! Kathryn got to her feet, slipped the psalter into her writing satchel, and made her way slowly down the library. This was not the darkened stairwell outside her chamber: The air was sweet, the sunshine pouring through the windows, the dust motes dancing, the gleaming woodwork catching the light. Nevertheless, Kathryn felt as if every stair she passed was like the mouth of some darkened alleyway. She heard a sound, paused, and stared at the door: The middle bolt was pulled across! The librarian couldn't have done this. Someone must have entered, pulled the bolt across, and be lurking here. There was no other door, the librarian had told her that, whilst the windows were too small and high for anyone to clamber through. Kathryn measured the distance and abruptly broke into a run. Feet thudding on the wooden floor, she fled down round the librarian's table and flung herself at the door.

'Mistress Swinbrooke?'

Kathryn pulled back the bolt.

'Please, Mistress Swinbrooke!'

Kathryn turned: Jonquil came out of the shadows of the bookshelves.

'Stay where you are!' Kathryn raised her hand.

The door to the library was open. She could hear voices outside, whilst the table was between her and this soft-footed friar who had stolen in like some cat bent on mischief. Jonquil, however, looked frightened, hands stretched out, tongue fighting for words.

'I am sorry. I am sorry.' He leaned against the table.

'What are you doing here?' Kathryn felt confident enough to walk back. She rested against the librarian's chair. 'You came in here. I called out. Why didn't you reply? Why did you bolt the door? Where is Eadwig?'

'Mistress,' Jonquil stretched out a hand, his face and manner all servile, 'I came in here with a message for the librarian. Ask him. Eadwig said you were not to be left alone, so when he left for the refectory, he asked me to stay and make sure you were safe. I drew the bolt across. You were so engrossed in what you were doing you never heard or saw me. The rule is that we have to whisper here, walk and talk softly. You became disturbed and agitated, and I didn't know what to do. If I suddenly appeared—' He shrugged. 'I heard what happened last night.'

Kathryn didn't know whether this lay brother was lying or just cunning. What he said made sense. She had been engrossed in Atworth's psalter. She had been aware of some sounds. Kathryn pulled back the librarian's chair and sat down.

'Well, Brother, perhaps I was mistaken. Next time I would advise you to declare yourself immediately, not lurk like some cat in the shadows waiting for the mouse to appear.'

'I am sorry,' he stammered.

'And are you sorry, Brother, when you climb the friary wall across Gethsemane and slip into the city?'

158

'Father Prior often sends me on errands.'

'And you have an aversion to gates and doors?'

Jonquil sighed; his farmer's-boy face was now pale, eyes constantly blinking, small beads of sweat lacing his forehead.

'Shall I tell you who you really are, Jonquil?' Kathryn continued. 'I don't think you are a friar any more than I am. You are a varlet, aren't you?'

Jonquil kept his head down.

'You are a retainer from the royal household, Duchess Cecily of York's man. You joined the Friary of the Sack as a lay brother, without taking vows, to guard and protect, even spy on, the Blessed Atworth. Prior Anselm, Brother Gervase, Simon the infirmarian, and possibly Atworth himself realised this. Look at your wrists. Go on, pull back the sleeves of your gown.'

Jonquil haplessly obeyed.

'Strong arms,' Kathryn declared. She picked up a quill and used the end to brush the red marks around Jonquil's wrists. 'Colum Murtagh loves Chaucer's *Canterbury Tales.* Have you ever read Chaucer's description of the yeoman? The archer with the wristguards? Is that what you were, Jonquil, an archer, a master bowman? You did your job well, didn't you? But now and again, the pleasures of the city called. Some tavern maid or merry-eyed girl who caught your fancy, a jug of ale, and a meat pie? You must be pleased Atworth's dead, and when this business is all over, you'll be trotting back to Duchess Cecily.'

Jonquil's head came up. 'I am a true lay brother,' he protested, his eyes harder, his face more resolute.

'Of course you are,' Kathryn smiled. 'You are not going to confess anything without the Duchess's permission. Nevertheless, I'll be talking to the Duchess sometime soon.'

Jonquil's eyes shifted.

'Did you really see a vision?' Kathryn asked.

'The Blessed Roger is truly a saint.'

Kathryn leaned back and scratched her chin. Jonquil protested that he was a lay brother, but he certainly hadn't denied her allegation. Had he been the one outside the stairwell last night? Had he killed Gervase?

'Tell me about Atworth.'

'He was a saint. I was his lay brother, his servant. Sometimes

he could be frail. He lived a good life and died a good death.'
Jonquil's nervousness had passed. 'More than that, Mistress, I
can't say.'

'And Gervase?'

'I disliked him. He disliked me. The reason was Blessed Roger.'

'And did Blessed Roger tell you about his life, his fears, his
anxieties?'

Kathryn chose her words carefully. She did not want to betray
the confidences Mathilda Chandler had entrusted to her. Jonquil,
his composure now regained, shrugged, putting the cord round his
waist.

'Mistress, I am a lay brother. Prior Anselm often sends me into
the city, and yes, sometimes I become bored with friary life. I have
not taken vows of poverty, chastity, or obedience. What I do and
where I go are my . . .'

He paused at a knock on the door. Eadwig burst through.

'Mistress, I am sorry I am late. You have visitors.'

He stepped aside hurriedly as Murtagh and Venables swept
through the door. On any other occasion Kathryn would have
jumped up. Colum was usually such a welcoming sight, yet his
appearance now surprised her: his face was shaved, his hair cut
and washed. He was dressed in a dark-green, velvet cote-hardie,
with a white shirt beneath, a gold-and-silver belt clasped round
the waist, and hose of the same colour pushed into his best Spanish
riding boots. He carried his war-belt in one hand, not the usual
one but a gift from the King, shining and smooth, the scabbards
cleverly brocaded with red stitching.

'Master Murtagh,' she teased, 'you look as if you are ready for
your wedding day.'

Colum came over, leaned down, and kissed her on the cheek.
He smelt of some fragrant oil he had rubbed into his skin, his
dark-blue eyes bright with mischief.

'It's good to see you, Mistress. It's time you returned. We have
business, haven't we, Master Venables?'

The Duchess's henchman came over, grasped Kathryn's hand,
and kissed it. He, too, was exquisitely dressed in all the finery of
a courtier: a jacket with puffed sleeves and ivory collar, tight
multi-coloured hose, and polished boots. His livery was adorned

with the favours or colours of the Duchess, and rings glinted on his fingers.

'Is it your wedding day, too?' Kathryn asked. 'What is this?'

Colum raised his head and gestured for the two lay brothers to leave.

'Why, Mistress, we are to meet the King.'

Kathryn got to her feet.

'Or rather his mother. Later this afternoon they are entertaining'—Colum's eyes held Kathryn's—'the Vicomte de Sanglier, the French King's personal envoy, in the grounds of the Archbishop's palace. We are all invited.'

Kathryn looked them up and down: She felt rather shabby and dishevelled in contrast to these two peacocks.

'We are not invited to the banquet,' Venables declared, as if revealing her thoughts. 'And, Mistress, you look as elegant as any lady at Court. Her Grace wishes to meet you: I am sure her beloved sons will be in attendance.'

'But I am not finished here.'

'It's not till late this afternoon.'

Colum grasped Kathryn's hand. 'Master Venables, if I could have a word in private with Mistress Swinbrooke?'

Venables gave a lopsided grin. 'I'll be outside guarding the door.'

He left, and Kathryn and Colum embraced.

'Thank God these books don't have tongues,' Kathryn whispered, extricating herself. 'I doubt if they see a kiss like that every day.'

'I hope not,' Colum teased. He pulled across a stool and indicated that she sit. 'We've just arrived, yet I can tell from Prior Anselm that something is wrong. What is it?'

Kathryn gave him a blunt description of everything that had happened since he'd left. Colum's good humour disappeared in the twinkling of an eye. He got up and paced up and down, pulling the dagger on his war-belt in and out of its sheath, a sign of his agitation.

'Anselm should have known better,' he snapped. 'Do you have that scrap of parchment?'

Kathryn opened her writing satchel and handed it across. Colum read it, then threw it back.

'I may not be your husband, Kathryn, but one thing I know is that you have spent your last night in the Friary of the Sack.'

'And Mistress Chandler?' Kathryn asked. 'You will do something for her?'

'If I can catch the King's ear, yes. But what do you make of it all?'

'Of the rats'—she tried to make him laugh—'I have vague suspicions.'

'Devil take the rats!' Colum barked. He glowered down at her. 'What about Brother Atworth? And Padraig Mafiach. God knows, tomorrow we'll hurry his body to a lonely grave.'

'How Mafiach was killed, Colum, I don't know. There is a loose thread, but I am in the dark searching for it. As for the verse from Zephaniah?' She shook her head. 'I have yet to study that again. It's no coincidence,' she added, 'that the Vicomte de Sanglier is here. Has he come to crow?'

'To crow and to collect,' Colum replied. He was still angry, gnawing at his lips and glaring at the door. 'And Brother Atworth?' he asked.

'He may have been a saintly man'—Kathryn scratched her hand where she had grazed it in pulling back the bolt—'but he was also a dangerous one. Duchess Cecily trusted him, perhaps even loved him. They both share some hideous secret.'

'Do you think Atworth could have been her lover?'

Kathryn raised her eyebrows. 'The great Duchess Cecily, "the Rose of Raby," deigning to bestow her favours on a mercenary? No, no, it's not that.'

'Then what?'

'Perhaps we should ask Duchess Cecily?'

Colum's hand snaked out and pressed a finger against Kathryn's lips. 'Never,' he warned.

Kathryn removed his hand. 'We may have to. However,' she continued briskly, 'Duchess Cecily confessed to Atworth. I suspect they were soul companions. But something happened: The secrets they shared may have leaked out. Dame Cecily became deeply concerned. She visited Atworth more often. She also became frightened for Atworth's safety. Whatever, that lay brother who calls himself Jonquil was sent here to guard and protect the Blessed Roger. I suspect Anselm, Gervase, and the infirmarian were also warned by the Duchess—you know how fiery and haughty she can be—to give Jonquil as much rope as he needed.' Kathryn leaned closer to Colum, lowering her voice. 'Others, now deeply interested, left the shadows to participate in this macabre dance. I have no proof,' Kathryn measured her words, 'but I suspect Gervase was bribed with gold, possibly preferment in the future. He was told to discover as much as he could about Atworth.'

'By whom?' Colum interjected.

'I don't know. Perhaps someone outside. Or does Prior Anselm also have allegiance to people we don't know? Anyway,' Kathryn sighed, 'Atworth died. Brother Gervase was no longer needed. In fact, he became a nuisance. He was lured out across Gethsemane, brutally murdered, his chamber carefully searched, and the killer then went back and burned Gervase's corpse. The same killer became alarmed at my presence here. He may have wished to frighten me. . . .'

'No, no,' Colum interrupted, 'he came to kill. But who was it?'

Kathryn spread her hands.

'Colum, you are a soldier, as is Venables. You could climb that wall, lurk in the undergrowth, and, disguised as a friar, go across the grounds.'

'Well, I know that can't be true.' Colum pointed to the door. 'What time did this assailant visit you?'

'Oh, between the hours of eleven and twelve. I remember the chimes of midnight came after Anselm had left me.'

'I was at Islip,' Colum replied, 'and so was Venables, with other members of the King's Council.'

'It must be someone here,' Kathryn said. She told him about Jonquil hiding in the library.

'I could take him out to Kingsmead,' Colum offered, 'and put him to the question.'

'Wrong in principle, my wild Irishman. Moreover, I suspect Jonquil enjoys a very powerful protector.' She patted her writing satchel, which contained Atworth's psalter. 'I'll show you Atworth's work later. Something was gnawing away at his soul. He released it in two ways: drawing pictures, thus wrapping his secret sin up in myth and legend, and by talking to Mathilda Chandler.'

There was a knock at the door, and Venables strode in.

'Mistress, Father Prior is all a-fluster: the so-called miracles

163

await us. Listen!' Venables picked up a small stool just inside the doorway, came across, and sat down. 'The Duchess is alarmed at the way matters are proceeding.'

'How are matters proceeding, Master Venables?'

The henchman smiled, eyes crinkling up. 'It's plain as a pike-staff,' he murmured. 'You entertain deep doubts, as I do, Mistress, about the Blessed Atworth's death. He may have been a repentant sinner, but God knows what else.'

'He was frightened,' Kathryn replied. 'He often talked to some-one else. He was frightened of giving up his secrets.'

'What secrets?' Venables queried, tapping his foot. 'I know Duchess Cecily is still deeply concerned by the death in the Tower of Henry of Lancaster. Rumour has it that all her sons were in-volved. Henry, or King Henry as the Lancastrians liked to style him, was a fool, but certainly a holy one.'

'And would the French be interested in that?' Colum asked.

'Perhaps; their Spider King would love nothing more than to portray Edward of England and his two brothers as the slayers of a saint, very similar to Henry II's murder of Becket. But'— Venables got to his feet—'God's work awaits us.' He gestured to the door.

'When do we have to be at the Archbishop's palace?' Kathryn asked.

'At about four this afternoon, when the banquet is over,' Colum replied.

'And you will speak for Mathilda Chandler?'

Colum was already helping her to her feet.

'Don't worry,' he reassured her, 'I'll speak to the King myself.'

They left the library to find that Anselm, flanked by Jonquil and Brother Simon, were waiting. The Prior looked highly uncomfort-able. He attempted a fumbling apology for what had happened the previous evening. Kathryn went to reassure him, but Colum brusquely intervened.

'Time waits for no one,' the Irishman snapped. 'The day draws on; people are waiting.'

'We have to be there,' Simon the infirmarian spoke up. 'We want to be present when Mistress Swinbrooke investigates these miracles.'

'And so you will be,' Kathryn replied. 'The more the merrier—though Cardinal Spineri is noticeable by his absence.'

'Cardinal Spineri has already made his mind up,' Venables retorted.

The henchman kept his face impassive, but Kathryn could see the humour in his eyes.

'His Eminence has affirmed that he will advance Blessed Roger's cause in Rome.'

Kathryn felt like adding how the good Cardinal could do the same for the Duchess's pet monkey, but she bit her tongue.

Anselm led them across to his parlour. The so-called miracles of Roger Atworth were waiting in the corridor outside, not the happiest group, nervous and ill-at-ease. Kathryn sat at the head of the Prior's table, Murtagh and Venables to her right, the three friars on her left. Each so-called miracle was called up and closely interrogated. A pox-faced young man, who claimed to have regained potency, spoke in halting, broken sentences. Kathryn kept her face grave, and Colum avoided her eye, whilst Venables hid his smile behind his hands. A mother followed, carrying her child, whom she claimed had been bitten on the wrist by a rat. Again Kathryn questioned her closely. The child, who had been sleeping, now awoke and added his own contribution to the discussion with loud squeals and yells. Kathryn was only too pleased to wish the mother well. A lay brother guided her out across the refectory, where refreshments had been prepared. A young woman with scrofula was followed by an old soldier who had suffered an ailment of the bowels. Again Kathryn asked them about their condition and their treatment, and then dismissed them. Once the door closed on the last of them, Simon the infirmarian raised a hand in protest.

'Mistress Swinbrooke, you were hasty and peremptory.'

'A miracle,' Kathryn retorted, 'and correct me if I am wrong, Father Prior, is the direct intervention by God to change the laws of the physical world and, in doing so, create wonder and surprise amongst the faithful. For the love of God, Father Prior, look at these so-called miracles! The young man who suffered a loss of potency: That is quite common amongst young bridegrooms who sometimes fear their virility may not be up to their expectations or those of their wives. Any man will confess that his potency can be affected by ale, disease, or fear.'

'You seem to know a great deal.'

Colum kept his face grave.

'Do I?' Kathryn teased. 'Five men sit in this room with me. All five of you who are on oath would agree with what I have said. This young man was nervous. He was seeking relief. He was too frightened to go to a physician, too embarrassed to discuss it with anyone. He hears about the Blessed Roger, comes here, and finds that relief.'

'And the young woman with scrofula?' Prior Anselm demanded.

'What the physicians call "King's malady," ' Kathryn replied, 'cured by the King's touch. Oh, I don't doubt,' she continued, 'that the young woman was cured at the Friary of the Sack. She was a guest here, yes? Did you feed her?'

Brother Simon nodded.

'And she brought her best gown? By her own admission she also bathed before visiting the so-called shrine. Her malady was light; I could have cured the same. Scrofula is often caused by a lack of good food, especially fresh vegetables. It is worsened by woollen clothes which seem to harbour fleas and dirt. Give the patient fresh fruit, a warm bath, a change of clothing.' She could tell from Brother Simon's embarrassed glance that the infirmarian knew all this. 'It's common knowledge,' Kathryn declared. 'I knew it before I questioned the woman. I have seen my father work so-called miracles amongst sailors from the Medway.'

'And the child bitten by a rat?' Colum asked.

'The skin is healed; the child is only a babe. True, such bites can kill an infant. At the time,' Kathryn replied, 'by her own admission, the mother was suckling the infant. According to the masters, a mother's milk will strengthen the child's humours, but I listened to the mother carefully. The woman has a wise head on her shoulders and doesn't realise it.' Kathryn ticked the points off on her fingers. 'First, she washed the bite with wine. Now that would make the child scream and inflame the bite, but actually do more good than harm. She then used an ancient cure, a mixture of dried milk and honey. This concoction can be found in many a book of remedies to cleanse what the physicians call a dirt-infested cut. I don't'—she dropped her hands—'I don't know how it works.' She shook her head. 'But it arouses the pus and cleans it out.'

'So,' Venables stirred in his chair, fascinated by what Kathryn was saying, 'she brought the child to Brother Atworth's tomb. The wound looked malignant, but it was actually healing?'

'Yes,' Kathryn confirmed. 'It's the same as when you drain a boil or carbuncle: the pus and the blood can look offensive, but as my father said, "Better out than in." To put it bluntly, the child's wound would have healed, Brother Atworth or not.'

She glanced at the three friars. Anselm and Simon looked embarrassed. Kathryn quietly vowed that, when the opportunity presented itself, she would have words with these two cunning priests. Jonquil had assumed his air of bemused innocence, but Kathryn wasn't fooled. She was more intrigued by why Jonquil was here in the first place. True, he had been Atworth's guardian angel and his servant, but he held no position of authority in the friary.

'And the old soldier?' Colum asked.

'That is difficult,' Kathryn said. 'And it intrigues me. He suffered from the flux. He came to the friary, stayed a day, and then left.'

'But by his own admission,' Simon interrupted, 'the distressing condition has not returned. And he claims to have been suffering from it for at least six years.'

'As I said,' Kathryn retorted, 'I don't know. I may have to ask the advice of others. Such an ailment can be caused by certain foods which may agree with me but upset another's humours. It could have been putrid water, or. . . .' she paused.

'Or what?' the infirmarian demanded. 'Mistress Swinbrooke, I agree with your diagnosis of the other three. A natural explanation may be logical, but they could still be miracles. This last one, however, is puzzling.'

Kathryn played with the buckle on her writing satchel.

'Master Venables, have you fought as a soldier?'

'Yes, both on land and sea.'

Kathryn studied the heavy-lidded eyes of this henchman, his smooth-shaven face, the hair neatly coifed, fingers beating a gentle tattoo on the table.

'You look in remarkable health, Master Venables. I don't wish to embarrass you but . . .'

Venables's secretive face creased into a smile.

'Mistress, I am in good health, body and soul. Thanks be to Heaven I have been brought through the most bloody conflicts without a scathe or a wound.'

'But you have been frightened?' Kathryn asked. 'You were at Tewkesbury where King Edward met the Lancastrians?'

'Yes, I was at that great slaughter.'

'And the morning before the battle did you eat or drink?'

Venables shook his head. 'My stomach felt like a cloth, tightly wrung. If I had eaten, I would have been sick. It happens to any soldier.'

'Of course it does,' Kathryn agreed. 'Now on this matter I am as knowledgeable as the pigeons outside. I do not know how the mind affects the humours of the body. To put it candidly, as you say, Master Venables, fear makes the heart beat faster, the stomach churn, the skin sweat.'

'Ah, I see,' Colum spoke up. 'You are saying this old soldier . . . ?'

Kathryn shrugged. 'He may have found peace here in the friary. He did say that he confessed and had been shriven by one of the friars. Perhaps the cause of his ailment was not so much a matter of the bowel or the stomach as of the mind?'

'In which case,' Prior Anselm declared triumphantly, hand raised, 'it is still a miracle. You may chatter on, Mistress, about your remedies, but God's will shall be done.'

Kathryn felt a spurt of anger at this prior whose lack of care had nearly cost her her life.

'God's will,' she retorted hotly, 'is more about compassion, Father Prior! I am to leave the Friary of the Sack, and I thank you for your hospitality. However, I would be most grateful if Brother Eadwig would keep a solicitous eye on Mistress Chandler.'

'The Accursed!' Anselm almost spat the words out. 'I have heard of your friendship with her.'

'She is a poor widow woman,' Kathryn declared, 'who has more than atoned for her crime. If I had my way, Father Prior, this friary would house her for only a few days more.'

'Very well. Very well,' the Prior muttered. 'But, Mistress, on these miracles?'

'Brother Simon is my witness. I will draw up an account.'

'You'll look for natural causes?'

'If I believe God's will has been made manifest, then the Blessed Roger truly looks on God and is in heaven interceding for us, sinners and all.'

'And there's the matter of the vision?' Brother Simon spoke up.

Kathryn refused to be drawn into another argument. 'I think we'll discuss the vision later.'

Kathryn could still feel her anger bubbling within her: She didn't truly care whether Brother Atworth was a saint or not. It was more the attitude of the Prior, his lack of compassion for Mathilda Chandler, and his determination to use the spiritual for his own advancement and that of his friary that bothered her.

'One thing I can't understand.' Kathryn unbuckled her writing satchel and took out a sheet of vellum on which she had made a summation of her thoughts. 'You claim, Father Prior, that Atworth died in his sleep? You broke the door down. He was lying on his bed serenely as any saint, almost expecting a visit from God or one of his angels.'

'Don't be sarcastic!' the infirmarian suddenly shouted.

'No, Brother, I am being truthful. According to you, the door was locked and bolted from the inside; that was common?'

'Oh, yes.'

'And the only people who approached Brother Roger were you three?'

There were nods of agreement.

'So what happened to the letters Brother Roger received from Duchess Cecily?'

'We told you, Brother Roger must have burnt them.'

'Ah, yes, so you did. And you have relics of Brother Roger?'

'What do you mean?'

'Come, come, Father Prior. If you have your way, Atworth's shrine will be visited by hundreds, perhaps thousands of pilgrims. They will bring offerings, stay at your guest-house. Money will flow like a river into your coffers. Your friary church will be patronised by the great and the good.' She ignored Venables's sharp intake of breath. 'Isn't it common to have relics the faithful can touch?'

'Brother Roger had two robes and a shift,' Anselm retorted. 'He was buried in one of them.'

'And the other?'

'It's somewhere in the friary.'

'Could you get it for me?'

The Prior gaped at her.

'Why? It's probably been taken to the wash-house.'

'The wash-house?' Kathryn exclaimed. 'So it will be used again? Given to another friar or some poor man who comes knocking at your gate?'

'Yes, that's the rule of the friary.'

'But this was the robe of the Blessed Roger!' Kathryn put the piece of vellum back on the table. 'I thought it would be folded up, specially kept, even hung up in your church so the faithful could touch it. Or you could have cut it up and sold the pieces as relics.'

Prior Anselm swallowed so fast and hard that he clearly found it difficult to speak.

'We have his rosary beads,' Simon the infirmarian interrupted. 'And his psalter.'

Kathryn patted her writing satchel.

'Not any longer. I have it here.'

'That's theft!' Jonquil shouted.

'I am simply borrowing it, Brother. But before I return it, you do realise certain pages have been cut out?'

All three friars stared at her.

'But let's continue with these relics. I am so pleased to have all three of you here at the same time.'

Kathryn ignored Colum's warning look. Venables was also growing visibly uneasy.

'Mistress Swinbrooke, where is this leading? Who's asking this?'

'Brother Roger died in his bed.' Kathryn joined her hands together. 'Now, when I visited his chamber, all I saw was a wafer-thin mattress on a small truckle bed. I do not deny that Brother Roger lived a life of austerity, but he did have a bolster, sheets, and a blanket. These were cloths touched by his holy body. What happened to them?' She lifted her hand. 'Don't tell me! The bed was stripped, and they were sent to the wash-house, yes?'

The Prior nodded.

'Didn't the thought occur to you,' Kathryn continued, 'to keep such precious cloths as relics? Here you are, Father Prior, advanc-

170

ing the Blessed Roger's cause; yet according to all the evidence, you appear to have destroyed or removed as many of Brother Roger's paltry possessions as possible.'

'What are you implying?'

'Nothing! I am just mystified.'

'You forget one thing.' Jonquil laced his fingers together and smiled at her out of the corner of his eyes. 'This is a house of friars; many good and holy men have lived and died here. When we discovered Brother Roger's corpse, we were distressed and sad, but death is a common occurrence. He was an old man. He suffered many ailments. We did not know he was going to be a saint. We did not have the gift of prophecy. True, there were certain phenomena, such as the perfume and the stigmata on Brother Roger's corpse, but we did not foresee the miracles, the visions. . . .'

His two companions chorused their agreement. Kathryn pulled a face and put the sheet of parchment away.

'In which case I am grateful for your advice.' She tightened the buckles on the satchel. 'Master Murtagh, if I could have a word with you in private?'

The meeting broke up. The friars, darting angry glances at Kathryn, swept out of the parlour. Venables announced that he was totally intrigued.

'I understand Brother Roger's body is to be re-buried?' he asked. 'The Duchess would like me to pay her respects.'

'Isn't she going to visit the corpse herself?'

'Tomorrow, Mistress, but I am still under orders.' Venables bowed and left.

'Well, well, well.' Colum pushed back his chair and stretched. 'I would say this is not a safe place for you, Mistress Swinbrooke. When it comes to priests, you have a sharp tongue.'

'No, Colum,' Kathryn leaned over and squeezed his hand, 'just when it comes to liars. We have to separate the wheat from the chaff. Atworth may have been a very holy man; I think he was. Miracles may have occurred, and I don't deny that. But the more I investigate his death, the more I reject the accepted story.'

'What? Are you going to say he was poisoned?'

'No, Colum,' Kathryn whispered, 'but I do believe he was murdered. A little more time, and I'll have my proof.'

'What makes you say that?' Colum insisted.

'Atworth himself. I never asked these good friars—well, not in a thorough way—why Atworth should burn his papers and lock his door.'

'Because he knew he was going to die? He may have welcomed death?'

Kathryn shook her head. 'No man welcomes death. Not even a saint. Our three friars are liars, and they are hiding the truth!'

Chapter 10

'Lordes in paramentz on hir courseres,
Knyghtes of retenue, and eek squieres . . . '
—Chaucer, 'The Knight's Tale,'
The Canterbury Tales

The Archbishop's palace had been transformed by the Court's presence. Royal Archers wearing the personal livery of York on their leather jackets, long yew bows slung over their shoulders, clustered around the gates and side entrances. Inside the grounds the Royal Standard depicting the Golden Leopards of England fluttered bravely in the late afternoon breeze. Knight bannerets, in full plate-armour adorned with the gorgeous tabard of the Royal Household, guarded doors, galleries, and entrances. A group of scurriers stood with their horses, ready to carry out the King's least whim. Messengers galloped in from London and elsewhere, bearing letters and reports from sheriffs, judges, and commissioners. The Cathedral precincts had lost their aura of sanctity, the fragrance of beeswax and incense replaced by heavy perfume and the stench of horses and leather. The quiet serenity of the buildings and the chanting of the monks were shattered by the clatter of steel and the raucous shouts of serjeants-at-arms.

Colum, Venables, and Kathryn were stopped virtually every twenty paces: war-belts were taken off them, they were searched for hidden weapons, and then only were they allowed through on the personal recommendation of the captain in charge.

'The King is wary,' Colum whispered. 'The country is still unsettled. The House of Lancaster has many a madcap with assassination on his mind and murder in his soul. Edward's particularly concerned about the Royal Children.'

Kathryn nodded. Colum often discussed the politics of Court and country. Edward of York had annihilated his enemies. The Lancastrian war captains had been executed barbarously in the market place of Tewkesbury and elsewhere, but the last Lancastrian claimant, Henry Tudor, still sheltered in foreign courts, together with his redoubtable war leader, de Vere, Earl of Oxford. Lancastrians who had escaped the bloodbath at Tewkesbury now hid out in wastelands or forests, whilst many of the great lords couldn't be trusted to enjoy the peace.

'They'd turn at the toss of a coin,' Colum had confided. 'But the wolf pack remains calm as long as the leader stays strong.'

'And you, Colum?' Kathryn asked.

The Irishman had grinned and quoted a proverb.

' "When you lie down with wolves, if you wake, you always howl!" '

Kathryn recalled these words as they passed through the hallowed precincts. She rarely thought of war breaking out again, of Colum dressing in the harness of battle and being summoned to the Royal Standard. She had met the Royal Family before. Edward the King was magnificent, towering over everybody, with his cynical blue eyes and full lips, his easy, slouched walk, the knowing glance at any pretty face, the lazy charm which masked a will of steel and a heart of iron. Edward could be magnanimous, generous, and open-handed, but if trapped or threatened, he was the most blood-thirsty of them all. Clarence, Edward's brother, had the sly, beautiful face of a woman; he would have been a truly handsome man if it wasn't for his scowl and sneer. George of Clarence was as attracted to treachery as a cat to cream. Richard of Gloucester, smaller than his two brothers, with russet hair, dark features, and green eyes, was a prince with a reputation for being both a stalwart warrior and the best of friends and the worst of enemies. Kathryn had also met Edward's Queen, Elizabeth Woodville, a truly remarkable woman and one of the comeliest Kathryn had ever seen, with her golden hair and strange, violet eyes. Some whispered that Elizabeth was a witch, skilled in the art of love. A widow, she had drawn Edward of York into her silken web and entangled him with her conniving, subtle games. Kathryn closed her eyes and hoped that this business would not bring some-one like herself, one of the "little ones," to their attention.

They went down a pillared portico, flanked on either side by Royal Archers, arrows strung to bows, through another gateway guarded by the King's own household Knights, their swords drawn, and into the Archbishop's pleasaunce or garden. Kathryn gasped at the sheer beauty of it. It was a broad square of lawn, screened by trees and flowerbeds. Behind these hung gorgeous cloths of gold, pulled tight across poles, to create an impression of an outside dining hall. Each cloth bore the Royal Arms and the White Rose of Yorkshire and was of a different colour: blue, dark scarlet, green, gold, murrey, and burgundy. The cloths rose at least four yards high; on the top of each supporting pole a pennant, bearing the different arms of the Royal House, fluttered lazily in the breeze. Carpets covered parts of the grass. At the far end of the square, the Royal Table had been set up on a makeshift dais covered with gleaming cloths. Another table just beneath the dais ran down the middle of the lawn. Kathryn was aware of the noise and chatter of servants scurrying about. The tables were littered with silver and gold platters, jewelled goblets, forks, spoons, and ladles of precious metals. On the Royal Table a pure gold salt-cellar, carved in the shape of a fairy castle, caught the sun and dazzled her eyes.

Kathryn was so surprised she had to shield her gaze as Colum pointed out the guests on the lower table, high-ranking courtiers and ecclesiastics. As her eyes grew accustomed to the light, she made out, at the high table, the King, with his Queen on his right and his mother on his left. Clarence, already deep in his cups, lolled over the table arguing with his brother Richard. Edward himself sat under a silver, red-tasselled canopy; he slouched in his chair of state, a goblet in one hand whilst the other covered the hand of his wife. Even from where she stood, Kathryn could see that the King's mind was elsewhere; he stared up at the sky, study-ing a swallow as if envious of its freedom. Behind the Royal Table ranged the heralds and knight bannerets. The air was sweet with cooking smells.

Kathryn looked for Bourchier and found him on the end of the table just under the Royal Dais. The Archbishop sat, eyes closed, hands joined as if in prayer. By the wine stains splashed along the ivory white cloth, it was obvious the banquet was coming to its end. Royal musicians behind the cloths of gold attempted to provide some music, but this was drowned by the clatter of plates and the comings and goings of servants, who moved amongst the guests with large jugs of wine.

'They have eaten and drunk well,' Venables whispered. 'God and his saints only know the King's mood.'

A chamberlain came and whispered to the King. Edward gestured for him to go away. Colum grabbed Kathryn's sleeve.

'Look at the man at the end of the Royal Table; he has just returned.'

Kathryn followed Colum's direction. A small, portly man with bright red hair, dressed like a peacock in a dark-purple cote-hardie with a high, jewel-encrusted collar, had re-taken his seat. His wine-flushed face looked as bored as the King's. He kept playing with a ring on his finger. Now and again he would turn to smile at a pretty serving girl holding a jug of water with which the guests could wash their hands. The King seemed interested in the man's return: He leaned forward and shouted something down the table. The man picked up his goblet, bowed, and toasted the King.

'The Vicomte de Sanglier,' Colum whispered, 'the envoy of Louis of France, come to bring the most loving messages, as well as the kiss of peace, for Louis's gentle brother in Christ, Edward of England.' Colum's words were rich with sarcasm.

The King picked up his own goblet, toasted de Sanglier, and sat back; then he murmured something to his wife, who simpered and lowered her head. The chamberlain returned and whispered in the King's ear. This time Edward agreed, languidly raising his hand. The heralds behind him flourished trumpets, and their harsh braying drowned the chatter. This was the signal for another chamberlain, resting stiffly on his staff of office, to come through one of the entrances between the screens. Behind him four cooks carried, on a broad silver platter, a beautiful white swan fashioned entirely out of sugared icing. The guests all clapped as the sweating cooks, holding onto the platter tightly, proceeded around the tables to where the King sat. Behind them walked pages carrying small bowls of sweetmeats. The chamberlain stood aside as the table was cleared and the swan was placed before the King. Again there was the flourish of trumpets, and the excited chatter and gossip died away. Edward lifted his goblet, his voice strong and carrying, though his words were slightly slurred.

'My lords and ladies! We welcome from France, envoy of our beloved cousin Louis, the Vicomte de Sanglier, who has come to reaffirm the great peace which exists between our two kingdoms.' The King sounded sincere, but his smile was a cynical one.

He lifted the goblet again and drank its contents in one gulp. The rest of the Court followed suit. The Vicomte made to rise, but Edward gestured for him to remain seated.

'There is no need for speeches.' The King beamed round. 'We offer peace, friendship, and brotherly love. This swan is a token of our esteem.'

He turned to the chamberlain, who drew his knife and handed it to the King. Edward leaned over and, in one swift cut, opened the swan. Six pure white doves burst out. The doves, hungry and frightened by the light and noise, rose up in a flurry above the guests, who 'Oohed' and 'Aahed' and clapped their hands. The King rapped out an order. The doves were breaking away when, from behind the silken tapestries, falconers released five of the Royal Hawks. These hunting birds, prepared and hungry, rose like black shadows against the sky. The exclamations of the guests died on their lips as they watched the hawks climb, pause for a fraction of a second, and then, wings back, plummet like stones on their chosen victims. One dove managed to escape, but the rest, frantic and terrified, were easy prey. One hawk took its quarry, seizing it in its cruel talons in a splutter of blood, some of which fell on the guests below. Similar killings took place under the blue sky with a slight patter of blood as each hawk, obedient to the whistle of its master, brought its quarry back. The guests clapped. Edward sat on his throne, smiling lazily down at them, amused by the occasional courtiers dabbing quickly at the specks of blood which stained their gorgeous apparel. Here and there the white table-cloths bore similar scarlet drops. De Sanglier was looking at the rings on his fingers as if unaware of what was happening. Kathryn turned away in disgust.

'A cruel act, Colum,' she whispered. 'That wasn't a hunt but a killing for the sake of it.'

'Aye, that's our noble prince,' Colum replied. 'He's probably been waiting to do that all day. It's a warning to de Sanglier. He can sup, and he can dine, he can watch the doves of peace be released, but if necessary, the hawks of war will constantly roam the skies.'

The King got to his feet. He clapped his hands as a sign that the ceremonies were over and, followed by his mother and brothers, left the Royal Enclosure; as he did so, he patted de Sanglier on the shoulder as a sign to follow. The rest of the guests relaxed, some getting up to join friends or calling for more food and wine.

'And now?' Kathryn asked.

Venables, who was standing on her left, gestured at them to follow.

They left the Royal Enclosure and crossed a cobbled yard into the Archbishop's private garden, where a sumptuous Royal Pavilion had been set up. A guard at the entrance stopped them, but after a brief conversation with Venables, they were allowed through. Inside, the pavilion was sumptuous, the ground covered in carpets. Chairs and stools of state had been arranged in a horseshoe fashion with small oaken tables before them. The King and his family had already taken their seats, and white wine had been served. Kathryn noticed that Bourchier and Spineri had joined the Royal Party. The Cardinal looked half-asleep, listening heavy-eyed as Bourchier whispered in his ear. The King sat moodily, his mother on his left, Clarence, Gloucester, and the Vicomte on his right. Up close, the Frenchman, with his russet hair and bright, dark eyes, reminded Kathryn of a little fox she had once owned as a pet. He seemed unruffled by the cruel mummery Edward had played at the banquet but cradled his cup and jabbed a silver toothpick into his mouth, as if a trapped piece of meat was the most important thing in his life.

As Kathryn and the others came in, the King gestured at the three cushioned stools placed just within the entrance. Colum went forward to kiss his hand, but Edward leaned his head back and snapped his fingers. 'I have had enough of ceremony, Irishman.' He smiled lazily. 'I remember you, Mistress Swinbrooke.' His voice rose, not only in greeting, but as a sign for the rest to keep quiet.

Kathryn took her seat. She felt as if she was entering a dangerous game. Edward lolled there, eager to dispense with courtesy and protocol, yet still a prince vigilant about his rights. Beside him Duchess Cecily glowered at Kathryn; her strong, beautiful face, emphasized by the arched, plucked eyebrows, was lightly coated with white powder; her lips, wet with wine, were full and red. Kathryn could see that the so-called Rose of Raby was not pleased with her.

'Well, well, well!' Edward leaned forward. 'My condolences, Murtagh, on the death of your friend and colleague Master Mafiach.'

The hushed silence became more intense.

'Who is this?' de Sanglier asked. He was now cleaning his mouth with his tongue, staring at Kathryn, then back at the King.

'Who is what?' Clarence drawled. 'The young woman is a physician. Now, de Sanglier, would you like to be examined by her?'

George of Clarence laughed, a noisy sound, shoulders shaking.

'Shut up, George!' Edward smiled at Kathryn. 'This, my Lord Vicomte, is Kathryn Swinbrooke. I am sure she already knows the Vicomte de Sanglier; your reputation always goes before you.'

The Frenchman bowed as if this was the most gracious compliment.

'And this death?' The Frenchman waved his hand. 'I know Master Murtagh,' he continued, 'and Venables, but Mafiach? I have not heard his name before.'

Kathryn glanced at this Frenchman, staring in round-eyed innocence at the King.

'Of course you wouldn't have,' Edward smiled. 'He was a messenger, murdered at a tavern outside the city.'

The Frenchman pulled a face and sat back in his chair as if the matter were of no consequence. The King's smile faded. 'You should have been more careful, Master Murtagh!'

'Your Grace,' Venables interrupted, 'Mafiach should have been more careful; he was unwary.'

'True, true,' Edward conceded, 'but now his soul has gone to God.'

'How was he murdered?' De Sanglier refused to stay out of the game.

Edward's gaze shifted. The King blinked. Kathryn glimpsed the fury boiling within him. 'His brains were dashed out.'

'I am sorry.' De Sanglier lifted his cup in a toast of condolence. 'They say, "In vino veritas": Wine always brings the truth. I am truly sorry, Your Grace, that you have been distressed.'

Edward nodded, about to speak.

'And you, Mistress Swinbrooke? This business at the Friary of the Sack? Our beloved mother'—he grasped the Duchess's wrist—'is deeply concerned. Should she be concerned? First, the Blessed Roger's death, and now there has been another murder! Come, Mistress, speak!'

Kathryn gave a succinct description of what had happened, omitting any personal details. She mentioned the so-called miracles and Atworth's corpse, but suppressed any reference to mystery or intrigue. As she talked, she glanced around. Colum remained silent. Venables sat staring at the Duchess as if communicating secret messages, nodding slightly in agreement with what Kathryn said. Spineri acted as if he was bored. Bourchier sat, his eyes half-closed, but Kathryn knew that he was listening intently, measuring her every word. The King just stared at her. Duchess Cecily glowered, whilst her two other sons seemed bored by the proceedings. The more she talked, the more certain Kathryn became that Edward of England was playing a game with everyone in the room. Spineri had to be there, as had the Archbishop, but there was some secret struggle between the King and the Vicomte. The French envoy must have had a hand in Mafiach's death. He could act the innocent, but Kathryn suspected he knew as much about Atworth as she did. When she had finished, the King sat back in his chair, swirling the wine round his cup.

'My Lord,' he smiled at the Vicomte, 'in your younger days you knew Master Atworth?'

'I had the pleasure of his company, Your Grace.'

The King leaned his elbows on the arm of his chair and steepled his fingers.

'If I listened to you correctly, Mistress, Atworth died a good death after a good life. You express doubts about the vision and the consequent miracles, but then again, you are the Advocatus Diaboli. His Eminence, the Cardinal, is ready to promulgate this matter in Rome. He has the ear of the Holy Father. He must faithfully report what he has found, which,' Edward's voice was tinged with sarcasm, 'must be a great deal. He must also report your conclusions! Would you, Mistress Swinbrooke, on the evidence you have studied, do anything to hinder the beatification of the Blessed Roger?'

Duchess Cecily was staring at Kathryn; her face had softened. Was that a beseeching look? Kathryn recalled what she knew about Atworth, his cruelties as a soldier offset by a life of penance and prayer; the compassion he had shown to Mathilda Chandler.

'No, Your Grace, I would not. True, there are mysteries here,' Kathryn added quickly. 'Atworth may have been born a sinner and lived his life as one, but I think he died a saint.'

Duchess Cecily clapped her hands and beamed at Kathryn. The Vicomte muttered something in French and lifted his goblet to Kathryn.

'And so the matter is ended?'

The King asked the question so quickly that instantly Kathryn knew why they were here. Edward of England didn't give a fig about Atworth. If his mother wanted to sanctify a hawk in the Royal Mews, Edward would have agreed. Something else was going on, but what?

The Vicomte spoke. 'May I say, Your Grace, that my noble master, Louis of France, will do everything in his power to promote this case before the Curia. You have my solemn word on that.'

Edward should have been pleased, but instead he stared long and hard at the French envoy.

'Oh, I am sure he will, my lord.'

'We will do everything in our power,' the Vicomte reassured him. 'My master has this matter close to his heart.'

'Our thanks.' Clarence stretched out his legs, stifling a yawn. 'Our deepest thanks for all you have done, Mistress Swinbrooke. This cannot have been a pleasant experience.' He pulled himself up in his chair, a lecherous smile on his face. 'You must have been vulnerable, Mistress Swinbrooke?'

'No, my lord, with men like you around I feel no danger.'

Clarence's smile faded. The others in the Royal Party just stared for a moment; then Richard of Gloucester smiled. Edward threw his head back and bellowed with laughter, and the rest of his companions joined in. The Vicomte shook his head slightly at Clarence, as if warning him to be careful. *I'll remember that,* Kathryn thought, and by the look on Clarence's face, so would he.

'Mistress Swinbrooke! Mistress Swinbrooke!' The King got to his feet, clapping his hands. 'We thank you for what you have done.'

The Duchess plucked at his sleeve, and Edward leaned down; she whispered to him, nodding at Kathryn.

'Very well. Very well. Mistress Kathryn, my dear mother wants a private word with you.'

Edward led the Royal Party out. Bourchier winked at Kathryn as he passed, tapping her gently on the shoulder. Colum said he would wait outside. Once the tent flap had fallen behind them, Cecily beckoned to Kathryn, tapping the chair of state her son had left.

'You can sit here.' She smiled. 'My son will not object. He has, on a number of occasions, had to vacate his throne for someone else.'

Kathryn obeyed. Duchess Cecily turned, her beautiful eyes scrutinising Kathryn.

'I am grateful for what you have done, Mistress.' She lifted her head and stared at the tent flap. 'What else have you discovered, Mistress Swinbrooke?'

'Your Grace, I need your help.' Kathryn decided to be blunt. 'Undoubtedly Roger Atworth lived a saintly life, but he was also a man of secrets. Others want to dig these secrets out.'

Duchess Cecily's face didn't change.

'I may assure you, Madam, that your late confessor is now in Heaven, but I can give no assurances that he took his secrets with him.'

The Duchess's eyes grew fearful.

'Madam, why don't you trust me?' Kathryn insisted. 'Do you know—' She bit her lip.

'Do I know what?'

'Why the French are interested?'

'You've plucked up the thread and followed it far, Mistress Swinbrooke.'

'Madam, do you know anything about Atworth's death? I need to know for both our sakes.' Kathryn forgot for a moment that this woman was the mother of the King of England. She touched the Duchess's hand, which was ice-cold. 'You are terrified, aren't you, Madam?'

Duchess Cecily's lower lip began to quiver.

'Prior Anselm assured me that Roger Atworth burnt my letters before he died.' She sighed. 'Not that there was much in them.' The Duchess glanced away.

'Is Jonquil your spy?' Kathryn asked.

Duchess Cecily didn't reply but gazed down at her brocaded slippers peeping out from beneath her costly gown.

'Not here,' she whispered, 'not now.' She grasped Kathryn's wrist. 'And you walk safely, Mistress. My son George of Clarence'—she shook her head—'does not take insults lightly. But now,' the Duchess's voice rose as if conscious of eavesdroppers outside, 'I thank you once again, Mistress. You have my favour.'

She rose to her feet and extended a be-ringed hand for Kathryn to kiss. As Kathryn did so, the Duchess leaned down and murmured in Kathryn's ear. 'Not here, not now!'

And then she was gone.

Kathryn left the pavilion to find Colum and Venables deep in conversation. The henchman broke off, made his hasty farewells, and followed the Duchess across the lawn to the wicket gate.

'Well, well.' Colum undid the buttons of his green jerkin and put his arm round Kathryn's shoulder. 'You made Clarence look a fool; he can be a bad enemy.'

'His mother said the same,' Kathryn remarked drily. 'And you've been rebuked.'

'Oh the King will forget. Unlike Clarence, he doesn't bear grudges.'

'Am I in any danger?' Kathryn asked. 'Clarence has the eyes and mouth of a spiteful child.'

Colum stared up at the dark mass of the abbey buildings.

'No. If I frightened you needlessly, it would be cruel. As they left, the King linked his arm through Clarence's. I suspect he will be warning him to leave you well alone. But come, Kathryn, let's be out of this silken web.'

They left the Cathedral grounds by a side entrance. Kathryn felt strange to be back on the streets of Canterbury after the silence of the friary and the gorgeous splendour of Edward's Court. The day was now drawing to an end. People hurried home as stalls were being put away, the merchants, traders, and apprentices thronging the taverns and cookshops. Kathryn and Colum walked arm in arm. She noticed how the streets were cleaner, the sewers empty, the refuse piles few, whilst the scavengers' carts were everywhere.

'It looks as if Malachi's war against the rats is succeeding.'

'Holbech is still a-feared of them,' Colum replied. 'He claims to have seen one the other night in a tavern so big he thought it was a cat.'

They went down alleyways pungent with the smell of boiled cabbage. Women sat at doorways in their dowdy gowns spinning wool. Children ran about screaming. At the corner of St. Peter's Street, Rawnose the pedlar, his disfigured face grubby and dirty, crouched with an empty tray, hand out begging. As Kathryn and Colum approached, he leapt to his feet, tears streaming down his poxed cheeks. The ugly scar where his nose had once been seemed redder and angrier than usual.

'What's the matter, Rawnose?'

'I have a demon in my belly.' Rawnose's eyes were frantic. 'Tom of Bedlam and Hot Dance cavort in my soul! Oh, Mistress Swinbrooke, a foul demon haunts me with the voice of a nightingale. He has led me through fire and flame, fall and whirlpool, bog and quagmire.' Rawnose scratched his cheek. 'This demon within me does not live in the real world but beneath a dark thicket; at twilight he comes to haunt me.'

Kathryn opened her purse and took out two coins.

'Rawnose, you've sold all your ribbons and geegaws, and you've drunk the profits, yes? Here, take this. Now go down to Father Cuthbert at the Poor Priests' Hospital; let him see you and do exactly what he tells you. You need bread and broth and, by the looks of you, a good night's sleep.' Kathryn squeezed the beggar's fingers. 'Promise, or I'll not talk to you again!'

Rawnose greedily took the coin. He lifted his hand as if taking an oath, swaying on his feet.

'Not another word,' Kathryn said.

Rawnose shuffled off.

'Good Lord!' Colum watched him go. 'He's got a face as pitted as cheese, and he smells like a compost heap.'

'Father Cuthbert will look after him.'

A child ran up, dressed in a ragged smock.

'Mistress,' she asked in a piping voice, 'can I have a coin?'

The little girl's eyes were cornflower blue and smiling.

'Why should I give you a coin?'

'I'll show you a fairy and the carriage she travels in.'

She giggled at Kathryn's frown of disbelief and brought her hands from behind her back. In one hand the little girl held a cracked pot full of soap suds from her mother's wash vat; in her other hand was a small stick with a ring on the end. She dug this into the suds, scooped them up, and began to blow bubbles. Kathryn laughed as the bubbles drifted up towards her. One landed on the corner of her nose, and she smelt the wood ash the girl's mother must have used.

'There are fairies inside,' the little girl said. 'I tricked you.'

Kathryn handed across the requested coin and walked on.

'I used to do that,' she remarked, wiping the tip of her nose, and then stopped abruptly, sniffing at her fingers.

'Kathryn, what is the matter? I want to be off these streets and out of these clothes. Holbech has been wondering where I am. I also want to pay my respects to Mafiach's corpse before it's buried.'

Kathryn just stood staring at her fingers.

'Kathryn'—Colum grasped her by the hand—'are you well?'

'Oh yes, I am.' And she walked on as if in a daydream.

'What did the Queen Mother want?' Colum asked. 'Does she know what you know?'

'She suspects,' Kathryn glanced up at him, 'that there is more to Atworth's death than meets the eye. One question she evades: Is Jonquil her spy? My mind's a jumble. I need to sit, Colum, and think about what I saw and heard today. One other thing puzzles me—the Vicomte's remarks about how the French would support Atworth's canonisation.'

They turned into Ottemelle Lane. Kathryn nodded at Goldere the clerk, who, as usual, scampered by, one hand clutching his codpiece, the other his shabby gown.

'Did you tell the Duchess about the psalter?'

'No.' Kathryn paused, her hand on the latch. 'The least I say in such silken, treacherous surroundings the better. Our Duchess will be reflecting. Perhaps we'll meet again.'

She opened the door and went in. The air was thick with the smell of cooking from the kitchen. Agnes was in the apothecary room scrubbing down a counter. As soon as she saw Kathryn, she dropped the brush, her thin, pale face lit by a smile. Wulf appeared from behind a chest where he had been hiding, his blonde hair all spiked, his face sticky and dirty.

'You've been stealing marchpane?' Kathryn asked.

'And a lot more.' Thomasina came bustling down the passage-way, arms naked to the elbows, covered in flour, her face brick-red from the fire. 'I've been baking pies.' She glowered at Colum. 'And I am glad the mistress is home.'

Thomasina led Kathryn into the kitchen, chattering volubly about what had happened and the patients who had called.

'I sent those down to Father Cuthbert. Most of them are stomach ailments. People are not careful about what they eat and drink.'

Thomasina brought the book of sales, and Kathryn was pleased at the purchases made. Thomasina, for all her hustle and bustle, had been well schooled in the horn book and knew more about the trade than she let even Kathryn know.

Thomasina forced Kathryn to sit down in the chair at the top of the table, bringing her and Colum ale and slices of cherry pie. Kathryn smiled at Colum and winked. Whenever Thomasina was excited, she chattered like a magpie, making it difficult for anyone to get a word in edgewise; all the news of the parish, the gossip, the petty scandal tumbled out. And then she began the questions: What had Colum and Kathryn been doing? Why was the Irishman dressed like a popinjay? Had they seen the King? What did he look like?

At last Thomasina, still talking over her shoulder, went down the corridors and dragged Wulf and Agnes in "for something proper to eat." Kathryn ate pie whilst Colum escaped up to his own chamber, claiming he had to change; but in truth he left to escape Thomasina's barbed remarks and constant chatter. Kathryn, however, sat listening with half an ear whilst she tried to marshal her thoughts. She got to her feet and excused herself. Thomasina, midway through a sentence, paused and smiled at her.

'I can see you are here in body, Kathryn, but not in spirit.'

Kathryn ignored her and walked down to her writing office just beside the apothecary room. She sat down at her father's table and stared out at the herb garden, then rose to open the door.

'You've done a good job, Wulf. The plots look well weeded.'

Wulf, his mouth full of pie, yelled something back. Kathryn closed the door. For a while she just sat, allowing the memories of the last two days to flit like birds through her mind. Gervase's grisly corpse; Atworth, his body waxen, that beautiful perfume; the conspiratorial faces of Anselm, Simon, and Jonquil; Mathilda Chandler whispering at her through the Judas squint; the strange pictures in the psalter; and the tense atmosphere of that Royal Circle. She recalled the hawks, the pathetic bloody remains of the doves.

'They are all hawks,' Kathryn muttered.

Yes they were, Edward, Richard, Clarence, and the rest: like peregrines on their perches, watching each other as well as the ground beneath them. She opened a small coffer and took out some parchment and a small writing tray.

'Atworth,' she wrote. 'The miracles? The apparition? The stigmata?'

'You certainly didn't die in bed,' Kathryn whispered.

There was a knock on the door.

'Oh, one thing.' Thomasina pushed her head round. 'Father Cuthbert sent a number of messages; he wants to see you.'

'When did these arrive?'

'This morning. He said it was rather urgent. Oh, and by the way, that Malachi Smallbones has been back: He's a gallows bird if there ever was one.'

No sooner had Thomasina closed the door behind her than Colum knocked and strode in. 'I was thinking about Atworth's canonisation. If he was acclaimed a saint, how would that benefit the French?'

'What I am worried about,' Kathryn replied, 'is not whether Atworth is a saint or a sinner, but what Atworth knew about the Royal Family.'

'Oh, sweet angels!' Colum breathed. 'You think it's as bad as that?'

'There are different sections to this puzzle,' Kathryn answered.

'Who is the spy at the English Court? Tonight, Colum, after I return from the Poor Priests' Hospital, I am going to study that verse from Zephaniah. Then there's Mafiach's murder. I believe the Vicomte knew all about it. He was baiting Edward with his witticisms, and the King knew it.'

'But what he doesn't know,' Colum interrupted, 'is that Mafiach had a second copy of that message.'

'True,' Kathryn conceded. 'Then we have the strange phenomena surrounding Atworth's death, not to mention who Jonquil is and what happened to Gervase. Somehow or other, Colum, I believe they are all linked, closely connected.' She smiled. 'One thing I have learnt, that beautiful fragrance round Atworth's corpse? Nothing more than bubbles in the air.'

'What do you mean?'

'I'll wait for a while to tell you.' Kathryn got to her feet. 'First I need to sleep. Just a little rest, Colum. Once it's dusk, we'll visit Father Cuthbert.'

Night was falling around the Friary of the Sack, the twilight time when, according to legend, hobgoblins, wood sprites, and all the creatures of the dark came into their own. It was a lonely time, with the whispering trees mourning the passing of the day. Those early hours of the night were specially hallowed by Holy Mother Church for special prayer, invocations to God against Satan and all his cohorts, who roamed the wastelands hunting men's souls. The deep copse of woods at the end of the Gethsemane Garden in the friary became a lonely, haunted place, but the assassin, crouched beneath the outstretched arms of an oak tree, had no fear of God, man, or indeed the terrors of Hell. His face was now blackened, whilst the brown robe kept him well hidden.

He stared across at the lights from the friary. Here and there a candle glowed in a window casement. A bell tolled, and he heard the distant sounds from the stables and kitchens. The assassin clutched the wineskin tighter. The deep pockets of his robes contained a piece of hempen string greased with oil and a sharpened tinder. Like a hunting animal, the assassin slunk forward, his sandalled feet creating no sound, his eyes sharp for any twigs or branches. As the trees and bushes began to clear, he passed the spot where Sub-Prior Gervase had met his hideous death.

He glimpsed the glow of light through the Judas squint of the cell where the Accursed was imprisoned. He placed the winesack full of oil down on the ground and crept forward. He reached the cell and, raising himself up, peered through the squint. A candle glowed. He could see the outline of Mistress Chandler on her cot-bed, fast asleep. The assassin crouched back down and, edging his way round, found the steel sheet used to block the door. He in-serted this back into its wooden wedges and returned to the Judas squint, picked up the wineskin, removed the stopper, and poured the contents through. The oil slopped and gurgled as it flowed out, an ominously dark stream. The assassin next took the hempen string and a piece of oil-soaked wood and threaded these through the Judas squint. He grasped the tinder, sharp and prepared. He struck once, struck twice, but the flame wouldn't hold. He struck again and watched the flames race up the hemp through the Judas squint. The assassin withdrew. A crackling echoed through the gap, and fire spurted up. Satisfied, the assassin retreated deeper into the darkness.

From his so-called eyrie, the Ancient One, Brother Timothy, stared out over Gethsemane. The old man was lost in wonderment. He prided himself on the fact that, despite his age, his eyesight and wits left nothing to be desired. Now he reflected that he could not recall Sub-Prior Gervase crossing Gethsemane that fateful af-ternoon. Or had he, but much earlier? And was there something else? On a night like this some weeks ago, around the Feast of the Annunciation, when Brother Roger had died, Brother Timothy was sure he had seen figures out there at the far end of Gethsem-ane, lanterns in their hands. Hadn't that been Father Prior and the infirmarian? What had they been doing out in the dead of night? He must tell Eadwig this. The Ancient One chomped on his gums and peered out at the dark trees and starlit sky. The woman phy-sician, Kathryn Swinbrooke, he had taken to her kind eyes and respectful ways. He suspected that the physician, who, according to rumour, had powerful friends, had released Mathilda Chandler from her cell. Brother Timothy was sure he had seen the Accursed walking amongst the trees and bushes earlier this evening. The Ancient One was pleased. He had been in the friary when the poor woman had been bound, fettered, and immured for life. Brother Timothy's gaze caught the glow of light in the trees. More lanterns? No, a glow like that must be another fire! Had the devil and his demons returned? Brother Timothy picked up his hand-bell and began to ring it vigorously.

Now that it was evening, the Poor Priests' Hospital lay quiet. Father Cuthbert, the white-haired, anxious-eyed supervisor, had welcomed Kathryn and Colum and led them through the long, well-lit dormitory smelling of soap, polish, and fresh herbs. Most of his patients lay here, on pallet beds, tended by servitors. The hospital was really meant for priests who had fallen on hard times, but Father Cuthbert's compassion was now famous: No man or woman who came through the hospital's arched gateway begging for help was ever turned away. Brother Cuthbert paused so quickly that Kathryn and Colum nearly jostled him; then his grey, cadaverous face broke into a smile.

'I know why I sent for you.' He lifted a bony finger. 'But I also want to ask you about these miracles at the Friary of the Sack.'

He led them into his office at the far end of the dormitory, an austere chamber with a crucifix on the wall, a shelf bearing some books, and a coffer containing small jars and phials. The floor was of polished wood. Father Cuthbert eased himself into a chair, specially padded and constructed for him, as he suffered constant back pain. Kathryn and Colum sat on stools.

'Do you want some wine?' Cuthbert asked. 'I have a jug somewhere.'

'Father, we have eaten and drunk our fill,' Colum assured him. 'I have come to pay my respects to Padraig Mafiach.'

'Ah yes, the poor Irishman.' Father Cuthbert's face wrinkled in concern. 'I said a mass for him, Colum. No, no.' He raised a hand, cutting short any protests from Colum. 'It was the least I could do.'

He sat puckering his lips. Kathryn felt a deep compassion for this old priest, probably one of the most skilled physicians in Canterbury. In his youth, according to Thomasina, Father Cuthbert had been the most handsome of men.

'The ladies positively swooned after him,' Thomasina had whispered, dewy-eyed. 'But then he went on his travels and found God.'

Kathryn suspected her friend's affection for this old priest ran very deep indeed.

'I heard about the cures at the Friary of the Sack. I love miracles!'

'No, you don't, Father,' Kathryn teased. 'You don't really believe in them, do you?'

'Yes and no.' Father Cuthbert eased himself up. 'I think we look for them in the wrong places. The sun rising; that's a miracle. How an egg gives birth to a bird; that's a miracle. A man laying down his life for a friend; that's an even greater one! So come, Kathryn, tell me what you know about these miracles.'

She gave a summary of her findings. Father Cuthbert nodded.

'I agree. I agree,' he sighed when she'd finished. 'Except for the last one: That could be strange; perhaps the power of the mind? I read once how the ancient Greeks used to put people to sleep to calm their humours and bring respite. An interesting question, Kathryn, isn't it? Did God use the Blessed Roger and give that old man comfort so his belly might recover? Ah, well . . .'

'You wanted to see us, Father?' Colum interrupted. 'Or rather Kathryn.'

'Yes.' Father Cuthbert folded back the sleeve of his gown. 'Rats, Kathryn! I heard on the breeze about your meeting with Bourchier, and I have met Malachi Smallbones.' A shift in the old priest's eye showed that Father Cuthbert had little regard for the self-proclaimed rat-catcher of Canterbury. 'Have you noticed, Kathryn, that no rats scuttle around here? Go along that dormitory, in the store-rooms-or even the charnel-house. You'll not hear the squeak or patter of tiny feet.'

'You've discovered some new poison?' Kathryn asked.

'Ah!' Father Cuthbert jabbed a bony finger into the air. 'That's why I wanted to see you. Don't use poison, Kathryn. You know I have a secret chamber?'

'Everybody in Canterbury knows about your secret chamber, Father.'

Father Cuthbert looked surprised.

'You carry out experiments?' Kathryn teased.

'Yes I do, and I use rats. I believe, Kathryn, they carry disease. Not only in their bite, urine, or faeces: something noxious lurks in their bodies, a fetid air or a malignant odour. I've tried to poison rats. Sometimes I am successful, but after a while, their bodily humours oppose the malignancy.'

'As can happen in men,' Kathryn added, and told him quickly about Roger Atworth.

'Yes, yes, I've heard of that.' Father Cuthbert straightened himself up, shaking his head. 'I never use arsenic for a stomach complaint. You see its properties. . . .'

'Father,' Kathryn intervened, 'you were talking about rats.'

'Ferrets!' Father Cuthbert replied.

'I beg your pardon?'

'Ferrets!' Father Cuthbert pronounced the word as if it had come directly from God. 'What you need here, Kathryn, are professional ferreters with their little trained foragers. They'll soon clean out the nests and kill the rats, especially if they're starved. After a while they'll drag the corpses out for you.'

Kathryn recalled Gethsemane.

'The same thing happened at the friary,' she declared. 'There were rats in the garden, but there's a great curtain wall which houses a colony of stoats.'

'They are as ferocious as ferrets,' Father Cuthbert agreed, 'but impossible to train. Now I want to tell you something very interesting. I keep my little ferret friends in the cellar. I call them "the Twelve Apostles." Each has a name: Peter, Bartholomew, Phillip. They are the holiest ferrets in Christendom. There are two surprising things about them: first, I used the ferrets only in this hospital and the surrounding buildings, and so far they haven't found a nest with young ones in it. Isn't that strange?'

'I don't understand,' Colum broke in.

'Rats breed like flies,' Father Cuthbert explained, 'so it's strange that they haven't set up colonies; the only answer is that they haven't had time. The second thing . . . well, come, I'll show you.'

He leapt to his feet like an excited young boy and led them down the staircase and across a cobbled yard to a small outhouse. He lit a lantern, and they went in. The pungent smell of herbs did little to conceal the whiff of corruption.

'Yes, yes, it's not too special. Anyway, I've been saving this.'

He lifted a wooden box on the table, walked away for a moment, and returned with three pomanders.

'Hold these to your noses.' He handed them over and lifted the lid to reveal the bloated corpse of a black rat. 'This gentleman,' Father Cuthbert explained, 'was killed by my beloved ferret, Thomas the Doubter. You don't have to touch it, Kathryn.' He picked up a small white wand and brushed the rodent's fur. 'This rat has also been badly singed.'

Kathryn peered down. Father Cuthbert was right: The singed fur was clearly visible.

'It was worse when I first saw it,' Father Cuthbert said. 'Very much like when I singe my eyebrows or hair when I get too close to a fire.'

Kathryn gestured at him to close the lid and walked away. Colum was only too pleased to follow. Father Cuthbert came over and made them wash their hands; he poured water into a small bowl and sprinkled this with herbs and rose powder.

'I've seen the same,' Kathryn explained, wiping her hands on a napkin. 'What does it mean, Father?'

'I know! I remember the farmers in Ireland,' Colum interjected. 'When the hay was stored, most of it was used, but what lasted through winter and spring became coarse with mildew.'

'A nesting place for rats?'

'That's right, Father. We set it alight. The rats would come teeming out, and we would kill them.'

'Precisely,' Father Cuthbert agreed. 'You'd get rid of the old hay, and the vermin it houses, before you bring in the fresh and sweet. To cut a long story short, Kathryn,' Father Cuthbert sniffed at the pomander, 'first, these rats have been burnt out of a building. Secondly, I think . . .'

'I know what you are going to say, Father. They've been deliberately brought into Canterbury.'

'Impossible!' Colum exclaimed.

'No, no.' Kathryn walked out of the outhouse and breathed in the cool night air. 'All credit to you, Father; I was beginning to suspect something similar.'

'It's quite easily done.' Father Cuthbert came up behind Kathryn. 'You find a place teeming with rats, the sewers or underground passages of some city. One thing rats fear above all things is fire. They flee by the hundreds. Only this time they were not killed but trapped in cages, baskets, and boxes, loaded onto a cart, and brought into Canterbury. At the dead of night one box was taken here, one box there. They haven't had time to nest or breed as yet, but a problem has been created, and everyone is looking for a remedy.'

'Malachi Smallbones!' Kathryn whispered.

'Malachi Smallbones,' Father Cuthbert agreed. 'Think, Colum, of a large cart covered with a canvas cloth kept out amongst the ruins around Canterbury.'

'A cunning man's trick,' Colum agreed, 'which would require little silver.'

'True,' Father Cuthbert replied. 'Wood for cages, a cart, a night like this, full of shadows. Who would suspect? Yet the rewards for such mischief are very, very great.'

'And the solution?' Colum asked.

'Holbech,' Kathryn replied. 'Take him into your confidence, Colum. Tell him what we suspect and have Master Smallbones carefully watched.' Kathryn stared up at the light in a hospital window. 'The sheer cunning of human minds,' she murmured. 'What made you suspect, Father?'

'Kathryn, all my life I've waged war against the cunning men, the conjurors, the quacks. Read your Galen or your Hippocrates to discover the most ancient trick of any charlatan. Some patients visit you: They are hale and hearty, but you tell them something is very wrong. You offer the cure. They take it, nothing more harmful than rose water, and of course the illness doesn't develop. You praise the charlatan, pay him good silver and gold for his trickery, and recommend him to your friends. As soon as I met Malachi Smallbones, I thought, here's a man who could sell fleas to a dog. He's created the problem. He knows how Canterbury is terrified of its pilgrim trade being interfered with.'

'I'll have him followed and watched.' Colum stamped his heel on the ground. 'I've spent hours out at Kingsmead chasing those rodents. Oh yes, he's been there. He's made his presence felt in important parts of the city: the Royal Stables, the Cathedral, the friary. And, what's truly unforgiveable, a hospital for sick people!' Colum gnawed at his lip, his hands tapping the hilt of his dagger.

'Don't, Colum,' Kathryn warned, 'don't take the law into your own hands. Every rogue has his day. Malachi has had his. We'll need solid evidence, and then he'll feel the full lash of the law in more ways than one.'

Father Cuthbert rubbed his hands together, pleased with her words.

'Come!' he urged.

They crossed the cobbled yard and went down a small alleyway into another square. Father Cuthbert pointed across at the small chapel.

'Your friend lies there, prepared for burial. I have done the best I can, both for the savage wound and to stave off corruption. Go on! The door's open, and candles have been lit.'

Colum took off his war-belt, walked across, and placed it on the steps outside.

'I want to show you something, Kathryn,' Cuthbert declared.

He led her across to a small, red-bricked building with a flat roof. He pushed open the metal-studded, black-timbered door, and they entered a white-washed chamber, bleak and cold. Tables stood around the walls. On each lay a corpse covered by a sheet. Incense was burning, and jars of herbs stood on every niche and shelf to sweeten the air; this was the charnel-house, where the corpses of strangers were brought for burial. Father Cuthbert stopped at one table and pulled back the sheet: The remains beneath were pathetic, nothing more than a skeleton with pieces of rotting hair still clinging to the skull.

'A fisherman found her on the banks of the Stour,' Father Cuthbert declared. 'Probably a young woman, but I've searched the records, going back months: There has been no report of a young woman being missing. But what are these?' He pointed to the feet.

At first Kathryn was mystified. She could make out the bones of feet and toes, but tied underneath the feet by a cord was another piece of bone, thick with a shiny surface.

'When she was alive,' Kathryn mused, 'she couldn't have walked on those. Why should a young woman have pieces of bone tied to her feet? Can I have a closer look?'

'I already have, but . . .' Father Cuthbert pulled one of the bones away and handed it to Kathryn.

The bone was a long cube, and both the top and bottom were smooth; the rotting cord had been threaded through metal clasps on the side.

'Oh, Father!' she exclaimed. 'Haven't you ever gone skating?'

Father Cuthbert shook his head.

'Never?' Kathryn persisted.

Father Cuthbert's crumpled face broke into a smile, and he smacked his forehead with the heel of his hand.

'Of course!' He breathed, 'I never thought of that!'

'I suspect,' Kathryn explained, 'that this poor woman died many years ago. She went skating on the Stour when it was frozen, but the ice broke, and she sank to the bottom, her corpse tangled in the mud and reeds. Years later the river gave up its dead.'

'Ah well, Kathryn, that's one mystery solved. I was curious; this is different.'

He covered up the skeleton, moved to a second table, and gently folded back the sheet. This time the young woman's corpse was whole and preserved. Despite the ravages of death, she must have been a beautiful young woman: Lustrous blonde hair framed an oval face with high cheekbones. The eyes were held closed shut by two coins, and her body was smooth and comely with generous full breasts and broad hips, all marred by the hideous wound on her left side, a deep, red-black gash.

'Who is it, Father?'

'I don't know. She was found on the edge of a marsh in Bean Woods, covered in slime and mud. The morasses there are not too deep. The water bubbles up, and eventually a corpse will rise. She was brought in this morning, and I had her washed. She is beautiful. And look, Kathryn.' He took the dead woman's hand. Kathryn felt the skin of the palms; it was soft and silky to the touch.

'A woman of substance, don't you think?'

Kathryn agreed.

'I've made enquiries.' Father Cuthbert shook his head. 'But again, I could discover nothing. Here we have a beautiful young woman who enjoyed certain wealth and status. Very recently she was lured to Bean Woods, brutally stabbed, and stripped of everything, and then her corpse was tossed into a marsh. Yet no one has been reported missing. I did find one thing.'

Father Cuthbert crouched and drew out a small wooden coffer from beneath the table. He opened this and took out a pewter hair clasp.

'Her hair must have been very thick and lustrous,' he explained. 'The killer missed this.'

Kathryn took it over to one of the thick tallow candles.

'It's a pewter hair brooch,' she observed.

She made out the emblem, a pilgrim carrying a staff, and the letters round the rim: CANTERBURY and, on the other side, FAL-STAFF INN. Kathryn's heart skipped a beat.

'What's the matter?' Father Cuthbert asked.

'Look, Father, here's a wealthy young woman, barbarously murdered, probably in the last two or three days. She was killed, her corpse concealed. She cannot be from Canterbury, otherwise a hue and cry would have been raised. She definitely stayed at the Falstaff, where Mafiach was also murdered. I just wonder if the two killings are connected. Father, can I keep this?'

'Of course.'

Kathryn slipped the hair clasp into her wallet.

'One other favour, Father. I want you to send a messenger to mine host at the Falstaff. Ask him to come here. Show him this corpse. If he recognises it, tell him to come and see me at first light tomorrow. Would you do that?'

Father Cuthbert agreed.

'A worthwhile visit.' Kathryn smiled.

They left the charnel-house, and a short while later Colum rejoined them. They bade Father Cuthbert good night. Kathryn surprised Colum by insisting on walking as swiftly as possible back to Ottemelle Lane.

'What is the matter?' Colum pressed Kathryn's arm. 'If I let go, you'd run!'

Kathryn paused and kissed him quickly on the lips.

'I will not be sleeping much tonight, Colum. You and Holbech deal with Master Smallbones. I have an assassin to catch, and trap him I will.'

They found the house in Ottemelle Lane all quiet. Thomasina, crouched over a piece of needlework, was talking to herself.

'Nothing's happened whilst you've been gone.' She lifted her head, eyes red-rimmed. 'How's Father Cuthbert?'

'Very well: He sends his regards.'

Thomasina smiled, rose, and kissed her gently on the brow.

Kathryn went along to her writing office and lit the candles and table lamp. She took a sheet of vellum and wrote at the top, MAFIACH. She closed her eyes, recalling everything she knew. She wrote facts down as she would a list of ingredients and picked up the copy of Mafiach's cipher. She wrote down all the names of the people she had met since this business had begun. She made good progress, despite Thomasina's constant interruptions to see if she wanted something to eat or drink. One by one Kathryn crossed off names, and, as she did so, the face of the assassin became clearer. She moved to a second piece of vellum, writing on the top ATWORTH. She heard a soft knocking at the door and then Thomasina's curses about patients and their cures. The door opened. Kathryn heard a woman's voice, hushed but firm. She looked at the crucifix.

'Thank you, Lord,' she whispered and, pushing back the chair, went out to meet the Duchess Cecily, cloaked and cowled, escorted by Venables. The Duchess looked pinch-faced, as if she had been crying.

'Mistress Swinbrooke, I apologise. Brother Atworth is dead, so perhaps you can hear my confession. Venables, you stay outside!'

And following Kathryn into the chamber, Duchess Cecily herself closed and bolted the door behind them.

Chapter 11

'Ye, sterve he shal, and that in lesse while
Than thou wolt' goon a paas not but a mile . . .'
—Chaucer, 'The Pardoner's Tale,'
The Canterbury Tales

Kathryn had finished her task and sat half-dozing. Dawn was breaking, greeted by the clanging bells of the Cathedral and the other churches of the city. A dog yelped in an alleyway. Carts, bringing fresh produce in from the countryside, trundled along Ottemelle Lane to the different markets. The Duchess had left in the early hours. Kathryn had refused to discuss her visit even with Colum. She had been sworn to secrecy, and she'd keep her word. But despite her midnight visit, Kathryn suspected Cecily had not told her the full truth.

The loud knocking on the door made her jump. Thomasina was not yet awake, so Kathryn answered it. Eadwig, red-eyed and pale-faced, his lean face unshaven, gazed beseechingly at her, stumbling over his words. Kathryn noticed the ash stains on his hands and face.

'Oh no.' She grasped Eadwig by the arm and pulled him through the doorway. 'Mathilda Chandler?'

Eadwig didn't answer but groped along the passageway, holding the wall. Kathryn helped him sit down on a stool and brought him a black jack of buttermilk. The lay brother drank it greedily, wiping his lips on the back of his hand.

'The Ancient One saw it first,' he gasped, 'a fire out in the copse. By the time we got there, Mistress, the fire was a furnace. Nothing could have survived. You'd best come.'

Kathryn put her face in her hands. If she hadn't been so tired, she would have burst into tears. All she could think of was Mathilda Chandler's sad eyes, her profound happiness at standing free under God's sky, smelling the bracken and the weeds, rejoicing in her new-found freedom. Kathryn stared at the crucifix.

'It's my fault,' she muttered. 'The killer must have known.'

'The steel plate was slipped back,' Eadwig explained. 'The poor woman must have been unable to escape.'

'And her remains?'

'Brother Simon said we would have to wait till dawn. I think it's best you come; so does Brother Timothy.'

Kathryn sat, hands to her mouth. She felt slightly nauseous, and a cold sweat had broken out on her back. She closed her eyes and begged forgiveness even as she cursed her own fecklessness.

'Mistress, are you all right?'

'No, I am not!' Kathryn snapped.

She got to her feet and, going to a shelf, took down a jar of camomile powder, poured herself some milk, and stirred a spoonful in. She lowered the wire bread basket and cut a slice for herself and one for Eadwig, who refused at first.

'No, no, eat!' she insisted, placing the bread on a wooden platter and sliding it across. 'It will calm your stomach. Go back and tell, well, tell Prior Anselm I cannot come immediately. I'll be there soon.'

Eadwig wolfed the bread down. He licked his fingers and stared appreciatively round the kitchen.

'Mistress, it's many a year since I've been in a place like this. Oh dear, I left my staff outside the door.'

Eadwig drained his tankard and got to his feet. He made Kathryn promise again that she would come.

'I'll pray for you, and I'll pray for her,' Eadwig muttered as he slipped through the door, grasping his staff. Kathryn watched him go. Goldere the clerk, standing in the mouth of the alleyway opposite, scratching his stomach, stared blearily across. Kathryn closed the door and drew the bolt across.

'Who was that?'

Thomasina, now fully dressed and smelling of lavender, came downstairs, a white apron already placed over her dress of dark sarcanet, a white, gauze wimple firmly planted over her hair and kept in place by a piece of green baize cord.

'Just a visitor.'

Thomasina peered at Kathryn. 'You haven't slept.' Her black button eyes scrutinised Kathryn's face.

Kathryn walked back into the kitchen. 'I can't explain.'

'Can't explain what?'

Colum, soft-footed as a cat, boots in his hand, came down the stairs along the passageway. He looked fresh-eyed and clean shaven, a new shirt under his boiled leather jacket.

'Will you take me to the friary?' Kathryn asked.

'I'll do better.' Colum took Eadwig's tankard, went across to the jar of buttermilk, and filled it to the brim. 'I've already sent a message out to Holbech at Kingsmead. He knows what to do. He'll keep an eye on Malachi Smallbones.' He slouched in a chair at the top of the table and drank, watching Kathryn carefully. 'What's the matter, lass?'

Kathryn, Thomasina towering over her like a guardian angel, described how Mathilda Chandler had been burnt alive out at the friary. Colum lowered the tankard to gape at Kathryn. Even Thomasina stopped her muttering and stood in horrified silence. Kathryn was almost pleased to hear the knock on the door. Thomasina bustled out.

'Let him in!' Kathryn called. 'I know who it is!'

Clitheroe, mine host at the Falstaff, came lumbering down the passageway, mopping his red face and bald head with a rag. He nodded at Colum and, without being asked, sat down on a stool just within the doorway. He sniffed.

'Is that buttermilk? Can I have some?'

Thomasina thrust a black jack at him. Kathryn sat, determined not to put words into this man's mouth.

'Well, I never! Well, I never!' Clitheroe smacked his lips. 'How did you know, Mistress? I mean, apart from the hair clasp?'

'Know what?' Colum demanded crossly.

'I've just been down to the Poor Priests' Hospital,' Clitheroe replied, 'about the woman who was stabbed, stripped naked, and thrown into a marsh.'

'Oh Lord in His heaven, more deaths!' Thomasina wailed.

'Hush!' Kathryn raised her hand.

'She was the same one,' Clitheroe continued blithely, 'the wife of the merchant who stayed in the chamber above Mafiach's the night he died. You don't think her death's connected with his? I don't want this being bandied about. With these bloody rats, trade is bad enough!'

'You are sure it was her?' Kathryn asked.

'Of course. Pretty as a picture she was. Even in death she's comely.'

'And what was her husband like?'

'Ah, he was secretive, grey-haired, much older. Didn't really clap eyes on him.'

'Are you sure it's her?' Kathryn insisted.

'Oh come, Mistress, pretty face, blonde hair. Ah, that's right.' He raised a hand. 'She came downstairs for the meal. Some customers ask for it to be sent up; others don't trust our scullions. I remember her coming down to the tap-room, all a-smiling and dove-eyed.'

'And what did she order?'

'Oh, Lord's sake, Mistress, it's some time now: bread, a bowl of meat and vegetables. I have the accounts back at the inn.'

'And wine?' Kathryn asked.

'Oh yes, a large jug for two.'

'Very similar,' Kathryn asked, 'to the one Mafiach ordered? Do you remember?' Kathryn leaned forward. 'You said that after you discovered Mafiach's corpse, you took the jug back to the kitchen, that you and your tapsters finished it?'

'Yes, that's right.'

'Colum,' Kathryn looked over her shoulder, 'was Mafiach a heavy drinker?'

'No, a goblet or two of wine, no more.'

Kathryn turned back to the taverner.

'So why should Mafiach, a wary man'—she smiled thinly at the description—'yes, a very wary man, who was on his guard, order a large jug of wine for two people?'

Clitheroe lowered the tankard. 'Do you know, Mistress, you are right. If you were staying at the Falstaff by yourself and you ordered wine . . .'

'I'd get a smaller jug,' Kathryn intervened.

'Yes, a measure for one person.' Clitheroe looked puzzled.

'So why should Mafiach get a larger jug?' Kathryn asked.

Clitheroe closed his eyes. 'But you are wrong, Mistress. I've just remembered. It was a small jug. I also recall Mafiach hadn't drunk much.'

Kathryn closed her eyes and swore under her breath.

'What's the matter, Kathryn?' Colum asked.

She stared at the taverner. 'No, no, I am correct,' she declared. 'Let me approach it from another path. You said that Mafiach hadn't drunk much? Yet I smelt wine from his mouth. You do remember that?'

Clitheroe nodded. Kathryn tried to concentrate. 'But you never found out if Mafiach ordered the meal and wine?'

'Well, he said that he would have an evening meal.'

'But you never recollected him sending down for it?'

Clitheroe shook his head.

'And you can't remember ordering a scullion to take it up?'

Again the shake of the head.

'And you have never found,' Kathryn spoke slowly, 'the scullion, pot-boy, or slattern who took that meal up?'

'No, Mistress, I haven't.'

'Kathryn!' Colum exclaimed. 'What are you implying?'

Kathryn raised her hand for silence.

'Master Clitheroe, if I was staying at your tavern, could I get a small jug and one of your standard wine goblets? I mean, empty? Would you charge me for it?'

'Well, of course not.'

'Can you remember the merchant and his wife asking to borrow such a jug and goblet?'

'Well no, Mistress, I can't, but they could come down and ask for such. I wouldn't give it a second thought. I mean, we are a tavern, Mistress, such jugs and goblets can be found on a table.'

Kathryn smiled. 'I am sure they can be.'

'What is this?' Colum asked in exasperation.

'Why, Master Murtagh, murder!' Kathryn got to her feet. 'The assassins were that young woman, whose corpse you have just seen, and her so-called husband.'

'And who could he be?' Clitheroe spluttered.

'Was he clean shaven?' Kathryn asked.

'No, he had a beard and moustache.'

'His hair?'

'Grey. I can't truly remember if there was much of it or not.' Clitheroe shook his head.

'He was in disguise,' Kathryn replied.

'Who?' Colum asked. 'One of the Friars of the Sack?'

'Possibly,' Kathryn replied. 'They have money and wealth enough. They leave their friary. They can disguise themselves and hire some courtesan.'

'A courtesan?'

'I suspect the dead woman was a prostitute of some wealth and status,' Kathryn replied, 'especially hired to act the role, lured into Bean Woods, and cruelly murdered. She was hired to act as the assassin's wife. Given enough gold and silver, she'd keep her mouth shut and do what she was told. The assassin was probably watching the Falstaff Inn. When did this merchant and his wife arrive, Master Clitheroe?'

'Oh, about two days before Mafiach did.'

'And I suppose they left the following morning?'

'Yes, they did. They gave a name, but I forget it now. They paid well.'

'Of course they would. The fewer questions asked the better. To answer your question bluntly, Colum, this so-called young wife went down to the kitchen. She ordered two bowls of food, some bread, a large jug of wine, and two goblets. She then took them back to her own chamber. In the days beforehand she or her accomplice had managed to obtain a small jug and a clean goblet. Anyway,' Kathryn picked up her tankard of buttermilk and drank from it, 'once she was back in her chamber, this young wife changed her appearance, putting on a ragged dress and sandals; perhaps she greased her face and hands, smeared on ash and dirt. She took the food. . . .'

'But that would be cold.' Clitheroe interrupted. 'I pride myself on serving hot food.'

'Each chamber has got a brazier, hasn't it? It can be kept hot over that.'

Clitheroe agreed.

'Moreover,' Kathryn continued, 'your young murderess is moving very quickly. She has to. She takes the tray, puts a bowl of food on it, takes the small jug and cup, and fills the jug with wine heavily laced with a sleeping potion. . . .'

'And takes it down?' Colum asked.

'Mafiach answers the door,' Kathryn explained. 'All he sees is some young slattern carrying a tray with some food, a jug of wine, and a goblet. Mafiach makes his one and only mistake, but it is his last. He probably wouldn't give the girl a second glance. Mafiach is expecting danger, but only from some assassin, a hired killer, not some dirty, greasy-faced slattern in a ragged dress carrying a tray. He is distracted, and his mind is on other matters. He ordered food, and food has come up. He sits down, enjoys his meal, and drinks a goblet of wine. Many sleeping draughts are tasteless; they give no odour. Mafiach's tired, so he loosens his clothing and lies on the bed.'

'But how did the assassin get into the room?' Clitheroe demanded, gazing in admiration at Kathryn. 'What you say is possible. Slatterns and maids are going up those stairs all the time. They are tired, hard-working, and they wouldn't give another a second glance.'

'Darkness falls,' Kathryn continued, determined to prove her theory. 'Yes, it would be nighttime. Customers leave, the tavern is silent, the cobbled yard deserted. Our assassin has hired the chamber above Mafiach's.'

'But how did they know which chamber Mafiach would have?' Colum asked.

'They didn't,' Clitheroe broke in. 'Now I remember! The merchant asked for two chambers on the top floor. He said his wife wished to be by herself. She acted the great lady.'

'So here we have this merchant and his wife,' Kathryn continued. 'They hire two chambers on the top floor. When Mafiach comes, they discover where he is staying. They have been watching the tavern for some time. The only thing the assassin had to do was discover that.'

'No, no!' Colum banged his black jack on the table. 'Why didn't they just release a crossbar or stab him on the stairs?'

'Too dangerous,' Kathryn replied. 'It had to be done by stealth. They needed time to search his chamber and make their own escape without provoking any suspicion or outcry.'

Colum agreed.

'Anyway,' Kathryn continued, 'Mafiach was not fast asleep.'

'How did they know that?' Colum asked.

'What are you,' Kathryn exclaimed in exasperation, 'a lawyer?' She sighed. 'No, I apologise; it's evidence. They would take a staff and tap at the shutters. If Mafiach opened those shutters, they would know their plan had failed. But he didn't, so they'd been successful! They have hidden a ladder. In the dead of night our merchant, the assassin, climbs up. He carries a long dagger. He slips this through the slit between the shutters and lifts the bar. The shutters are now released. He pulls up the ladder and climbs into the room. Mafiach is fast asleep. He's dragged from his bed, and his brains are dashed out. The assassin now has as much time as he needs. He's brought a sack with him. The wine jug is replaced, so is the goblet, and the tainted wine is poured out onto the cobbles below. The assassin makes one mistake. He fills the fresh jug a little too much. He seizes Mafiach's psalter. The tainted wine goblet and jug are placed in a sack. The assassin leaves, but as he does so, he ties a piece of thin cord around the bar.'

'Ah, and I know why—' Clitheroe broke in.

'One shutter is pulled closed, then the other one, and using the piece of twine, the bar is lowered. The twine has probably been tied in a slip knot and can be pulled free. Everything is as he wants it.' Kathryn paused. 'They'd been waiting for the Irishman. Mafiach didn't help matters; he was tired. On reflection he made two mistakes: He used his alias, and he trusted that slattern. Whilst the assassin was in the chamber, she would keep a look-out. A very clever murder! The assassin drew Mafiach's sword and dagger to complicate matters and make it look as if a fight had taken place. Yet he also made mistakes: Mafiach possessed a second copy of that cipher; the killer filled the jug too full, and he was too hasty in tying up the points on Mafiach's hose.'

'Ah, yes!' Colum exclaimed. 'I remember that!'

'Anyway,' Kathryn continued, 'the assassin returns to his chamber; the tainted jug and goblet are scrupulously washed and left on the table. The following morning, whilst Mafiach's corpse stiffens in his chamber, this precious pair leaves. She probably moved to another tavern or hostelry. Later that night the woman goes out to Bean Woods to meet her accomplice and receive the rest of her reward. Instead she is murdered. The assassin makes a further mistake: Unbeknownst to him, the woman has bought one of those pilgrim brooches at the tavern. She has this in her hair, which is rich and luxurious; when he strips the corpse, he fails to notice this.' Kathryn smiled. 'Who says the dead don't speak?'

Thomasina, who had been standing in the corner listening to it all, approached Kathryn.

'But, Mistress, how did they know about the gap between the shutters?'

'Oh, I can answer that,' Clitheroe declared. 'Very few taverns have windows; their upkeep is too costly. In spring and summer, shutters are used. There's always a gap between to allow air in.'

'And in winter,' Kathryn went on, 'you have a roll of leather covering the inside, which is let down like a curtain. Thomasina, go round our house; I haven't yet seen a pair of shutters which fit snugly together.'

'It has to be that.' Clitheroe nodded vigorously. 'What Mistress Swinbrooke says is correct. Any of us could do that. You climb a pair of ladders carrying a long Welsh stabbing dirk. You push it between the slits beneath the bar. You prise the bar loose from the clasp. In fact, you could even lock it again the same way, no need for thread or twine.'

'I suspect,' Kathryn got to her feet, 'the assassin is the high-ranking spy. He knew Mafiach was going to stay at the Falstaff, where he was to be collected by you, Colum. If he could disguise himself once as a merchant, then why not later as a chapman or a wandering tinker? He could study the Falstaff for any weakness and soon find it. He would realise how silent the tavern became in the early hours and profit accordingly.'

'But this young woman?' Clitheroe asked.

'It's only been a matter of days,' Kathryn replied. 'Perhaps someone will report her missing or . . .'

'Or what?' Colum demanded.

'Nothing,' Kathryn said. 'Master Clitheroe, I thank you for coming. What you heard is secret and not to be discussed.'

'Oh, don't worry about that.' Clitheroe got to his feet. 'I want people to forget as quickly as possible that a man was murdered at my tavern. I've already slapped the slatterns and scullions for talking about ghosts.' He went across, hand extended; Kathryn clasped it. 'What you say makes sense, Mistress. Poor Mafiach! He thought he was safe.'

'And he was,' Kathryn declared. 'He simply made a few mistakes and paid for them with his life.'

Clitheroe left, and Colum, shaking his head in disbelief, went to fetch his cloak and war-belt. Kathryn left instructions with Thomasina.

'If any patients come, send them to the Poor Priests' Hospital.'

Thomasina grabbed Kathryn by the arm and held her fast. 'You know who it is, don't you?'

'Yes, Thomasina, but trapping him is another matter!'

Kathryn, escorted by Colum, walked quickly up Ottemelle Lane. A weak sun was struggling through an early morning mist, and the city was not yet fully awake. They walked down the centre, well away from opening windows and the shouts of 'Gardez loo!' as chamber-pots were emptied into the street below. Heavy-eyed apprentices were setting up the stalls under the watchful gaze of their masters. Two street-walkers, skirts held high to reveal dirty legs and thighs, ran shrieking with mocking laughter away from a fat, red-faced, perspiring beadle. A Capuchin friar begged for alms, his cadaverous face peering out from under his deep cowl. Two debtors from the castle prison, shackled together, carried a basket from door to door for provisions for themselves and their companions. A roisterer who had drunk too much was being escorted down to the stocks with an empty beer cask over his head. The doors to cookshops and taverns were flung wide open, allowing the savoury smells from their ovens to waft out and tempt the early risers. Horses neighed in stable yards as the carts of peasants and scavengers trundled noisily over the cobbles. Colum found it difficult to speak, whilst Kathryn was in one of her tight-lipped moods.

They arrived at the soaring gate-house of the Friary of the Sack. A lay brother let them through and escorted them round the buildings to the Garden of Gethsemane. Prior Anselm, Simon, and Jonquil were already there with other members of the community. The smell of burning was rank. Plumes of grey smoke still wafted across the dew-fresh lawn and frightened the birds into noisy fluttering round the gables and spires of the friary.

Prior Anselm came across, all anxious-eyed. 'A terrible act! A terrible act!' he wailed. 'The poor woman!'

'A hideous death indeed!'

Kathryn turned round. Venables, wrapped in a brown military coat, stood behind her, one hand resting on the pommel of his sword.

'Her Grace the Duchess asked me to come here.' He pointed to the trees. 'Another murder, eh, Mistress?'

'Truly a place of death,' Kathryn replied. 'Let's see for ourselves.'

When Kathryn reached the prison cell, her heart sank. The fire had been so intense, the door and steel plate had buckled, the walls were cracked, and the bricks round the Judas squint had crumpled away. The smoke was still fairly thick and acrid, stinging her nostrils and throat. Kathryn, taking a rag offered by Prior Anselm, pulled at the small door, which gave way in her hand as the inside panels had crumbled. Kathryn crouched down and peered in. 'It's like an oven!' she exclaimed.

The walls and ceiling were black; everything else had been reduced to ash, still hot to the touch. Kathryn, ignoring Colum's protests, made her way gingerly in. Now and again a hot cinder scored her ankle or the edge of her hand, and every time she moved, puffs of acrid smoke made her cough and sneeze. A little light was provided by the Judas squint and the open door. At one point Kathryn had to pause, fighting for breath. She panicked and blinked quickly; her eyes were stung to tears. She reached what must have been the bed. Again, there was nothing but black cinder and feathery ash. Kathryn searched carefully, and then grinned and made her way out. For a while she stamped away the ash, cleaning it from her gown and sandals.

'You look a bit like Thomasina after she has burnt the bread.' Colum's smile faded. 'I'm sorry, Kathryn.'

'Well, I'm not.' Kathryn pushed by them onto the lawn. 'Mathilda Chandler!' she shouted. 'Mathilda!'

She walked along the edge of the copse, the rest following.

'Mathilda, don't worry! It's me, Kathryn!'

Nothing but the raucous cawing of crows and the chatter of a jay answered her. Kathryn quietly prayed that she wasn't wrong.

'Mathilda!' she shouted. 'You have nothing to fear! I will take you to a safe place!'

Kathryn had almost reached the end of the copse: A bush swayed, and Mathilda Chandler stepped out onto the lawn, shrouded in her thick cloak. She hastened across to Kathryn, eyes glittering, face white and pinched. Kathryn grasped her cold hands.

'Don't say anything,' she whispered. 'Don't say anything at all. Just agree with whatever I say.'

Mathilda nodded. 'I . . . I . . .'

'Hush!' Kathryn urged.

'What is this?' Prior Anselm strode forward. 'We thought you were dead!'

'Don't question her.' Kathryn put an arm round Mathilda's shoulder. 'She's frightened enough.'

'This is my friary.' Prior Anselm boomed. 'I am Father Prior!'

'You are also a liar,' Kathryn retorted.

'How dare you?'

'Oh, I dare everything. I am here on the orders of the Queen Mother, Cecily, Duchess of York.'

Prior Anselm blanched, his Adam's apple bobbing like a cork on a mill pond.

'I will see you, Brother Simon, and Jonquil in your parlour. Not at my request, Father Prior, but on the Duchess's orders. If you refuse,' Kathryn gazed up at the sky, 'the King's men will be here within the hour.'

Prior Anselm spun on his heel, whispered to his two companions, and walked across the lawn without a second glance. Kathryn indicated that Colum and Venables should approach no further. She led Mathilda away and gave her a squeeze.

'I am so glad,' Kathryn whispered, 'so happy!'

Mathilda sobbed quietly.

'Comfort yourself,' Kathryn whispered. 'You are safe.'

'I've become like an animal,' Mathilda replied. 'I stayed in my cell, but I felt an unspoken, unseen danger, like one of those cold morning mists which gathers round and clings to your skin like a shroud cloth. Yesterday afternoon I wrapped what little provisions

I had in a rag. I left my cell, closed the door, and put the steel sheet back in its place. I hurried to the end of the copse, and like a fox being hunted, made myself a new lair.'

'Did you see anything?' Kathryn asked.

Mathilda shook her head. 'The first I knew was when I smelt the smoke and heard the crackling. I was terrified. I could hear the flames roaring. If I hadn't moved, my body would have been consumed and my soul sent to God.'

'Well, listen,' Kathryn replied, 'listen very carefully. You are not to say anything, not even to Master Murtagh, but when I ask you a question, agree with whatever I say. Do you understand that?'

'Do I have to go back there?'

Kathryn gave her another hug.

'You can be sure of two things, Mathilda Chandler: The sun will set today, and your imprisonment is over. I promise you that.'

Kathryn turned and led Mathilda back to Colum. The Irishman was full of questions, but Kathryn pressed her finger against his lips.

'You are not to ask her anything.' She smiled at Venables. 'I would be grateful if all three of you would wait in the small chamber near the Prior's parlour. I assure you this will not take long.' She grasped Colum's wrist. 'Don't let Mistress Chandler out of your sight. Where she goes, so must you.'

Colum agreed. Kathryn kissed him quickly on the lips, smiled at Mathilda, and hurried back across the lawn.

The three friars were in the parlour, sitting like scholars waiting to be chastised by a master. Kathryn closed the door behind her, turned the key, and sat across the table from them.

'I'll come swiftly to the point, and I am not bluffing.'

'I would like to object.' Prior Anselm raised a hand.

'Shut up!' Kathryn banged the table with her hand. 'You've wasted enough time with your lies and fables. Brother Jonquil, your real name is Edmund Brotherton. You come from Pickering in Yorkshire. You are York's man, body and soul. You were a page in Duke Richard's household and later a retainer in Duchess Cecily's.'

Jonquil's face paled, his fingers went to his lips.

'How did . . . ?

'The Duchess told me,' Kathryn cut him off. 'You were placed here to protect the Blessed Roger Atworth. You are no more a lay brother than I am an abbess. Prior Anselm, Sub-Prior Gervase, and Simon the infirmarian were the only members of the community who were informed of your true identity and your real task here at the Friary of the Sack. That is the truth?'

Jonquil agreed.

'You found it irksome,' Kathryn continued, 'but now and again at night you crossed Gethsemane, climbed the wall, took off your habit, and became another young man out to enjoy himself in the taverns and cookshops or wherever else you wanted to go. Whilst you were gone, Prior Anselm, Gervase, and Brother Simon kept an eye on the Holy Roger.'

Jonquil put his face in his hands.

'Now,' Kathryn smiled at Prior Anselm, 'regarding Brother Roger's death and the miracles'—she shrugged—'I think Brother Simon here knows that they are as much the work of nature as they are of God, but they don't bother me. The perfumed smell—' Kathryn opened her wallet and took out a small piece of membrane, transparently thin. 'Do you ever blow bubbles, Brother Simon? When they burst, you can smell their soap. You did the same, didn't you? You are an apothecary. You filled pieces of membrane, very similar to this, with some perfume concocted in your infirmary.

'You placed them in your pocket and, when appropriate, let two or three fall on the ground. You crushed them under your sandalled foot, and the smell became pervasive.'

Brother Simon sat, eyes closed.

'I've heard of schoolboys doing the same,' Kathryn declared, 'but with a substance not so sweet. You went into Brother Roger's chamber. You allowed three or four pieces to fall on the floor and quietly crushed them under your foot. You placed these in Brother Roger's coffin, and, when the tomb was opened and no one was looking, you did the same again.' Kathryn waved a hand. 'The air became sweet with some mysterious fragrance. If you search for the source, you can't find it. The membrane is very thin, and, of course, it can be kicked under soil, between a crack in the floor-boards, or under a bed. Whatever.' She glanced at the young lay brother, who still sat with his head in his hands. 'As for your vision, Brother Jonquil—I have knelt in the Lady Chapel when the sun comes pouring through the window. That's all you saw, wasn't it? The rest was mere fable, like the perfume, to gladden Duchess Cecily's heart and prevent her asking too many embarrassing questions about Brother Roger's death. All three of you must have got on your knees and thanked God when Atworth's corpse was exhumed and found to be uncorrupted. Brother Simon may throw his hands in the air, but I think he knows the effect of arsenic as much as I do. Brother Roger was taking very minute grains for a stomach ailment. I am sure that did not kill him, but it did keep his corpse intact.' Kathryn sighed. 'So, am I to tease it out of you, like some clumsy thread of tapestry?'

'We have sinned.' Prior Anselm's hands went together. He bowed his head. 'Mistress Swinbrooke, we have sinned, and we have lied. Not because of greed!' He spread his hands. 'Well, perhaps that did play a part.'

'The truth?' Kathryn demanded.

'Very well.' Prior Anselm sat back in his chair. 'Roger Atworth joined this community and soon won a name for holiness of life. In many ways he was an excellent companion: humble, pious, always ready to please. I liked him. I knew about his former life, the hideous deeds he'd committed. Yet if there was ever a man searching for God, it was Roger Atworth.' He paused. 'The war between York and Lancaster ended. We soon realised that Brother Roger had very powerful friends. Duchess Cecily became a constant visitor here. Brother Roger was her confessor. They used to greet each other like brother and sister and go walking in Gethsemane. Duchess Cecily warned me to keep Atworth well and safe: If he suffered any distress, threat, or danger, I was to tell her immediately. Gervase and Simon were similarly instructed. Gervase didn't like Brother Atworth. He often wondered what secrets Atworth held. He was certainly jealous of the intimacy between this holy friar and the mother of the King of England. Now and again we would have visitors, particularly from France: merchants, messengers. Even though they disguised it well, their interest in Brother Roger was noticeable. A few months ago I informed Duchess Cecily.' He gestured towards Jonquil. 'So he was sent to protect Roger.'

'And?' Kathryn asked.

'An easy task,' Jonquil spoke up, taking his hands away from his face. 'Atworth was a holy man. He wanted to do nothing but pray, walk in Gethsemane Garden, and write in the small psalter you have seen in the library. It was not an onerous task, but I did find the life here stifling. Prior Anselm was kind enough to turn a blind eye to my occasional departures into the city.'

'We didn't think there was any danger,' Prior Anselm took up the story. 'Brother Roger went to church, to the refectory, the library, his own chamber, or to walk in Gethsemane. He struck up a friendship with our poor prisoner, but I thought that posed no danger. And then,' he snapped his fingers, 'suddenly, one night, everything changed.' Prior Anselm laced his fingers together. 'The Feast of the Annunciation falls on the twenty-fifth of March. On the evening of the twenty-third Brother Jonquil left for the city. Brother Roger, we thought, went for a walk in Gethsemane. No one really paid much attention until the morning of the twenty-fourth. Jonquil went to Brother Roger's chamber and found it empty, his bed unslept in.'

'We were terrified,' the infirmarian spoke up. 'Roger Atworth had been placed in our special care. Jonquil had been out in the city, and in that time, Brother Roger had disappeared. His chamber was undisturbed. He only had a few paltry possessions, and we know he kept the Duchess's letters in a wallet on a cord. We had to keep this secret from the rest of the community. We thought he might have gone into the city or been in another part of the friary. We had to work discreetly, quietly. As the day progressed, we could find no trace.'

'But you found him, didn't you?' Kathryn asked.

'Yes, after dusk. We began to search Gethsemane and the copse beyond.'

Prior Anselm sucked on his lips. Kathryn could see his hand was trembling.

'We found him dead in the disused cellar, lying on the floor, hands crossed. We waited till it was dark and the rest of the community had retired. We brought his corpse back in the dead of night and laid it on his bed in his chamber. Only then did we notice something was wrong.'

'Let me see,' Kathryn interrupted. 'First, he was dirty and dishevelled, yes? So you had to strip the corpse and, of course, the bed, now stained from the dirt on Brother Roger's habit, yes?'

214

'True.' Prior Anselm kept his head down.

'You took off his habit, washed the corpse, and as you said, sent his robe and the dirty blankets, sheets, and bolster to the wash-house.'

Kathryn paused at a sound from outside.

'Even then, Brother Simon, you must have recognised something exceptional about Brother Roger's corpse, already that waxen, sponge-like texture. What really frightened you, however, were the cord marks round his wrists and ankles. True?'

'We realised'—the infirmarian closed his eyes— 'it was no accident. Brother Roger hadn't simply gone down that cellar, become ill, collapsed, and died.'

'He had been abducted, hadn't he?' Kathryn asked. 'Atworth went for a walk in Gethsemane, and the assassin struck. God knows how he did it, but Atworth had been enticed into the copse, perhaps struck on the side of the head. When he regained consciousness, he found himself lying on a dirty slab, hands and feet lashed to some pole or clasp in the wall. The assassin didn't want to kill Atworth. He wanted to interrogate him, question him about the secrets—he also took Atworth's letters, didn't he? Brother Atworth was terrified. Now a frail man, under the shock of such ill treatment, his heart gave way. The assassin released him from his bonds and left the corpse for you to find. You knew Duchess Cecily would demand an explanation. She would come to see the corpse, so that's when the charade began: clean sheets, blankets, fresh robes, the story that Atworth had burnt the letters, locked the door, and lay down on his bed to wait for his God.'

'We had no choice,' Prior Anselm wailed.

'Of course people would be suspicious,' Kathryn declared. 'Why was the door locked? Why didn't Atworth, if he knew death was near, summon his brothers? Make his farewells? Ask to be taken down to your church? But that would be forgotten, wouldn't it, once the marvellous stories began to circulate? The bed was changed, the corpse washed and re-clothed, the brazier lit; some parchments were burnt. Brother Simon brought his small sacks of perfume; some he broke, others he would leave for the morning. The only problem remaining were those awful red marks round the wrists and ankles. You, Brother Simon, are a physician. When death occurs, the blood flow stops. You had the marvellous idea of providing Roger Atworth with the stigmata, a rare mark of Christ's approval for great saints like Francis of Assisi. Those wounds in his wrists, ankles, and side, as well as to his head, were your work, weren't they? And, being a pious man, you had these holy wounds covered by strips of cloth. Consequently, any suspicious person would simply say that the marks on the wrists and ankles were caused by these miraculous stigmata and the cloths you used to bind them. Similar marks were placed round his forehead.'

Kathryn laid her hands on the table and stared at the three friars.

'What people want to see,' she murmured, 'they will see. What people want to believe, they will believe. Atworth is hailed as a saint. Duchess Cecily is sorrowful, but she has two consolations: First, the man who knew all her secrets has taken them to the grave. Secondly, the man who was her confessor is now a saint in heaven. Duchess Cecily would like that, and so would you. You would win her patronage. Atworth's tomb would become a shrine for pilgrims. The only suspicious person was our wily old Archbishop Bourchier, who, perhaps, knew more than he told us. He decided to use the process of canonisation to discover the real truth behind all this. Brother Roger is hurried to his grave. Duchess Cecily is eager for his canonisation. At the same time she becomes less confident that the secrets Atworth held are safe once and for all.'

Kathryn got to her feet to ease the cramp in her back and arms. She walked over the crucifix.

'Duchess Cecily would have welcomed the process of canonisation. It would give her not only to a saint but surety that all was well.' She looked over her shoulders at the three friars. 'You, of course, had a lot to hide and a great deal to gain. The charade continued until I arrived at the Friary of the Sack.'

'It's true,' Prior Anselm blurted out. 'God forgive us, Brother Roger was murdered!'

'And his assassin?' the infirmarian demanded.

'Yes,' Jonquil added plaintively, 'and poor Gervase? What happened to him?'

'That,' Kathryn retorted, 'is not for you to know, at least not yet!' She went and stood over Jonquil. 'One final thing, that note pushed under my door in the guest-house, that was your work, wasn't it?' Kathryn punched him on the shoulder. 'You were waiting on the stairwell.'

'I was just trying to frighten you.'

Kathryn leaned down, her face only a few inches from his.

'Well, Brother Jonquil, you did! Now all of you, get out!'

Chapter 12

'The leoun sit in his waayte alway
To sle the inocent, if that he may.'
—Chaucer, 'The Friar's Tale,'
The Canterbury Tales

I might call them the three Wise Men,' Colum remarked as he sat down in the parlour. Venables had taken the seat at the table. 'But they are neither wise nor happy! Oh, there seems to be some disturbance outside.'

There was a knock on the door, and then Prior Anselm came sheepishly in!

'Mistress Swinbrooke, Royal Archers now guard every entrance. A serjeant-at-arms and a group of pike men patrol Gethsemane.'

'Yes, I know, Father Prior.' Kathryn re-took her seat. 'They are here for your protection and mine. I'd be grateful if you would leave.'

The Prior hastily withdrew.

'What is this?'

Venables undid the clasp of his cloak and threw it over the back of his chair. He loosened his war-belt and, half-rising, pulled it from his waist and placed it on the table before him.

'Why, Master Venables, this is a court of enquiry.' She ignored Colum's sharp intake of breath. Kathryn stared down at this most treacherous of henchmen. 'You are the assassin, aren't you, Master Venables?'

The only change in Venables was the way he straightened in

the chair, a quick downward glance, a nervous licking of the lips. He leaned his elbows on the table, hands half-covering his face.

'Why Kathryn . . . ?'

'Mistress Swinbrooke to you.'

'Ah, so that's how the wind blows.'

'We found her, you know,' Kathryn continued conversationally. 'The poor woman you murdered in Bean Woods. You stripped her corpse and threw it in the marsh, but items were found near her body. Where was she from, Master Venables? A courtesan from London? Hired to help you with murder?'

'What things were found?' Venables jibed.

'Enough to send you to the gallows. You hired her, and you waited at the Falstaff Inn for poor Mafiach.'

'I didn't know he was going there. Only members of the Royal Council or your love swain, Master Murtagh, were party to that.'

'True, true.' Kathryn smiled thinly. 'And a member of that Royal Council told you that Mafiach was to be there at a certain time. You had the Falstaff watched, slipping in and out in your disguise.'

'Disguise?'

'Yes, an elderly merchant with greying hair, moustache, and beard. For a man with your wealth, Master Venables, such disguises are easy to buy or make. I won't waste time.'

Kathryn gave a brief description of Mafiach's death and Venables's hand in it, how he killed the Irishman, stole the cipher, and the following evening murdered his own accomplice. Venables shook his head in mock disbelief.

'I understand your logic, Mistress Swinbrooke, but where's the proof? The evidence?'

'Let's move on,' Kathryn responded, 'to the Friary of the Sack. How did you first contact Brother Gervase, the sub-prior? Was it by secret letter? Or a meeting out in the city? Or in that dense copse at the far end of Gethsemane Garden? Brother Gervase didn't like Atworth; he resented him, jealous of his intimacy with the Queen Mother.'

'And I just walked up to him,' Venables jeered, 'and introduced myself?'

'Well, no. You first spied out the land, by letter or a meeting where you kept your face, name, and character well hidden. Gervase was a contentious man.'

Kathryn looked at Colum, who had not yet overcome his surprise at Venables being named.

'Gervase would object, he'd quarrel, yet there's nothing like sacks of gold and silver to ease a greedy man's conscience, are there, Venables? To put it bluntly, Gervase became your spy here. You met him out in that lonely copse across Gethsemane. He would tell you all the chatter and gossip of the friary, the doings and sayings of Brother Atworth. Two things became obvious: First, Atworth held secrets, and secondly, he kept those secrets close to his heart.

'Despite the gold and silver you paid him, Gervase was not very helpful. So like a weasel stalking a rabbit warren, you decided to take matters into your own hands. You watched the friary, and you noticed how Atworth's protector and guardian, Brother Jonquil, would sometimes shirk his duties for the fleshpots of the city. One evening you pounced. Brother Atworth liked to walk in the garden by himself. You assaulted him, struck him unconscious, and dragged his body into that underground cellar near the friary wall. You had all night to question him. The poor man's wrists and ankles were lashed, held secure. Time and again you'd come back. What did he know about Cecily, Duchess of York? What great secrets did he hold? You didn't even have to torture him. Atworth was a frail old man, and you simply hoped that the loneliness, the dark, being held prisoner might loosen his tongue.'

'This is nonsense!' Venables interrupted.

'Oh no, it isn't. You overlooked two matters: First, Atworth really had converted to God. He was a friar, a priest, a confessor. He would no more give up his secrets than he would return to his former life. Secondly, Atworth was more frail than you realised. He didn't survive very long. He was a frightened old man, and his heart simply gave way; he slipped quietly into death. You could claim some success. You removed the letters from his wallet, loosened the bonds, left his corpse in that dank, stinking cellar, and fled across the wall.'

'And I just wandered into this friary whenever I so wished?'

'Of course. You had the help of Brother Gervase, who supplied you with one of his gowns and cowls, not to mention a pair of sandals. In a place like this, one friar looks like another, especially with a cowl pulled over his head. Brother Gervase was of some use to you, wasn't he? He gave you Brother Atworth's psalter.'

'I don't know what you are talking about!'

'Gervase took it from the library for you to inspect. You found certain pages interesting and removed them before giving the psalter back.'

Colum got up from the bench, went across to the side table, and poured a goblet of wine. He put this into Kathryn's hand; then, instead of re-taking his seat, he went and leaned against the wooden panelled door, closer to Venables, hand resting on the pommel of his sword. Venables ignored him, eyes on Kathryn.

'Gervase was a nuisance,' Kathryn continued. 'He didn't know who you were, but he hadn't been of much use. However, if this matter'—Kathryn waved a hand—'began to crumble, Gervase might decide to tell someone what he knew. On that afternoon, when I first arrived here, you sent the pre-arranged signal to Gervase to meet in the usual place in Gethsemane. He went across, and you murdered him, as you did that young woman in Bean Woods. A dagger through the heart or his throat cut from ear to ear. We can't truly tell because such wounds would be hidden by the fire. Disguised as a friar, you took Gervase's keys, slipped up to his chamber, and carefully went through his possessions. You removed any incriminating evidence, including the quite considerable amount of gold and silver you had paid him. Satisfied, you walked back across Gethsemane. You couldn't leave Gervase's corpse as it was. You recalled his opposition to Atworth, so you decided to muddy the waters by making it look as if the sub-prior had died a mysterious death. You soaked his corpse in oil specially brought in a wineskin and propped his body up against a bush. Master Murtagh,' Kathryn looked at the Irishman, 'you have fought in sieges. You have seen the King's miners light a slow fuse, a piece of hempen rope soaked in some flammable solution or powder. Master Venables did the same. Hidden by the screed of bushes and trees, he lit the rope, picked up the wineskin, made sure there was no trace of him left there, and slipped into the deserted alleyway beyond the friary walls. Who would give a second glance at a cowled friar hurrying down a lane? A common enough sight. Meanwhile, the Ancient One, Brother Timothy, whom Gervase must have told you about, was staring out across the garden. All he saw was Gervase standing there one moment, the next being engulfed in a sheet of flame.' Kathryn paused. 'I have studied the place where Gervase's body was burned. The copse is so dense and thick that you could do all this without being detected from the friary.'

'This is very interesting.' Venables lowered his hands. He kept moving in the chair, agitated and nervous. 'But where is the proof? Why should I betray Her Grace, the Duchess?'

'Perhaps you can answer that better than I can. Finally, we come to Mistress Chandler. Only you, apart from Master Murtagh and Lay Brother Eadwig, suspected how much Mistress Chandler had told me. I let it slip yesterday before we left the Archbishop's palace. You became alarmed, nervous of what she might have seen or heard. Had Gervase confided in her? So in the dead of night you returned, once again garbed as a friar, armed with oil and a piece of hempen string. You replaced the steel sheets and the wooden slats. You poured the oil in, lit the rope, stood back, and watched your bloody handiwork. You made one mistake. Mistress Chandler, by the grace of God, suspected you might return. She was hiding nearby. She saw your face.'

'That's im—!'

'What were you going to say, Master Venables?' Kathryn steeled herself for what she knew was a downright lie. 'You may have had your cowl pulled up, but you were not meeting anybody. No Gervase, no accomplice. Your face wasn't masked: You turned your head. Mathilda Chandler, hiding nearby, saw your face in the glare of the fire. She will go on oath and swear that you are responsible.'

'Who would believe a murderess?' Venables sat back in his chair, hands griping the arms. 'Is that all the proof you have to convict me,' he jibed, 'Duchess Cecily's confidant and henchman?'

'Oh no.' Kathryn emphasized the points on her fingers. 'First, whilst you are in here, your chamber and possessions are being searched. I am sure the disguise you wore at the Falstaff will be discovered. Second, you will be taken back there. Mine host Clitheroe is a sharp-eyed man. We may disguise you again and ask him to look at you. If he doesn't recognise you, perhaps one of the servants will. Third, the King's sheriffs will make a careful search

222

amongst the courtesans and doxies of London. I am sure someone will claim the corpse of that poor woman, and, perhaps, point the finger at you. Fourth, when they search your possessions, they may find the gold and silver you took from Gervase's chamber.'

Kathryn's bluff had struck home.

'Fifth, I will point out that, apart from myself, Master Murtagh, and Brother Eadwig, you were the only one who knew what possible dangers Mistress Chandler might pose. Sixth, she will identify you. Do you believe in ghosts, Master Venables?'

The henchman leaned forward, fingers not far from his war-belt.

'Say what you have to, woman!'

'The dead will convict you,' Kathryn continued. 'Especially Master Mafiach. When we met in the King's pavilion at the Archbishop's palace, you said in the presence of witnesses, "Mafiach was unwary." How did you know he was unwary? You were not supposed to know about him.'

'It became common knowledge.'

'Yes, but you actually used the word "unwary," not unfortunate, hapless, or unlucky. You said "unwary," as if you knew Mafiach was on guard but had made the mistake of trusting that so-called slattern and compounded his error by drinking drugged wine.'

'You are playing with words!' Venables spluttered.

'Oh no! Finally,' Kathryn opened her purse and took out a small scroll of parchment, 'Mafiach carried two ciphers. Shall I read them out to you?'

Kathryn proceeded:

' "Regis regum rectissimi prope est dies domini
dies irae et vindictae tenebrarum et nebulae
diesque mirabilium tonitruorum fortium
dies quoque angustiae meroris ac tristitiae
in quo cessabit mulierum amor ac desiderium
hominumque contentio mundi huius et cupide.'

' "The day of the Lord,
The Kings of Kings most righteous, is at hand:
A day of wrath and vengeance, of darkness and cloud:
A day of wondrous mighty thunderings:

A day of trouble also, of grief and sadness:
In which shall cease the love and desire of women:
And the strife of men and the lust of this world." '

'Finally, we have that enigmatic phrase: "Recto et Verso." You do realise,' Kathryn tapped the sheet of paper, 'that both the Latin and English text contain letters which spell out your name.'

She crumpled the parchment up and threw it down on the table. Venables caught it quickly.

'I have another copy.' Kathryn plucked up the second scroll. 'I have scored, in both versions, the letters which spell out your name.'

Venables sat like a man stricken.

"Recto et Verso": forwards and backwards. The "forward" refers to the Latin text; the "backward" to the English translation. Both spell out the name of the spy at the court of Edward IV of England, Venables. Your accomplice, of course, did not help matters.'

'What accomplice?' Venables snarled.

'Why, the Vicomte de Sanglier. He couldn't resist the jibe at us. "In vino veritas; in wine the truth": That's what he said when the death of Mafiach was being discussed. The Vicomte was actually confessing, in his own mocking, secretive way, that he knew exactly how Mafiach had died. How he had been drugged with tainted wine so the shutters of his chamber could be opened and you could steal in to finish the task.'

'I demand to see the woman.' Venables wiped the bead of sweat running down his left cheekbone.

'Master Murtagh, she is in the hall outside.'

Colum opened the door, his eyes never leaving Venables.

'Mathilda Chandler!' he called.

They heard the sound of soft footsteps as Chandler entered the room. Kathryn stared hard at her, praying that Mathilda would have the wit to co-operate.

'Mistress Chandler, look at Master Venables.'

The woman did so.

'Have you ever seen him before?'

Chandler stared at Venables, back at Kathryn, and drew closer to Colum.

'Mistress, I have told you that already. He was the one who started the fire last night, the fire which could have killed me.'

Venables sprang to his feet. Kathryn thought he was going to protest, but it was only a ploy. He grasped his war-belt, quickly drawing his sword. Chandler fled. Colum, slamming the door shut, threw himself sideways. Venables lunged. Kathryn, horrified, watched Colum slip and crash against the side table, sending the wine jug flying. Venables then drew a dagger from its sheath. His face red with anger, he hastened round the table, shouting curses. Kathryn jumped up, the chair crashing back. Her foot slipped on the spilt wine, but she picked up the jug and threw it at Venables's head. He dodged it as Kathryn felt herself being pulled away. Colum was on his feet. He'd grasped a stool and pushed Kathryn along the chamber.

'My war-belt!'

Kathryn tried to grasp it, but again, Colum pushed her aside to protect her from Venables. The henchman was now moving more slowly, jabbing the air with sword and dagger. Colum, grasping his war-belt, backed further round the room. Venables reached the door, and with the side of his hand, pushed the top bolt across. Colum now had his own sword drawn. Venables, confident, followed slowly. When he attacked, his speed and ferocity surprised Kathryn. Venables believed he had both of them trapped. He even allowed Colum time to draw his dagger and throw the empty war-belt onto the table.

'How good are you, Irishman?' Venables taunted. 'A prickle of steel, eh?'

Once again he lunged. A confident swordsman, a professional man-at-arms, Venables thought he had Murtagh at a disadvantage. Time and again he lunged and parried. Colum acted clumsy, using sword and dagger to fend off these deadly parries and feints. When they reached the end of the room, Colum stood his ground. Both men crashed in whirling arcs of scraping steel, swords out, daggers up. At one point their weapons locked. Venables tried to knee Colum in the groin, but the Irishman was too fast; he disengaged and moved away. Venables was no longer so confident: narrow-eyed, the sweat streaming down his face, he stood at a half-crouch. This time Colum attacked, leading with his sword. Venables went to meet it with his own. Colum dropped to one knee. Venables's weapon scythed the air, whilst Colum drove his dagger into the henchman's belly. Venables swayed slightly, eyes staring, his mouth opening to speak. He took a step forward, sword and dagger slipping from nerveless fingers. He grasped Colum's dagger, thrust almost to its hilt in the soft, fleshy part beneath his left rib, before giving a long sigh and crumpling to the ground.

For a while Colum stood leaning against the wall, gasping for breath. Kathryn went up to him and undid the top lace of his shirt.

'Well, well, my fighting man!'

Kathryn felt nauseous, and her legs seemed to have lost all strength. Colum kissed her quickly on the forehead and pushed her gently aside. He walked across the room and turned Venables's corpse over with the toe of his boot. The room now looked like a battlefield. Colum dropped his sword and dagger and slumped down on a stool.

'He's dead,' he whispered throatily. 'The misbegotten traitor's dead! Kathryn, you have taken years off my life! Why didn't you have men-at-arms here?'

Kathryn came and crouched beside him, wiping the sweat from his cheek with the palm of her hand.

'Colum, I knew he was guilty. He knew he was guilty, and God knows he's guilty. But if the truth be known, it was a matter of logic rather than evidence. I had little real proof. I had to watch his eyes and face. I wanted to count on his arrogance and, when that failed, the violence seething within him. To be caught by a woman, to have evidence laid against him by the likes of Mathilda Chandler . . .'

Colum grinned. He put an arm round her shoulder, drawing her close.

'Oh, Kathryn, as they say in Ireland, we have seen the days! You know the hearts of men better than you claim.'

He took his arm away at the thunderous knocking on the door.

'Mistress Swinbrooke! Mistress Swinbrooke!'

Kathryn got to her feet and pulled back the bolt. A serjeant-at-arms almost struck her with the door as he threw it open. Garbed in the gorgeous hues of the Royal Livery, he swaggered into the room, helmet in the crook of his arm, his other hand on the pommel of his sword. He reminded Kathryn of an angry cockerel as he stared round the room. He glimpsed Venables's corpse sprawled in its widening pool of blood.

'By Satan's tits!' he breathed. 'That's Master Venables! Is this your work, Irishman? Do I have to take you in hand?'

'He's a traitor'—Colum snapped—'not to mention an assassin and a thief. And I can prove it. Take his corpse in hand; I will answer to the King.'

The news had spread quickly. In the hallway outside, Prior Anselm, surrounded by the members of his community, stood wringing his hands as if the heavens had fallen and all lay in ruins. Mathilda Chandler sat on a stool in the corner, quiet as a mouse.

'What's the matter? What's happened?' The infirmarian bustled forward.

Colum pushed him gently away. 'Nothing to trouble you, Brother. Come, Mistress Chandler, we are finished here.'

He led Kathryn and their new-found companion out of the friary, its grounds now packed with men-at-arms and archers. A courier galloped into the courtyard, swinging himself out of the saddle. He wiped the sweat from his face and peered at Kathryn.

'Mistress Swinbrooke, I come from the Duchess!'

'Tell the Duchess she has nothing to fear,' Kathryn replied. 'Search Master Venables's corpse. Oh yes,' she saw the surprise in his face, 'he lies in his own blood; his soul has gone to judgement. Tell your mistress to have Venables's possessions carefully searched by her and no one else.'

The messenger made to object.

'Do as you are told, man!' Colum snapped.

They left the friary and made their way through the busy street. Mistress Chandler, frightened of the noise, the bustle, and the smell, pushed her way gently between Murtagh and Kathryn.

Once they were back home, Kathryn handed Mathilda over to Thomasina, who gently put an arm round her and took her upstairs to the guest-chamber at the back of the house. Wulf and Agnes were busy in the herb garden. Kathryn told them to stay there. She found it difficult to talk to Colum. No sooner was she in her own chamber than she began to shake. Despite the warmth, her body was racked by shivers. Thomasina came in, took one look at her, bustled out, and returned with a goblet.

'Some powders to make you sleep.'

Kathryn drank it slowly. She felt tired and slightly nauseous. All she could think of was Venables's hate-filled face and that abrupt violent struggle in the Prior's parlour. Colum came in and sat beside her on the bed; he spoke, but she wasn't aware of what he was saying. He seemed calm enough.

'Don't think, Kathryn.' Colum stroked her hair. 'Venables was a killer. He would have taken your life and mine without a second thought, even though I still find it hard to believe he was a traitor.'

Kathryn kissed Colum absent-mindedly on the cheek.

'It's not over yet,' she whispered.

She turned to lie down and noticed the small scroll on the table beside the bed. It was tied with a piece of black cord, sealed with blobs of red wax. Kathryn picked it up, undid the cord, and broke the seal.

'What is it?' Colum asked.

Kathryn gnawed at her lip, tears in her eyes. She read the message once again and pushed it into Colum's hand.

'Read it out loud, Colum!'

'To Mistress Swinbrooke, physician and apothecary at Otte-melle Lane in the city of Canterbury. Monksbane, her loyal servant, sends cordial greetings. I write this from the Golden Wyvern tavern, which overlooks the market place at Cirencester. For a man skilled as myself, the search was neither long nor arduous. Your husband, Alexander Wyville, is dead and lies buried in a pauper's grave in St. Dunstan's Church-Outside-the-Gates.

'I have not seen his corpse, but I have spoken to Parson Crispin, who buried your husband after he was killed in a tavern brawl in the market place below me. I have it from good testimony that Alexander Wyville joined the Lancastrians in their march to the west, hoping to join up with other traitors in the company of Margaret of Anjou and Beaufort of Somerset. Your husband, however, was more interested in plunder, food, and drink. His death, God assoil him, was without grace or favour. He deserted his companions and, with a few others of his coven, became involved in a game of hazard when the dice were found to be loaded. Harsh words and a drunken brawl led knives to be drawn. Alexander Wyville was slain immediately, his corpse identified by letters and warrants in his wallet. His possessions were sold for a meagre sum, and the money was given to Father Crispin; he was buried the following evening. I shall return to Canterbury with the sworn testimonies that this is God's own truth. May His blessing be with you. Farewell. Monksbane."

Colum went to embrace Kathryn, but she pushed him gently away.

'Not now,' she whispered. 'God forgive me, Colum, I feel no grief, only that a shadow has been lifted.'

Kathryn lay down on the bed, and Colum pulled the coverlet over her. She heard him say that he would be out at Kingsmead, and then she drifted into a deep sleep, waking late in the afternoon. Thomasina and Mathilda were in the kitchen, chattering merrily as two sparrows on a rooftop. The change in Mathilda's appearance was remarkable. She had lost that wan, grey look; colour now bloomed in her cheeks, and her eyes sparkled. Kathryn went into the buttery and brought out a jug and bowl of water which she used to wash her hands and face. She still felt sleepy, and her arms and legs ached, but she pronounced herself better.

'Where will you go?' Thomasina asked Mathilda. 'I mean, you are welcome to stay here.'

'And you will stay here.' Kathryn sat down at the table. 'Until these matters have been cleared up, you are my guest, Mathilda.'

'I already have plans,' the woman replied. 'Thomasina mentioned Father Cuthbert at The Poor Priests' Hospital. I'll not marry again, Mistress. If the King is good, I wish to thank God for my deliverance. I would like to work there.'

Kathryn was drawn into their conversation, interrupted now and again by Wulf running in from the garden, the arrival of patients with a list of minor ailments, or customers wishing to buy herbs and spices. Kathryn slipped easily into the ordinary routine of her life. Thomasina took Mathilda out to the garden, still chattering and gossiping. Darkness began to fall. Colum came striding into the house, his face wreathed in smiles.

'I have just arrested the rat king,' he announced, standing over Kathryn. 'Master Malachi Smallbones is now with the other vermin in the dungeon beneath the Guildhall. He has made a full confession.'

'Let me guess,' Kathryn said. 'Master Smallbones worked in Oxford, where he drove rats out of the sewers by using fire.'

'There and elsewhere,' Colum grinned, taking off his war-belt and straddling the bench. 'Good Lord, Kathryn, the man is more to be pitied than hated. He's such a rogue. Apparently he boxed these vermin up, fed them, and brought them down to the ruined village of Luxmoor about a mile from Canterbury.'

'How many?' Kathryn asked.

'Well, Holbech followed him there late this afternoon. He reckons at least a few score.'

'I don't believe this.' Kathryn shook her head.

'It's easily done,' Colum laughed. 'Rats can be caught and boxed as easily as snails on a path. There's no infestation of rats in Canterbury. What Smallbones did was bring a few boxes in and release them in Westgate, Southgate, and near the Cathedral. The rest depended on rumor, gossip. . . .'

'And fear,' Kathryn interrupted.

'Apparently he has done it elsewhere,' Colum remarked. 'Colchester, Oxford, Gloucester. He creates the problem and then offers to solve it.'

'I hope the City Council remembers Father Cuthbert.'

'Luberon is hopping with rage,' Colum said. 'Imagine a fat pigeon striding up and down the eaves of a roof.'

'What will happen to Smallbones?'

'The return of all monies. He'll probably have to work until mid-summer clearing every rat from the city and pay a large fine. He's also to be whipped at the tail of a cart and taken, to the sound of bagpipes, to sit in the stocks every day for a week.' Colum grinned. 'That's the least Luberon can think of at the moment.'

'You must send a message,' Kathryn declared. 'Luberon must speak to Father Cuthbert. Ask him to hire the Twelve Apostles.'

Colum promised he would. He got to his feet.

'And shall we talk about Wyville?'

'When this is all over, Colum, we will talk about Wyville.'

'It's not finished, is it?' Colum asked. 'There's something else?'

'We have one more visitor coming,' Kathryn said, getting to her feet. 'And I must prepare for her.'

She returned to her chamber, where she changed her clothes; then she went downstairs to join the rest for the evening meal. Colum's joy at the news from Monksbane was ill-concealed. When

Thomasina found out, she crossed herself and insisted on going down to the cellar to broach the best cask of Bordeaux. Kathryn still hadn't made her mind up about what to feel. She ate and drank, listening to the chatter of others. Colum and Wulf were now teasing both Thomasina and Mathilda, only giving them respite when they turned on Agnes. But Agnes gave as good as she received, being an ardent student of Thomasina's manner of speech. Kathryn felt sadness but no real grief at Alexander's death. Both of them had closed the door on the past; Alexander had followed his path, and she had taken hers. What was left to do? Grieve? Over what? Why act the hypocrite? Kathryn quietly vowed that she would ensure a cross was set up in that pauper's churchyard in Cirencester. She would pay Father Cuthbert to sing Requiem Masses for Alexander's soul. Engrossed in her own thoughts, Kathryn hardly heard the knock on the door. Thomasina came back into the kitchen all a-flutter.

'Mistress, you have a visitor.'

Kathryn told the rest to stay. Cecily, Duchess of York, waited in the hallway, escorted by a knight banneret, a dark-blue coat covering the Royal Livery. Through the half-open front door, Kathryn glimpsed the rest of the escort. The Duchess murmured instructions to her protector and followed Kathryn into the writing chamber. She closed the doors behind her, pulling across the bolts and turning the key, then handed Kathryn her cloak. The Queen Mother's face was white and drawn. She was dressed in widows' weeds, black from neck to toe, except for a gold bracelet round her left wrist and a jewelled cross on a silver chain about her neck.

'Do you wish wine?' Kathryn offered.

The Duchess shook her head and took the offered seat.

'We can't be heard in here, can we, Mistress Swinbrooke? Kathryn, I will call you Kathryn.'

'Your Grace is well?' Kathryn sat on a stool and stared up at the Duchess's face.

'When we spoke last night, I did not know it was Venables.' The Duchess's face took on a vindictive cast. 'I trusted him!'

'Why are you here, Madame?'

'How much do you know, Mistress Swinbrooke?'

Cecily studied Kathryn, who repressed a shiver at the hard-eyed look. The Duchess was obviously deeply disturbed by what had happened at the friary, and Kathryn wondered how safe she was. Duchess Cecily was a powerful woman, but the secrets of her past could bring her and, perhaps, the House of York into hideous disrepute.

'Your Grace must trust me,' Kathryn replied. 'And you must listen to me. You must only tell me what you want, though I can guess what nightmares haunt your soul.'

'You tell me, Mistress,' Cecily whispered.

'You are of the Neville family,' Kathryn began, 'and made a rich and prosperous marriage with Richard, Duke of York. Your late husband went to France some thirty years ago as Keeper of Calais, and you accompanied him.'

'I told you that last night.'

'You also said that while your husband was away with the English armies, a certain knight in his retinue plagued you with his attentions.'

'Again, as I told you, it was fashionable for members of my husband's retinue to pay honour to their lord's lady. But as you know, the matter got out of hand. He was a tempestuous, fiery young knight who demanded more than courtesy, etiquette, or the vows of marriage would allow.'

'He tried to force himself on you?'

'Yes. In one of the towers of Calais Castle I described how Atworth, who was then in my retinue, apprehended that man and slew him.'

Kathryn nodded, recalling the scrawled, illuminated miniatures she had seen in Atworth's psalter.

'Is that the truth, my lady?'

Dame Cecily's mouth quivered. She blinked to hide her tears.

'Your Grace, what was that knight's name?'

'I cannot tell you,' came the whispered reply. She glanced quickly at Kathryn. 'But perhaps you can tell me?'

Kathryn swallowed hard. Could she trust this woman?

'Whoever that knight was, Your Grace,' she replied slowly, 'he was more than just some fervent admirer. He may have had a relationship with you which was improper.'

Dame Cecily sat, hands on her lap, as if carved out of stone.

'He may have also become threatening,' Kathryn continued, 'so Atworth killed him. I have done some reckoning.' Kathryn looked up at the ceiling. 'Your eldest son, Edward, was conceived in Calais. Your Grace, I'll come bluntly to the point. If you had had an affair with this knight, particularly around the time you conceived Edward, some people might claim the present king is not the true offspring of Richard of York. If that is the case, he has no claim to the Throne of England.'

'Who would be so malicious as to maintain that?'

'Venables, for a start. The secret between you and Atworth was not just the murder of a knight who had dared to over-reach himself, it also touched on the conception of your eldest son. Atworth was captured by the Vicomte de Sanglier. God knows what happened in that castle where he was imprisoned. Atworth may have been tortured, bribed. Somehow or other de Sanglier suspected that secret. The years passed. De Sanglier, like the rest, grew old, but he never forgot. In 1471, Edward of York sweeps the board clean: the Lancastrians are defeated in two bloody battles at Barnet and Tewkesbury in the West Country. Edward is now King, conqueror, ruler of a united kingdom which, once again, might threaten France. Louis XI is alarmed, and Vicomte de Sanglier whispers rumours about a possible scandal. Like two dogs with a bone, Louis and his vicomte search about. They want to learn more. They need a traitor high in the Royal Circle.'

'But Venables wasn't that!'

'No, Your Grace, he wasn't. He was only the instrument of a much more sinister figure, your beautiful-faced, golden-haired, blue-eyed son George of Clarence.'

Dame Cecily's face crumpled in pain as her body began to shake with sobs.

'George of Clarence,' Kathryn declared, 'is as treacherous as he is beautiful. During the recent civil war, he sided, for a while, with the Lancastrians. George's mind teems like a box of worms. If Colum is to be believed, he has bounding ambition but not the talent to match. If this story can be proved, George might lay claim to the Crown of England.'

'He would have to fight Edward,' Cecily snapped, 'and fight Edward he would!'

'Clarence might be prepared to take that risk. He certainly was susceptible to the Vicomte's treachery. He listened to the story with some delight and recalled other whispers he may have heard.

You know your son better than I, Your Grace. He's attracted to treason as a cat to cream. He cannot spy on his mother, who trusts him no further than the length of her arm. So Clarence turns to your confessor, Roger Atworth, and your henchman, Venables, whom he suborns with gold and silver, the offer of protection, and the hope of preferment. Venables is like many of the men around your sons, killers all, falcons who roam the sky looking for prey. Venables agrees. Disguised and masked, Venables enters the Friary of the Sack. He, in turn, suborns Gervase and obtains Atworth's psalter.'

'I have heard of that,' Dame Cecily replied. 'Roger was indiscreet, but his paintings prove little.'

'Clarence realised that, and Venables was sent back. He abducted Atworth—despite the care of Jonquil—and interrogated him, but Atworth's frail heart gave way. The trickery I described to you last night is no longer a hypothesis; it is the truth.'

Duchess Cecily's mouth was now a tight, bloodless line.

'Meanwhile,' Kathryn paused, 'your son Edward the King becomes aware that Clarence, in return for the French support, is selling secrets to Louis.'

'He does not know it's Clarence?'

'No, but he suspects, so Edward contacts his own agent in Paris, Padraig Mafiach, also known as Robin Goodfellow. Mafiach is very good. He learns the names of both the English spy in the Royal Council and that spy's accomplice. Mafiach takes a verse from the Bible, Zephaniah 1:16, both the Latin text and its English translation. He writes on the bottom "Recto et Reverso," backwards and forwards, with that enigmatic phrase, "Veritas continet Veritatem; the Truth contains the truth." Now, Your Grace.' Kathryn rose, unlocked a coffer, and took out a scroll of parchment. "Recto et Verso." You can see how in both the Latin and the English text Venables's name can be detected.'

'And the phrase: "The truth contains the truth"?'

'The same can be said about George of Clarence; the translation spells out his full name. Clarence is the one who contained or held Venables, just as the English text contains the meaning of the Latin verse.'

'He was always a spoilt brat!' Duchess Cecily looked out at the darkness beyond the small window. 'Beautiful as an angel with a heart as black as sin! He told Venables when Mafiach would arrive at the Falstaff, yes?'

Kathryn agreed.

'Why didn't you tell me all this last night, Mistress? You told me about the friary and hinted at other things.'

'Your Grace,' Kathryn replied sweetly, 'I was as honest with you as you were with me.'

The Duchess gave a lopsided smile.

'And now what?'

'Oh, I am sure your son the King will frighten Clarence, who will, perhaps, forget this matter for a while. The Vicomte de Sanglier will regret coming to England. He will certainly regret being so bold and confident at not only contacting these traitors but openly baiting you on the matter of Mafiach's death. He will go hunting different quarry.'

'And you, Mistress Swinbrooke?'

Duchess Cecily pulled back her cloak and opened a small jewelled purse on the gold cord round her waist. She took out a petite, silver glass case.

'This is a relic, Kathryn.'

The physician laughed. Duchess Cecily glanced at her sharply.

'You find such things amusing?'

'Yes, I do.' Kathryn gazed up at the ceiling. 'Will the Blessed Roger be canonised? Will his shrine be set up in the Friary of the Sack?'

Duchess Cecily smiled thinly. 'Perhaps, perhaps not. I truly believe Roger is with God, whatever sins he may have committed. However, these rumours, which Clarence would love to publish, have cooled my support for the canonisation.'

'Of course,' Kathryn agreed. 'That explains de Sanglier's spiteful remark. The French would love to spread such scandal and claim its source was no less a person than your own confessor, a saint of the Universal Church, a man whose cause you so vigorously promoted!'

'I understand the Pope in Rome is busy.' Cecily looked at the reliquary case and shook her head. 'I just can't believe a son of mine would dare to rake up such filth!'

Kathryn was tempted to ask her if there was any truth in the rumours but bit her tongue.

'Madam'—she picked up the English translation—'read for yourself.' She handed the piece of parchment across. 'See, I have scored the letters.'

The day of the Lord,
The King of Kings most righteous, is at hand:
A day of wrath and vengeance, of darkness and cloud:
A day of wondrous mighty thunderings,
A day of trouble also, of grief and sadness,
In which shall cease the love and desire of women
And the strife of men and the lust of this world.

Dame Cecily did so, tears in her eyes, her finger spelling out the letters. She handed the piece of parchment back and thrust the reliquary at Kathryn.

'Swear, Kathryn, on this piece of the True Cross, that what you have told me, and what you have learnt, will be shared with no one else this side of Heaven.'

Kathryn brushed the reliquary with her fingers.

'I swear,' she murmured. 'Your Grace has nothing to fear from me.'

The Duchess got to her feet and stared down at her.

'But I have got a great deal to fear from you, Mistress Swinbrooke! Leave George of Clarence to me! As for the rest, ask whatever you want!'

Kathryn and Colum were betrothed on the eve of Corpus Christi, at the door of St. Mildred's Church, very close to the font where Kathryn had been baptised. The guests gathered round to witness this solemn exchange and the promises of both that they would be married before the summer ran its course. Kathryn felt sublimely happy. She was dressed in a beautiful gown of blue satin fringed with white, a jewelled crucifix Colum had given her around her neck, her black hair covered by a silver-white, gold-edged veil. She watched Father Cuthbert bless the ring and the candles to be used at the nuptial mass. Thomasina, Agnes, Wulf, Holbech, Mathilda Chandler, and all their friends from the parish clustered in the warm porchway of the church; they cheered as Colum took Kathryn by the hand and led her out to the top step, where they

236

repeated their promises in public. Kathryn stared at the sea of faces smiling up at her. Here she had been baptised, come with her father for Sunday mass, and once, almost an eternity ago, believed she loved Alexander Wyville. As she stared down at the throng, a movement at the back caught her eye. Her heart skipped a beat. Was that Wyville's face she'd glimpsed? She glanced away, dismissing what she had seen as simply a ghost from the past. Colum, the love of her life, was standing holding her hand, smiling lovingly down at her.

Author's Note

This novel develops a number of very interesting themes. First, medieval medicine was perhaps more advanced than it is given credit for. Like today, quacks and charlatans flourished, but many physicians were keen observers and often diagnosed and, sometimes, even successfully made a prognosis of serious ailments. It is easy to assume that in the medieval ages the status of women was negligible and only succeeding centuries saw a gradual improvement in their general lot. This is certainly incorrect. One famous English historian has pointed out that women probably had more rights in 1300 than they had in 1900, whilst Chaucer's description of the Wife of Bath shows a woman who could not only hold her own in a world of men but travelled all over Europe to the great shrines and was a shrewd businesswoman, ever ready to hold forth on the superiority of the gentler sex.

In this novel fiction corresponds with fact, and the quotation facing the title page summarises quite succinctly how women played a vital role as doctors, healers, and apothecaries. Kathryn Swinbrooke may be fictional, but in 1322, the most famous doctor in London was Mathilda of Westminster; Cecily of Oxford was the royal physician to Edward III and his wife, Philippa of Hainault; and Gerard of Cremona's work clearly describes women doctors during the medieval period. In England, particularly, where the medical faculties at the two universities, Oxford and

Cambridge, were relatively weak, women did serve as doctors and apothecaries, professions only in later centuries denied to them.

History does not move in a straight line but often in circles, and this certainly applies to medieval medicine. True, as today, there were charlatans ready to make a 'quick shilling' with so-called miraculous cures, but medieval doctors did possess considerable skill, particularly in their powers of observation and diagnosis. Some of their remedies, once dismissed as fanciful, are today in both Europe and American regarded quite rightly as alternative medicine.

Medieval physicians recognised the dangers posed by rats and viewed them as the carriers of disease. Medieval municipal authorities also waged war on this versatile rodent, though with little success: The position of official rat-catcher was common in many towns and cities. Indeed, the most successful way of eliminating the vermin was either by fire, as proved by the Great Fire of London in 1666, or the use of ferrets to wipe out both the vermin and their nests. The idea of someone bringing rats into a certain town is based on fact. Such 'forced infestations' were common, whilst Malachi Smallbones is based on that eternal confidence trickster, the person who secretly creates a problem and then publicly offers to resolve it!

Medieval physicians knew a great deal about the properties of arsenic. They saw it as dangerous but believed that, in small quantities, it could be useful. Indeed, this practice continued well into nineteenth-century Europe. Arsenic does have certain unique properties. The slow corruption of a victim poisoned by arsenic, and the red dust often found in their coffins, sent a number of notable murderers to the scaffold.

In the Middle Ages shrines and relics were big business, a veritable source of revenue for many churches. Naturally, there were many religious orders who prayed that one day their church would house the relic of a great saint. The cures at these shrines should not be summarily dismissed. True, some are laughable; others bear powerful witness to the power of mind over matter; whilst a few, like those of Lourdes, must be considered as genuine.

The rumours about Duchess Cecily of York are not fiction. George, Duke of Clarence, was a treacherous prince, and, later in Edward's reign, he was arrested for plotting against his brother and spreading such scandalous rumours about his mother and the conception of his kingly brother. In 1483, when Richard of Gloucester usurped the throne and imprisoned his nephew, Edward V, in the Tower, his henchmen allegedly resurrected this story. They pointed out that Edward IV may have been illegitimate, and therefore, his sons had no claim to the throne. Accordingly, the story may be salacious, but it did become a powerful political weapon in the turbulent politics of the House of York. In the end, those who spread such scandal received very little comfort. Clarence was murdered in the Tower, allegedly drowned in a vat of malmesey. Richard of Gloucester, later Richard III, was defeated and killed by Henry Tudor at the battle of Bosworth in 1485.